SORRY
YOU MISSED IT...

A COMING-OF-AGE
NOVEL

FRED HOSLEY

Backwater
Bayou Books

Sorry You Missed It…
Published by Backwater Bayou Books
Inglis, Florida

Publisher's Cataloging-in-Publication data

Names: Hosley, Fred, author.
Title: Sorry you missed it… / Fred Hosley.
Description: Inglis [Florida] : Backwater Bayou Books, 2020. Also published in hardcover.
Identifiers: ISBN 978-1-7347111-0-3
Subjects: LCSH: Bildungsromans. | Adventure fiction.
BISAC: FICTION / Coming of Age.
Classification: LCC PS490 | DDC 813 HOSLEY—dc22

Cover Art by Stephen Littlefield
Cover and Interior design by Victoria Wolf

For Jody ...
Dads were once boys.

PROLOGUE

"I'M NOT A COWARD."

The drive-in theater spotlights illuminated the parking area, and the rows of cars became a blur of headlights.

Mr. Parker placed the speaker back on the stand, turned the key in the ignition and started the car. "I don't think you are either," he answered.

Sitting in the back seat of the '39 Ford coupe, seven-year-old Matt Parker leaned forward between his Dad and Mom and rested his chin firmly on the back of the front seat. "I don't think I'll ever be one. I want to be like Marshal Kane. What do you think about that, Dad?"

"Let me get out of this Sunshine Speedway we seem to be in, son, and then we can talk."

"Okay, Dad." Matt turned his head to the right. "Hey, Mom, I think "High Noon" is the best movie I've ever seen. Did you think his wife was really going to leave on that train? I didn't."

"I was hoping she wouldn't, Matt. She showed she wasn't a coward, didn't she, dear?"

"Yes," Matt said. He sat quietly and waited until they reached the main road. "Dad, are cowards fraidy-cats?" he asked.

"They usually just don't have confidence," his dad answered. "You'll learn about the word coward as you get older, Matt."

"I'm a real good wrestler."

"Lawrence Fraley has told me."

"I always win. Now, there's an older boy that wants to fight me—maybe tomorrow. I can beat him."

"Confidence is good, son. You're learning how to take care of yourself."

"Yes, sir! I'll tell you how Marshal Kane does tomorrow when you come home from work."

Fifteen minutes later, they drove down the oyster shell road to their "Cracker Villa," a craftsman's dream house that his dad had resurrected with his carpentry skills in the neighborhood of old frame homes.

Early the next morning, Matt opened the screen door carefully, slipped out on the porch and let the door close without a sound.

The screen door spring twanged behind him and the door reopened. "Wait just a minute."

"Yes, ma'am." He shook his head and turned with a smile.

"Where are you going and what's your plan?"

"The bull pen, Mom, to wrestle with the older boys. Lawrence Fraley's there to watch. How did you hear me?" he said and he laughed.

"You taught me well. Your dad fixed the squeaking nail alert, but I still hear you when you step out on the porch. Now, be good, especially with the older boy, if he comes calling your name."

She released the door, and it slammed shut as she turned and walked back inside.

Matt walked down the shell road and belted out the song he'd heard Tex Ritter sing at the drive-in, "Do Not Forsake Me," as he jumped over puddled potholes. Some puddles already showed little waves from tiny tadpoles as they surfaced and gulped air for breaths. A dragonfly rested on a small piece of wood floating in another puddle like it was on its own boat. Matt bent over, flicked it with a thumb and finger and watched it fly.

Fifteen minutes later, Matt sat on the back of the older boy and pushed his arm high into his shoulder blade. The boy winced and let out a loud moan.

"Say give ... or I'll break it."

Lawrence Fraley jumped to his feet and swatted Matt on the head. "Ease up, Mattie—Now! You won. C'mon, all of you. Let's go over to the big oak tree. I've got a new story for you today, and you're gonna love it."

Lawrence shook his head as the boy Matt had beaten walked ahead of them. "You're something, beating these older kids, Mattie. You don't let that wiry body rest. You're stronger than you look for sure. And most important you're still a good kid."

"Thanks, Lawrence," Matt said softly.

PART 1

Chapter 1

WHERE'S BILLY?

LIGHT-CRACKLING THUNDERHEADS with ominous black bottoms rose high in the east. Their rolling white-gray tops looked like great stone monuments in the pink-blue sky—not an unusual sight for late afternoon on the west coast of Florida at the end of August, but something for twelve-year-olds on bicycles to keep an eye on.

Matt looked at the formidable line of storms and felt its quiet strength as it grew before his eyes. He pedaled faster and hoped it might dissipate as storms that time of year sometimes did. "You stay over in Tampa," he said to the clouds. "We have a ball game to play."

A solitary meadowlark sang in the nearby pasture, and boys laughed in the distance.

Matt grinned. He pedaled faster toward the laughter and for the first time noticed the sound of his bicycle chain rubbing on the guard. He banged on the chain guard hard with his heel and the grating sound stopped.

The streets of the new subdivision were empty and the only equipment visible was an old gray 8N Ford tractor with a box blade, standing in the front yard of a partially completed, concrete block, ranch-style home. The workers had left for the day—no buzzing skill saws, no banging hammers, no men on scaffolding yelling, "More mud!"

At the vacant subdivision lot used by the boys for sandlot baseball games, Matt jumped a puddle of dried concrete left by a cement truck and wobbled through the soft gray sugar-sand to a large pine tree. Bikes lay scattered on the ground. He leaned his own against the tree and approached the group of boys standing around the faded red boat cushion that marked second base.

Bob Walton and John Hollis were playing catch. Jonathan Andrew Brown, nicknamed "JB" by John in the second grade, was hitting balls to Brad Hammond and Robin Goodman while John's neighbor James Applewhite, nicknamed "Appie" by John, sat on the ground and watched the action.

"You guys ready to pick teams?" Matt asked.

"Where's our little farmer?" John asked.

"He's not here?"

"Nope ... no bike, no Billy."

"That's strange. He hasn't missed one game this summer."

"Are you worried, Matt? You sound worried."

"I'm not worried, John. Something probably came up. Let's play ball."

John grinned. "Okay, let's pick teams. It's you and me today, buddy. 'Rock-Paper-Scissors' to see who picks first?"

Matt smiled and put his fist over the open palm of his other hand. "Ready to lose? One, two, three ..."

John kicked the ground. "How do you always win?"

"You're a scissors kind of guy."

Bob laughed. "Should have chosen paper."

John shot him a bird. "I'd have beaten you."

"I pick JB," Matt said.

"I pick Bob ..."

Two hours later, Matt stood at home plate waiting for a pitch from Bob. His bat ripped through the air and met the baseball as it crossed over home plate. Smack! The ball curved foul. Strike two!

"We've got you now, Matt. Come on, Bob, strike him out," John yelled.

Matt popped up the next pitch behind home plate, and John caught it with a laugh. "Gotcha now, ol' buddy. One more out and we've still got a chance to beat you."

JB stepped up to the plate next and connected with Bob's first pitch. "Yes!" he yelled, and he started to run as the ball soared over second base.

John flipped off his mask and Brad shouted to him from the third base coach's box, "You can kiss that ball goodbye, John."

JB tossed his bat into the fresh cut weeds and raced down the path toward the blue boat cushion that marked first base. As he rounded first, the ball dropped deep into the freshly planted azalea bushes in front of the living room picture window of the almost completed house across the street.

"Get it, Appie!" John shouted to the center fielder.

Appie disappeared behind the bushes. "I'm looking!"

JB jumped up and down, and his race to first base became a joyful stroll toward second.

"Find it, Appie? Go help him, Bob," John yelled.

Bob left the pitcher's mound and ran across the street, his glove still on his left hand.

JB rounded second and picked up his pace.

"Hurry!" John yelled.

"What a hit, JB! You're the Bambino today!" Matt yelled.

Appie stood up behind the bushes and held up the ball. "I got it!"

John shook his head. "Yeah, you got it. Good job, Appie. Wanna throw it in?"

JB approached the flat, dirty cardboard box that marked third base, jumping and waving his hands back and forth. He rounded third base continuing his theatrics, clicking his heels for John who stood dejected at home plate.

"Take your time, JB," Matt yelled. "We've got this game in the bag!"

A wide grin flashed across Matt's tanned face as JB loped past John, jumped high in the air, and landed on the ragged outdoor furniture cushion that marked home plate, creating a dust explosion that flew into the air like a busted bag of dry mortar.

Matt hopped up and down. "JB, way to go. Brad, Robin, nice double play in the eighth to give us a chance. Eat your heart out, John." He raised his fist in victory and shouted, "Game over! We won!"

John threw his catcher's mitt down in the dirt. "Screw you."

Bob walked back toward home plate. "John, it's just sandlot. Who cares who won?"

"Maybe not you," John said. "But I play to win—even with Appie— and besides, this is our last baseball game this summer."

"John, first is best, but fun's the test," Matt said.

JB glanced up at the sky and pointed to the tall mountain of dirt on the adjacent lot. "How about one last game of King of the Mountain? I don't think the storm's going to hit us."

John grinned. "Yeah ... I'll win *that* game. Let's go. You in today, Brad?"

"No," Brad said. "Got to get home. I'll see you guys tomorrow at the dock."

"Yeah, sure," John said with a laugh. "Afraid you'll get your hands dirty?"

Robin climbed on his bike. "See you tomorrow. Call me and tell me what time, Bob."

The five remaining sweaty boys ran to the adjacent lot and crawled up the mountain of dirt standing beside an idle drag-line and a shallow pool of muddy water.

At the top, Matt rubbed John's blond flattop. "You can't win every time, buddy."

"You got all the good players this time," John said. He pushed the chubby, brown-haired boy standing closest to him. "Appie, you're the worst. Go play checkers."

Appie tumbled down the dirt mountain.

Bob jumped on John's back and tried to twist him to the ground. John swung around laughing and shoved Bob backward. "You gave JB that home run with the lousy pitch you threw, you little midget. Go cool off."

Bob tumbled down the dirt mountain into the muddy water. "You're a turd," he yelled. "No fair. You caught me off guard."

John caught JB and pushed him off. Then he turned and grabbed Matt in a headlock and tossed him over the side. Matt sailed into the air and rolled to the bottom.

John lost his balance and slid down the steep incline, landing in the shallow brown water at the edge of the dirt mountain next to Appie. He stood up and raised his fist with a big grin. "Last one in the water—I'm King of the Mountain!"

"Okay, Big John. You won. Congratulations," Matt said, laughing. He moved back to the edge of the shallow pool of water next to Bob. "What time are we leaving for Hog Island tomorrow?"

"Not sure yet," Bob said. "Got to check with Dad and see when I can use the boat. Probably mid-afternoon. I'll call you and let you know."

The boys stood up and stomped the mud off their shoes.

On the corner, the street light flickered in its daily ritual of trying to turn on.

"Dinner time," Matt said. "Let's go home."

"Well, the farmer never showed," John said. "Still not worried?"

"He's fine … probably got wrapped up in feeding his snakes and forgot what day it was."

The mud-encrusted boys headed for their bikes, laughing and shoving each other. They picked up their baseball gear and rode off in different directions, yelling.

"Later."

"Bye."

"See ya."

"Later, gator …"

"Junior high here we come!"

Twenty minutes later, the old red American Flyer bicycle sailed down Tangerine Street, leaned, turned and rolled up the driveway.

Matt smashed down his wet tennis shoe hard on the metal rod of the pedal without a rubber footpad. The brake locked, the back wheel slid out to the side and the bike skidded, leaving a black trail on the concrete driveway. The bike's loose kickstand hit the ground in front of the skid mark, and Matt jumped off and ran to the front door. He heard the bike crash on the hard cement. He closed his eyes tight and pulled his cheeks taut. The sound meant loose handlebars that would need to be tightened along with the pedal repair that already needed to be made.

The screen door slammed behind him. "I'm home," he yelled.

"Matt, come out here, please, and help me get these clothes off the line before it rains," his mom said from outside the kitchen screen door, a half-filled clothes basket at her feet.

"I'm pretty dirty, Mom. I don't think you want me touching those clean clothes," Matt said from inside the kitchen. "Hey, it's not going to rain."

"Okay."

Mrs. Parker walked into the kitchen carrying the clothes she'd taken down. A puddle of dirt and water pooled around Matt's wet tennis shoes.

His mom frowned but Matt could see a smile hiding in her bright blue eyes. "You're filthy and wet. That's not from playing baseball. It looks like you went swimming in the mud. Take off your shoes right there. Don't you dare track any more mud through this house—King of the Mountain?"

"Yes, ma'am, and John won. He tossed everybody off the mountain, including Bob and me."

"Well, get washed up. I'll finish getting the clothes. Your dad will be home soon, and dinner's almost ready."

"Yes, ma'am."

Down the street, a muffler rumbled in the distance. Its loud hollow sound and the accompanying vibration echoed in the neighborhood. The noise increased as it neared.

"That's Dad's truck," Matt yelled from the bathroom.

"I know. I hear it too. You made it just in time. Next week school will change that."

Matt walked into the kitchen. "Smells good, Mom. Can I help?"

Mrs. Parker looked out the kitchen window. She smiled. "Yes. Set the table, please."

Chapter 2

AUSSIE NEWS

THIRTY-SIX-YEAR-OLD HARRY PARKER tapped the door-jamb with his hand and walked through the kitchen door. "I'm home, honey. Something sure smells good."

Mrs. Parker looked up from the stove with a hot pad in her hand and an apron tied around her waist. "Pork chops, peas and potatoes, and a lemon meringue pie I baked today. Go get cleaned up, dear. Dinner will be served in ten minutes."

She tilted her head back for a quick kiss as he walked past her. He looked over at Matt and smiled. "Hello, rascal."

"Hi, Dad." Matt pushed the sleeping cat off his chair. "Get off, Smoky. Okay Mom, table's set. What else can I do?"

"Please pour the iced tea."

Mrs. Parker opened the oven and checked on the biscuits. A buttery aroma filled the kitchen. "Almost ready … mmmm … Bet the queen's not eating this well tonight."

Matt put the dishes of food on the table and handed her the straw basket lined with a red-and-white-checked cloth napkin. "Ready for the biscuits, Mom. Yours are the best ones ever."

She filled the basket with puffy, brown, sweet-smelling biscuits. "Thanks, Matt. Okay, Harry, dinner's on the table. Let's eat while it's hot."

Mr. Parker said the blessing and they filled their plates.

"How'd the baseball game go today, son?"

"My team won. JB hit the longest home run, Dad—all the way into the front yard of the new house on the lot across the street. John was the catcher, and he didn't like it. Typical John. He was so mad."

"Why?" Mrs. Parker asked.

Matt laughed. "Because the home run won the game for our team, Mom—and John hates losing. He's our competitor-in-chief."

"Speaking of competitors-in-chief, guess who I saw today at Hamrick's Lumber Yard picking up wood for his next boat-building project?" asked Mr. Parker.

"Bill Peart?" Mrs. Parker said.

"Yep."

"To get him to fishing holes ahead of you?"

"Yep. We were laughing about that "Twenty Years Ago Today" article in the Clearwater Sun a couple of days ago. It was about the big heist and the lost treasure we were all looking for in high school. People were digging holes in the sand from Cedar Key down to St. Pete Beach and Pass-A-Grille."

"I bet that old green metal box with the map and newspaper article about you and Bill is still up in the attic," Mrs. Parker said.

"It's up there somewhere. Guess I'm guilty of a little nostalgia," Mr. Parker said. "And, if the treasure is ever found, I'll know how close we were with my almost secret map. So far, nothing."

"I remember you showing a map to our Cub Scout troop a long time ago, Dad," Matt said. "Wasn't there supposed to be something on Hog Island?"

"Yes, the other half of the map. Bill and I looked there, but we didn't find it." Mr. Parker pushed back his chair and stood up. "Another great supper, June. I've got to run over and pick up a trailer at the Washingtons'. Pie and coffee when I get back?"

"Sure ... but before we get up from the table, I have some news," Mrs. Parker said, "and it's not good news. I got a letter from Australia today. Mum said they won't be able to come over this fall like they'd planned. My dad has developed a heart condition. He's okay but his doctor thinks the long trip is too much for him."

Mr. Parker sat back down. "I'm sorry, honey. I know you've been looking forward to their visit. It's been a long time since you've seen them."

"I know what we can do," Matt said. "Let's go see *them* and I can finally meet all my cousins and aunts and uncles. Maybe we can go at Christmas."

"It's a long trip, Matt. It would take your whole Christmas vacation just to get there and your dad has a business to run." His mom wiped away a tear. "Someday we'll go, but not this year."

"In the meantime," Mr. Parker said, "I'm going to learn how to operate a ham radio and then at least we can hear their voices."

Mrs. Parker smiled. "I like that idea. Now go run your errand and I'll have pie and coffee ready when you get home."

Chapter 3

THE PHONE CALL

MATT SLIPPED OUT OF HIS ROOM and followed the fragrant coffee trail down the hallway, past the still black pane of the picture window and toward the gleaming strip of hardwood floor at the other end of the room. He pushed open the saloon doors that separated the living room from the kitchen.

Mr. Parker sat at the kitchen table with a bowl of cereal in front of him, a spoon in one hand and the Tampa Tribune folded in half in the other. He looked up and smiled.

Matt patted him on the shoulder as he walked past him to the refrigerator. "Morning, Dad."

Mr. Parker snagged the last cornflake floating in the milk. "Morning, son. I thought you'd sleep in today."

"No, too much to do. Got to get ready for our camping trip to Hog Island this afternoon."

Mr. Parker put the paper down. "An article in the paper this morning says a prisoner escaped from the county jail yesterday. He won't be sunbathing out on Hog Island, but you boys stay alert."

"Yes, sir, we will. Thanks for giving me Saturday off, Dad. The last weekend before school starts is going to be so much fun."

His dad stood up. "You're welcome, son. You've worked hard every Saturday all summer. You're due a day off. The men are going to miss you. I've got to get going. General Ready Mix has two concrete trucks scheduled for me at seven o'clock. We're pouring a big floor slab this morning."

"Want me to take Mom her tea this morning?"

"No, let her sleep. It was a long night. She's really disappointed your grandparents aren't coming."

"Okay, Dad. Bye. I'll try to cheer Mom up if she gets up before I leave."

Matt sat at the table, rubbing his sleepy eyes as he poured a glass of cold orange juice from the pitcher.

The wall phone in the kitchen broke the early morning silence.

He put the glass down beside his bowl of cereal. *Who's calling so early? Mom's counting sheep in the bed. Must be a work call for Dad—probably a question about the early concrete pour.*

It rang a second time. It sounded louder.

He reached above him and lifted the receiver. "Hello?"

"Hi, Matt. We farmers are early to rise. Did I wake you up?"

A smile stretched across his face. "Justin?"

"Yep, your ol' buddy with the tractor connected to his ass."

"How's everything in Indiana?"

"Fine, but not so sure about things in Clearwater."

"Why's that? It's great here. A bunch of us guys are starting Labor Day weekend with a camping trip on Hog Island tonight, and I talked Billy into going with us ... and on Tuesday we start junior high school. We're excited!"

"I know, Matt, and thanks a lot. Billy *is* excited. I know he comes across as a little bit square, but that's because he's such a little bookworm. He's a great kid. Can't believe you've got him playing baseball. You know, you're really his only true friend in Florida."

"You coming home?"

"No. That's why I'm calling. I have a big favor to ask."

"What's the favor?"

"I need your help with Billy."

"Billy? Trouble? Here?"

"Going to be. Heard of Wayne Tyson?"

"Older guy. In your class, right?"

"That's him, but he didn't make it to high school with me. He's almost sixteen and still trying to get out of junior high."

"Yeah, I remember him. His dad worked for my dad a few years ago. Don't recall ever seeing him, but I've heard he's big and mean."

"He's bigger than you, but you can hold your own with him. Ready for a story?"

"I like good endings."

"That's why I called you."

"You mean I'll help you write the ending?"

"Matt—you *are* the ending."

Matt laughed. "Oh great. Okay, I'm ready, I guess."

"Well, I had a run-in with Wayne Tyson early this summer … started as a pissing contest, ended with scraped knuckles. We fought, and only his favorite cousin, Bruce, witnessed the blood and mud."

"I didn't know anything about that."

"I didn't tell anyone but my dad, but you'll be happy to know I dropped that duck-butt sucker to his knees. He walked out of the woods with a blood-soaked handkerchief pressed to his broken nose. We didn't shake, but I told him, for me, the whole thing was over, and he could go back to his cave and leave me alone on my mountain. He didn't like my suggestion of where we each lived, but he didn't seem to want a rematch—not anytime soon, anyway. You liking my story so far?"

"I'm standing on the stage just behind the side curtains, waiting for my entrance. Is it coming soon?"

"Yep. Billy called me last night. His bike tires got slashed. Wayne did it. He stood under the streetlight near our house, like he wanted to be seen."

"So, he was seen. Maybe he was just standing around, hanging out, you know."

"Billy watched him nail a note to the street pole, Matt. He read it after Wayne was gone."

Matt grinned. "Did it say, 'I want to be your friend?'"

"No. It said, 'See you soon.'"

"I'm tired of standing behind the curtains, Justin."

"Well, come on out. Your part starts now. I need you to watch out for Billy while I'm here finishing up at the farm with Dad ... only a couple of weeks."

"Justin, you're not serious. Tyson's a hood and he's trouble."

"I'm as serious as I can be. Matt, will you help me? Wayne Tyson is crazy! In his twisted mind, there's *nothing* he won't do to get even with me."

"I don't know if I can, Justin."

"Come on. You can do it. You're not a regular kid, Matt. You've concealed your secrets very well, but I know about you. You've tossed me more than once like a rag doll when we've been horsing around at swim practice. The power, the quickness ... I've felt it. No one I know at Clearwater Junior High can handle Wayne Tyson except you.

"You're a Samson, Matt, but no one's cutting off your blonde hair, beach boy. Plus, you're a thinker. I get all of this. I do. That's why I'm talking to you now. Please, I need you to look out for my little brother.

"I've heard the story about your fight with Jimmy Knox in elementary school. I *know* you can do this! You've got the stuff and the guts to keep him safe until I get home!"

"Well, guess what, Justin? After that fight, I decided not to fight anymore. I can see that end of the story, and—no thanks—I don't want the part. I've got to focus on grades and athletics. You know I want to go to West Point. I can't be fighting with some hood at school."

"I understand, but this is only until I get home. It won't affect you going to West Point, and you won't have to fight him. Just be there. He'll leave Billy alone if you're there."

Matt rolled his eyes. "Justin, I need to think about this—I need to *pray* about it. No promises. I told you ... no more fights for me."

"That's fair. Just remember that you're the only guy in junior high who can do the job and you won't have to fight. Wayne likes to use intimidation and he's good at it. He won't mess with you or hurt Billy, if you're there standing guard."

Matt's stomach stirred and he heard the churning. "Justin, don't say that. You're making me feel bad. Get somebody else."

"There isn't anybody else I trust. Remember, I know you—I *really* know you—and you're the only person I know who can shut Wayne down and help Billy. Please? Hey, Dad's here. Gotta go back to being a farmer. Remember, I'm counting on you."

"Bye, Justin … nice talkin' to you."

Matt stared at the little specks moving beside his cereal bowl—ants, tiny sugar ants. He mashed one with his thumb. *That's what Wayne could do to Billy—but I'm not going to let that happen! I'll tell him this morning.*

His thoughts drifted back to his Mom and her sad face at the dinner table the night before. *I'm not even going to think about Billy's problem right now. Wish I could think of something to cheer Mom up.*

Suddenly the missing treasure that his dad had talked about at dinner flashed across his mind—and like lightning coming down out of the sky—he had the answer. He lifted his glass of orange juice with a smile and toasted his good fortune. *The answer's up in the attic!*

His dad said the green ammo box he'd shown him a few years ago was packed away somewhere up there. The box contained half of a treasure map that his dad and some of his friends found when they were in high school, and an old newspaper clipping with a picture of them. They thought the map would lead them to a treasure a diver had recovered from a sunken galleon in the Florida Keys and had stored in a St. Petersburg bank. It was stolen in a robbery from the bank and never recovered.

That was it! He needed to find that buried treasure. If they had that much money, his dad wouldn't have to work and they could go to Australia and spend the whole summer there. *Concentrate on finding the treasure map! You won't have to deal with Wayne Tyson until next week. Go get the stepladder. Go find the ammo box so you can take the map to Hog Island this afternoon. Hog Island is where our trip to Australia begins!*

Chapter 4

THE ATTIC

SOFT SNORING FROM BEHIND the bedroom door and the faint hum of the refrigerator in the kitchen were the only sounds disrupting the silence in the house.

Matt opened the stepladder he'd brought in from the garage. The early morning rays of sunlight had not yet made their way to the hallway in the center of the house, and the top of the ladder rested in darkness twelve inches beneath the painted plywood that covered the opening to the attic. *I feel like one of the Hardy Boys trying to find the tower treasure.*

He put his foot on the first step of the ladder and stepped carefully so the ladder wouldn't creak and wake his mom. He slid the plywood to the side, climbed the next step and peered into the black cavernous space.

The heat enveloped him. He rubbed his nostrils and buried his nose in his hands, pinching it tight before letting out a muffled sneeze. Then came a second and a third. He reached for the light cord. *Find the ammo box and get out.*

The forty-watt bulb flicked on. The attic remained almost dark except for the circle of light under the bulb. Somewhere stored with all the other stuff not yet ready to be thrown away lay a small box, a little smaller than a shoebox, a green military ammo box that contained a treasure map and a newspaper clipping. When he found the map—and he knew he would—he'd be the next one to search for the hidden treasure. *It has to still be there somewhere. It's my turn. I'm going to find the treasure.*

His eyes adjusted and on the outside edges of the room he saw silhouettes of stacked boxes, an erector set in a cardboard box with a picture of a crane holding a steel pipe in its bucket, old lampshades and faded duck decoys. He felt like he was in a derelict spaceship storage locker in a Flash Gordon story.

It's out there. Don't bump your head and don't slip. Dad said you could fall through the ceiling. Go slow. Have to find that ammo box so you can take it to Hog Island this afternoon.

He kicked the hatbox on the floor in front of him. The hatbox rolled. There it was—the green ammo box—covered with dust.

A shiver ran down his back. *I found it.* Holding the box under one arm, he returned to the opening, turned off the light, climbed on the ladder and slid back the attic cover. "Darkness once again rules in the attic," he said quietly, and he grinned as he descended.

Sitting on his bed with the door to his bedroom closed, he opened the ammo box and took out the wrinkled map that had been scribbled with crayon on a piece of old brown paper bag. A large X marked where the second half of the map and some coins from the treasure were buried. *Wonder why they went to all that trouble? Maybe the other half will lead to the treasure itself.*

Matt carefully folded the map, softly kissed it and slid it into a pocket of his shorts. He'd be the next one to search for the hidden treasure. *It's my turn, and I'm going to find it! We're going to Australia!*

Before he closed the ammo box, he unfolded the yellowed newspaper and saw the article, "Possible Hidden Treasure," with a photo of his dad and some other boys. He put the old newspaper back in the box and hid it on a closet shelf behind his hunting boots and bird vest. He'd tell his dad later that he'd found it.

In the hall, he looked at his watch. He had to hurry. In twenty minutes he had to meet Billy. A snore interrupted the silence. He blew his mom a kiss, picked up the ladder and walked out to the garage to put it away. Mission accomplished.

Mullet, a brown and white pointer—the family's bird dog—waited behind the garage at the kennel gate, whimpering and looking downcast.

"I know Dad's fed and walked you so don't give me that sad look." He topped the bird dog's dish with fresh water from the hose, patted his head, kissed his nose and walked into the kitchen, not looking back. Mom would be up soon and give him some more attention. *You found the treasure map. Time to go meet Billy ... and don't worry about some hood that doesn't even know you!*

Chapter 5

MR. WELLER

STANDING MOTIONLESS on the front porch, touched by the serenity of the morning, Matt forgot for a moment about the treasure map in his pocket and Billy's problem with Wayne. The damp air hung close to the ground and the moist grass glistened in the rays of the early morning sun. Perched on a nearby TV antenna, a mockingbird sang his collection of other birds' songs while the neighborhood slept.

He allowed the sensation of the peaceful moment to grow inside him. It was the Friday before Labor Day. He and his buddies planned to go downtown and then leave the docks at four o'clock and head to Hog Island for their last campout of the summer. On Monday, he was going deep-sea fishing with Billy, and on Tuesday, he'd be a seventh grader at Clearwater Junior High. *No bully's going to spoil our fun. If Billy needs to be rescued from Wayne Tyson, I'm ready!*

He stepped onto the sidewalk and began singing "Jim Dandy," snapping his thumb and finger to the rhythm. Dressed in plaid Bermuda shorts and a short-sleeved blue T-shirt, he bounced down the street, staying on the sidewalk to keep his tennis shoes dry. He looked like a young version of the lifeguards on the beach with his sun-bleached blond hair, dark tan and sunglasses.

The white frame house with peeling paint at the corner of the street belonged to Mr. Weller, the grumpy old man of the neighborhood. The house, with its green shingled roof and a dormer window with green shutters, stood separate from the garage. Mr. Weller's car, an old green Hudson, was parked in the driveway. The tires sagged. They weren't flat, just low on air.

Billy sat on the sidewalk across the street from Mr. Weller's house, his legs crossed, his glasses on his lap and his face in his hands. As Matt approached, the backfiring lawnmower behind Mr. Weller's house stopped. Matt could hear Billy sobbing. *Boy, he's letting this Wayne guy get to him.*

Mr. Weller pushed his Blue Boy mower from behind the house and walked through the open garage door past a leather boxing bag hanging from a rafter and shelves lined with paint cans. He stopped at a jumble of garden tools that were crammed into a corner.

He emerged holding a shovel. He was shirtless. Suspenders held up his pants and a red rag hung from his back pocket. His wrinkled skin was deeply tanned, his white hair cut short, his belly flat and his muscles rippled on his chest and arms.

"Good morning, Mr. Weller. Not even eight-thirty and you've already finished mowing."

Mr. Weller leaned on the shovel like it was a cane. "Who are you?"

"You know me, sir. I'm Matt Parker. I live one street over. I'm Harry Parker's son."

"I know your dad. He's a good man—you tell him I said that." He looked down and began digging. "Who's that kid over there bawling, Matt Parker? What did he do—put a hammer to his thumb?"

Matt had assumed that between attention to Mr. Weller's task and the hearing aids he wore, the old man didn't hear or see Billy. Wrong—twice. Matt paused and crossed his fingers. "His name's Billy. His dog died."

"Well, he's too old to cry. Boys leave the crying in the crib."

Matt ignored the comment about Billy's crying. "You have a beautiful yard, sir."

Mr. Weller stuck his shovel into the ground, grabbed the garden hose and dragged the sprinkler to a new place. "You new hatch of kids are babies. That crying is irritating, embarrassing and it's disturbing the neighbors."

Matt smiled. "How about your lawnmower?" he said carefully.

"Engine sounds are music to my ears," Mr. Weller said as he pulled the red rag out of his back pocket. He pointed an outstretched arm at Billy. "The sound coming out of that boy's mouth makes me want to turn off my hearing aid and stuff this rag all the way back to his tonsils."

Matt shook his head and walked toward Billy, who looked small in a red T-shirt that looked like it was a hand-me-down from Justin. "Talk to you later, Mr. Weller," he called back over his shoulder.

Mr. Weller bent down, pulled up a weed, dropped it into a Red Ryder wagon sitting on the grass beside the driveway and returned to his garage without turning around.

"I'm going to help my friend bury his dog," Matt said just loud enough for Billy to hear. "Sad, isn't it?" He winked at Billy. "We're digging the hole right in the middle of your front lawn."

Billy stopped crying, wiped his eyes, put his glasses back on and smiled. "I don't even have a dog."

"No wonder he's nicknamed grouch of the neighborhood," Matt said. "My mom says he changed when his wife died last year, but long before she died, he always yelled at us kids if we put a foot on his property. He's lucky Halloween comes only once a year. You okay?"

Billy wiped his sleeve over the mixture of tears and sweat still on his nose. "No."

"Never seen you cry like that. Justin told me all about Wayne Tyson. Did something else happen?"

Billy sniffed and rubbed his nose. "No, but Matt, he's big and scary."

Matt smiled. "Is he a giant or something? Does he have big old fangs hanging out of his mouth?"

"No, he's not a giant, but gosh, is he scary. Maybe he does have fangs. He's not real tall, but he's bigger than you and lots bigger than me. Man, compared to him we're little kids. He's older—a lot older, and he likes to fight. Justin took him on, but Justin's not typical. Right, Matt?"

"Right, but Wayne's not going to fight you, and if he's in junior high, he can't be that old. Besides, we're getting bigger by the day, so stop crying. We're going to Hog Island today."

Billy sniffled. "He's been held back a bunch of times."

Matt laughed. "Maybe he'll join the Navy."

"That's not funny, Matt." Billy wiped away a tear. "First you say 'fangs,' now you say 'Navy.' Wait 'til you see Wayne Tyson. Your jokes will stop then."

"You may be right," Matt said. The name made goose bumps appear on his arms. He reached down, plucked a blade of grass and stuck it in his mouth. He hooked his thumbs in his front pockets and flared his fingers on the outside of his Bermuda shorts like he'd seen James Dean do in "Rebel Without a Cause."

As he chewed the grass, he casually smoothed the ground in front of him with one foot and packed down an anthill. He hoped he looked confident. He wasn't. "Let's start walking. You've got to get your mind off that hood. Plus, now you've got me worrying a little. I want you to start thinking good thoughts."

"You're right. Where are we meeting the guys?"

"Downtown at Brown Brothers."

The low baritone sound of a truck horn pierced the air. A Pet Milk truck slowed as it approached the boys and the milkman stuck his arm outside the open door and waved. "Morning boys."

Matt waved back. "Hi, Mr. Dulligan," he yelled as the milk truck sped back up and hurried down the street.

"What time is it, Billy?"

"Almost nine."

"Wow, he's late. He should be home by now."

Matt noticed Billy staring at him. *Probably comparing me to Wayne Tyson or Justin. Probably wondering how I can even help him. Wonder if Wayne will be downtown? Settle down, Matt—you can deal with this without fighting.*

He wiped the perspiration beginning to form in the corners of his eyes and put his sunglasses back on. "Shake it off, Billy. Like my new sunglasses? Pretty cool, huh?"

"Yeah, they're cool." Billy looked at his watch. "What time are we supposed to be there?"

Matt patted Billy on the back. *Maybe I can cheer him up. Put one foot in the water and check the temperature.* "Nine o'clock," he answered. "Listen, Billy, I know you're worried about Wayne. I've been there with someone like him. I can't protect you like Justin can, but I'll help you if you need me. I hope that makes you feel a little bit better."

"It does, Matt. Thanks."

Matt's stomach churned thinking about Wayne. He wanted to be on the train headed for West Point one day. Wayne's train led to a bad station. *Got to get Billy thinking about something else. No time for distractions today.*

Chapter 6

WHO'S BEHIND THE TRUCK?

THE TWO BOYS WALKED at a brisk pace as drops of sweat fell from the tips of their noses onto the hot pavement.

"It's too early to be this hot," Matt said. "Where's a cloud when you need one?"

"I can't wait to get to Hog Island this afternoon," Billy said. "Over there I bet we'll love having no clouds."

A group of chimney swifts flew overhead in tight formation, with a long string of high-pitched chirps all running together. They peeled off like F-86 Sabre jets on a strafing run. The two boys looked up and as the birds disappeared, another group appeared in the sky.

Matt grinned and saluted them the same way he'd salute the planes flying over at an air show. "Do you think those birds are eating or just having fun?"

Billy smiled for the first time. "Those birds are having fun!"

"That's right and that'll be us in a few hours, Billy."

"Hog Island?"

"You got that right."

Down the street, the American flag on the post office flagpole lay limp and motionless instead of waving in the saltwater breeze from the bay that usually provided relief from the heat downtown.

A '56 black Thunderbird convertible with the top down swung into a parking space in front of the post office with the voice of Chuck Willis blaring from the radio singing his new hit song, "Hang Up My Rock & Roll Shoes."

The teenage driver, wearing sandals and a swimsuit cover-up, jumped out of the car and ran up the steps of the post office with a letter in her hand, leaving the driver door open and the engine running.

Matt hit a parking meter with his hand. "I love that song—and I love that car. The way she's dressed, I bet the beach is her next stop. And the way she's waltzing up those steps, I bet that letter is headed to a boyfriend. What do you think, Billy?"

"A pen pal in New Zealand? I have one from Auckland. His name is Louis Aiken."

"Pen pal? No way. She's a looker—definitely a boyfriend, and not a Wayne Tyson type. Jeez, I've gotta quit thinking about that guy. Once you think about snakes in the woods, every stick is a snake. I'm not even sure I'll recognize him and here I am thinking about him as someone's boyfriend."

"Yeah, she's too classy for him," Billy said. "She reminds me of my cousin in Indiana."

Just past the post office, the driver of a delivery truck put a load of newspapers on his dolly and rolled them into Mel's Newsstand.

"Look at those stacks of newspapers," Matt said. "That guy has a big job ahead of him. Ever been in Mel's? It's a cool store."

"No, but my dad goes in there to get the *Indianapolis Star.*"

"I can see why. Anyone who wants a different newspaper than the Clearwater mullet wrapper or the *Evening Independent* goes there. Plus, you can get chewing gum, candy bars, peanuts and all kinds of Lifesavers flavors, every cigarette known to man, not only American but English, Australian and lots of others, pipe tobacco that smells like sweet cherries, magazines, comic books ..." Matt stopped and took a deep breath. "He has everything in there."

"Sounds like it," Billy said.

Matt's heart began beating fast. He saw someone slip past the driver and disappear behind the truck. He stared at the wheels and undercarriage. Jeans and boots. The boots stopped then stepped back out of view. He felt like he was at the top of a roller coaster track ready to plunge. *That could be Wayne. There I go again, seeing snakes—but better not take a chance.*

"We need to hurry," Matt said. "We were supposed to meet John and Bob five minutes ago. I hate being late, plus I'll have to listen to both of them cry. The first words from Bob's mouth will be, 'It's about time,' and John will say, 'Where have you been?' You mark my words. I bet I'm right."

Matt glanced down the street. "Hey, there they are by the railroad tracks beside Brown Brothers. Look at them laughing and chasing each other around. No worries for them." Matt shook his head. "Four days from junior high and look at them. They look big enough, but they act like they're still at South Ward Elementary. They're funny though.

John always says not to ever let maturity take away your fun. Let's sneak up on them. They won't even see us coming."

Billy stared at the back of John's tight Dodger T-shirt and his tanned, muscular arms. "Gosh, Matt, I don't think I ever realized how husky John is. He makes me feel like a sick midget."

"He'll probably be the strongest boy in seventh grade," Matt said, "and probably captain of the football team like his brother when he gets to Clearwater High School. Quiet, let's sneak up on them."

They walked up behind John, and Matt grabbed his arm. "We're here."

John jumped. "Where have you been? It's hot standing out here in the sun." Bob's damp hair clung tight to his scalp. He glared at Matt. "It's about time."

"Do I know these two or what?" Matt said.

Billy nodded and smiled. "Yep, you're clairvoyant without a doubt."

"You look like 'The Thing' chased you, Bob," Matt said.

Bob pulled his fingers through his hair and his glare turned into a smile. "You're late—and I'm hungry."

John's grin changed into a frown. "Matt's been telling you we're immature, right Billy? We're embarrassing him and that's good! Don't believe too much unless you wanna be a priest ... or a goody-goody."

He looked at Matt. "And it's hot standing out here in the sun. We started to think you two weren't coming. We're standing around here sweatin' our balls—and where were you? Sipping lemonade somewhere?"

"Quit your belly-achin.' We're here. Who are you? Sgt. Friday?"

John grinned. "Just the facts, sir. Nothing but the facts."

"It was a hot Friday morning. We were working the day shift ... Hot and muggy. Got a call ... two boys disrupting the people downtown by Brown Brothers Dairy Store. Someone said they looked crazy," Matt said in his best Joe Friday voice.

"That's a good one," John said.

"Thanks—and just so you know—we're late because Billy and I needed to talk."

"What were you talking about?" Bob asked. "No secrets in this group. Right?"

"Right," Matt said. "Billy's bike tires got slashed last night by a hood named Wayne Tyson. That's what we were talking about."

"I've heard of that guy, Billy. He's bad news," John said. "Let's go inside Brown Brothers and cool off in their new air conditioning and we can talk about it while we get some food."

Chapter 7

MEL'S NEWSSTAND

WAYNE TYSON TURNED SIDEWAYS and let the truck driver pull his dolly through the opening of Mel's Newsstand with his last load of newspapers, but his eyes never left the two twerps as they ran between the slow-moving cars on the other side of the street.

He watched Billy MacDonald, Justin's little brother, and Matt Parker, the son of the homebuilder his dad had worked for before his dad died, as they walked down the sidewalk and disappeared into Brown Brothers. They were going to be easy targets and he was glad they were downtown. *It's going to serve Justin MacDonald right when I get his little brother.* He touched the ridge high up between his eyes and rubbed the bump. *Justin broke my nose. I hate that sonofabitch and that twerp is going to pay for it.*

Wayne licked his lips. *Take it slow. Yeah, that's right. Savor it all. Remember, big predators play with their food, sometimes for a long time. Then they finally kill and devour their prey, one limb at a time.* His game was playing out the same way, and except for Justin, his technique had served him well.

Wayne was the top dog within his group of friends. They were the hoods—tough guys dressed in white T-shirts, leather jackets, Levi's jeans with leather belts and boots. They slicked their hair back on the sides. They were "bad." Their heroes were James Dean, Sal

Mineo and Marlon Brando, the rogues of the movie world.

He liked the title "bully" even more than "hood," but picking on these little ones could cause a backlash. He didn't care. Bullies are cats. Cats bat little mice back and forth, back and forth, hurting them first with only the fear that they can't escape. He was the big tomcat of the school. Time had passed, memories had dimmed and the guard dog had left for a farm in Indiana. He had new mice, unprotected—a dream come true.

Mel stood behind the shop's large cash register—etched like a Browning shotgun—that stood front and center above a glass-topped cabinet. "Can I help you?"

"Gimme a pack of Lucky's and some Juicy Fruit gum," Wayne said.

"Cigarettes for you," Mel said, "or your boss?"

Wayne glared at him and in a surly voice answered, "The boss wanted the gum."

"Anything else?"

Wayne shook his head.

"Thirty cents."

Wayne bounced on his feet to get his hand to the bottom of the pocket of his tight Levi's jeans and struggled to get his fist out. He opened his palm and between his grease-stained thumb and little finger lay a quarter, dime, two nickels, a blue ball of jean washing lint, a nut, a washer and a silver box lighter.

He picked out the quarter and nickel and tossed them on the counter. He stopped the nickel as it rolled like a free tire heading for a ditch, smacking it down against the glass of the countertop as if he'd squished a fly.

Mel picked up the money and dropped it in the cash register. The register dinged as the drawer closed and Mel looked up with a dull, straight face. "Thanks."

Wayne pulled the red string of cellophane with his teeth and opened the pack of cigarettes. Out on the sidewalk, he hit the edge of the pack on his open palm and pulled out the two protruding cigarettes, placing one over his ear like a pencil and tapping the other against the lighter.

He took a final drag on the cigarette, the burning tobacco less than an inch away from his lips, threw it on the sidewalk and ground the cigarette butt down to an ashy black smear with his heavy boot. He'd pay Justin back for the bloody, broken nose and the embarrassment.

He went back into Mel's and wandered to the back, found a hot rod magazine and glanced through it. Let the twerps relax and enjoy their milkshakes. Yeah. Let them laugh and carry on—all the more fun for him to bust them up and take them into the realm of the mouse.

Chapter 8

BROWN BROTHERS DAIRY STORE

JOHN PULLED OPEN THE DOOR of Brown Brothers Dairy Store and swept his hand forward. "After you, future junior high seventh graders, members of the secret Order of Ming, open Order of the Grill, silent Order of the Timid and no order at all. Let's get in here and cool off."

Matt poked John in the stomach with a finger as he walked past him. "Whatever that meant, John ... thank you." He felt John's muscles tighten, hard as a brick. No matter what happened with Wayne, John was the friend he knew he needed by his side. He stepped into Brown Brothers, relaxed, and sucked in a long smooth stream of air. "Ahhhhh. Back in our oasis and my sweat has turned to ice."

John closed the glass door and sighed as the cool air hit his hot cheeks. "Oh boy, this beats the attic fan in my house. I could stay here the rest of the day and just drink chocolate ice cream sodas 'til they rolled me out the door."

Billy's eyes scanned the long room filled with booths and counter stools upholstered in pale green vinyl.

"Been here before, Billy?" Bob said.

"No, this is my first time. It's cool."

Conversations of customers already seated sounded like bees

moving around in a flower garden. The smell of vanilla and cinnamon floated in the air. Fresh baked pies with glazed crusts, some sprinkled with cinnamon, waited on a glass countertop, ready to be sliced and delivered to tables.

Mr. Brown, the co-owner of the dairy store, sat at the counter on the first stool, wearing a long white apron over his shirt and slacks, sipping a steaming cup of black coffee. He looked up over the newspaper spread out on the counter and smiled. "You boys find a seat. It's early and there are still plenty, but it'll be jammed in another hour."

John sat down in a booth beside the window overlooking the railroad tracks. "How about this one? I can face the front door like Wild Bill Hickok—you know, keep an eye out for bad guys."

Matt watched Billy's eyes dart around. "Wayne won't be in here, Billy. Relax."

Behind the long counter, a waitress in a white uniform pulled the shiny metal container out from under the long mixing rod of the jadeite green Hamilton Beach milkshake mixer that matched the room's décor and poured a chocolate milkshake into a tall glass. "Billy, look at that milkshake. I'm having one of those," John said.

Bob pointed to the sandwich board menu attached to the wall behind the long counter, under the sign that read BROWN BROS DAIRY STORE in bold red letters. "Billy, take your pick. Egg salad sandwich forty cents or banana split forty cents."

"No hamburgers?"

"Hamburgers at the Owl Diner or the Park Terrace Grill. Here, you get great sandwiches, pies, fountain Cokes and malted milkshakes."

"No music either, Billy," Matt said.

"Sincerely? No jukebox?"

"Nope," Matt said. "Only good food and conversation. No music. Let's sit."

John grinned and winked at Billy. "Listen to this—Oh, Mr. Brown, I see you still don't have a jukebox. Where's your rock 'n' roll spirit?"

Mr. Brown snapped the paper wide open so hard it popped. Without looking up, he said, "No, I don't, John."

Matt's chest tightened. John wasn't done.

"Why not?" pressed John.

Mr. Brown folded his paper and took one more sip of his coffee. "Like I tell you every time you ask me that question, John. If I had to hear that screaming music you kids love, they'd ship me off to Chattahoochee in a day. That screaming, what's his name? Little Jack? And that 'shaking' Elvis drive me nuts. I have to listen to it at home on Sarah's radio, but I don't have to have it here. Comprende? Find me a jukebox with only Frank Sinatra and the Ames Brothers and I might reconsider."

"Sir, excuse me," John said. His face flushed and he suppressed a laugh. "Little Jack is Little Richard."

"Mr. Brown?" Bob said.

"What, Bob?" Mr. Brown answered, ignoring John.

"Do you know you're the only one in town that doesn't have a jukebox? The Park Terrace Grill has one, and even the Owl Diner."

A big smile filled Mr. Brown's face, and Matt relaxed.

"Yes, I do and I'm quite proud of that. If I had one in here, we'd all go deaf. I've watched people coming out of the Owl holding their ears. Bottom line, it's my decision. We live in America."

John grinned and held his ears. "What did you say, sir?"

Mr. Brown walked over to the boys' booth, scowling. He was a big man, and the long apron that fell below his knees made him look even bigger. He laughed and rubbed John's head. "Who's this young man? Do his parents know he's with you?"

The boys laughed, John the loudest.

"My name's Billy MacDonald, sir."

"You have a brother named Justin?"

"Yes, sir."

"Justin's a fine young man, just like the boys you're with today." He patted Matt on the back. "Keep 'em straight, Matt. You're the adult here."

"Yes, sir. Thank you."

Mr. Brown turned away. John scowled. "He's probably right, Matt, but the truth hurts," John said. "You're a dork, you know."

"Hey Matt, did you see Dee and Maggie and those other two girls sitting way back there in a booth laughing?" Bob asked.

"Yes. The short one with the wavy dark hair sitting beside Maggie is Elaine. She went to Skycrest with Dee and Maggie, but I don't recognize the girl with the ponytail sitting beside Dee. Want to go say 'hi' to them?"

"Not now," Bob said. "I'm hungry."

"I'll go with you," John said. "Haven't seen Elaine for a while. She's not happy with me. We were at the beach and I ran after her friend Ann, yelling 'fatty on the beach.'"

Billy rolled his eyes. "John, you're always getting in trouble."

"How can you say that, Billy? Why … I'm the perfect gentleman. Hey, Matt—is Dee the cute one with the short blonde hair and big smile?"

"That's her. Bob and I know Dee and Maggie from church. Let's go over and see why they're laughing."

"Girls laugh for no reason," John said.

"Like you?"

John flipped Matt the bird. "Up yours, Matthew. Let's go see the girls."

Dee looked up from a picture album as Matt and John approached. "Hi, Matt."

"Hi Dee, Hi Elaine, Hi Maggie. Long time no see—not since Sunday School last week." His eyes circled the table. "This is John Hollis, my buddy from South Ward."

"Hello, John. It's a pleasure to meet you," Maggie said.

"I'm glad to meet you too, John," Dee said. "Matt, who's that over there with Bob? Should we know him?"

"Billy MacDonald," Matt said. "Went to Belleair Elementary last year."

"We heard you all giving Mr. Brown the business. You guys ready for school to start?"

"You bet. Junior High here we come," John said. "We heard you all laughing and said, 'Let's go over there and break up the party.' Hi, Elaine, are you still mad at me?"

"Hi, John. No, I'm not mad at you, but it's a good thing Ann got over what you said or I would be."

"Come on, Ann knew I was kidding. I've made her blush since nursery school."

"Yeah? She chased you out into the water."

"I told her I was sorry."

Elaine laughed. "After she threw a giant shell at you. Too bad

38

John's not nice like you, Matt. Well, maybe you're not *always* nice. Remember playing musical chairs at Dorothy Hood's birthday party in second grade?"

Matt glanced over at the blue-eyed, sandy-haired girl with the ponytail and the cute figure that he hadn't met yet, closed his eyes tightly and grimaced. "What did I do, Elaine?"

"You pulled the chair right out from under me so you could win," Elaine said. "I flopped right to the floor and my dress went over my head. I could have killed you. I hardly knew you then. Remember? I was so embarrassed."

Matt's face turned red. "You weren't supposed to fall. I'm sorry."

Elaine laughed. "You're forgiven, but in the future whenever you gentlemanly pull out a chair for me to sit down, I'm going to be on guard."

Dee touched the shoulder of the girl beside her. "Boys, this is Bonnie Curtis, our friend from North Ward. Bonnie, Matt and John went to South Ward."

"Hi, John, nice to meet you," Bonnie said. She looked over at Matt and extended her hand, looking into his eyes. "Hi, Matt. Remember me?"

Matt looked at her, trying to remember her face. He shook her hand and suddenly, his heart galloped like a racehorse on the home stretch. Her warm hand triggered unfamiliar feelings inside him and he felt tingly all over. Little goose bumps erupted on his arms. It was new and crazy. Bonnie was maybe the cutest girl he'd ever met.

"Sailing prams?" she said with a coy smile.

"Oh wow … my gosh … yes, that was a long time ago … fourth grade?"

She laughed. "Yes. I don't think you liked sailing, especially after you rammed into me."

"Oh, that's right. I thought I sank you. Boy, I made a quick tack, peeked under the sail and bam—I hit you broadside. That was a bad accident."

"Ah, I didn't see it that way," Bonnie said with a playful look on her face. "I was winning that race. Someone was beating you and you couldn't stand it. I think you crashed into me on purpose so you could win."

"Matt!" Dee said. "Shame on you."

Matt looked at John and cringed. "Oh man, why did we come over here, John?"

"Because you said, 'Let's go over there and talk to those good-looking girls,' but I'm glad we did. I like it when somebody else sees you're not perfect."

"And once again, John sees the open wound and reaches for the salt shaker. Thanks a lot buddy," Matt said. "Okay, Bonnie, you got me. Will you accept my apology?"

Bonnie smiled. "I guess so—you're forgiven."

"Thank you. Do you still sail?"

"Yes, Snipes."

"Well, you're safe. I fish now. No more sailing …"

"Why?"

"Sometimes I can't wait on the wind."

"Guess what? I fish too—with my dad."

"Really? I'm going out fishing on the Miss Buckeye on Labor Day with Billy, the boy sitting over there with Bob." Suddenly, he felt lightheaded and his head spun. *Why did I say that?* The words just popped out.

"Really?" Bonnie said. "We just went fishing on that boat two weeks ago. My dad knows the captain."

"Well, if you're free, maybe you could go fishing with us on Monday." He was surprised at his boldness. He was floating in the clouds. He looked at Bonnie closely and tried to remember more about the sailing mishap. He had a vision of a little girl with blue eyes and pigtails. The girl he stared at was nothing like the girl in that long-ago vision. Beyond the blue eyes—nothing, but yet—something. He wanted to know this girl. He really wanted to know her.

Dee grabbed Matt's arm, the smile back on her face and a twinkle in her eyes. "Isn't it exciting? Next week instead of being in separate schools, we'll all be in one school together."

"It's going to be cool," Matt said.

"It was nice to see you, Matt," Maggie said, "and I'm delighted to say you've always been a perfect gentleman around me. Maybe I've been lucky," she added with the hint of a smile.

"Well, we're out of here and headed to Frank's to buy some girl stuff," Dee said. "And then a slumber party at my house tonight—you know—hair in curlers, popcorn and soft drinks and no sleep." She fluttered her eyelashes. "We're going to the movies at the Ritz tomorrow afternoon. Maybe we'll see you there."

Matt and John returned to their table just as the waitress brought a tray of food and drinks. Matt watched the girls walk past them, his eyes never wavering from Bonnie. The girls waved as they opened the front door and left the store.

"Okay, let's get serious," Matt said. "We've got our food and we're alone. Billy has a big problem with Wayne Tyson. He threatened Billy last night. Justin called me this morning and asked me to watch out for Billy at school until he gets back in a couple of weeks. I may need your help."

"You've got it, Matt. You know that," John said.

"Mine too," Bob said.

"Okay. Thanks, guys. Billy and I will tell you more about his problem tonight around the campfire when everybody's together, but I want to talk to you right now about something exciting … this treasure map I just found." He pulled the folded map out of his pocket. "There's an old stolen treasure buried around here. This half of the map shows where the other half of the map is buried on Hog Island. My dad found this half when he was in high school. I say we dig for it tonight. We find that half and then we find the treasure and we're in the money—lots of money."

John took a bite of his sandwich and wiped the mayonnaise running down his chin. "Who's 'we,' Kemo Sabe? Just kidding … you know we'll help. Sounds like a cool adventure. Moolah—ka-ching, ka-ching."

"If we find it, we split it," Matt said. "John, you could buy one of those Army Surplus Jeeps you always point out in the *Popular Mechanics* ads, you know, the Jeeps stored in crates. Bob gets his dreamboat, Billy gets a serpentarium and I'll use my share for a trip next summer to visit my mom's family in Australia. Sincerely, the treasure is real, guys."

"Cool," John said. "I like that idea of the Jeep—I could even buy one for my buddies, Crow and Bum."

"The stash hidden is mind-boggling," Matt said. "You could buy a ton of Jeeps."

"I'm ready," Billy said. "I could use some more room to keep my snakes."

"I hate snakes," said John with a shudder. "Don't tell me you're one of those guys that wraps them around your neck."

"Yep, I even kiss 'em."

"That's sick, Billy," John said.

"Yeah, Matt," Bob said, "I could get my own boat instead of having to use Dad's. If I put a hole in that boat, no worry about a spanking."

"Well, let's not forget about the guy who's trying to scare Billy," John said. "I say he needs to worry about a spanking."

Matt banged his fist on the table. "Let's do it."

"Let's do what?"

"Spank him."

"You and what Army, Matt? Have you seen him?"

"I was only kidding, John. I haven't seen him, but I'm not worried about him. Enough about who we can spank and what we can do with that treasure. There's something else we need to talk about. There's an escaped prisoner on the loose and we need to be on the lookout when we're on the island."

"My dad said that guy's got family in Alabama and he's probably halfway to Tallahassee by now," Bob said.

"Hey," Billy said. "No talk about escaped prisoners. I've got enough on my mind with Wayne Tyson." He picked up his milkshake and sucked on the straw.

"Okay, Billy. Sorry to bring that up. Dad wouldn't be letting me go if he was worried about it. And, let's not ruin this day worrying about Wayne Tyson. He's just trying to scare you. We won't let anything happen to you, right boys?"

Bob banged both hands on the table. "Right! Attention. Blow the trumpets. Assume battle stations. We'll protect you, Billy."

"Right on," John said as he lifted his fist.

Matt held out his hand, palm down, and the others placed their hands on his. "All for one, and one for all."

Bob took back his hand and stared through the front window with his eyes open wide. His chin dropped. "I hope you're ready, because I see a hood that could be Wayne Tyson jaywalking across Cleveland Street right now—in the middle of all that traffic—and he's coming this way."

Matt squinted his eyes. "Leather jacket in the dead of summer and walking like a wannabe tough guy. I bet that's him. I thought he might be downtown today."

Billy slumped in his seat. His face turned pale and his body trembled, like he'd fallen through the ice on his farm pond in Indiana in the dead of winter.

"Settle down, Billy," Matt said. "It's going to be okay."

Chapter 9

TROUBLE

THE FRONT DOOR OF Brown Brothers opened. Bright sunlight flooded the entry and silhouetted the figure of Wayne Tyson wearing a black leather jacket. He remained motionless in his own shadow. He looked like a statue out of a wax museum.

He took a step forward, pulled the door closed and stuck his thumbs into the front pockets of his Levi's.

"That's got to be him," Bob said under his breath.

Wayne looked at the boys with a blank expression. His green eyes and long eyelashes stood out and made him look coldly handsome, in spite of a prominent Adam's apple and pimples along his jaw line and down his neck.

"He thinks he's Marlon Brando in *The Wild One*," Bob mouthed.

John whispered, "Is that prick for real?"

Wayne took three steps. The upholstery tacks on the heels of his boots hit the black and white checkered linoleum floor like a hammer hitting a sixteen penny nail. He stopped ten feet from the boys' table and stared at them.

Matt moved to the edge of the seat and said without moving his lips, "He thinks so."

A drop of perspiration rolled down the side of Wayne's nose and formed a bead of water in the indention above his upper lip, but he didn't touch it. "Well, well … you boys think you're hot stuff because you're starting junior high?"

Matt folded his arms on the table. "Actually, probably not as hot as you, kid … but we *are* excited."

"You commenting on my jacket? I'm Wayne Tyson, and don't ever call me 'kid' again."

"My friend Billy, here, tells us some kid named Tyson is going to get him at school," Matt said. "You know anything about that?"

"I asked *you* a question—so-called boss of the table."

Matt rubbed his bare leg below his Bermuda shorts. "It's still a little warm the end of August."

John's eyes flashed at Wayne. "I've seen your name carved on bathroom stalls … You think you're bad?"

Wayne's eyes turned to John. He didn't blink. "This morning I drowned a kitten in the toilet and kicked a crippled dog that was limping along down the street. His cries brought a smile to my face. Does that answer your question?"

"I guess you eat raw meat," Matt said before John could respond.

"Matt Parker, right? I know who you are. My dad once worked for yours—went to high school together—said your dad was an asshole."

Matt tensed. *Better cool it.* "Yeah, I'm Matt Parker, and these are my friends. Hope you find an open table because our booth is already filled."

Wayne took another step and stopped a few feet from the boys. Cool air blowing from the air conditioner fluttered the paper napkins secured by forks on the table, but not a hair on his head moved.

Matt sat quietly watching him. "Want me to introduce the table? That's John and Bob. And that's Billy."

Wayne looked at Matt closely. "Didn't know you were so young, Parker. You could pass for a fifth grader."

"Oh … I'm growing fast," Matt said, matching the tone of Wayne's voice. He could handle Wayne, but he had to be careful.

"Where's Justin?" Wayne asked. "I hoped he'd be here too. Yeah, it's my bad fortune he's gone."

"Oh, he's coming back," Matt said. "He loves picking low fruit, you know, the ones not able to cling to a branch—that are soft and mushy."

Wayne's eyes closed into slits and he pulled himself up straight and tall. "I can't wait for both of you … and baby brother too."

Matt tightened his fist under the table. "You mentioned a relationship between our dads and you tried to disparage mine. Here's the rest of the story. … From time to time my dad needed to purge the riff raff and the unproductive. Didn't he fire your dad?"

Wayne lunged toward the table but stopped just beyond reach and pointed his finger at Matt. "I don't need to tell you anything, but I will. First of all, my dad said he got screwed, and second, I'm going to do something to little Billy here, just because I want to, okay? And the way you're making me feel right now, you're next." He closed his hand and made a fist. His knuckles turned white. "You want trouble, you little fucker? Come here and I'll kick your ass right now."

Matt and John stood up simultaneously. A plate crashed to the floor.

"Hey!" Mr. Brown yelled. He ran up from the back of the store and stepped in between Wayne and the boys. "There'll be no trouble here. Do you hear me, Wayne?"

"These little twerps are getting under my skin."

Mr. Brown pointed to the front door. "Well, you're getting under *my* skin. Get out, and don't let the door hit you on your way out."

Wayne glared at Billy who had slumped in the booth. "I'll see you at school, Billy-boy. I've got plans for you and your cocky friend. You better watch your backs."

"Did you hear me?" Mr. Brown said.

"I'm leaving."

Wayne walked toward the door, removed the cigarette from above his ear and popped the back of his arm, making the cigarette flip and land in his mouth.

Bob gave Wayne the finger, and Billy pulled himself back into a normal sitting position. "That trick might get you into a sideshow at the fair," John said.

Wayne turned around, his face flushed. He bit into the cigarette and smiled through clenched teeth, looking like he'd swallowed a bad oyster. "Your asses are mine."

"So long, Wayne. It will be a pleasure to see you again," Matt said in the mild manner he imagined Clark Kent might use. On the inside, his stomach knotted up.

Wayne walked out and slammed the door behind him.

The window rattled, the door vibrated and the clock hanging above the door fell to the floor.

Mr. Brown yanked off his apron and ran out the door after Wayne.

"My, my," John said. "That's one pissed-off Mr. Brown."

Matt's eyes opened so wide his eyeballs looked all white. In all the years he'd known Mr. Brown, he'd never seen him lose his temper. "Whoa! Did you see how red his face was? I think Wayne's in big trouble."

"Did you see his eyes?" Billy said. "Flames could have shot out of them."

Bob laughed. "Wayne better be over the railroad tracks and gone."

"He must have disappeared," Matt said. "Here comes Mr. Brown and he's smiling."

Mr. Brown picked up the clock, examined it and walked behind the counter. "Wayne Tyson is going to buy me a new clock—just for starters. This one will now only work twice a day, eleven-fifty a.m. and eleven-fifty p.m."

"I think that guy's all talk," Matt said. "Dressing tough doesn't make you tough, and talking tough doesn't make you tough. He's just a typical bully—gutter talk and all."

"You're dreaming, Matt," Bob said.

"It costs nothing to dream, Bob."

"Matt, this isn't the time for philosophy," John said. "And by the way—what's with the word 'disparage'? I've never even heard that word before. You pissed him off—you *really* pissed him off. You'd better watch your ass. You know I'll be there, but damn ..."

"You didn't do so bad yourself," Matt said with a grin. "Maybe you should say "we" instead of 'you.'"

"Oh my gosh," Billy said, "this is worse than I ever thought it would be. All that blood-curdling talk scared me to death. I'm still scared."

"Billy, I think Matt short-circuited him," John said. "He wasn't expecting a seventh grader to stand up to him—excuse me, the 'Waynster' said 'fifth grader.'"

"Well, that's what he needed," Matt said.

"Makes me want to steer clear of him," Bob said.

Matt stood up. "Makes me want to expose him. Let's get out of here."

"Hold your horses," John said. "Sit back down, Matt. Let's talk about this guy for a minute. I'll help you watch out for Billy, but it looks to me like we need to get serious about this. I was thinking we might have some run-ins with him at school and that would be the end of it. And here we are, having something to eat at Brown Brothers and—shazam—through the door he appears." John grinned. "I heard last summer that Justin beat him up. What should I know besides that?"

"I bet the word was going out that Wayne got beat up," Bob said.

"Yep, and I bet it embarrassed him," Matt said. "You know the saying is that embarrassment can hurt more than a fist."

"John wouldn't know," Bob said.

John's face froze. "What do you mean?"

"You're always the 'embarrasser' not the 'embarrassee.' There's a lesson to be learned here," Bob said.

"Says who?"

"My dad."

"Learn what?" John said with a louder voice. His face showed signs of irritation.

"I'm just saying embarrassment creates strong inner feelings," Bob said.

"And?"

"Watch out who you embarrass."

"I love to tease people. If they blush, so what?" John looked over at Matt. "So, the Waynster was embarrassed. What does that mean? I'm supposed to be scared?"

"He was probably embarrassed because Justin showed that Wayne wasn't as tough as he wanted everyone to believe. Now he needs to prove it," Matt said. "This is serious, John. No laughing anymore. Okay?"

Chapter 10

ADVICE FROM
MR. BROWN

MR. BROWN WALKED OVER and placed one hand on Matt's shoulder and the other on Billy. "The food's on me today, boys. You did well. You were tested and you got an A. Sometimes, you must take a stand or forever be subject to a consequence not wanted. You'll be tried again by Wayne, but today you caught his finger in the car door. Always close the door."

"Thanks, Mr. Brown. We're glad to have you on our side," Matt said.

"Thank you, Mr. Brown," John said. "And think about that jukebox."

"I just did."

"And?"

"Learn to enjoy my singing."

Bob stuck his head out the door and looked both ways. "All clear. I hope we don't need fast feet."

"Goodbye, air conditioning—hello, heat," John said.

Matt took in a deep breath and exhaled slowly. "Wasn't expecting anything like that today."

"Wow, anyone as scared as I was?" Bob said.

"Hell, yes—*I* was scared," John said. "That boy knows how to hurt you."

"I told you Wayne was scary," Billy said. "Believe me now?"

Matt looked up at the white clouds. Wayne's comment about their dads brought forward the disturbing reality that he had a connection with Wayne. He hadn't thought about that, and now he was another blip on Wayne's radar screen.

"Good thing Mr. Brown was close by," Bob said. "We might have been mincemeat."

"Bullshit," John said. "We can kick his ass. What's the worst that can happen? A black eye, bloody nose, split lip? Maybe it'll be like Shane in the barroom fight with us throwing the punches."

"That was a great movie, John, but that was a gunfight," Bob said.

"Don't confuse the story with facts, Bob," John said. "The point is we'll score too."

"And I'll help you, John," Bob said. "I'll be right behind you—scoring you on how well you throw your punches."

"Let's forget about that prick and help Matt find a treasure. I'm ready to dig for a Jeep," John said.

Bob's blue eyes sparkled in the bright sun. "I'm ready to relax by the pool for a while and then go dig for a new boat. Let's wash that hood out of our brains and start thinking about moolah."

Matt glanced over at the clothing store on the corner. Dee said she and the girls were going to Frank's. Maybe they had stopped at Lerner's too.

"Hey, what are you looking over there for?" Bob asked.

"Nothing." Matt tried to act nonchalant. Bob never missed a thing, and Matt didn't want him teasing him about Bonnie. "I've got to get a haircut," Matt said. "Mom will pick you up at three o'clock, Billy, and we'll see you two at the dock at four."

Chapter 11

THE BARBER SHOP

MATT WALKED ALONG the sidewalk in front of the Fort Harrison Hotel, thinking about how he loved the times he'd been there swimming at the pool with Bob, and the times when he and his dad saw the hotel on the horizon when they were returning from fishing out in the Gulf. The hotel was an important navigational sighting for the captain of a boat—but this walk was all about getting a haircut.

Across the street at one of the shops along the side of the Grey Moss Inn, the spinning red and blue stripes of a barber pole signaled Cecil and Jerry's Barber Shop. He loved to go to Cecil and Jerry's and listen to the men talk.

Jerry stood behind the first chair, his back to the mirror, running his clippers up the neck of a customer. He looked up and waved at Matt through the black letters stenciled on the large picture window of the shop.

Matt waved back, walked in and headed for the only vacant seat in the long narrow room—a worn, dark oak chair pushed up to a wall scarred from years of chair-backs rubbing or hitting it. On the back wall, a mounted twelve-point buck's head watched him walk all the way to his seat. On the side wall, colored bottles lined the counter at the base of the mirror, their images doubling all the way down the wall.

"Good morning, Mattie," Jerry said as he pulled away the black and gray striped cloth draped over the shoulders of the man sitting in his chair and gave it a quick snap. "Be with you in a minute. Ready to start junior high? Doesn't seem like very long ago I was putting a board on this chair for you to sit on."

"Morning, Jerry," Matt said.

Jerry swung the barber chair around to face the mirror. "How's that look, CJ? Close enough over the ears?"

CJ studied himself in the mirror, stood up and dug his billfold out of his back pocket. "Thanks Jerry ... looks good. Reminds me of my army days when I was in the motor pool. Back then I used to say, 'Just leave my ears, please.'"

Jerry laughed. He opened the cash register, slipped CJ's five-dollar bill into the bottom drawer and handed him some change. "Thanks."

CJ left a tip on the counter behind the chair and said, "I'll call you tomorrow before the Oklahoma game starts. You'll know it's me. I'll say, 'This is the four-forty-four double clutching truckin' outfit ... you call, we haul, no job too small ... Private Valentine reporting, sir.'" CJ laughed. "Another favorite memory from my army motor pool days."

"That's a good one, CJ—Okay, Tucker, you're next."

Matt picked up an old copy of *Look* magazine from the disorderly heap on a small table beside him. He'd already seen it, but he didn't care. He enjoyed flipping through the pages and looking at the pictures while he waited and listened to the barbershop talk.

Cecil, the barber at the second chair and Jerry's partner, slapped his razor up and down, sharpening it on the leather strop that hung from the side of the chair, while his customer lay back with a towel over his face, like a barbershop scene in a Western movie.

"So, Doc, you back to the pari-mutuel page yet?" Cecil said to the man sitting beside him in the third barber chair.

Dr. Haygood pushed his glasses back up on his nose. "No, still studying the front page." His tie was pulled loose with the top button of his shirt open, and his suit coat hung over the clothes tree in the corner.

"You look a little tired this morning, Doc," Cecil said.

"It was a long and *much* interrupted night of sleep. Just got home and had to go right back to the hospital," said Dr. Haygood.

"Anything interesting in the paper, Doc?" Jerry asked.

"Well, there's a story here says there's a prisoner on the loose, and he might still be in the county."

"Yeah, I heard about him," the man sitting beside Matt said. "He's supposedly one bad rascal. Escaped late yesterday afternoon. I heard about him last night on the radio while I was listening to the Clearwater Bomber softball game. The Bombers beat the Raybestos Cardinals one to nothing, by the way. Herb Dudley pitched a no-hitter. Joe Everett scored the winning run."

"They play again tonight," Jerry said. "I think John Hunter's pitching."

"Go Bombers," Matt said. "I know Junie Trombley. He's our coach in six-man football."

"This morning they said the prisoner's still on the loose," Tucker Thompson said.

"Well," Dr. Haygood said, his head still deep in the paper, "I think we've got another Rastus Russell on our hands."

Matt moved out on the edge of his chair. "Rastus Russell? I've never heard of him before."

"No, probably not. You'd have been a toddler when he broke out of jail and brought fear to every household around here."

Jerry pointed his scissors at Matt. "I remember him. He was a cold-blooded murderer. What does it say about this guy, Doc?"

"His name is Jeremiah C. Rennolds Jr., and he was charged with assault and battery. He escaped from this jail a month ago and stayed on the lam until they caught him a few days ago around Lake Butler, near Jackson Groves. Charlie Jackson saw him sneaking around and called the sheriff.

"He escaped again?" Tucker Thompson said. "They need to be thinking about getting a new jailer."

"He escaped last night around sundown," Dr. Haygood answered. "According to the paper, they think someone may have helped him. It says here he's mean and crazy. What's the difference? How can you be mean and not be crazy?" He chuckled. "But I'm not a psychiatrist."

"Well, old Rastus was crazy, but he's got green grass growing over him now," Charlie Short said.

Matt's eyes opened wide. "Really?" he said.

"Yes, Matt. When Rastus was ten, they sent him to Chattahoochee. Said he drowned kittens. Had a penchant for doing that. But they eventually let him out."

"Then what happened, Mr. Short?"

"He later killed some people up in Palm Harbor. They said it was a grisly scene."

"Did he escape from jail?"

"Yep. He escaped from this same jail and they finally found him and shot him in a grove out in Thonotosassa. You know what they say were his last words?"

Jerry put down his scissors and clippers and looked at Mr. Short. "What?"

The whole barbershop got quiet.

"He said, 'You fellows killed me and I'm glad you did.'"

"Wow," Matt said. "Where did you say this Jeremiah guy might be hiding now?"

"The radio said they think he's probably headed way up north around Pasco County or Hernando," Tucker said.

"That's good," Matt said. "Glad he's not around here. We're going camping at Hog Island tonight."

Jerry combed through Tucker's hair, his scissors snipping like cricket legs rubbing together. "You're not scared, Matt?" Jerry asked him. "What if he doubled back? Maybe you should take a rain check until they catch him."

Matt laughed nervously. "This has turned from a barbershop to Edgar Allan Poe's *House of Usher*."

"Those were stories, Mattie. This is real," Jerry said. "At least take your bird gun with you. Pepper his ass with birdshot if he shows up—So Doc, what else is on that front page?"

"Same old politics and world news."

"Well, don't tell me about that stuff. This is a good Friday. Tell me about the good stuff."

"President Eisenhower has started his plan to build super high-ways that are going to be inter-state. How 'bout that?"

"Thanks, that's something I like to hear about. Now, turn to the sports page. Stay away from the financials. We can read that and cry on our own. Besides, that paper isn't very informative on financial information. The *Wall Street Journal* is around here somewhere."

"I've got it," Charlie Short said from back in the corner of the shop. "Want to know about the bond market?"

"No," Cecil said. "How about some news about the Phillies? They've won three in a row."

"Yeah," the man sitting next to Matt said, "and tell us about Dagwood. Turn to the funnies."

"I was at the track last night," Tucker said. "The fifth race had a real long shot—'Eatin' Grass' was her name—and if she won, I was ready to win thirty-five on her and eight hundred on the quinella."

"The way you're telling the story, you're not sounding happy, Tucker," Jerry said.

"She came around the last turn, ready to take the lead and got bumped. She flipped ass over teakettle and I ended up ripping up the bet. It was so close. I love the dogs. That would've made my night."

"I wish kids were allowed to go," Matt said. "I don't care about the betting, I'd just love to watch them race. They're so fast."

"Well, *you* better be fast, Matt," Jerry said, snickering a little. "I hope you can outrun that escapee if he's hiding on the island. I hope he doesn't join you kids for dinner tonight."

Matt knew the men were trying to scare him, not keep him and the others from going. "I'm sure it'll be a topic around the fire tonight," he said.

Dr. Haygood folded the newspaper and looked at Matt. "You boys are something else."

"You on call again tonight, Doc?" Jerry asked. "Seems like you doctors are always on call. All that education and training so you can be kept up all night?"

Jerry powdered Tucker Thompson's neck with a soft brush, powder going everywhere. He picked up his razor and carefully cut a straight line at the bottom of his sideburns. He pulled the sheet away, shook it out and folded it over his arm. "Okay Doc, slip over here. You're next. I know one thing—I don't begrudge you one penny for what you make and have. I just hope someday you get to enjoy it."

"I'm only on call through the weekend," the doctor said, "so there's an end."

"When's the next time?" Matt asked.

"Every two weeks with the hospital, but I'm still pretty much responsible for my own patients."

Jerry rang up another bill, placed it into the register and slapped his customer on the back. "See you soon, Tucker," he said.

Fifteen minutes later, Dr. Haygood walked over to the mirror, buttoned the top button of his shirt and tightened his tie, adjusting it so it was full at the knot. He walked over to the clothes tree, grabbed his suit coat and put it on. "Thanks, Jerry."

"You're next Matt," Jerry said.

Dr. Haygood put his money next to Jerry's cash register and patted Matt on the shoulder as he climbed into the barber chair. "Have fun camping and keep an eye out for ole Jeremiah."

"Yes, sir."

"Get some sleep, Doc," Jerry said.

Dr. Haygood opened the door and gave a backward wave over his shoulder. "Going to go finish my rounds and then head to the office."

Jerry watched him walk out. "If I ever need to be cut on, that's who's going to do the cutting on me."

He stepped behind Matt. "Watch out for the cowlick, right?"

"Right," Matt said with a grin.

Jerry picked up the electric clippers, pushed Matt's chin down into his chest and turned on the switch. "I'll see what I can do," he said as he began trimming the peach hair, as he called it, on Matt's neck. "So, Mattie, ready for school? Out of elementary and now on to the next level—getting closer to adulthood, right? Some advice: work hard, study hard, play hard. Become a barber, if you love it. Or be a doctor, plumber, teacher, truck driver, carpenter or engineer … whatever. Just do something that you enjoy and makes you happy."

The clippers moved from Matt's neck up to his head, and buzzed in shallow tracks through his hair. "Enter these adolescent years with a serious understanding of how important they are. You kids are special. Some of you don't know it. I think you do. So, get on with it. Keep your drive. Reach for the top."

Matt smiled and nodded.

"It's fun talking to you. You get it," Jerry said.

Matt felt older and special because Jerry didn't treat him like a kid. Other barbers didn't talk to him like that. Jerry was different. He listened to Jerry. The others in the room just heard his words.

Jerry combed across the top of Matt's head and said with a laugh, "Wow, this is some swirl you've got here."

"You know what I think it looks like?" Matt said, his chin again pushed down into his chest. "I think it looks like an ant lion's hole." Matt waited for Jerry's response. He knew he had stumped Jerry—he stood still and the scissor noise stopped.

"A what?" Jerry asked. "A lion hole? Never heard of one."

"An ant lion's hole." Matt looked up at Jerry in the mirror. "The ant lion lives in the sand. He makes a hole like a funnel. He hides under the sand at the bottom. When an ant falls in, he flips sand up along the wall, creating a little landslide, and the ant falls to the bottom. The ant lion grabs him and eats him. I think my cowlick looks like the hole."

"That's a new one on me," Jerry said, and he started cutting again. "I won't disturb the ant lion's hole. You're something, Matt. How old are you? Thirteen yet?"

"Not 'til May."

The door opened and a big man in a white, cement-spattered T-shirt that showed his round stomach entered the room and sat down. His tanned muscular arms were flecked with dried cement. He wore tan work trousers with holes at the knees, and rubber boots that, like the rest of him, were caked with cement.

Matt knew John Kelly well. He was one of the masonry contractors his dad used frequently, and Matt saw him often. "Hi, Mr. Kelly," he said.

"Hi, Matt. Hi, Jerry."

"Hi, John. I was just telling Matt, he and his friends shouldn't go camping on Hog Island tonight because that escaped prisoner is on the loose."

"Got to go on the island," Matt said, a little urgency in his voice. "It's important. My dad knows about that guy, and he didn't say anything about not going tonight."

"There you go, Matt," Charlie Short said from Cecil's chair. "I know your dad. He knows what's best."

"Don't you think it might be a little risky, Charlie?" Jerry asked.

"They don't really know where the guy's hiding."

"My dad would laugh and say, 'Think we should all lock ourselves up in our homes until he is caught?'" Matt said.

"What does that mean, Matt?" Jerry said.

Matt grinned. "It means—we're going camping."

Charlie Short chuckled.

John Kelly looked at Matt and his laugh roared through the room. "That's his dad. You listen to your dad, Matt." The laugh stopped and the smile left his face. "When your dad and I were your age, Matt, we didn't know that in six years we would be in the South Pacific fighting the Japs. Young men are always our fighters—some are good shooting a gun, some can fly a plane. Some drive a truck, some bang on a typewriter. We all have talents, but we need to be decision-makers. We need to think fast and face fear. Not just in war. It will carry you through all facets of your life. Keep going on those campouts. Learn about adversity firsthand. That's my speech to you, Matt. You boys build a giant bonfire out on the sand, listen to music and the island sounds that pucker up bumps all over your body. That convict is not on your island. But if he is, be calm and deal with it."

All eyes were fixed on John Kelly. As quickly as he became serious, he turned his smile back on and picked up a magazine. "When I see you on a job site the next time, Matt, I'll ask how it all went."

"Yes, sir," Matt answered. He had listened to every word, and everyone else in the room had also.

Jerry poured some hair tonic from one of the colored bottles in the palm of his hand. He rubbed both hands together and massaged the oil into Matt's scalp. With a comb, he pulled Matt's hair forward until it almost reached his eyes, parted his hair and made a wave in the front. He patted the waved area with his free open hand. "Left the cowlick alone. Watch out, girls."

Matt blushed. He touched the wave with his hand. The hair was already hard and stiff and felt solid to his touch. Jerry slowly turned the chair, letting him inspect the results from different angles into the mirror. "Thank you, sir."

"You're welcome," Jerry said. He picked up the soft brush and powdered Matt's neck, pulled the sheet away from Matt's body, gave the matador cape a wave and stepped back. "See you soon, Mattie. Keep up the good work in school this year."

"Yes, sir."

Matt paid for his haircut and turned for a last look at Mr. Kelly, who appeared deep in his magazine article so Matt didn't disturb him. He walked to the door, quietly opened it and stepped out onto the sidewalk. The door closed behind him with a soft bang. As he left, he heard Jerry say, "Okay, John. You're next."

Chapter 12

WATCH OUT FOR
THE SEAWALL!

CLEARWATER BAY GLITTERED in the bright afternoon sun; two weathered, green-bronze WWI memorial statues of a sailor and a doughboy at the base of the bluff cast strong shadows across the neatly cared-for flower gardens inside the circular brick and cement sidewalk.

In the channel of the intercoastal waterway, a large sailboat under power circled slowly on the north side of the drawbridge, waiting for the bridge to open. Behind it, a sports fisherman with outrigger poles and a tall radio antenna also waited for the bridge to open, its captain sitting on the flying bridge.

Drawbridge bells dinged and red lights flashed as the bridge tender lowered the crossing gate. Brake lights of the beach-bound cars lit up.

Mrs. Parker's green and white '53 Buick crawled down the bluff toward the bay with the speed of a sick turtle. "Oh dear, I should have taken Pierce Street to get to the dock," she said, her hands gripped tight around the steering wheel.

"No worries, Mom. We'll be able to turn. There's plenty of room on the bridge for the cars in front of us." He turned up the volume of the car radio. "Listen to this one, boys," he said to Brad and Billy, who were sitting in the back seat. "It's a new Del-Vikings song, 'Come Go with Me.' I love it."

Matt sang the first few words and Brad joined in.

"Please turn that radio back down, Matthew," Mrs. Parker said. "Sounds like a bunch of cockies in the car and I need to concentrate."

"What are cockies, Mrs. P?" Billy said.

"Cockatoos," Mrs. Parker said. "In Australia, they live in flocks in the wild, and they're bloody noisy."

"Mrs. P, we're smart like cockatoos, but we were singing, not screaming," Brad said.

Mrs. Parker looked in the rearview mirror and smiled. "Don't flash that smile and those handsome baby blue eyes at me, Brad Hammond. I don't call that singing."

The Buick reached the side street at the base of the bluff, and Mrs. Parker stuck her hand out the open window to signal a left turn. Matt pointed to Elk's Nursery School on their left. "It all started there with Mrs. Narum, buddy," he said to Brad.

"Yep. Remember that day on the playground when you and John were pulling Mike Sanders on the Red Ryder wagon so fast it flipped over and he split his head open? Boy, we saw lots of blood that day. It was gushing from his head."

"I remember—blood everywhere. He was a redhead for a few minutes," Matt said.

"And then, John said the buzzards would be coming and his cousin Larry's face turned white. He thought Mike was going to bleed to death."

"So did I, at first. Mike didn't even cry," Matt said. "He just sat there quietly and let Mrs. Narum wash the blood out of his hair."

Mrs. Parker shook her head. "Too right! I was there that day. Poor Larry—I think he was more upset than Mike. Mrs. Narum was so sweet with him."

"Well, we'll all be together in school again," Brad said.

"You guys went to nursery school together?" Billy asked.

"Yep," Brad said. "Haven't gone to the same school since then, but we're still good friends. In July he went to North Carolina with me and my family, and we fish together at Crest Lake and hang out with the girls on the dock."

Matt blushed. "Brad's the one with the girlfriends at Crest Lake, Billy." He wished he was comfortable in conversations with girls like

Brad was, but he was shy around them and his conversations with them felt like forced talk. He pointed back in the direction of the drawbridge. "Look at that big schooner and the sports fisherman behind it. The drawbridge is going to be up a long time. Glad we're not on our way to the beach."

Ten minutes later, Mrs. Parker pulled into the paved lot at the city dock, braked hard and stopped. Only a narrow swath of dry grass separated the front wheels of the Buick from the concrete seawall. "I'm a little nervous here."

A strong aroma of dead seaweed became part of the salty breeze as the seaweed sloshed back and forth at the seawall, finally resting in dark mounds on the brown sand at low tide. Its sweet, distinct smell blew in the car's rolled-down windows.

"We're here," Matt said. "Smell that seaweed? I love it."

"A little strong to my liking," Brad said.

"You're definitely not an old salt, my friend."

Brad leaned forward in the back seat. "Mrs. P, I can only see water through the windshield. Be sure you only go backward from here when you leave."

Matt got out and examined the car's close proximity to the water of the bay. "Yeah, Mom, you're really close to the edge, but you're okay—just remember to have the car in reverse before you let out the clutch."

Mrs. Parker turned off the key to the engine and started to laugh. "Thanks, boys. Am I that scary behind the wheel? My next car will be an automatic. That will help me."

Matt walked around to his mom's open window, leaned in and kissed her on the cheek. "You're no race car driver, Mom. Let's just say we don't want any tragedies like Bill Vukovich."

"Who's he?"

"He's a famous Indy 500 driver."

Mrs. Parker lifted her hand. "I don't want to know what happened to him."

"Let's just say he went over a wall."

"Matt!"

"That's all I'm saying," Matt said. His sad look changed into a grin.

"Mrs. Parker, thanks for the ride," Billy said. "Reverse please, when you leave, and I hope you don't stall on the hill if you hit the red light."

"You're welcome, Billy, and don't make me nervous. You boys get your stuff out of the trunk. Have fun, but no foolishness. Hear me?"

"Yes, ma'am," they said in unison.

The three boys piled their camping gear on the seawall next to the deserted boat dock. Matt waved. "We're good, Mom. The bridge is still up. If you hurry, you'll be able to get back up Cleveland Street with no traffic behind you. Don't forget to back up. Love you."

She waved through the open window and started the engine. "Here I go. See you tomorrow."

The car lurched forward.

"Mom!" Matt screamed. "Stop," Billy yelled, waving his arms.

Mrs. Parker stuck her head sheepishly out the window and smiled. "No worries. I've got it now." She backed up slowly and turned the car around.

"Pray for a green light," Matt said. "If the light is green, no problem; if the light is red, big problem. The drawbridge is still up. At least she won't be in a line of cars. A car behind her—or John and Bob in the back seat—really gets her going."

Brad put his hands together and looked up to the sky. "Please, Lord, give Mrs. P a green light and don't let her stall the car on the hill by Calvary Baptist."

The Buick started up the hill and the boys watched.

"She's got a green light—she made it!" Matt said.

The boys cheered.

Matt looked down the street and saluted the statues of the soldier and the sailor by the bridge.

"Why'd you do that?" Billy asked.

"I've seen my dad do it. Don't know why; he never gave a reason. I know he called my grandpa a doughboy and said the statue of the soldier was dedicated to him and all the rest."

"I didn't know that," Brad said. "My grandfather was a dough-boy too."

Chapter 13

THE CITY DOCK

IN THE FIRST SLIP of the Clearwater City Dock, in the center of the cockpit of an old custom fishing boat, a "For Sale" sign lay on a mahogany fighting chair, its slats weathered and gray from the sun.

"That is one run-down boat," Brad said.

Matt shook his head. "I bet she was a beauty in her time. Looks like a Boca Grande tarpon boat and that chair needs a good coat of varnish for starters."

Hack Ward, a mechanic who worked for Bob's dad, popped his head up from the engine compartment of the boat, holding a wrench in his hand. The shirt pocket of his short-sleeved blue work shirt said "Gulf Marine" and contained a pack of Chesterfield cigarettes. The grease smeared on his forearms and face looked like camouflage. Sweat dripped off his nose. He wiped a red grease-rag across his mustache and looked at the boys.

"Hi, Mr. Ward," Matt said. "Have you seen Bob?"

"Nope, haven't seen him, but I heard him about an hour ago when I was fighting with the carburetor down here."

"Got her running?"

"Not yet. About a year too late, I'm afraid. Salt's taken a toll down here. The owner just let it go. The boss wants me to check her out for a friend who wants to resurrect her. I need a smoke."

Matt pushed his foot down on a loose plank. "A big guy could fall through here."

"You boys be careful. I saw Mr. Walton here earlier. He said the dock's a mess—all from that last hurricane." He smiled and stroked the end of his mustache. "He said it a little different than that—a little too rough for your tender ears."

"We're okay, Mr. Ward. We're teenagers now."

"Well, don't go barefoot until you're in the boat." He coughed and lit a cigarette. "City told me they were getting to it. That was a month ago. Between the warped boards with rusty nails sticking out, and pelican and cormorant shit, it's a disaster. You boys remember if that white stuff is still wet, it's slippery." He laughed and started coughing again.

"Where's the *Sea Fever*? On the waves?" Matt asked.

"Yep. I saw Captain Couch down here this morning. He said it's in dry dock up on the Anclote River. They're scraping and painting her while the city fixes the dock and it'll be ready to take people out fishing soon. And he told me they're going to rebuild Mary's Bait House out at the end of the dock. I'm not holding my breath. Ole Mary's not a young chick anymore. She's not moving too fast on things."

Mr. Ward flicked the cigarette into the water. "Back to work," he said. He grabbed another tool out of the metal toolbox on deck and disappeared in the engine compartment.

A large, dark brown bird sitting on the end piling lowered its head and bobbed it up and down.

"Yuck! Matt, did you see that bird just squirt white poop out its butt?" Billy said.

"That's a cormorant lightening its load. He's saying, 'I'm out of here.'"

"Guess I know why the tops of pilings are full of that white stuff."

The big bird flew off the piling, dropped down and almost hit the water before gaining enough speed to fly away.

"They're better swimmers than flyers," Matt said, "but when they get some air speed, they zip along."

Matt jumped in the Waltons' eighteen-foot Stamas. "Looks like Bob dropped off a few things when he was here earlier. Mr. Walton sees that this boat is cared for. When we return, it better look just as good as it does now."

"Cool boat," Billy said. "That's a big outboard on the back. What kind of wood is that?"

"It's not wood. It's called fiberglass. With that big Johnson motor, they say the boat can pull two skiers at one time. Usually there's a slalom ski tucked along the inside of the gunnel, but the rule is no skiing on campouts. Our parents don't want any skiing accidents when we're out on an island. Hey, here comes our second boat."

Robin, barefoot and wearing red shorts and a white T-shirt, pulled his fourteen-foot skiff into the open slip beside the Waltons' boat, reversed the engine, slowed to a stop and turned off the key. The bleached hair on his bronzed legs looked white in the sun.

The tide and light wind pushed the bow of the skiff toward the dock. Robin tied a spring line around a cleat, sat down on the back gunnel and rested a bare foot on the side of the engine. "Hi, guys. Where's Bob?"

"Hey, buddy, you look as relaxed as you did yesterday at the baseball game," Matt said. "You played a great game. Glad you were on my team. Bob should be here soon. Came early to get the boat ready, but I bet right now he's at the Fort Harrison Hotel eating a snack around the pool, nourishing his tapeworm."

"Hi, Robin. Nice boat," Billy said.

"Thanks, Billy. First time camping on an island?"

"Yes. I camped a lot in the woods in Indiana, but this is a first for me, and I'm really looking forward to finally seeing Hog Island."

"You heard there's an escaped prisoner on the loose?" Matt said.

"Yeah, Mom told us about that this morning," Robin said.

"My dad was talking about it too," Brad said. "Guess we need to be extra careful tonight." Brad looked back at the parking lot. "Hey, I see Mrs. Walton's station wagon. Bob, John and JB are here."

"How about a hand?" Bob shouted from the seawall.

Matt turned around and clapped.

Bob shot him a bird and yelled, "We've got all the food. Come on, you lily-livered bums, or I'll hide the marshmallows."

Matt started down the dock toward the pile of boxes.

"Looks like you got enough food for the town," Brad said.

Bob rubbed his stomach in circles. "I hate being hungry."

JB picked up the gun leaning against Matt's sleeping bag. "I see you brought your shotgun."

"Yep. My four-ten. Dad said it was a good idea."

"What shells? Double-aught buck?"

"No, eight-and-a-half birdshot."

"For protection?"

"If we need it. With John with us, who knows what we'll see."

"And we've got shovels," John said. "I can split a head with one of them."

"What are the shovels really for?" Robin asked.

"Digging for something special. I'll explain on the island," Matt said. "Let's get this food down to the boats and get it stowed."

Fifteen minutes later, Bob shoved the last box of food in the locker under the bow of his boat. "You riding with me, Matt?"

"Yep, Billy, JB and I with you. John and Brad with Robin."

"Okay," Bob said. "Let's get going."

The boats backed out of the slips, turned in a tight circle and headed north in the light chop of the channel.

South of the dock, out in the bay, a two-story dredge with pipes suspended above dried white-gray sand belched out thick, chalky fluid as it moved sand to shore from deeper water and created silt that made the water cloudy.

"My dad says this water reminds him of the Mississippi River down near where it opens into the Gulf," Matt said to Billy. "Just wait. On the north side of the bridge the water is clear as spring water."

The schooner that had stopped the traffic on the bridge moved toward them under engine power, its sails still furled. The boys waved and the captain, alone in the back at the helm, tipped his hat as they passed him.

"Come up front on the bow, Billy," Matt said. "Listen to the cars cross that metal span when we go under the drawbridge. The rumble is loud and it sounds neat. And look along the bridge fenders. See the sheepshead munching on barnacles? If we had a pole and some fiddler crabs, we could catch 'em."

They kept the engines at idle speed, and the boys waved to the bridge tender as they came out on the north side of the bridge.

Bob pulled up right into Robin's stern. "Are you planning on poking over there to the island like a tugboat pulling a barge?"

"If I want to—what's the hurry?" Robin said.

"Push that throttle to the floor or just let me pass you so we don't have to smell your fumes. What's wrong with being in a hurry? Gives us more time to set up camp."

"Okay, pass me."

Bob pulled around Robin's boat and eased up beside him. The waves sloshed between the two boats as the gunwales almost touched.

"You're too nice to him, Robin," Matt yelled over the sound of the engines.

"I heard that, Matt. Don't be a goody two shoes," Bob said. He twisted his fist around his nose. "What a brownie. You're getting a poop nose."

"Remember the last time you were in a hurry and you ran aground? I'm just saying … stay in the channel, please," Robin said.

John laughed. "Yeah, Bob, I remember. I had to help push you off the sandbar."

"Watch him close, Matt," Robin said. "Maybe we should have brought your boat instead."

The smooth water in front of the boats reflected the clouds in the sky like a mirror.

"It's so calm today I bet we can make it in twenty minutes," Bob said. He shot Robin a bird and pushed the throttle forward.

Robin twisted the handle of his tiller and both boats jumped up on a plane and took off across the bay.

Matt picked up the rope tied to the bow cleat. "It's calm on this side, Billy. Stand up here on the bow and hold this. You'll think you're flying on a magic carpet." He pointed over to the bluff. "See that white house with the green roof? That's Robin's house. You should see the sunsets from their dock. I'm happy where I live, but Robin's house tests me. It's not the house … it's the sunsets. I love sunsets like I love rainbows."

Bob pushed his throttle further forward and they entered St. Joseph's Sound, screaming along on the millpond flatness of the bay.

It was a good tide with ample water in the bay. Fish shot out from under the boat as it passed over them.

Matt crawled in front of Billy and straddled the tip of the bow, letting his feet splash in the water sailing up and off the front third of the boat. "Dee—lightful!" he yelled, as the boat sliced through the water, forming waves that tugged on his bare feet. "There's a big ray," he said, pointing it out to Billy.

"What are the other fish scooting out of our way?"

"Mostly mullet … that one was a trout … there's a big snook."

"This is so cool."

"Hey, Bob," Matt yelled, "there's enough water. Want to go through Scharrer's Pass?"

Bob nodded, held out a fist with the thumb up and turned out of the channel, flying over the flats in three feet of water.

Matt looked behind the boat. Robin was in their wake.

After a ten-minute run, Bob slowed down, and Robin pulled up beside him. Sitting in the middle of the small pass between two mangrove islands, a boat sat anchored with two men fishing.

"Whoa," Matt said. "They're right in the middle of the pass."

"We could get real close to the north mangroves and idle by them," Robin said.

"I guess," Bob said. "But I was thinking, maybe, follow the mangroves south, around the outside."

"Okay, need to get way outside of it, and remember the oyster bar at the end."

"I remember. Let's go that way. Don't want to piss off those fishermen."

"Aw, toss an orange grenade and soak 'em," John said.

"Sit down, John," JB said. "We don't need to get in trouble today."

"This time, you follow me," Robin said. He turned the throttle on the tiller and the boat popped up on a plane.

Bob did the same. He hugged Robin's rooster tail with his bow and the two boats rounded the bar and shot up along the other side of the mangroves.

"There's Hog Island, Billy," Matt shouted over the noise of the engines. The barbershop talk spun in his thoughts. He kept a keen eye along the mangroves, secretly watching for a boat hidden under the bright green leaves of the overhanging branches.

After they got to the campsite, he'd tell the rest of the boys the purpose of the shovels, and the scary part about the escaped prisoner doubling back to hide on the island. And he'd tell them what Mr. Kelly said about staying calm and dealing with it, if the prisoner showed up.

Chapter 14

HOG ISLAND

"BILLY, AHEAD OF US IS the north tip of Clearwater Beach," Matt said. "The water that separates it from Hog Island to our right is a deep channel. You can see the sandy bottom through the clean water. And if you look closely, you can spot live conch shells and the pompano that are attracted here along the path out into the Gulf. That's the way we'll go fishing on the Buckeye on Labor Day."

"Is that island called Hog Island because there are pigs on the island?" Billy asked.

"In the 1800s, settlers tried to raise pigs there. I think that's when it got its name, but the pigs are all gone," Matt answered.

"How big is it?"

"A couple of miles long and almost a mile wide at its widest point," Matt said. "In 1921, a hurricane split the island in two. The northern island is now Honeymoon Island and they named this part Caladesi, but we locals still call it Hog Island like our dads do. See all those trees? A stand of pine trees grows in the interior of the island, and mangroves cover the southern tip."

"And lots of fishermen beach their boats and wade along the edges fishing for snook," Bob said. "It's our favorite camping spot."

The boats closed in on the southern edge and both young captains eased off the throttles. The brown roots of the mangroves were about one-third exposed.

Matt stood up and walked back to Bob. "Water's running out of the bay now, but look at the mangroves. There's still enough water to beach the boats."

"Looks good," Bob said. He dipped into Robin's wake, pulled out alongside and increased his speed enough to go ahead again. He turned toward the island and ran perpendicular to the beach, still a couple hundred yards away. "Enough water over the bar?" he asked Matt.

"Plenty. You can do a Normandy landing."

Bob sped up, the bow stayed on plane and they ran over the sand bar, watching the pattern of sand waves on the bottom as they crossed it. As the water got deep again, he cut the power, the boat slowed and its momentum carried the bow up to the dry sand on the beach.

"At your service," Bob said with a sweep of his arm. "We can push the boat off after we get the supplies on the beach. Don't want a stranded boat high and dry with this outgoing tide."

Matt jumped onto the sand, anchor in his hand. "No wet shoes today," he said. He carried the anchor forty feet up on the beach and planted it in the soft white sand, leaving some slack in the rope to push the boat back into the water after the supplies were unloaded.

Robin ran parallel to them about thirty feet away, but he slowed near the water's edge instead of driving all the way up on the sand. John dropped the bow anchor in the water and looked at Bob with a grin. "We're not afraid of getting our feet wet."

"Robin's afraid one little coquina shell will scratch the bottom of his boat," Bob said. "Right, captain?"

Robin just smiled and shook his head.

Matt went up the beach toward the tall sand dunes dotted with clumps of sea oats. The snowy-white sand squeaked as he walked. "This is perfect," he yelled. "I'm on the path to the pines. Let me check it out before we carry all the stuff from the boat up there."

He followed the narrow path of packed white sand that meandered around palmetto clumps, under a tangled sea grape tree and snaked back toward a stand of tall long-needle pines.

The path ended at a fire pit gouged in the sand. Inside the circle of small rocks, black charred remnants of pine logs and palmetto stems lay in an uneven stack of burnt rubble, and ashes from the last campfire filled the bottom. Beyond the fire pit, in the stand of pine trees, pine needles covered the ground.

The campsite looked just like they'd left it. He walked back to the opening in the sea oats, climbed up on the top of a dune and yelled, "Okay. The boats are fine right there."

With the supplies on Bob's boat unloaded, John waded through the water, carrying his second load from Robin's boat: his sleeping bag and two shovels. "I should have put everything on Bob's boat," he said.

"JB and I've got the boat secured," Robin said. "Cool your jets, John. We'll be relaxing on the beach while they're still anchoring their boat."

"What's da matter, John?" Brad said in a high-pitched voice. "'Fraid you might have to sleep in a wet bed tonight?"

"Kiss my arse, pretty boy," John said.

Bob waded back to the stern and lifted out the second anchor. He carried it back a short distance and sunk it in about two feet of water. The line tightened, and a slight wind and wave action moved the boat until the boat stopped and the anchor dug deeper into the sand. "Fine back here," he said.

"Same on the front," Matt said. "We're good." He loved these campouts out on the island, independent and free. Since their first campout without adult supervision, they had followed what they had learned as Cub Scouts from Matt's dad: "Everyone is responsible for the campout's success. Blend what you like to do with what you don't." They had no rules. Not one person gave an order. They just pitched in and worked together.

Just short of the dunes, John screamed. "Owww!" Holding one foot in his hands, he jumped around in circles on the other one. "Shit, I stepped on one."

Bob laughed. "John, the barefoot boy, got a sandspur. Listen to the crybaby."

John dropped to the sand and looked at his big toe. "Shut up, Bob, you pissant. Oh damn, I hate pulling these out."

Bob whimpered, using baby talk like Brad. "Is the big boy about to 'cwy'?"

John's face got red and he started to laugh. "If I could catch you now little boy, you mealy-mouthed blowfish, I'd kick your ass and knock the air out of your bony butt."

Bob covered his mouth with his hand and snickered. "You're such a pussy. Be a man, John."

"I hate … I hate … I hate pulling out a sandspur. It's not funny, Bob."

"It is, when it's you. You always look funny when you're mad. Your face bloats, you get red and your mouth foams like you have hoof and mouth."

"Cut the chit-chat and just pull it out, John," JB said.

John grabbed the burr with his fingers and carefully pulled. He gritted his teeth. "Owww! Oh God—that hurts. Shit."

"Don't be such a baby, John," Bob said, "and you better stop that cussing before school starts."

"I'll get you when I pull this out, Bob. You're a dork. I have to be gentle or I'll leave in the sticker. Did we bring tweezers in the kit?"

"Come on John, pull it out. You don't need tweezers," Brad said.

"The afternoon is moving on fast, John," JB said. "We've got stuff to do."

"Quit rushing me. You're all dickheads." He grasped the sandspur again and pulled gently, hissing like a snake.

"Pull, dang it," Matt said loudly.

John pulled and let out a scream. "Owwwww!" He got up smiling and held out the sandspur. "Look, I got it all. My, my …"

"Now put on some shoes," Matt said. "We're going."

"Yessir, you wannabe drill sergeant."

He reached over and socked Bob hard on the arm. "Hope that hurt."

Chapter 15

ROCKY AND PORKY

MATT STOPPED AT THE EDGE of the clearing, closed his eyes and breathed in deeply. "Smell that? Pine smell … beach smell … and the smell of an old fire. Mix it together and what do you have? Paradise."

Robin nodded his head in agreement. "I love this place."

The sound of gentle waves reached the campsite and the smell of the salt air clung to the pine needles and cones that swayed in the soft breeze. Around the scarred bark of pine tree trunks, a brown pine needle carpet covered the ground. Scattered pinecones and occasional patches of bare sand created a patchwork of colors on the floor.

A few feet from the fire pit, a pine stump that served as a table was all that remained of a tree hit by lightning. "Made in the shade," Matt said. "Just like we left it. We don't have to do anything but put our stuff out."

"How can I help?" Billy asked.

"Put your gear over there by the fire pit where Brad's setting up his stuff," Matt said. "How about gathering some firewood with a possible side bonus?"

"Sure. What's the bonus?"

"You might find a snake—hopefully not John's favorite variety."

John looked up from the kitchen area where he was arranging the food. "If you find *any* variety, don't you dare bring it back here or your supper tonight is what you and the snake fix up together at the other end of the island."

"I didn't know you were that afraid of snakes, John," JB said.

"Let's just say they're not my favorite life form."

"Don't worry," Billy said. "If I find any kind of snake, I'll leave it alone. Thanks, Matt. Gathering firewood will be fun."

"Don't put your sleeping bag too close to the fire, Billy," JB said. "John's almost caught on fire one time."

"But that was wintertime and we froze. The temperature that night set records. Why, Brad called me 'Sam McGee.'"

Robin shook his head. "Poor excuse."

"You know, Robin," John said, "sometimes you're too serious. Cool it. You and Matt both need to let your hair down. You know—fart and let it be heard."

Robin grinned. "You're the one that had to explain at school how you singed your hair."

"I remember that now," Bob laughed. "John, you smelled like a bug zapper."

"You do what you have to do to stay warm. We were the boys of the infantry in a foxhole—stay warm or die."

In thirty minutes the campsite was set up, just the way they'd done it in Cub Scouts. Seven sleeping bags circled the fire pit at a safe distance, and a portable radio sat on the pine stump.

Matt sat down on his sleeping bag and opened his knapsack. "Hey guys, we're done. Before we do anything else, I have something to share with you—a new adventure while we're here on the island. Bob, John and Billy already know about this and they're in. If you want to join us, you'll be rewarded equally. If you don't, I'll be surprised, but I'll understand."

The boys plopped down on their sleeping bags and watched him.

"So, lay it on us," Brad said as he stretched out. "We're all ears."

"You've got my attention," Robin said.

"Mine too," said JB.

Matt pulled the wrinkled map from his knapsack and waved it in the air. "We're going to search for a treasure—a buried treasure that's worth tons of money. It was stolen twenty years ago from a bank and never recovered. In my hands is one-half of a map that leads to the treasure. It belongs to my dad. He and a friend found it when they were in high school. They searched all summer trying to find the other half of the map on this island, but they finally gave up."

"So, it's not here?" JB said. "Why would we dig here?"

Matt frowned. "Just because they didn't find it, doesn't mean we can't. We're new map readers with new interpretations and a lot of storms have changed the topography of this island in twenty years. These dunes might not have even been here twenty years ago. Remember how that bad hurricane divided the island in half thirty-five years ago? I say it's worth a try. What do you think? Want to dig for the mother lode of gold and jewels hidden by the bank robbers who heisted the fortune?"

He stood up, kicked the sand and slid the ball of his foot back and forth until it was smooth again. "I really want to find this treasure."

"So first we have to find the missing half of the map, right?" Brad said. "And *then* we look for the money. Does that half show where the other half is?"

"Yes."

"So that's why you brought the shovels," Robin said. "I'm ready. Let's get started."

"I'm in," JB said. "You've convinced me it's worth a try. That would be so cool to find it."

"But maybe before we get started," John said, "we should check up the beach to see if Rocky and Porky, our old buddies who like to scare us late at night, are here. Right, Matt?"

"Good idea, John. We don't need them to see us digging and start asking questions. This is our secret mission. Let's go check on them right now."

"Who are Rocky and Porky?" Billy asked.

"Old South Ward boys, a year older than us—cocky and tough," Matt said. They live on Clearwater Beach. We know where they usually camp."

"They're fun, Billy, but they're tricksters," JB said. "If they're here, we'll know to be on the lookout."

"For sure," Robin said. "They put ghost crabs in my sleeping bag once."

"How about when they threw firecrackers in our campfire and about a hundred of them went off at one time?" Brad said. "That got us going."

"I remember that," Matt said, "but we weren't choir boys either. The week before, John and Bob had put a cherry bomb in their fire. Listen, it's not about that. We don't want them snooping around. This treasure hunt is our secret."

Billy shook his head. "Sounds like your camping trips are pretty exciting."

John patted Billy on the back. "This is the best playground we have."

Robin looked directly at John. "But we don't do anything that's foolish or could get us in trouble. No one wants to deal with our dads. We don't want this privilege to come to an end. Right, John?"

"Robin, don't be a party pooper," John said.

"All I know is we've heard our dads' stories and most of the stuff we do, they've already done," Bob said.

"Yeah, we're tame compared to them," John said.

Matt smiled. "Very true. Now let's go! I want to see if they're here."

Small waves rolled up onto the beach. The two boats remained in the same position they had left them—bow anchor ropes taut.

"Boats look good, Bob," Robin said.

"Dad said his charts showed the next high tide will be late this evening, and then the following low should be a weak one on this quarter moon ... so there should always be good water here where our boats are anchored."

Brad grabbed a flat scallop shell and heaved it out along the water, watching it skip along the surface three times before it dropped out of sight. "I love this island. Only thing missing is a girl or two to watch the sunset with."

"Always thinking about the ladies, Brad. Who's your girlfriend this week?" JB said with a grin.

"Junior high means a new school of fish. Ask me at the end of next week."

"Uh-oh, Clark Gable is turning into a shark," John said.

"C'mon Brad. I know you've got a warm spot for Dee," Matt said.

Brad skipped another shell across the water and his long black lashes fluttered over his blue eyes. "Maybe so. When are you going to find a girlfriend, Matt?"

Matt blushed. "Let's get our minds back on finding Rocky and Porky."

"I saw you giving Bonnie the eye at Brown Brothers this morning," John said.

Matt blushed again. "Okay, end of that subject. Let's go."

The seven boys started up the beach at the water's edge, spreading out and then coming back together like an accordion. They kicked the water at one another, threw a football, skipped shells, chased sandpipers, intimidated gulls and in between talked, laughed and sang songs.

"Let's play *Name That Singer,*" Bob said.

"What's that?" Billy asked.

"Our version of the show on TV, *Name That Tune,*" Bob said. "I'll start … 'Just Because.'"

"Lloyd Price," John yelled. "That's easy. Everyone knows that one."

"I know that, pissant," Bob said.

Matt interrupted Bob. "Who sang 'That'll Be the Day?'"

Bob laughed. "Easy. Buddy Holly and the Crickets."

"Right," Matt said.

"Okay, how about this one?" Robin said. "'Ain't Got No Home?'"

"Duh … Clarence Frogman Henry," John said in a deep, froggy voice.

"Bet you can't get this one," Brad said. "'Raunchy.'"

"Bill Justis," Matt answered.

"Here's an old one," Bob said. "'Black Denim Trousers and Motorcycle Boots.'"

"The Cheers," Brad said. "I can sing that one in my sleep."

"Come on, Brad, give us a chance," John said. "You and Matt are getting all of them."

"Okay, John. Here's my favorite 'oldie goldie,'" Brad said. "Give you a hint. This guy's going to be a great R&B singer—'I Got a Woman.'"

"Ray Charles," Billy said. He winked at Brad. "I'm not surprised that song is one of the ladies' man's favorites."

"How about 'Money Honey'?" JB said.

"Elvis," John shouted. "'Money Honey'—that's what we're going to find tonight."

"I've got one," Billy said. "'Boney Maroney.'"

"Larry Williams," Matt said, laughing. "I love this game. We're so good. Can't stump us."

Ahead of them the dunes flattened out and the beach narrowed. The pine trees grew close to the water and the sea oats thinned out.

"Okay, I've got one last one," Brad said. "'Brown Eyed Handsome Man.'"

"Chuck Berry," JB said with a smile. "I know that one. It's a song about me."

"Shhh, we're getting close to Rocky and Porky's camp. We need to be quiet," Matt said.

"I don't see a boat around," Robin said.

Matt looked out over the open water. "Maybe they're coming later. I've seen them not get here till almost dark."

"Wow," Billy said. "That's a neat place to camp."

"Yeah, they like it here. The campsite is close to their boat. It's perfect for them—no walking."

Two sleeping bags lay on the ground with a stack of firewood nearby.

Matt's eyes scanned the area like a cavalry scout. Behind a palmetto, about fifty feet beyond them, he saw movement. He caught a glimpse of brown hair, cut in a short flattop. It was Rocky. He and the boys needed the island to themselves. Maybe he could talk about the escaped prisoner and scare Rocky and Porky into leaving. *We don't need them watching.*

"This is Rocky and Porky's stuff, all right," he said in a loud voice. "I'd know it anywhere. A year older than we are, and still don't know what they're doing. Probably had to go back to the mainland to get something they forgot. One time they came over here and forgot all their food. Another time they ran out of gas after they got here. They're just scatterbrained. I wouldn't be surprised if they're in our class in another year or two."

Matt winked at Bob and, with his hand out of view, pointed a finger toward the palmetto. Bob looked, saw Rocky's head and turned away quickly.

"Listen, everyone," Matt continued, raising his voice enough for Rocky to hear. "I was going to tell you later, but I think I should tell you now. A very dangerous prisoner escaped from the county jail last evening. A boat was reported missing this morning and they think he might be hiding on one of the islands. Rocky and Porky probably heard about it and saw something suspicious—and like the big scaredy-cats they are, left the island without even taking their stuff."

"Maybe they saw him," Bob said and he winked at Matt.

"Well, we're safe. Dad let me bring my bird gun and said if anyone comes into our camp after dark, pepper them first and ask questions later."

John realized something was going on. He'd played this game before. With his back to the palmettos where Matt had pointed, he whispered, "What's up?"

"Rocky," Matt mouthed.

John glanced over at the palmetto clump and with a loud voice got into the act. "Maybe we should go home too. I know those two are both mommies' boys, scared of their own shadow, but maybe the prisoner *is* on this island. Let's get out of here."

Porky must be somewhere in his boat. Gotta get out of here before Rocky jumps out and spoils my plan. "You're right, John," Matt said. "Let's go. Race you back to the boats."

He turned around and started running. The other boys followed. John passed Matt and yelled, "Last one to the boats has to buy Rocky new underwear."

"Why underwear?" Billy asked.

"When he heard there was an escaped prisoner on the island, he pooped his pants," John said, laughing.

They ran all the way back to the boats. Everyone except Matt and Bob ran into the water, lifting their knees high, and one by one diving forward, hitting the water head first, their hands stretched out in front of them. Each head surfaced and shook to shed the saltwater.

"We got Rocky," John laughed. "We got him so good."

"Would you please explain to us what's going on?" JB said.

"Yeah," Brad said. "I'm confused."

"Well, I missed something," Robin said. "All of a sudden, you guys turned around and started running."

"Did you see Rocky?" Billy asked.

"Yes, he was hiding back at the campsite and Matt was trying to scare him so they'd leave, John said. "Now let's see if that happens."

"What are Bob and Matt doing up on the beach?" Brad said.

"I don't know, but they're looking at us," John said. "Wonder why they stopped?"

Chapter 16

BLACKTIP SHARKS

BOB AND MATT'S GAZE drifted over to the old barnacle-coated wood tripod that once marked the channel fifty feet off the beach on the Hog Island side of Big Pass, where the color of the deeper water changed to dark green.

They nodded at one another and bolted for the water. "First one to the marker wins! See you later, fellas, here we go!" Matt yelled.

They ran into the water until it was too deep for running. They stretched out and hit the water on their bellies, coasting as long as their momentum carried them.

Bob's arms smacked the surface hard and water flew everywhere. With Matt's stroke, very little water sailed in the air. He opened his eyes and saw the brown sand bottom in a blur. The sand disappeared and the color of the water changed. He knew he'd reached the deep water near the marker.

The marker's wooden ladder, smooth from time spent in the sun, was in his reach when Matt felt a hand on his ankle. He grabbed the wood and pulled both him and Bob up to the marker. Bob released Matt's ankle and surfaced beside him. They rubbed their red eyes to clear away the stinging saltwater.

"You barely won," Bob said.

Matt stepped on the bottom rung and pulled himself out of the water. "Oh sure. I was always ahead. I felt my feet kicking you all the way out."

They climbed the ladder and sat down on the space where a navigation light once set, letting their feet dangle over the side. "Come on out, you chickens!" Bob yelled to the other boys.

A light sea breeze blew, and the air moving over his wet skin made goose bumps pop up on Matt's legs and arms. "Ready to head back?" he said.

Without a word, Bob climbed the narrow wooden section to the top of the marker, balanced himself out on its edge and peered down into the water. "Watch this."

He jumped, projecting himself out and away from the wooden structure, and grabbing his knees, executed a neat flip. He landed flat-footed in the water with a loud pop and sank out of sight, but a moment later floated up to the surface. He shook his head and wiped the water out of his eyes. Floating on his back, he yelled up to Matt, "You do a one and a half! The water is plenty deep."

Matt climbed to the top and balanced on the side of the highest section of the old marker. "Okay, here goes." He stood there for a while thinking about the dive, using the time for getting up his nerve. From the shallow water, the bantering began. "We're all watching. You can go now. Hope you don't do a pancake. God, you're bowlegged!"

Matt ignored the comments and jumped up and away from the channel marker, turned the first flip and snapped open, entering the water headfirst. One minute later and way down the beach, he surfaced.

"That's not funny," Bob yelled. "You didn't come up and I thought you broke your neck."

"You knew I didn't break my neck."

"Okay, wait for me on the beach."

Five minutes later, they lifted their hands high in the air, smacked them together and walked back with arms draped over each other's shoulder to join the other boys who were standing together in a circle in the chest-deep water, laughing and slapping water into each other's face.

"We thought you all would come out there with us," Bob said as they waded toward the group.

"We were talking about Rocky," JB said.

Bob laughed. "Did you all see him hiding in the palmettos?"

"I didn't," Robin said.

"I didn't either," Billy said, "until I saw Matt pointing. Then I spotted him."

Robin jumped. "Hey, something bumped my legs. Watch out! I see them—a school of blacktip sharks—a couple of them are pretty big."

"I see them," Matt said. "Quick, let's get to shore. They're not real big, but they have sharp teeth. They're aggressive and they bite."

"There must be twenty of them," John said. "Damn, they're not that small. Let's go. Hurry! Go! Go! A shark's a shark ..."

Matt took a step and felt a sharp pain like somebody stabbed his leg with an ice pick. He saw the head of a shark attached to his calf. He kicked and the pain stopped. A green cloud swirled in the water below his knee.

Green meant blood. A feeling of apprehension rolled through him. A shadow followed him as he waded toward the beach behind the rest of the boys. In ankle-deep water, he looked down. Blood poured down the side of his calf.

John looked at his leg. "Oh my God, one got you."

Matt gently splashed water on his leg and got a look at the deep gash before blood covered his leg again.

"Is it bad, Matt?" Robin asked.

"Not too bad," he lied. "It's just the initial bleeding making it look bad."

"Looks bad to me. Bet you'll need stitches," Brad said.

"Sit down, Matt, and let's take a look," Robin said.

"I'm okay, just a couple of superficial cuts. Get a towel from the boat. I'll wrap it up. No worries."

John squatted by Matt. "Let me see it—I know you."

"John ... *I said* ... I'm okay."

"Well, let's get back to camp so you can put a bandage on it," John said.

In the distance, a small boat appeared, headed in the direction of the island.

"That boat looks like it's coming our way," said Robin.

"That's Porky's boat," John said. "Maybe we should stop him and get you to the hospital. There's your ambulance. His boat is already running."

"I said I'm okay," Matt said sternly. "Don't stop him, John."

"Okay, if you say so."

"I wonder if Porky heard about the escaped prisoner," Billy said. "It made all the newspapers."

"If he did," JB said, "when he hears that Matt said the guy might be around the island, they're both going to flip."

Bob laughed. "If we see them pull camp and leave the island, we'll know why. Boy, we can get them at school on Tuesday!"

Robin handed Matt a towel. Matt wrapped it tightly around his calf and stood up slowly. "Let's go," he said.

When they reached the campsite, Matt grabbed the first aid kit his dad made for camping trips and sat on his sleeping bag. His dad always said the worst accident probably causes bleeding, and the simplest probably causes bleeding, and you mostly need supplies for that kind of event. He should have everything he'd need.

He pulled out a roll of gauze, a silver tube of Ichthyol, a skinny bottle of Mercurochrome, cotton balls, peroxide, scissors and adhesive tape. The sight of the Mercurochrome brought back painful memories of childhood injuries. He always asked, "Are you going to put the red stuff on it?" holding back his tears. "Probably," would be the answer, and that always opened the floodgates. Before the antiseptic would be applied, Matt would say, "Blow on it."

He unwrapped the bloody towel and looked at the side of his leg. Blood had clotted everywhere except in one large gash. He wet several large cotton balls with peroxide and pressed them on the bleeding area. When he lifted them, a clot had formed, but fresh blood started to ooze around the edges.

John walked over and knelt beside him. "Can I look?"

"Sure," Matt said as he readied to apply the wrath of the crying juice. John knew the routine. "Do you want me to blow on it?"

Matt smiled. "That might help."

"Or you can kiss it," Bob chimed in.

"Shut up, Bob," John said. He looked closer at the leg and squinted his eyes. "Matt, that top one looks bad. Don't you think it needs stitches? I don't like the way it looks."

"No stitches. The cut might leave a little scar, but as my dad would say, 'It will give the leg some character.'"

He stayed away from the clot as he dried the cuts again with another cotton ball, and before the blood returned, he dabbed on the Mercurochrome while John blew.

His face flushed. "Oh God! Blow harder."

John started to laugh. "Helping?"

"Kind of," Matt answered through tightly clenched teeth. He pushed another cotton ball on top of the cuts. "It'll ease in a minute, I hope."

John laughed harder. "Matt, you should have bitten down on a stick and swigged a bottle of whiskey. That's what the pirates do in the movies when they cut off someone's leg. 'Argh, matey, whaddya think about that?'"

Matt started to laugh. "What would I do without you?"

"Cry?" John said with a little snort.

Matt handed the rolled-up tube to John.

John held the tube with the end of his thumb and forefinger like it had germs on it. "What's in this?"

"Good stuff, John. It's made at the drugstore. Dad says 'Ick' is the best ointment to put on a cut. Hey, Brad. Tell John about 'Ick.' Your dad's a pharmacist."

"Ichthyol?" Brad said. "My dad sells it in tubes and little jars. He says it's nasty looking, but it works."

John looked at the cracks on the surface of the metal tube and the black remnants dried and stuck to the area around the cap. "How old is this? This tube maybe belonged to your grandfather."

"I don't think it's that old."

"Well, the tube looks old and icky."

A blank stare replaced the smile on Matt's face. "Take off the cap, John, and help me put it on the cuts before I cover them with the bandage."

"Why so serious? I just said it looks old, it might not work anymore and it looks like axle grease."

"John, please open it up so we can get this over with."

"Okay, but when I open it up, don't be surprised if whatever is in here is solid like an old tube of caulking compound, or whatever that stuff is you put between cracks."

John squeezed the tube. Some yellow-brown oily liquid came out. He squeezed harder. Out came black ointment. He laughed. "Are you sure you want this on your leg?"

Matt pressed another cotton ball on the area that was still bleeding. "You know, John, this was funny at first, but sometimes you don't know when to stop. Just squeeze some along the cuts so I can get this bandaged."

"Who's being funny?" John said. "This tube maybe came over on the Mayflower."

John squeezed and more black ointment oozed out. He put it over the cuts. "Oh my God, what is this stuff?" He laughed again. "Matt, this looks like axle grease and it smells like we are on an oil well in Texas."

"I know how it smells, John, but it works. It helps the healing."

John held the tube up but more ointment came out and got on his hands. "It's not stopping," he yelled. "If my hand falls off, you're to blame."

Matt gave in. A smile returned. "John, try to let it go over my cuts. Don't waste any of it. It's valuable in spite of how it looks and smells."

John focused on the largest cut again. He got serious. "Just place it along all the cuts? What about that big one?"

"All of them, John."

John pushed out more of the ointment and let it run on Matt's leg. "You spread it. I'm not touching it." He looked away and took a deep breath. "I have no desire to be a doctor."

"I know," Matt said. "You did good. Thanks."

John shook his head as he put the cap back on the tube. "I can't believe that's medicine. That is some ugly, smelly, stinky stuff."

Matt spread the salve all over the wounds with his finger. The black oily substance covered a large area on the side of his calf. "Just remember—it works. And that's why it's in the kit. Press the end of the gauze and I'll wrap it around my leg and then tape it so the cuts are completely covered."

John looked at Matt without a smile and quietly said, "I think this might be a mistake."

"Why?"

"I think you need to see a doctor."

"I'll be fine. Now please help me."

In two minutes, the tape was wrapped around the gauze and the dressing completed.

John smiled and announced, "Matt's going to be okay."

The boys clapped.

"You had us worried," said Billy.

"I guess this means we're staying," JB said.

"Matt, you covered that leg before we got a good look," Robin said. "Are you sure it's okay? It sure was bleeding on the beach."

"Honestly, I'm fine," Matt said. His leg ached, but he didn't want anyone but John to know how bad the cut was.

He looked at Robin. "Before the sharks interrupted us, you asked why I said all that stuff about the prisoner for Rocky to hear. When I saw him hiding, I thought it was a good opportunity to try to keep them away from our campsite tonight."

"Why didn't he come out?" Billy asked.

"That's what I meant about opportunity," Matt said. "If Rocky was hiding, he wasn't coming out. That would be a 'you won.' And he wasn't going to let us win."

"I bet it was really hard after we called them scaredy-cats," JB said. "He's one tough cookie."

Matt lifted his hand like a policeman stopping traffic. "Listen, beyond the teasing there was some truth in what I said. A dangerous prisoner did escape from the county jail."

"Do you swear?" JB said. "I haven't heard about that."

Matt stood up slowly. "Dad saw it in the paper this morning. Just said to be careful. I said all that other stuff for Rocky's ears. A prisoner did escape, but he didn't steal a boat. The talk at the barbershop was that he's headed to north Florida. I just wanted to give Rocky and Porky something to think about instead of us. I hope we can start digging before dinner. We don't want them snooping around. Right now, we keep this map our secret."

"How did the prisoner escape?" Brad said.

"He jumped the guard, stole a key and escaped out the back door.

The cops think he got hurt somehow and they found bloody finger-prints on the corner of the building. They have a posse and blood-hounds on his trail."

"Hey, peg-leg Pete," John said to Matt. "We should be on the alert. You know this island could be a perfect hiding place. I'll take the first watch tonight—just a precaution."

"I doubt he'll come over here," Matt replied. "But, you're right. Why take a chance?"

"Is he armed, Matt?" JB asked.

"Don't know, but they say he's big and mean. They called him a giant."

"Let's booby-trap the campsite," Billy said. "I'll 'build a perimeter,' as the Marines say."

"Not a bad idea," JB said.

"And remember," Matt said, "they think that guy's headed north. I said that about a boat being stolen for Rocky to hear. Relax."

"Not sure your shotgun will do us any good if we need it, Matt," JB said. "You're the dead-eye, but you're too nice to pull the trigger."

"Thanks for the compliment," Matt said. "But, don't test me." The sound of Billy hammering interrupted his thoughts. "What's all that noise, Billy?"

"I found these cans when I picked up firewood, and I'm using the ice pick to make holes in them. I'll tie a shell inside and then tie them on a fishing line around the campsite. When the cans move, the shells will hit the side and make a racket. It'll let us know if someone's trying to get into the camp. Good idea?"

"Yes, that's a good precaution, but I bet it stays quiet," Matt said. "This is a lucky group."

"How can you say that?" John said. His voice sounded a little annoyed. "There's an escaped prisoner on the loose, a bully is threat-ening Billy and you just smeared 100-year-old axle grease over a nasty shark bite on your leg. Trouble all around you and you say we're *lucky*?" He stopped and began to chuckle. "It's more than I can take, pilgrim."

"Well, look around. We *are* lucky," Matt said. "Here we are, camp-ing out by ourselves and enjoying this adventure on an island that's special to us."

Bob took out his machete from its canvas scabbard and lifted it in the air. "Look, we have this to protect us tonight. I used it to cut some sea grape branches for roasting hot dogs and marshmallows."

"Great," said Brad. "We'll see how brave we are tonight when the sun goes down and it's real dark."

JB looked at Billy who was jabbing the ice pick into another can. "And Billy is protecting us like John Wayne against the Japs on Iwo Jima. What happens when the prisoner hits the string and the cans go nuts, Billy?"

"I'm telling you—that prisoner's not coming here," Matt said. "Let's face it. At times like this sometimes we miss our dads here, but we're fine. Today at the barber shop, one of the men told me it was highly unlikely that guy would show up on this island, but if he did, to just deal with it."

John flexed his biceps in a muscle man pose, reached down and picked up a small branch and broke it over his knee. "Yeah, we're tough."

"We better be," Brad said.

Bob walked over to John and squeezed his bicep. "Not big enough if the guy looks like 'The Thing.'" He lifted his arms and let his hands hang limp with ten stiffly curled fingers that looked like rigid claws. Dragging one foot behind him, he moved slowly around the campsite, eyes wide open, staring blankly skyward like a zombie. He lumbered past John and turned his head backward like a screech owl. Then with blinding speed, he whipped around, lunged and stopped with his face a foot from John's face. *"You picked—the wrong night—to come—to this island,"* he said in his best Bela Lugosi voice.

John jumped, and then everyone jumped. No one laughed except Bob. Then the tension broke and everyone began to laugh.

"Boy are we jittery or what?" Matt said. "Good job, Bob. You got us. Now are you guys ready to talk about digging for the other half of this map so we can find the treasure?"

"Matt, sure you feel like digging now?" Brad said. "You don't look too good. Get off your leg and we can dig tomorrow."

"I'm fine," Matt lied again. "Let's get going."

"Argh, matey," John bellowed. With one eye closed and a lisp in his voice, he softly and slowly enunciated, *"Give me a shovel—and point*

*yer fin-ger toooo the ground. I'll dig—'til I heer—the sound—of the blayde—
smacking—on the lid—of the treasure chest. Whaddya think—about that?"*

Robin laughed and threw a shovel in the air toward John. "Show
him where to dig, Matt."

John caught it on the fly and grinned at Matt.

From behind his back, slyly, like a magician exposing a colored
scarf, Matt pulled out the brown crumpled paper and jiggled it high
in the air. "Follow me, boys," he said with a forced grin. He tried to
conceal his limp as he headed out of camp.

Chapter 17

DIGGING FOR TREASURE

DEEP IN THE STAND of pine trees behind the campsite, one tree towered above all the others. From the water, the tall pine stood out like a beacon, and years ago the boys' dads had shown them how to use it to find the campsite.

Matt walked over to the huge tree, the largest tree on the island. It had to be the one indicated on the map. Holding his compass out flat on his hand, he checked the map and began to walk away from the tree with large, deliberate steps, counting out loud. "One, two, three, four, five, six." He took a smaller step. "And a half."

At his feet, a piece of weathered wood with a dark brown metal circle attached to it protruded from the sand, a perfect marker. He must have started at the right place.

Billy bent over and touched the wood. "What's this?"

"Looks like part of a derelict boat, probably washed up by the hurricane of 1921 that created Hurricane Pass up to the north of this island. This map took me right to it."

"Oh my," John said. "I think we're getting warm."

"We're getting hot," Matt said. He stepped over the wood plank and scuffed the dry gray sand with his heel, looked at his compass again and marked off ten more steps at a right angle. The ground in front of him was a level clearing.

"One, two, three, four." He stopped, looked at John and made an X in the sand with his heel. "Dig here, matey," he said, forcing a grin. His leg throbbed and he knew he needed to sit.

John placed the edge of his spade on the ground. "How big a hole?"

"I'll mark the area, but that's a good place to start."

The boys found four large sticks and Matt pushed them into the sand, marking an eight-foot square.

"Start in the center, John, and dig out to the corners, two feet deep," Matt said. "See if you hit something."

"I hope it's a treasure chest and not someone's bones. We're not close to that burial mound they say is out here, are we? JB, grab the other shovel and get in here and help me, okay?"

"You got it," JB said.

Bob looked at Robin. "This is a good time to go check the boats. Tide's coming in and the evening breeze will push the water even more."

"Good idea. We'll be back in a bit, Matt."

"I'll go with you," Brad said. "Digging is not one of my favorite things to do. Makes you sweaty and tired. Plus, sweat mixed with dirt gives you acne. That's why I'm pretty, John."

John threw the next shovel full onto Brad's shoe. "If you want a share of this treasure, you're going to have to do some digging too, pretty boy."

"I'll stay here and help with the digging," Billy said.

Thirty minutes later, piles of moist, dark sand lined the edges of a large square hole. Billy and JB sat down on the edges, dejectedly. "No luck, Matt," JB said.

John looked over at Matt and jammed his shovel into the center of the hole. "Nothing," he said. "Maybe that's why your dad gave up."

"This isn't a survey map," Matt said. "We can't give up, but let's take a break. Bob, Robin and Brad can take over in the morning. They can dig a little deeper and wider, and I can dig too."

"You're crippled," John said.

"I'll be better tomorrow," Matt said. "Let's go back to camp and get something to drink. The other guys are probably already having a snack. Leave the shovels here."

Matt thought about the tall oak tree deeper in the island that you

94

could see from the water. Maybe that's what the mapmaker meant by the biggest tree on the island. He'd find the tall oak and start there in the morning, but he wasn't saying anything to the others until then. His leg ached. Let the oak tree be the one.

"No treasure map, huh?" Bob said when they walked into camp. "We're just eating some crackers with peanut butter … appetizer for the seven-course meal served later."

"We need something to drink," John said. "That was a lot of digging and sweating and we found nothing but the bottom of the hole. You guys get your turn at digging in the morning."

Bob picked up the radio from the pine stump. "Want to join us and rest for a while? We can listen to music. The radio is ready to go."

"WTMP former WIOK, the colored station? They play the best blues," Brad said.

"I love that station," Matt answered. "See if we can get it. We can try WALT too. Their signal will be strong until the sun goes down, and then by nine or ten we should get WLAC in Nashville."

Bob pulled out the antenna and tuned in WTMP.

"Turn up the volume, Bob. I love 'Jim Dandy.'" Matt said.

"What song don't you love?" John said.

"Not too many, when it comes to rock 'n' roll."

"Be honest with you," John said, "sometimes, I'd rather listen to the Dodgers."

Matt went up to John and popped him on the back of the head. "Well, no Dodgers game tonight, John. You gotta listen to music."

"John loves music," Bob said, shaking his hips as he danced to the song. "He just has no rhythm. That's why he likes baseball."

John stood up and began to shake his body. "Eat your heart out, Elvis," he said as he tried to move his legs and hips to the music.

Brad laughed. "John, your dancing looks like somebody standing on a bed of red ants. Each ant takes a bite—you lift a foot off the ground and start jumping. Ants don't bite in rhythm and neither is your jumping."

"You have no beat, John. Admit it," Bob said, watching John's performance. "You're pitiful."

John jumped and stomped and exaggerated his movements. "Put

me in a dance contest and I'd win hands down. Why, I'm the new Sammy Davis Jr."

The song ended, and John stopped slowly, like a toy soldier with the battery going dead. He turned in a circle and bowed to each person. They responded with a slow clap-clap.

"Listen," Robin said, "that's an outboard engine cranking up. Bet we can guess who that is."

"Porky and Rocky. I bet they're leaving," Bob said. "Let's go give 'em some trouble before they cut out over the sand bar into deep water."

Not far down the beach, thick blue smoke surrounded the engine of Porky and Rocky's boat. The uneven sound of the sputtering engine could be clearly heard over the surf and shore birds. Porky stood in the boat. In the waist-deep water, Rocky shoved the bow and jumped on the boat, sprawling across the deck on his stomach, his feet dangling in the water.

Bob ran to the shoreline and waded out knee deep. Billy, Robin, JB, Brad and Matt stood at the water's edge, like fishermen on the beach waiting for tarpon to roll.

John came running from the campsite with a fishing pole in one hand and his T-shirt in the other. As he ran, he threw the white T-shirt over the tip of the pole to create a surrender flag.

"Here they come. Here come the big babies," Bob giggled. "We gotta get 'em good."

"Just give them a wave when they go by," Matt said, "and Bob … a wave, not the finger."

John lifted his improvised flag in the air. "I've got something better than a bird for them. I call this a special sendoff—to go along with my bird." He splashed past Bob, the pole in his hand.

The boat had to stay inside the sandbar, close to the shore. Blue smoke puffed from the back with each cough of the motor. They had no choice but to go past Bob and John at a slow speed.

Porky tilted the engine so part of the propeller was out of the water. Brown sand churned up behind the boat as the blades hit the bottom. The spinning prop shot water high into the air. The distinct sound of the engine—loud and raw, not muffled by water—reached the ears of the boys.

"Poor water pump," Matt said, hearing the engine's cylinders with no water circulation. "Better get that prop back down into the water, Porky, before it heats up and quits on ya."

Just then, Porky lowered the prop and the normal engine sound returned.

"He knew," Robin said.

"Where you babies headed? Back to mommy?" Bob yelled through his hands cupped around his mouth.

John lifted the pole and yelled, "You forgot your flag."

"Yeah," Bob chimed in. "Scared?"

"Surrendering?" John waved his flag.

"You wusses. We got the big kahunas," Bob shouted. "Look at the babies, here they come. You're both shaking. I can see it from here." Bob gave a big belly laugh and slapped his knees. "Look at them—here comes the sissy brigade, guys. They've got little dicks and fat asses."

Porky lowered the prop again as the boat crept into deeper water, and the boat began to move a little faster, but they still had to get past Bob and John. Standing in the front of the boat, Rocky looked at the boys and laughed at them.

"If we had a movie camera, we could take movies of the chickens headed home to mommy." John laughed, still waving his flag.

Bob pushed his thumbs up into his armpits and flapped his elbows like a chicken strutting along the ground. "See you later, chicken boys. When you get home, Rocky, hide under the sheets."

The bow started to lift and water peeled off on either side. The boat sliced through the still water. Rocky shot them a bird. "Scratch my ass."

"Now I know why you two have high voices," Bob said. "You pull your dungarees up too far. Bye-bye, sissies. When you're at Frank's next time, shop in the girls' department."

Rocky stood up laughing, and waved at them. "I'll see you two fuzz balls at school on Tuesday."

"You got an open wound, Bob. Reach for the salt shaker," John said.

"There go the tough boys," Bob yelled, "but we know the real toughs—it's us. We got fuzz. You guys are ball-less. Go home and listen to Johnny Mathis." Bob slapped his knees again and belly-laughed, rubbing his stomach.

Rocky shot them a bird with both hands. "Hey, candy asses. See you Tuesday. We'll see who's laughing then."

"Sleep tonight with the lights on in your bedroom," Bob yelled, as the boat made a sharp turn and headed over the bar.

Porky gave the engine full throttle and the flat-bottomed custom plywood skiff jumped up on its final plane with only the back half in the water. It was a fast boat. Its bottom popped as it hit the incoming waves. Rocky remained on the bow—holding the anchor rope like he was riding a horse—and the bow dropped into water. The engine screamed and the last remnant of blue smoke drifted back over the sandbar.

Matt turned to JB who was beside him up on the beach, watching the show. "If we were closer, I bet we'd see red faces on that boat."

"I bet it'll be all laughs Tuesday at school," JB said. "You can't be mad at Bob—maybe John, but not Bob."

"I don't know," Matt said. "They both sometimes take it to the edge."

Bob and John slapped each other's hands and jogged back to shore. "That was fun," Bob said. He shook his head and looked at Matt. "They believed you, Matt. They actually think that prisoner could be here. The eighth graders left and this group of seventh graders stayed."

Matt picked up a small broken shell and skipped it across the water. "You know, we knew the prisoner didn't really steal a boat. They didn't. That's the only reason we aren't leaving the island with them. Yeah, we got them—they fell for my story—but don't lose the perspective of what happened."

John looked at Matt with a grin. "Sometimes you think too much. We got 'em, and you're still thinkin'."

Matt threw another shell into the water. "Just pointing out feelings, John. We all have them."

"So, now you feel sorry that you told them the story and made them leave?" Bob said.

"I'm glad I told the story. I hoped it would make them leave because

98

we're going to discuss things tonight around the fire that they don't need to hear. But I feel sorry they left."

"You're too nice, Matt. Are you getting ready to cry?" John said, wiping pretend tears from his eyes.

"I wouldn't cry in front of you, John."

"Sounds to me like you're ready to cry."

Matt lunged at John, quickly putting him in a headlock. With his knuckles he gave him a quick Dutch rub. "Let's see who shows some tears."

John started laughing. "Stop! I give. Stop! I'm not fightin' a cripple." He tried to pull away. Matt held him firm and knew John felt his strength. He loosened his grip and gave John a little push. It was over.

John shot him a fast, curious look. "I know what lives in your body," he said.

Rocky and Porky's boat was just a speck as it left Big Pass and headed for the intercoastal waterway that hugged the eastern side of Clearwater Beach. On the horizon, the sun passed through the last tip of a cloud just above the water's edge and slipped into the Gulf. No noise, just silence as it finally disappeared.

"Well," Robin said with a sigh, "No green flash, but there's always tomorrow night. My dad saw it once out on his boat, so it does happen."

"What is it?" Billy said.

"Some people say that with the right conditions, just at the instant that the sun completely sets, you see a green flash of light on the horizon."

John laughed. "Well, Billy, you didn't see a green flash, but later you will see a blue flame."

"A what?" Billy asked.

"You'll see tonight," John answered, laughing harder.

Bob kicked the water with his foot, sending a splash into the air. "And Billy, if you want to take a swim tonight, you'll see a different kind of light—phosphorus in the water. It's cool. Anybody want to go?"

"Let's pass on that," Brad said. "We've already had one shark bite today and we know blacktips are in the area."

SORRY YOU MISSED IT...

The group walked through the last dune. "Remember our perimeter," Billy said. "Don't trip over my string."

Just as Billy said the words, John tangled his foot in the fishing line, and a loud tinny sound reverberated around the campsite. "Shit! I thought I stepped over it."

Matt covered his ears. "Stand still, John. That's annoying."

"Well, now we know it works," said Brad. "Let's hope no one trips it tonight."

John untangled his foot from the line and patted Billy on the shoulder. "That sound would wake us up on a Saturday morning. The snake man does it again."

"I'm hungry," Bob said. "Let's get dinner going."

"Good idea," John said. "Matt, you go sit down and get some music on the radio. We can handle the cooking tonight without you."

In one hour, they had completed their meal of hot dogs, beans and baked potatoes, and put everything neatly away like they'd learned from Matt's dad in Boy Scouts. A sea breeze developed over the Gulf and the evening cooled off. The temperature was in the seventies, but the heat of the fire still felt good.

Chapter 18

THE BLUE FLAME

OUTSIDE THE CAMPSITE, a circle of darkness began to eat up the light. In the West, the first star appeared with a pink and blue-black sky around it.

Billy pointed to the sky. "It's going to be a great night to see the stars. There's Venus. No moonlight tonight until later."

"Venus, huh?" John said. "What don't you know a lot about, Billy, my boy?"

Bob put more logs over the cooking coals to create a campfire for the evening. He stirred the coals with a branch and the flames burst to life.

Matt sat down on a log beside the fire. His injured leg throbbed. The faces of his friends glowed and shadows moved across their cheeks and noses. Who was who? The effect was cool but almost scary. They looked ghoulish. They were waiting … waiting for him to say something.

Bob tossed a large pine log into the fire and flames lit up the campsite.

The faces became people, identifiable like a flash bulb went off. No smiles in the picture—just serious faces—waiting to hear a twelve-year-old give them a story of triumph and optimism.

"I'm happy you joined me in looking for the other half of my treasure map, guys," Matt said. "I hope tomorrow we'll hit the jackpot.

SORRY YOU MISSED IT...

Now, I need to ask for your help next week at school. A nasty ninth grade hood named Wayne Tyson is after Billy, and his brother asked me to watch out for him until he gets back in a couple of weeks. It's a long story, but the bottom line is I need some help keeping Billy away from that guy. We had a run-in with him today at Brown Brothers, and he's a bad dude. That's about it. Want to ride with Custer?"

"Sounds kind of scary to me, but you know I'll help," Robin said.

"I'm with you," JB said. "I may not be tough, but I'm scrappy when things get crappy."

"I'm a lover not a fighter, but you can count me in too," Brad said.

"Thanks," Matt said. "I don't think it's going to be a huge problem."

"Won't be easy," said Bob. "Before school, after school, okay—but other times?"

"Yeah, like pee breaks," John snorted. "What if he's hiding in a stall and you got your tally-whacker out?"

"Your what?" Bob said and began to belly laugh.

"You know, your companion, your doo-dinker, your donkey ear. Heck, everybody's got their own name for it. But if it's out and Wayne jumps out, what do you do—spray his shoes? And what if he's in Billy's gym class? Oh God, then he'd have showers to worry about too."

"You're not funny, John," Matt said, but he bit his tongue to hold back a laugh. "This is serious."

"I'm serious Matt. Sincerely, it could happen. I don't trust that guy."

"Well, it sounds to me like the answer is one of us must stay with Billy the whole first day of school," JB said.

"I know the schedule," Billy said. "And it's not good. I saw it at orientation night."

"Oh God," John said. "Are you and Wayne in the same gym class?"

"Yes, *Kemo Sabe,*" Billy answered. "Sixth period gym. Can you believe my bad luck?"

"Wait," John said. "Bob and Matt and I have sixth period gym. That sounds like good luck for you and bad luck for us."

Matt frowned at John. "Actually, John, that's good luck for us too. We'll all be together and Wayne won't be able to isolate him."

"Damn it, John," Bob said with a frown. "Why did you say that?"

"To make you cuss," John laughed. "Get out the soap."

102

Bob threw a marshmallow that was partly melted from the heat and hit John on the nose. It stuck. "I said that to make a point, John."

John laughed. "I was just clowning around, Bob."

"Well, right now you look like a clown," Matt said. "Do you know the marshmallow is still on your nose?"

John pulled it off and looked at it, lifted his chin and opened his mouth. "Down the hatch," he said, "sticky but yummy. Thanks Bob." He moved over to the fire. "Throw me the stick with another marshmallow on it, Bob. I think I'll cook up another, crisp and black—that's my recipe—with the center oozing out like white lava."

Bob tossed him the stick and then a marshmallow. "Okay, so, back to Tyson the hood. We're all together in sixth period gym? And you're sure Wayne's on the list?"

"Positive," Billy said.

"Oh my, that's not so good," John said, waving the stick over the flames. "But with Coach Smith and Coach Shank, he won't think about doing anything. Right? Unless it's in the showers."

The marshmallow stretched out like taffy as John pulled it off the stick and popped it into his mouth. "I'll be ready for him with my towel and the tightest rattail you've ever seen. I'll pop his white ass with that and watch him jump off his toes like Tinkerbell with a red butt."

"You're dreamin,'" JB said. "I remember Wayne Tyson. He's …"

"Okay guys," Matt interrupted, "enough about Wayne and how tough he is."

Bob lifted another pine log from the woodpile, walked to the fire and tossed it on. Sparks flew high into the air and the pinesap popped like firecrackers.

"Okay," Matt said. "JB, you ride the same bus as Billy so you stay with him after you get off the bus until Bob, John and I meet you. We'll stay with him until the bell rings for first period. Then we'll walk him to the bus stop after sixth period. That leaves lunch. Bob, do you have first lunch?"

"I don't know. I think so."

"I think I do too," John said.

"That's good," Matt said. "You two look for Billy and keep your eyes open for Wayne. I'll be there too."

"Right, and Billy, you look for one of us when you get to the cafeteria," Bob said. "We'll save a table and all sit together the first day. Then we watch and see if Wayne is there or not."

Billy stood up from his sleeping bag. "Thanks guys. I appreciate your help. Wayne Tyson is like no one I've ever known. If something happens, just help me survive."

"Okay, Billy. It's cool. We have you under our protection," Bob said. "Now we need to talk about tonight and taking turns staying awake in case that escaped prisoner is around."

"There's no prisoner on this island," John mumbled with his mouth full of marshmallows. "I think you're hoping there is, Bob."

"Why take a chance?" Billy said.

"You're right, Billy," answered Robin, "and Bob's right too."

"Want to draw straws to see who goes first?" Matt said. "One hour each, until morning?"

"Good idea," said JB. "We don't want to just depend on banging cans to let us know if an escaped convict is about to enter this campsite."

"How do we stay awake?" asked Billy.

"Listen to the radio," replied Bob, "and keep the fire going."

Billy yawned. "Can I take the first watch? I'm afraid I might fall asleep."

"We usually draw straws," Robin answered, "but I say, we should let you be first, since you're the one who set up the noisemaker. Let's draw straws later, right before we go to sleep."

"We should have good radio reception tonight," Bob said with a glance at the sky.

Billy looked up and pointed. "Good atmospheric conditions, maybe. Look at the stars. Not a cloud in the sky, not even a mist yet."

"How do you know about that?" John said.

"I read it in my amateur radio book," Billy said.

Matt grinned. "Billy, I think you know about everything."

"Mainly science stuff."

"Science stuff, huh?" John said. "Do you know what makes a blue flame?"

Billy squinted his eyes and wrinkled his nose. "A what?"

"A blue flame," John repeated with a sly grin and a snort.

"Never heard of that. Are you serious John, or are you kidding with me?"

"I'm not kidding. Tell him, Bob."

Bob just smiled.

"I'll show you a blue flame right now," John said. "Do you have the matches, Robin?"

"Yes."

"Throw me the box. One act is worth a thousand words!" He pulled a green wool army blanket from his Army-Navy duffle bag and neatly spread it on the ground over the pine needle mat, taking care to remove all the pinecones first.

Robin rooted around in the brown paper bag with the utensils and pulled out a small box. "Here, John. Catch."

John sat down and began to laugh. "This is perfect. Great timing. I feel one coming on right now." He stood up and unbuttoned his Levi's, dropped them to his ankles, stepped out of them and stood there with only his underwear and a T-shirt on.

Billy watched him soberly. "This is quite a production, John."

John sat down on the blanket, rolled back and extended both legs up toward the stars. His white underwear shone in the light of the campfire. "You can't hurry a blue flame. Ready, Dr. Scientist?"

Billy still looked confused.

John lit a match and pulled his legs straight back to his ears, his face looking right at his crotch. "Ready? Here goes."

"What am I looking for, John?" asked Billy.

"A blue flame." He held the lighted match an inch from his underwear. The match flame crept toward his thumb and finger. "Watch, here it goes."

John let out a big fart, the sound deep and loud, and with a whoosh, a brilliant blue flame shot from his butt, out into the darkness about a foot. It looked like the flame at the end of a welder's torch, dark blue with a yellow orange point at the end.

Billy's mouth dropped open.

John lay on the blanket laughing, covering his mouth with his fist and snorting. "That, Billy my man, is a blue flame."

SORRY YOU MISSED IT...

Laughter exploded around the campfire. They laughed and rolled on the ground, holding their stomachs.

"Oh my gosh, where did you learn that, John?" Billy said, still laughing so hard he could barely talk. "That was the funniest thing I've ever seen in my life."

"He learned it from a kid in camp," Matt and Bob said almost in unison.

"You even burned your skivvies this time, John," Brad said. "Never seen you do that before."

"I feel another one coming," John said. He lit another match, held it near his butt and another blue flame shot out as he farted again. The brown burned spot on his underwear grew and John rubbed the singed spot on his butt.

"Your mom must think you're having bathroom issues when she sees brown spots on your underwear," JB said, and everyone started laughing again.

Billy continued laughing hard. "What if it ignites the gas in your body? You could blow up."

"It's like a jet engine, and jet engines don't blow up. I might singe a few hairs, but mostly just burn a spot in the underwear. It's like blowing out a candle on a birthday cake." John stood up and pulled up his Levi's, jumping in place to get them over his hips. "Okay, you're next, Matt. What kind of show have you got tonight?"

Matt got up from his seat at the edge of the campsite and picked up the lower end of a palm frond that they used for kindling. He put his arm around John's shoulder and held the wide end to his mouth like a microphone. "I can see it now ... at next year's Pinellas County Fair: a new attraction on the midway ... John's Freak Show.

"Attention. Attention. Step right up, folks! Come close. Welcome to the midway. There beside the Fat Lady Show, we'll see John's tent. The picture on the outside will show a half human, half dragon with his tail sticking up into the sky and a blue-red flame shooting out his butt, melting a steel girder of a skyscraper under construction.

"And beside the tent door with its canvas flap closed, on the sawdust floor, is a podium. Standing on a wooden 'Taylor Groves' fruit box is a five-foot-four carny, with a two-day beard and mustache, wearing a fancy Sam Snead hat, a microphone pushed up to his lips, almost touching the Lucky Strike cigarette hanging from his mouth, the exposed package visible in the plaid flannel shirt's front pocket.

"He'll say, 'Come right in, folks … See him light up and shoot flames across the room. Just one thin dime … One tenth of a dollar … Step right up, folks.'"

Matt pointed his stick mike at John. "A hand for the freak, please."

The boys laughed, clapped their hands and waited, ready for Matt to entertain them like he always did. John bowed and sat down.

Matt put down his stick mike and picked up the leaf of a palm frond, strumming it once like a make-believe guitar. "Thank you, boys. Here is my rendition of the Bill Parsons' song, 'All-American Boy.'"

Gather round boys and I'll tell you a yarn
About how to become a real all-American carn.
Get you some matches, light up a few
And you'll be blowing a flame or two.
Impressing the girls and that kind of stuff.
Well, he was shooting blue flames
He had what it takes
Everyone said his blue flames were great.
When up came a carny with a Pall Mall dangling from his lips
He said, 'Boy, I'll put you on the midway.
Buy you a Jeep …
Sign here, sonny.'

"Go, Daddy-O. That was cool," John said.

Well, he signed his name, became a star…
Shooting blue flames near and far,
Driving along in his Jeep
Fighting blue flames off the seat.
The flames kept a coming…
And he liked it.

The tent was full, the blue flames never dimmed
The money just kept rollin' in.
And then one day, came a knock on the door
A man standing on the sawdust floor.
He said, 'Uncle Sam needs you, son
We need flame throwers.
Ah, I'm going to give you a flattop
And put you in the infantry, kid.
Yeah ...

"Bravo, Matt! That was great," Brad said.

Billy rolled over holding his stomach and pleaded, "Stop, Matt. I can't laugh anymore."

The boys sat on their sleeping bags laughing and clapping.

Matt bowed from the waist and sat down on his sleeping bag. His leg still ached, but he put it out of his mind and enjoyed the laughter.

Several times, the laughter stopped for a minute, and then the silence initiated another round of laughter. Finally, the silence won. It wasn't cold, but the night air, pushed by the soft wind from the Gulf, made the warmth from the fire feel good to their bare skin. They turned off the lanterns and settled in around the fire, laughing themselves into peacefulness.

Beyond the light of the fire, the island turned pitch black. Heat lightning periodically flashed far away on the eastern horizon, illuminating the clouds in the sky. Stars lit up the heavens, the Milky Way actually looked milky, constellations were easily identified and some planets shown as bright as the moon, which would rise out of the East later.

Robin stretched out on top of his sleeping bag with his knees bent and his head nestled in a soft feather pillow. "Holy smokes, heaven is beautiful tonight. I see more stars than sand on the beach. Which star do you think is God's home?"

"All of them," Matt said, stretched out now on his sleeping bag and looking up into the sky.

"He does some moving around then," John said.

JB threw another log on the fire. "John, He's everywhere—the whole universe, stars behind stars."

"Yep, over there in the Big Dipper," John said, pointing his finger straight toward the constellation.

"And follow the two stars on the bottom a few inches, and that's the North Star," Billy said.

"From snake man to astronomer," John said. "You should have a big head like Einstein, Billy."

A long silence followed.

The smell of the campfire blended with the aroma of pine trees and salt spewed by the waves breaking on the beach, a part of camping on Hog Island that their dads had taught them to appreciate early on. The waves breaking down on the shore seemed to affect all the boys. Their voices softened and they spoke in quiet tones.

"Hear the owl?" Matt said. "Somewhere deep in the pines."

An answer came from the other direction, the same call but a little more hoarse.

"I love that sound," JB said. "Owls in the night ..."

"Great horned, I believe," said Bob.

"I concur," said Billy.

The flame deep down under the logs barely illuminated the campsite. A low layer of clouds covered the stars. An eerie silence engulfed the campsite.

"Quiet," said JB, looking out into the darkness past the light of the fire. "I hear something."

"I just heard something too. Over by the pines," Robin whispered. "Where did the stars go?"

"Are you bullshittin' us?" John said.

"Shhhh," Bob said. "I hear it—beyond the pines."

Chapter 19

THE INTRUDERS

MATT'S HEART POUNDED. He clenched his teeth. The fire suddenly flared and let them see better into the chasm of darkness. "Even the fire hears it," he said. "It's trying to help."

"Oh God, do you think it's Wayne?" Billy whispered.

"Maybe it's the escaped prisoner," John said in a low voice.

"Shhhh, don't talk," Matt whispered.

Snap—something broke a twig. *Snap*—this time a little louder.

Matt listened. Whatever was coming toward the camp stopped. No movement. No sound. His hands tightened into fists.

Billy held his hand to his chest. "Oh God," he said. "I can feel my heart beating."

"Brad, get the flashlight," Matt said. "Point it toward the pine trees but don't turn it on 'til I tell you."

Snap—the sound was moving and coming their way.

Billy crouched down. "It sounds like someone big. Maybe it's the escaped prisoner. Should we run?"

"No," Matt said. "Hold your ground. Where's the machete?"

"I've got it," Bob said.

Matt could see the machete in Bob's shaking hand. "Bob, give the machete to JB, and get the keys to your boat just in case we need to make a run for it. Robin, be ready to head to your boat too."

Robin reached for a small waterproof box that held all of his valuables. "Ready."

"John, my four-ten is beside my sleeping bag," Matt said. "I don't think I can get to it quick enough with my leg. Scoot over, take it out of the case and hand it to me, okay?"

"Is it loaded?" John said.

"Yes."

"It stopped," Bob said. "Maybe we should run before it starts moving again."

"It sounds big, Matt," John said. "Here's the gun. I'm going to get a shovel and walk over to the other side of the fire."

"What can I do?" Billy asked.

"Nothing right now. Just be ready to run for the boats," Matt whispered. "We're okay. Got the flashlight ready, Brad?"

"Yes."

"Get ready with the machete, JB."

Matt checked the safety, breached the gun to be sure the shell was in the chamber and closed it, holding it with both hands, ready to fire, if necessary. He listened, but all he heard were the waves breaking on the beach, the shrill call of a sandpiper as it ran on the sand and the breeze moving through the pines.

Another twig snapped in the pine trees. The intruder was getting close to Billy's perimeter.

"Get ready," Matt whispered.

Cans rattled in the darkness. The sandpipers on the beach flew up in the air, their voices piercing the night.

Matt pushed the safety off and pointed the shotgun toward the sound. "Brad, get ready. We need to see it before it gets to us."

"Now?" Brad said.

"I'll tell you when …"

Bang! CRASH! A deafening sound like a rock slide hitting a tin shed rolled toward them.

"Now, Brad!" Matt yelled. "Get ready, Bob! … Robin!"

John lifted the shovel like a bat waiting for the next pitch. "I've got a shovel," he yelled.

The oystercatchers on the beach scattered—their high-pitched shrieks mixed with the screams of the boys.

The beam of light lit up the darkness and the boys burst into uncontrolled laughter. Twenty feet in front of them stood two of the largest raccoons they'd ever seen, one tangled in the string, the other free and standing up on his hind legs, red eyes staring into the light beam.

Matt pushed the safety back on. "Well, Billy, your perimeter string worked."

"Two bandits," John laughed, "but not from our jail."

JB put the machete back in the scabbard. "Thank God—I was expecting a big, ugly, scary prisoner, lines tangled around his feet, ready to attack us with a knife in his hand."

"That's a relief," Billy said, wiping perspiration off his forehead. "I just knew it was Wayne."

The tangled raccoon flipped on itself and spun around chattering with high-pitched squeals.

"You did well, Billy," Matt said. "Now, let's see how you're going to get that one untangled from the fishing line."

"He's not happy," Bob said. "Listen to him hiss."

"I do snakes, not raccoons," Billy said, laughing. "Where's the other one?"

"Our screaming scared him to death. I saw him heading for the trees," Robin said, "and we're in luck, the other one is getting loose himself."

The second raccoon broke free and then waddled into the darkness at a leisurely pace.

"That's how freedom makes you feel," Matt said. "Always remember that."

"Turn on the radio," Brad said. "Let's chill out and listen to some music on the night stations for a while."

"Good idea," Matt said, "and then let's all go to sleep. We don't need to worry about anyone staying up. We've got things to do in the morning. The raccoons were our convict."

John picked up a large log lying on the ground beside the fire. "Might as well put this last one on the fire. We can go to sleep watching it."

"I think I'll be up for a while just thinking about all that's happened tonight," Robin said.

Matt turned on the radio. "Let's try WLS in Chicago first." He turned the dials. "Nope, not tonight. Not clear."

"Try WLAC-Nashville," Brad said. "John R can help us unwind. It's eleven o'clock. He's starting right now."

An announcer from WLAC came in loud and clear. "Hey, John R— Whatcha going to do? Come on, John R, man, play me some rhythm and blues."

A second voice answered. "All right there my friend. I got to do it. John R way down south here in Dixie … Let's kick this show off with the Blue Ribbon Special and Jimmy Reed, 'Baby, What You Want Me to Do' … Randy's Record Mart, Nashville, Tennessee. I gotta do it."

When the song ended, Matt showed Brad his arm. "Now that's music. I love that harmonica. Look at my goose bumps."

"Yep," Brad said. "Great song, and hopefully no runnin' for us tonight."

"Matt and Brad, the musical pair," John said.

After an hour of listening to rhythm and blues, the WLAC signal began to fade and the boys settled into their sleeping bags. Matt turned the volume down. "Put us to sleep, Brad. Recite us a poem."

"No sonnets tonight, please," Bob begged, and everyone laughed.

"No," Matt said. "I meant some Robert Service stuff and the one by the other man that Service inspired. The one your dad taught us."

Brad stood up. "Okay, just one," he said in a low, soft voice. Behind him, the fire glowed and crackled. "Tonight it's 'The Ballad of Yukon Jake' by Edward Paramore Jr."

"Oh, the North Countree is a hard countree
That mothers a bloody brood"
Brad stopped. "That one okay, John?"

"Yessiree," John said. "You're the man, Brad."

Brad continued to recite the poem about the transformation of Jacob Kaime, the hermit of Shark Tooth Shoal, from an honest young boy in Keokuk, Iowa, to Yukon Jake, a wicked Klondike bully in Alaska who sold his girlfriend, Ruthless Ruth, to Dan McGrew for a dog and some eggnog.

The boys hung on every word as the story unfolded, and five minutes later as Brad finished, everyone stood up and clapped. "Bravo,

Bravo!" said John. "Now do the Robert Service one, 'The Cremation of Sam McGee.'"

Brad sat back down. "Too tired. My brain's done. Stick a fork in me."

"Then just start Sam McGee," John pleaded. "You should have recited it first."

"I'm done. Next campout I'll recite that one and maybe 'The Shooting of Dan McGrew.'" Goodnight everybody. Sweet dreams and no nightmares."

JB pulled his sleeping bag over his shoulders. "That was great, Brad. Now I'm relaxed and ready for some shuteye."

Matt lay on his back and looked at the stars. "Thanks Brad. 'Night everyone."

"Stay warm boys," Brad said in a deep, bloodcurdling voice.

The rhythmic sound of the waves and slow breathing replaced the campfire poetry. Slowly the flame from the last log died and all that was left were occasional fireflies flying up into the sky.

Robin lay quietly watching the fire, with one foot sticking out of his sleeping bag.

Matt tapped Robin's foot with his own. "I think everybody else is asleep," he whispered. "Want to go down and check the boats one last time? The moon can be our flashlight."

Robin flipped the top of his sleeping bag off and sat up. "Sure," he said quietly. "I was just thinking the same thing. How's your leg?"

"Still hurts a little, but I can make it without a problem."

The moon cast enough light to illuminate the path to the beach. The mist had disappeared and the air felt dry to their skin.

The two boys put on their tennis shoes and followed the path past the stand of pine trees, through the palm trees, around the clumps of palmettos and between the dunes. Ahead, they could see the water and hear the waves running up onto the shore.

The waves slapped the two boats, smacking them almost broadside like an open hand. The tide and waves had pulled the stern anchors through the sand and turned both boats parallel to the beach.

"Glad we came down here to check. Those boats would have hit one another before long," Robin said. "We need to move the bows tight again. The incoming tide shifted them."

"Let's pull the anchors a little farther up on the dry sand and that should make the waves come up under the stern," Matt said.

They moved both boat anchors and the boats turned.

"I think we're good," Robin said.

Matt stood staring out over the water, watching the moonlight sparkling on the waves. "Want to sit on the beach for a while and let me rest my leg?"

"Sure," Robin answered.

A white ghost crab darted along the sand, and down the beach a lone sandpiper worked its way toward them, running up and down the wet sand, feeding, always running clear of the incoming waves.

Matt sat with his legs stretched out in front of him and leaned back on his arms with his flat hands sunk in the sand. His leg throbbed. "Feel kind of insignificant?" he asked Robin.

"Makes me feel close to our Maker," Robin said.

"Me too," Matt said, "kind of ..."

"What do you mean?"

"We're a speck in the universe—look outward to the stars, look inward to the atoms. Wow! My dad says we're not supposed to understand it all. Just appreciate its wonder and give thanks. Someday we'll be given the answer by God Himself."

"I believe that," Robin answered.

They sat there a long time in silence. The sandpiper walked right by them, so close to their feet that their big toes could have flicked a shell and hit him.

The moon was starting to show a ring and the stars appeared behind a haze. The breeze picked up a little, the sea oats waved and the damp salt air filled their nostrils. The late summer night was cooling off.

"I think I'm ready to go back and go to sleep," Matt said.

"Me too," said Robin.

They stood up and walked back to the campsite without talking.

Under the dark ashes of the campfire, the hot embers glowed and crackled. It slept now like the boys surrounding it.

As dawn approached, the stars in the east were still visible, but losing their luster. In the pines, the great horned owl hooted. Toward the west, the gentle waves produced a soft, rhythmic sound as they rolled up onto the beach, and shore birds talked to the beginning of the new day.

Matt opened his eyes. It was still dark, but he knew it was close to morning. Only a slight breeze blew out of the west, and the soft sound of the waves told him they were only footers. He lay there and listened, guessing it was probably around five o'clock.

By now, his dad would be with his best friend, Bill Peart, probably launching their boat on Lake Butler. On days when they didn't have to work, they loved to set out early and drive to one of the lakes in the area for a day of freshwater fishing. Matt knew if he wasn't on Hog Island looking up at the stars, he'd be with them. He was always invited. Sometimes making the choice was hard. Earlier, he had wished his dad was with them, but they'd all done fine and he knew their dads would be proud of them.

The stars quickly began to fade and only the Morning Star was prominent. Soon, the sun would greet them.

Somewhere Matt's watch rested on the edge of his sleeping bag, but he didn't try to find it. Most times on camping trips, just before falling asleep, he would take the watch off. He liked the feeling of nothing touching him. Unless it was really cold, he just slept in his underwear and that seemed good. He was right where he wanted to be. He was ready for a new day. He had drunk a lot of hot chocolate around the fire and now he felt the urge to go to the bathroom.

Billy stood up and quietly pulled his sheet from his sleeping bag.

Matt remained still. He knew what that probably meant.

Billy headed for the water with his sheet draped loosely over his arm. When he was out of sight, Matt slipped out of his sleeping bag and headed for the privacy of a palmetto bush. His leg felt better.

When he returned, Billy was sitting on his rolled sheet. Matt sat down beside him and whispered, "Good morning." He could barely see a tear on Billy's cheek. He rested his arm on Billy's shoulder. "Don't worry, you'll outgrow it."

"Our secret?" Billy whispered.

"Our secret. I'm going for a walk. Be back in a little while."

Matt got up and limped toward the beach. He would give Billy time with his thoughts, and he'd enjoy his own solitude. As he walked along the water's edge, small waves lapped at his ankles, and the particles of sand and broken shells, moved by the water, tickled his toes as they ran between them. A pair of sandpipers ran along just up ahead, darting away from him and the waves as they searched for food in the wet sand.

The ongoing cycle played out as Matt watched in amusement. Sometimes the birds misjudged their timing, ran prematurely, and abandoned the morsel of food to the next incoming wave. He watched the birds and thought of himself.

Forces moved him, like the birds, quicker than he wanted. The birds rolled with it, but he wasn't willing to accept being at the mercy of those forces, especially when it came to Wayne. But then again, sometimes being pushed was a good thing. Wayne's consequences would come. A little pressure was okay. It would keep his blood hot.

He walked, following the sandpipers, toward the southern end of the island where the mangroves began and the beach ended. Was that a boat beached up on the sand near the first mangrove? Probably just an early morning fisherman ... But what if it was someone else? He fought the urge to panic. What if it was the escaped prisoner? A giant of a man, they'd said.

Matt returned to the quiet camp, climbed back into his sleeping bag and pulled it over his head as he did earlier to protect him from a mosquito whining around his ears. He wouldn't say anything to anyone. No need to worry about a fishing boat. He listened to the slow breathing from all the other boys, including Billy. Everyone else seemed to be asleep. His bandage felt damp. Probably bleeding a little, but if he stayed still, it should stop.

He lay there, dozing, clearing his mind, and he, too, fell asleep.

Chapter 20

THE SMELLY BOOT

A NASTY SMELL AWAKENED Matt. Lying still with his eyes closed, he pictured flowers, long dead in a heap, topped with intestines of roadkill baked in the summer heat. He heard only the sound of the waves on the beach and the regular breathing of the sleeping boys, but he sensed a grotesque presence near him.

Without moving, he opened one eye and peeked out from under the sheet. On the sand, inches from his nose, he saw an enormous dirty boot with untied laces frayed at the ends and a tongue curling out over the toe area. The boot stank and made him want to gag.

He imagined yellow, two-week-old grunge caked between the toes inside the boot, sweat-stained clothes and a hot breath emerging from green teeth and gums caked with days-old food.

He lay there holding his breath, afraid he might start dry heaving. The boot remained motionless.

What was the giant inside the boot doing? Some partially chewed food dropped beside his nose. He was rummaging for something to eat. The giant smacked his lips and swallowed.

What next? Matt made his fingers slide down his side inside the sleeping bag. They touched the bandage on his leg and then the wooden stock of his shotgun that he'd stuffed in the sleeping bag after the raccoon scare. Moving the gun was smart, but with the cut on his leg, he'd have trouble getting it out so he could use it.

The giant moved his boot and stepped over Billy's sleeping body. The stink remained.

Matt thought if the smell could be seen, a green-yellow cloud would be clinging to the man's body and falling off his clothes like bubbles blown through a wire wand. He felt the bubbles on him. He still thought he might vomit, but he didn't. His eye saw the silhouette of the man and his knees suddenly started banging together—so much for staying calm.

The massively built man looked like a giant. His wide shoulders stretched far beyond his hips and his hands came nearly to his knees. If he wasn't the escaped prisoner, he must be an escapee from a mental hospital, or worse, a mad scientist from the three-story house, deep in the woods, its flickering dim yellow lights illuminating the windows, and a moon partially covered by fast-moving clouds sweeping past its tower, just like in the scariest of movies.

Matt's heart pounded, and it seemed so loud, he feared the giant could hear it. Whoever the man was and wherever he'd come from, at that moment, he was there, in their camp on Hog Island.

The giant quietly moved away.

Matt wondered if anyone else was awake.

The giant stepped over John, reached down and picked up the bag of marshmallows lying beside the smoldering embers of the fire. He pulled them out in handfuls and stuffed them into his mouth.

John became restless and turned in his sleeping bag.

The giant straightened up from his bent position, glanced down at John and dropped the empty bag.

The outline of his body was sharp and clear. Matt studied the enormous frame and a tremor ran through him. He was looking at a Yeti in clothes. He wanted to be home safe in his own bed with Dad only one room away. But he wasn't. He pulled on the gun's wooden stock and to his relief, found it moved easily.

Billy groaned beside him and Matt thought the groan must mean Billy was also awake. He wanted to say something but knew he needed to remain silent.

The giant turned back in his direction and moved like a ghost between the boys. Dirt blended with remnants of food and bits of marshmallow clung to the man's unshaven face.

Matt's eye saw the giant's face, so high up in the air that it almost touched the branches of the nearby pine tree. The ugliness almost overcame him, and for the first time, he wanted to scream and bolt from his sleeping bag.

The giant stood motionless. Above him, a beam of light suddenly flashed through the pine needles, sweeping back and forth, followed by the long yelp of a dog. The man let out a loud, bloodcurdling shriek that shot through the camp.

All seven boys bolted up in their sleeping bags, saw the huge, ugly man and screamed.

The giant raised his arms high in the air, shook them violently, howled and turned and ran toward the thick palmettos, plunging into them like a water buffalo escaping his captor. He was gone.

A moment later, two armed deputies hurried into the camp. A bloodhound on a leash was pulling one along. The other carried a flashlight, long and narrow, about a foot in length.

The beam of the flashlight moved across the ground in the dim early morning light, stopped at each sleeping bag and the boy sitting in it and then scanned the rest of the campsite.

"Are you boys all okay?" yelled the deputy holding the flashlight, continuing to move it erratically back and forth.

"Where did he go?" yelled the other deputy with the dog.

The boys all pointed into the thick palmettos beyond the pines.

"You boys stay put. The sheriff should be right behind us and you can tell him which way we went."

The sun was beginning to brighten up the dark sky in the east, and dull gray pink began to change the color of the night. Two more uniformed men carrying shotguns came into the camp.

"Did you boys see Jeremiah Rennolds, the prisoner who escaped from the county jail two days ago?"

"Tall and ugly?" John said. "We saw him all right. He was eating our food."

Matt pointed to the palmettos and dense undergrowth just beyond the pines. "He went through there and your men followed him. I think

I saw his boat early this morning before first light down on the beach at the edge of the mangroves."

"We saw it. Lost track of him last night in the woods south of town and then had a report of a missing boat, so we decided to take a chance and see if he was out on one of the islands. We got lucky. You boys stay here now 'til we tell you it's safe."

"How big is that guy?" Matt said.

"He's almost seven feet tall," the sheriff said, "and he is one sick cookie."

"He's sick? He had a big appetite for somebody sick."

"Not that kind of sick, son," the sheriff said. "We were going to move him to the state hospital and he got out of a holding cell at the jail.

The men left and the boys jumped out of their sleeping bags and threw on their clothes. Matt sat and watched. His leg ached. He looked down at the bandage and saw blood beginning to soak through. "I think we'd better forget digging for the treasure today," he said. "Let's get everything ready and get out of here as soon as the sheriff gives us the 'all clear.'"

"Good idea," Bob said. "C'mon guys. Let's break down camp."

"I'll get the shovels," John said.

"I'll clean up the cans. Do you remember how scared we were when the raccoons got into these?" Billy said. "Can you imagine if it had been that escaped prisoner? I'm glad the booby trap had already been tripped. He'd have flung cans into those palmettos he just annihilated. Look at them. They look like they've been destroyed by a tractor pulling a bush hog."

"I don't want to think about it," Brad said. "We'd have been toast."

They heard the dog barking and the sound of muffled voices deep in the island. A human howl reverberated through the campsite.

"He sounds like a werewolf," Bob said.

They waited for a gunshot.

"Do you think he doubled back?" Matt said. "That sounded closer."

John returned to camp with the shovels. "Have you got the shotgun, Matt?"

"I do."

"That little bird gun wouldn't kill that giant," JB said.

SORRY YOU MISSED IT...

"It wasn't for me to kill him," Matt said.

"What was it for you to do?"

"Shoot off his baby-maker," Brad said. "That would slow him down."

"Oh my," John said with a laugh. "It's probably long enough to tie into a birthday bow."

No one else laughed.

Fifteen minutes later, one of the deputies strode into the camp, the shotgun in his hand and a revolver visible in its holster. "Well, everyone can relax. We got him."

"Thank you, sir," Matt said. "That's good news. We're going to take our stuff to the boats now and head back to the mainland too."

"Are you all right?" the deputy asked. "That bandage on your leg looks pretty bloody."

"It's fine. Just a little cut. I need to re-bandage it."

The deputy smiled. "Okay boys, we're going to get this guy back to jail, and maybe you better stop by the hospital on the way home and have the doctor check out this young man's leg. Looks like it needs a new bandage and maybe some stitches."

"Wow," Bob said. "I've never been so scared. Matt, I don't know how you stay so calm, but I think the deputy is right. We'd better get going and get that cut on your leg checked out."

Matt held out his hand so Bob could see how it was shaking. "Bob, no one escaped being scared this morning ... and my leg is fine."

John laughed. "Well, Billy, after this encounter, Wayne is a pussy cat."

"It changes your perspective, that's for sure," Matt said.

"Boys," the deputy said, "your dads should be proud of you. You didn't panic. You did better than most adults."

"Where's Jeremiah the Giant, sir?" John asked.

"They're hand-cuffing him so we can get him in our boat and take him back to the mainland. He'll be on the beach shortly."

"Is he a killer?"

"Broke a guy's neck."

"Did the guy die?"

"Not yet. You got a lot of questions, son. I just came to tell you it's safe now," the deputy said. "I've got to go help them. We're going to get that guy back behind bars as soon as possible."

"Thanks, sir," John said.

"Wow, what stories we'll have to tell at school on Tuesday," JB said.

"Yep," Bob said, "our own Jack and the Beanstalk story. Wait 'til Rocky and Porky hear it. They won't believe it."

"Yeah," Matt said, "and they'll be glad they left the island last night."

John sat down beside Matt and said quietly, "Those shovels were in a different place than where we left them and the hole was about twice the size. Somebody was digging there during the night."

"Thanks, John," Matt said. "Let's not say anything about this to the other guys yet, okay? I just want to get home right now."

"Sure," John said.

Matt let his mind run with all that had just happened. Why had Jeremiah Rennolds come to Hog Island? Was he looking for the treasure map? Had he found it? Was it just a coincidence? Should they come back and dig again? He needed to think, but his leg hurt too much.

"Let's get the boats loaded," said Bob. "I'm ready to get out of here."

"Me too," Robin said. "C'mon, guys."

Ten minutes later, the boys stood on the beach by their boats and watched the sheriff's boat, still visible in the distance.

"Think Jeremiah is preparing for another escape?" Matt said, limping slowly toward them. The bandage was soaked red and the other boys stared at it.

"It's okay," Matt said in a calm, quiet voice. "I must have hit against something in all the commotion."

"No, it's not okay. We need to get you to the hospital," Robin said with alarm in his voice.

"First," Matt said, his voice a little louder, "I want to thank you guys for helping me look for the other half of the treasure map. I hoped we would be able to find it this weekend ..." he hit the gauze-wrapped leg with an open hand, "and then this happened. I just wanted to say I'm sorry. Maybe we can come back next weekend and try again. The treasure is real and it's hidden someplace."

John sat down on the sand beside Matt. "JB, Billy and I dug a hole in the place you said matched the star on the map. You know that. We did dig."

"I know, but I looked at the map again later and I think I may have started at the wrong tree. I just didn't want to say anything last night."

The boys all sat down around Matt. "Guess what, Matt?" Billy said. "I have something quite interesting to say and it makes me wonder."

"Wonder what?"

"I'm wondering if we're not the only ones looking for that treasure. Someone else dug in that hole after we did."

"For sure?"

"When John was finished," Billy said, "he stuck the shovel in the pile of sand beside the hole, and I stuck mine right beside it. I went back there this morning while we were waiting for the sheriff and the hole was wider and deeper—no doubt about it—and one of the shovels wasn't in the hole."

Billy looked around the group. "If it wasn't any of you, someone else was in the hole digging. I don't call that weird, I call that interesting."

"I went back there and picked up the shovels," John said. "Guess you were there before me. I agree. That hole was way bigger than the one we dug."

"It could have been Jeremiah the Giant," Robin said. "But he was trying to get away from the sheriff. Who else could it be?"

"Well, Rocky and Porky are gone, and the deputies were busy chasing Jeremiah. Is there someone else that could be a suspect?" Billy said, a finger touching his chin. "Sincerely, there is only one real possibility."

Matt nodded his head in agreement and looked at Billy. "Had to be Jeremiah."

"Bingo," Brad said. "Maybe he's not crazy after all."

"Maybe not. I need to find out why that prisoner would be looking for the treasure," Matt said. He moved to get up and grabbed his leg. "I think we better head home now."

"Let's wrap more gauze around your leg first," Robin said. "That's fresh blood flowing out the edge of the gauze."

Chapter 21

THE HOSPITAL

A STIFF BREEZE PUSHED white-capped waves from the west. Offshore, elephants danced on the Gulf's horizon.

Bob and Robin started their engines. "Glad we're not going out there today," Bob said. "Hang on, Matt, going to be a little bumpy 'til we get on the other side of the sandbar, and real bumpy when we get to the open water."

The tide was out and waves broke in the shallow water and crashed on the shore, but in a minute, the boats were over the bar and into deep water and Bob and Robin got their boats up on a plane. Three-foot waves broke over the bows and sprayed water into the boats. The boys' T-shirts were soaked before they left the pass.

John stood on the bow of Robin's boat and the mist from the waves fell on his face like light rain. "Goodbye, Hog Island," he said with a big grin on his face. "I think I feel a blue flame coming on—or maybe I pooped my pants. Giants can do that to me."

Whitecaps covered St. Joseph's Sound, but the rough chop ended at the bridge. The two boats slowed to an idle. South of the bridge, the water calmed, and they turned into the dock easily.

Bob eased into his slip, Billy sitting by Matt, and John standing on the bow with a rope in his hand. "Back where we started," Robin shouted over to him as he pulled his boat up parallel to the dock.

"A little bumpier ride home. Our patient's not complaining though," Bob said.

Brad and JB jumped off Robin's boat and except for an occasional cough, his engine purred quietly as it idled beside the dock. "Need me to help, Matt? I can tie up," Robin said.

"No need," Matt said. "You're running out of water. Head on so you don't get stuck getting to your house. Go—I'm okay."

"Sure? My boat only needs six inches of water to idle and four inches if I'm racing."

"I'm sure," Matt said. "Hey, it was great—another great campout except for the escaped prisoner and the sharks." He forced a smile. "That's why we camp out, right? Adventure, excitement and dealing with whatever happens. Teamwork and camaraderie, right? Get home and clean your boat."

Robin reversed his engine and eased away from the dock. "Take care of him, John. Matt, call me tonight."

A pain shot up Matt's bandaged leg as he attempted to stand up. He fell back onto the seat. "Sorry," he said.

"John," Billy said. "Come over here and take a look."

John stared at the spongy red bandage. "Matt, don't move. You're really bleeding. We need to get you to the emergency room fast!"

"It feels okay," Matt said, "but maybe I do need a stitch or two."

Bob helped John pull Matt to his feet. Matt squeezed his eyes together.

"Hurt?" John said, covering a smile with his free hand.

"Heck, yes. Quit laughing."

Bob slipped his head under Matt's arm. "Get under his other arm, John. Let's get him off the boat. I see Mr. Ward's truck. He must be back working on that old boat. He'll give us a ride to the hospital."

"Should I call your mom?" Brad said. "There's a phone booth in the corner of the parking lot."

"Yes, but don't mention the bandage," Matt said. "Just tell her to come get us at Morton Plant."

"I'll call my mom to come here," JB said. "Billy, Brad and I can load all the stuff in her station wagon and meet you outside the hospital."

"Great idea," Bob said.

Matt sat on the hospital bed with John and Bob standing beside him, their bare feet spreading sand on the linoleum floor.

A doctor with a stethoscope draped around his neck picked up a chart at the emergency room nurses' station and walked into Matt's room with a male nurse right behind him. "Hello, Matt. I thought that was you. Nice Boy Scout bandage. What's going on underneath?"

Matt grinned. "Hi, Dr. Haygood."

"Let's have a look. Didn't expect to see you again so soon. Do this on your camping trip at Hog Island?"

"Yes sir. I got kissed by a small blacktip shark in the shallow water over there yesterday afternoon."

The doctor turned to the other two boys. "You pirates go to the waiting room. I don't want anyone to pass out on me."

"Out, out," the nurse said. "You heard the doctor. Scoot."

John walked out of the cubicle and turned. "Dr. Haygood?"

"Yes, son?"

"If you need help with the saw, Bob and I are good. And if he gets delirious and talks about capturing an escaped prisoner, it's all true. Honest to God."

Dr. Haygood slowly unwrapped Matt's leg and lightly probed the area with his fingers, pushing the cut skin together. "How big was this shark?"

"Between three and four feet."

"Well, he got you good." He poured iodine over the area. "It's sure clean."

Matt tensed and gritted his teeth. "Yes, sir, very clean. Need stitches?"

"I believe so. This one is near a large vessel. It's weeping but could have been gushing. You were close to having a real emergency." He reached on the table and picked up a syringe. "Let's put this area to sleep. It might hurt a little. Sorry."

Matt closed his eyes. "Okay, I just don't want to watch."

The doctor injected Matt's leg, waited for it to get numb, and with a gloved finger explored the renewed bleeding. "I need a sponge, Smitty."

"You found an oil well," the nurse said.

"Yep. Matthew, there's a large vessel here and that shark must have nicked it. You did all the right things. You should be fine tomorrow. You're lucky that shark didn't cut any large muscles."

Half an hour later, the boys came back in the room and admired the new bandage. "Nine stitches," Matt said. "Three inside the gash and six to close it up."

"Did it hurt?" John said.

"Not really—once it was numb. And guess what, Long John Silver? He liked my Ichthyol dressing, and guess what else? He told me the prisoner escaped from the sheriff down at the dock this morning. Said he's been taking care of the man that Jeremiah the Giant hurt. Said it's better a shark got me than if he did."

"Oh my," John said. "Did you tell him we looked for a treasure and think the prisoner did too?"

"No, I don't want to mention the treasure to anyone. I need to find out more about Jeremiah the Giant, though, and I know someone who maybe can tell me more about him."

"We're going to the movies this afternoon. Think you can go?" Bob said.

"Sure. Dr. Haygood said I just have to take it easy and not pull out his pretty artwork. I can talk mom into letting me go."

"Good. We saw her earlier. Where is she?" Bob said.

"She didn't want to be here after he told her what needed to be done. Went upstairs to visit a friend already in the hospital and said she'd be waiting outside in the car. Paperwork's already done. Let's get out of here."

The three boys linked arms and headed out of the emergency room, laughing and singing "Transfusion."

"All right!" Matt said. "I'm glad I didn't need any juice."

Mrs. Parker waited by the curb outside the Emergency Room entrance with Brad and Billy in the back seat. Her blue eyes twinkled as they walked up to the car. "Matthew, your chauffeur is here. Bob and John, Mrs. B is waiting for you two on the corner."

Chapter 22

THE RITZ THEATER

SHOPPERS PACKED THE SIDEWALKS in downtown Clearwater on the Saturday afternoon of Labor Day weekend. Cars going to the beach filled the westbound lane of Cleveland Street, and a freight train engine working cars onto the side tracks in town created a greater traffic jam, blocking cars and blowing its horn every time it crossed the street.

"My, my, it's crazy here in town," John said as the boys stopped on the crowded sidewalk outside Brown Brothers. "We should still be on Hog Island, digging for treasure and enjoying the beach."

"I agree. Sorry we had to come back early because of me," Matt said.

"It's okay," Bob said. "I'm glad we're back and get to go to the movies. Maybe we can go dig for the treasure next weekend."

"Can you believe it was only yesterday we walked out of there worried about seeing Wayne?" Matt said.

"Hope we don't see him today," Billy said. "I'd rather be on Hog Island too."

Matt pulled his sunglasses back over his eyes. "If he's downtown, he won't try anything. This is my take on Wayne: He needs an audience of his peers. Why try to beat up a twelve-year-old, or for that matter, take on four twelve-year-olds, with only strangers watching?"

"Because he can?" John said with a laugh.

"He wants his pals around. That's his reward, trust me." Matt reached over and rubbed Billy's short brown hair, messing up his part. "Smile, Billy. We'll keep an eye out for Wayne. Can't worry about him and ruin this pretty day."

"Let's get to the movies," John said. "And no more talk of Wayne. Damn, this guy is driving us all to the funny farm."

Billy stopped at the display window in front of McCrory's Five and Ten. A model train with cars pulled by a steam engine, with smoke puffing out the stack and a train whistle loud enough to be heard through the glass window, moved around a track surrounded by mountains, tunnels, rivers and bridges, towns with homes and buildings and a countryside with forests and farmlands.

"I've got a model train," Billy said.

John watched the train enter the tunnel and disappear. "Me too, but mine's a simple one—just an engine, three cars and a caboose. Engine doesn't smoke, it has no whistle and it only runs around and around on the circular track hitting branches on the Christmas tree and de-railing. Most of its life it's in the attic in storage, waiting for the next Christmas."

Bob smiled. "Mine's like John's, a Christmas train mostly. When we try to play with it at other times, it never works. Dad fixes it every Christmas."

"Mine's like the one in this window," Billy said. "But a little more involved."

"A little more involved?" Matt said. "In what way?" *Got to keep Billy off the subject of Wayne, and talking trains seems to work.*

"I have more than one train running at the same time on a lot more track. I'll show it to you all sometime. It's one of my favorite hobbies."

"Didn't you say you have a pet snake?" John said, shuddering like someone had touched him with a hot wire.

"Yes."

"I thought so. Just send me a picture of your trains."

Billy reached over and hit John on the back, playfully but hard. "They're all in cages."

"All?"

"I have four."

"I hate snakes," John said, shuddering again.

"But you can protect me from Wayne?"

"He's a different kind of snake," John said.

"Guys, let's get going," Bob said. "Okay, Billy?"

"Sure."

A few stores down at the main city bus stop, three buses sat in a line, engines running, doors open, waiting to be filled. On the benches on the sidewalk, every available space was tightly filled with someone, rear end touching rear end, shoulder touching shoulder.

People shouted, waved their hands and bumped into each other trying to get to their bus before it left. The sign in the front of the first bus said *Clearwater Beach*. The second bus sign said *Largo,* and the third read *Safety Harbor*.

"Get us through this bottleneck, Bob," John said. "We're right behind you."

About a half block ahead of them, obscured by a sea of heads and shoulders, Matt caught a glimpse of a black leather jacket draped on the shoulder of a dark-haired teenager wearing a long-sleeve white shirt with the sleeves rolled all the way up onto the upper arm. He sat on a sidewalk bench in conversation with another boy, tightly squeezed together by others sharing the wooden seat. All had leaned forward— not enough space to settle back on the backrest.

Matt realized it was Wayne. Who was he talking with? Moving heads blocked his view. The next time there was a break, he saw red hair. It had to be Wayne's cousin, Jimmy. They were talking, but he suspected their eyes were watching for him.

John, Bob and Billy were busy getting through the crowd and never once looked in Wayne's direction. As they neared Wayne and Jimmy, Matt got ready to sound the alarm.

Wayne scowled as he watched the three boys walk by him laughing. It looked like their laughter irritated him, but he didn't move. He turned his head and looked at Matt. When their eyes met, he looked away and said something to Jimmy. He stood up and walked the opposite direction, looking at Matt one last time. Jimmy remained seated.

Matt watched Wayne walk away. *He looks frustrated. Maybe his intimidation isn't producing the fear he wants. If he'd heard us talking, it would have given him some satisfaction, but he has no way of knowing.*

Matt caught up with the others as they stopped at the main intersection of town where a policeman stood to help people cross the street. A convertible with the top down drove up and stopped right beside them.

"Look at that 1955, red-and-white, two-door Bel Air Chevy convertible," John said, rattling off the description like an auctioneer. "An eight-cylinder engine, four-barrel carb, spoke wheels, leather seats and dual pipes with glass packs. The girl inside is optional. What a car."

"And what a radio," Matt said. "Listen to that song." He snapped his fingers and tapped his tennis shoes on the pavement in time with "Susie Q."

Joe Langford, the new owner of the "Pure" gas station and garage, was in the driver's seat of the car, wearing a white T-shirt, Levi's and sunglasses. When the old owner retired at the beginning of the summer, he sold the station to Joe, his mechanic. Nestled up close to Joe, sharing the driver's side of the car, was a pretty young blonde.

Bob looked down into the car and said in a quiet voice. "Look—a lot of space between the gal and her door. She obviously is not just a front seat passenger."

"Music and cars—what else is there?" John asked.

"I think the driver would say—women," Bob said.

"Well, not for us—yet," John said.

"Hey Joe, give us a little rubber on the green light," Bob said to the driver.

Joe smiled, took his arm from around the girl, grabbed the gearshift on the steering column and pulled the gearshift down into first gear. With the clutch in, he pushed the accelerator down just enough to hear the beginning sound of the mufflers.

"I love that sound," Matt said. "And look at that car. Looks like it just came off the showroom floor of Dimmitt Chevrolet, not a speck of dirt anywhere, not even on the white walls. What a machine."

Joe's left arm rested on the door, just the elbow in contact, and one finger of his left hand was all that touched the knob on the steering wheel.

"That guy is cool," Bob said. "Burn some rubber when you leave, Joe."

Joe didn't react, but his companion turned her head, looked up at Bob and smiled.

The traffic light turned green and Joe looked at the boys, gave them a hint of a smile, pointed his finger toward the cop and pulled away slower than an old lady.

"Boo," John yelled. "If you're going to drive like that, buy a Rambler."

Joe didn't look back. He just lifted up his arm behind the girl and waved.

The "All Walk" light came on and the boys crossed the street. They approached the policeman and Matt closed his eyes for a second. He knew John was about to say something.

John didn't let him down. "Sir, you ever shot that gun before?"

"Yesterday at the range."

"Did you hit the target?"

"Most of the time." The policeman put his hand on top of the holster. "Come out to the pistol range sometime, and I'll show you."

"That's a deal."

"Let's go, John," Matt said. "You're the one who wanted to get to the theater early."

John looked at his watch and picked up the pace. "You're right, Matt, and I want to get there for everything, even the 'World News Today.'"

"Hey, cool your jets, John. We've got time," Bob said.

"I know why John's in a hurry," Billy said.

"Why would that be?" John said without a smile. He stared at Billy and began to close one eye.

Billy swallowed hard. "You want to be sure you're in your chair and seated to sing along with the bouncing ball if that's the Cartoon of the Day, right?"

They all stopped. Since they'd left Woolworth's, Billy hadn't said a word. They looked at him like they couldn't believe what they'd heard, and everyone laughed.

John laughed so hard his face turned red. "Billy, you're okay."

"Billy, John also wants to be there early so we can sit in the balcony and he can watch the kissing going on in the back," Bob said.

"Shut up, Bob," John said, "or I'm going to give you a fat lip."

The group moved down Fort Harrison Avenue toward the Ritz Theater with sweat beading on their foreheads.

In the sky, the clouds, once separate, were beginning to connect. Instead of stationary white powder puffs, they moved with the breeze, grew as they came together and began to darken on the inside. In the shadows of the clouds was the first coolness of the day.

The theater was close and a large crowd of kids milled around the entrance. Somewhere within the crowd was a line that led to the ticket booth. The line ended on the curb at the edge of the theater building, snaking back and forth until it finally stopped in front of the glass window with a small opening on the bottom.

"We should have gotten here sooner," John said. "The line goes on forever."

"We're okay," Matt assured John. "I love sitting in the front row."

John missed Matt's jab. He looked at the booth and kicked the ground. "We should be in there, relaxed in our seats, eating popcorn and sipping on a Coke. Thanks a lot, Matt. It's all your fault." He kicked the ground again and popped Matt on the arm. "I told you we should have gotten here sooner."

"What's that for?" Matt said, smiling. "Hey, we're here and I'm sure you'll be happy in the front row with the third and fourth graders. You can scream together."

John popped Matt a second time. "You made us late. It's your fault."

Matt laughed and rubbed his arm. "Quit it. Mom wouldn't let me walk downtown with these stitches in my leg and I had to wait until she was ready to leave. You're the one that wanted to walk around first."

The only time the Ritz had a crowded sidewalk of patrons was for Saturday matinees when the kids filled the house to watch the movie, and one other time when 'Gone with the Wind' was showing. It was the oldest theater in town and "kid shows" were the main attraction that kept it open.

All new movies played first at the newer movie houses in town, the Capitol and the Carib, and the Ritz showed them the second time. John said that was why the films always broke at the Ritz. He was convinced it was because the film got weak from being run so many times through the projector.

"I don't care if the films break," John said. "I like it because it's cool knowing old Westerns like a Tom Mix film showed here first or even Flash Gordon."

Matt liked going to the Ritz too. He loved the building more than the movies. It reminded him of the pictures he'd seen of theaters on Broadway. Even in the daylight, thousands of lights on the marquee sparkled like stars, and the lights in the "Ritz" sign blinked in unison.

Bob put his hand in his pocket and pulled out a five-dollar bill. "Mom said the movie today is her treat."

The lady in the ticket booth leaned forward and said, "Next?"

Bob stood beside an adult couple. He extended his hand and said, "You first."

The gentleman stepped up to the window and pulled out his wallet.

In a voice like she had pinched her nose, the ticket lady said, "Are you sure you want to see this movie now? It's mostly kids." Before he could answer, she said again, "It's mostly kids. If you buy a ticket, you're crazy. I'm just warning you." He looked at his wife, and the ticket lady added, "You'll be making a good decision."

The man put his money back into his wallet, and the couple walked back into the crowd. "Excuse me. Excuse me," he said as they moved away from the boys.

From under the small opening in the glass window of the booth, the small, white-haired lady with a high-pitched voice said, "Next?" Her head was even with the counter where money was pushed in and change and tickets were pushed out.

Matt leaned into Billy, cupped his hand around his mouth and whispered in Billy's ear. "The lady in the ticket booth is Miss Ellen Tompkins. She was selling tickets before "Gone with the Wind" was shown. A lot of kids make fun of her. Look at her glasses and you'll start to figure out why. Bob and John will probably show you how it's done."

"Why does she let it happen?" Billy asked.

Matt frowned. "I don't think she has a clue."

Billy leaned around John and tried to see her face. She seemed at least seventy or maybe even eighty. Her wrists were tiny like her body, but the thinness was striking. Blue, rope-like veins protruded from her white glistening skin and the rich blue lines connected to one another like synapses in nerve cells he'd seen in textbooks. One shake of her arm would probably fling her watch with the loose gold band across the room with ease.

Billy's eyes moved to her face. For an instant, Billy felt a laugh inside him when he looked at her face, and he immediately felt badly he reacted that way. He knew what Matt meant. John and Bob would have a hard time ignoring a face like that, and his impulse to laugh was the testament.

John stood right beside Bob. "Four, please," Bob said.

"Four?" Miss Tompkins said in a squeaky voice.

"Yes, ma'am, four."

Matt watched John. John looked intently at Miss Tompkins and Matt realized John's stomach was starting to shake. John put his hand up to his face and with his thumb and forefinger pinched his nose. His stomach shook violently. Matt heard a little fart, but held back his laugh. John squeezed harder on his nose and farted again. "Hope those aren't stinkers," Matt whispered.

"That will be one dollar, please, for four tickets," Miss Tompkins said, oblivious to what was going on outside her little window.

Matt could clearly see that Miss Tompkins was looking at John— but she was looking at Bob at the same time. Her thick glasses magnified her eyes. The right eye looked over at John while the other eye looked straight ahead toward Bob.

Bob slid the five-dollar bill under the window.

Matt jabbed his finger into John's backside. "Don't say a word, and stop laughing."

Matt and Billy pressed closer and all four heads were up against the window watching Miss Tompkins. Behind her glasses, a gray eyebrow hair swooped down beyond the level of the eyelash over her right eye and looked like a curled-up squid tentacle ready to grab anything that came near the eye. Billy didn't know which eye to focus on. John's belly was moving and his face was redder than a ripe tomato.

Matt moved away before he started laughing and Billy covered his mouth.

Miss Tompkins pushed the tickets and four one-dollar bills under the window. "Thank you, boys," she said. "Next?"

Bob felt the movement of John's shaking body. He grabbed the four tickets and the dollar bills and moved away from the window before he laughed. He covered the laugh with a cough.

They moved out of the line and headed for the velvet rope leading to the usher who was taking tickets. "You're bad, John," Bob said. "That's someone's grandmother."

"Matt's supposed to say that, not you, Bob," John said and held his nose tighter.

"Thank you, John," Matt said.

"Thank you for what?" John said, still holding his nose. "Did you see that hair? I could not keep my eyes off of it. It was worse than trying not to look at a wart on somebody's face."

"She's a nice lady," Matt said, "and I'm glad you didn't make her feel bad by laughing."

"I saw your belly moving," John said. "You didn't know which eye to look at, did you?"

"I know," Matt said. "When I saw why your belly was shaking, you made me start to laugh." Matt sighed. "We've been looking at that lady a long time and we still laugh when we get that close to her. May the Lord forgive us."

At the velvet rope inside the lobby, Matt walked through the turnstile and handed the usher his ticket. "Hi, Zeke."

Zeke tore the ticket and returned half of it. "Hey, Matt. See you're with the two troublemakers today. Who's the new kid with you?"

"This is Billy, Justin MacDonald's brother. Billy, this is Zeke. He's a diver on the swim team."

"Hi, Billy. I know Justin well. Matt's okay, but be careful if you're sitting next to these other two. You might get kicked out of the movies."

"You're screwing with us, Zeke," John said. "You know I'm a model moviegoer."

In the lobby behind Zeke, Mr. Black, the theater manager, stood watching everything going on at the turnstile. Matt and the other boys were well acquainted with the tall, slim man. He kept a tight rein on the theater's operation, and on Saturdays he made sure the kids walked on the path of sainthood.

Mr. Black pushed off the wall and headed toward them. The white socks that he wore with his black shoes and black slacks stood out like white legs on a crow. A deep wrinkle formed above his brow as his eyes fell on John. "This isn't a tea party. Move along. And you, young John, don't make me call your parents today."

"No sir."

"You know—I had good reason to run you out a week ago. You and that other boy—what did you call him, 'Crow?' I know you two released the pigeon in here."

"Crow worked at his dad's garage last week and he's working there today too," John answered.

Being only half correct seemed okay to John when it came to telling a white lie to Mr. Black.

When the boys moved on, John looked at them and smirked. "Why, he must be mistaking me and Crow for someone else."

Matt shook his head in disbelief. "All these kids here, John, and he knows you by name. What does that tell you?"

"It tells me my popularity is widely known," John answered with a straight face.

In the corner of the concession stand, with a muffled pop-pop-pop like a shotgun, popcorn exploded and fell from the suspended metal pan onto the floor of the glass-walled popcorn maker, piling up in mounds.

The attendant handed them four bags of popcorn, four paper cups of Coke, a Powerhouse bar, black licorice, Milk Duds and a Clark Bar.

John stopped at the door into the movie. "I hear the newsreel. The cartoon and serial haven't started."

Bob pushed open the door. The expansive room was as dark as a moonless night. The aisles sloped down to the stage with a screen that reached almost to the ceiling and sat ten feet back from its edge. A black-and-white newsreel narrated by Lowell Thomas lit up the room with periodic strobe light bursts of scenes of tanks and planes, revealing rows of seats and heads sticking up in them and chandeliers hanging from the ceiling.

The usher on duty inside the door pointed his flashlight down and to the left. "Still four seats together on that row. See them at the end?"

"We'll take them," John said, giving Bob a push.

"John, are you sure you don't want to sit in the balcony? Now or never. Smooch, smooch."

"That's not funny anymore, Bob. You sound like a broken record."

After the cartoon played, numbers appeared on the movie screen. The whole audience began counting down with the numbers to zero, complete with catcalls and whistles. "Rocket Man" flashed across the screen and the clapping began. He flew out of his secret mountain, turned the propulsion dials on his chest and the wisecracks began.

Bob loved the Ritz ritual of shouting one-liners. He stood up, cupped his hands around his mouth megaphone-style, and as Rocket Man flew through the sky, yelled up toward the screen, "Your head is a welding helmet, and your boots came off a Greek sponge diver."

The theater erupted in laughter. From high in the balcony someone else yelled, "That's not Rocket Man, that's Mr. Black."

The film stuttered, the picture shook and the screen suddenly turned white.

"Aww," Bob yelled, "the film broke."

"No shit, Sherlock," John answered.

The chandeliers flooded the dark room with bright light. All the room needed was cobwebs to turn it into a haunted castle. Mr. Black jumped up on the stage and clapped his hands. "Okay, everybody, sit down and quiet down. They're working on the problem and will have it fixed presently."

Two rows in front of the boys, Dee and Elaine turned around in their seats and waved. "Hi, Matt. Hi, Billy," Dee said. "Glad to see you made it. Hi, Bob. I heard you. You're a riot."

"I heard *you* too, John," Elaine said. "I don't think Mr. Black tolerates that kind of language."

Bob climbed over the empty seat in front of him and sat down right behind Elaine. He whispered in her ear and she looked back and smiled at John. "John, I was surprised to hear you. We thought you'd be up in the balcony."

John shook his head and turned red. "I heard last week you and Bob were up there playing a private game of post office with slobbery kisses."

"John ... you're bad! I knew I should have left that alone," Elaine said.

The girls laughed and put their hands over their faces.

"Don't get caught climbing over seats, Bob," Matt said.

"I didn't get caught."

"You still have to get back."

"Come on down, Matt. There's another seat here. Mr. Black isn't around. Come on. Don't be a chicken."

"Don't say that, Bob." There was a chance he might get caught and pay an embarrassing consequence, but Bonnie was sitting next to Elaine. It was worth taking the chance. He carefully climbed over the seat in front of him and sat down beside Bob, a mixture of emotions flooding through him. "Hi, Dee. Hi, Bonnie. Hi, Elaine. Long time no see."

Dee flashed him a big smile. "Not since yesterday at Brown Brothers. I can't wait 'til next week when we get to see each other every day. Where's Brad? I thought he was coming with you today."

The lights flickered.

"Not sure where he is," Matt said. He looked over at Bonnie. "I'll talk to you after the movie."

Back in his seat, Matt gave no thought to where Mr. Black might be. He remained in a daze. He hoped she hadn't forgotten about the invitation to go fishing with him on Monday.

He glanced at Billy and saw him looking up in the balcony at a red-haired boy with a freckled face standing at the railing. Jimmy pointed to the exit and mouthed to Billy, "I'll be waiting for you outside."

Matt looked up at Jimmy and yelled, "I'll be waiting outside too, buddy."

Jimmy smiled at Matt and turned away. The smile looked strained and fake.

"Don't pay any attention to that guy, Billy," Matt said. "That's Jimmy Knox. I'll take care of him."

"I think I saw him with Wayne the other night," Billy said.

"I think he's Wayne's cousin. Look, everything will be okay, trust me. Wayne's been messing with you, but now he's messing with all of us. You heard the guys at the campout last night. You'll be okay. I know Jimmy well. Believe me, that kid is just poop trying to stick to the sole of your shoe."

The lights in the chandeliers flickered one more time, the picture flashed on the screen and the theater went dark again. The audience roared with cheers and everyone sat down.

Rocket Man reappeared on the screen, and at the end, he was in danger again and his fate would not be known until the next installment of the story on the following Saturday.

To Matt, John looked a little tense. "He'll be okay, John," Matt said. "He'll pull out a sponge filled with something stinky from inside his boots, spread it over his tin suit and walk through the bad guys. As they hold their noses, he flies away to his cave."

"Don't make fun of him, Matt. He's cool," John said. "Right, Bob?"

"It's a little corny. Right, Matt?" Bob said.

"A little, but remember, it's for kids and that's us today."

"Well, I don't care what you two turds think," John said. "It's better than 'Godzilla.' Hey, is this movie in color?"

"Black and white," Bob said.

"I think it's in color," John said.

"Then why did you ask?"

"Keeping you alert. Okay, I saw the previews last week. It's black and white. It looks scary."

"Scary? You thought Flash Gordon was scary. Don't make me laugh. You'll be sitting on someone's lap before it's over. Probably mine," Bob said. "Hehehe …"

"No. This one is really scary. It's about a creature that lives in the water, but comes on land sometimes."

"Hey, don't tell the story," Matt said.

"I'm just telling you what was in the previews. Besides we've already seen it."

Seventy-nine minutes later, "The End" filled the screen and the credits began rolling.

"I think that movie was even scarier because it was in black and white," Bob said. "It always seemed dark. Made me shiver. When I start making movies, they'll all be in black and white: rain in the night—in black and white—is scary 'n' hairy."

Matt nodded and said to Billy, "And here you have … the next Cecil B. DeMille."

Chapter 23

JIMMY KNOX

THE THEATER DOORS OPENED to rain falling. Hard drops splattered up from the pavement, water moved along the curb and flowed into the storm sewer and cars drove through the rain and swished through the puddles and water along the curbs, sounding like jet engines.

By the time the boys walked through the tiled alcove and reached the street, the glare of bright sunlight had returned.

"Wow," John said, shielding his eyes with his hand. "Bright. The clouds are gone."

Matt looked down at the puddles scattered on the sidewalk and the water along the curb. "Yeah, and so is the rain. That was a hard shower. I heard a few claps of thunder during the movie."

"All I heard were screams," John said, "mainly mine."

"Where's Billy?" Matt asked. "I see Jimmy Knox over there and he said he'd be looking for Billy after the movies."

"He's still talking to Dee and the other girls. He should be out in a minute."

"Jimmy's waiting for Billy?" Bob asked. "Is he by himself?"

"Yes, to both questions," Matt answered.

"Better than Wayne," Bob said.

"Listen guys, here we go again," John said. "Wayne here, Wayne there, Wayne watching, Wayne hiding. Is this our future? On guard all the time? I don't like it … I'm done with it."

"I agree, but Billy needs my help right now and I'm committed," Matt said. "We can't let our guard down. Sorry, John, but that's the way it is."

John hit Matt on the back. "I'm also committed, Matt, but is somebody going to get a broken nose, or worse?"

"Possibly," Matt said, "but maybe we can handle it in a different way."

"So where does the curly red-haired tough guy fit into all this? Brown-nosing Wayne?" John asked. "This is all bad news. Next week, *we* might be on World News."

"Jimmy's just an opportunist," Matt said. "My dad says there are leaders and followers. Jimmy fits into the latter category. He doesn't make new trails. He follows opportunities not secured by himself."

John laughed. "What are you saying? You lost me. Sometimes you say things that you only should be thinking, but you say them anyway and you make my head spin."

"Sorry," Matt said, "my brain is spinning today."

"There's Billy," Bob said.

"I see him and there goes Jimmy. You guys wait here. Billy and I will be right back."

A red flag waved in Matt's subconscious. Since their fourth grade "disagreement" as he called it now, he had always had his way with Jimmy. The truth—hidden somewhere within him—sometimes tugged on his inner psyche and roared to the surface, saying, "Don't make waves. Leave altercations alone." He hadn't seen Jimmy all summer and Jimmy was now as tall as John. *Get this over with.*

Matt walked through the crowd at the Ritz. "Here comes a roadblock, Jimmy," he muttered to himself.

He and Jimmy reached Billy at the same time. Matt stepped in between them with his arms folded and his feet separated and firmly planted. "Hi, Jimmy. What's going on? You're not part of your cousin Wayne's little plan, are you? You need to stay away from Billy."

Jimmy gave Matt a big smile, but when Matt was around him, his insecurity always seemed to show. "Don't talk tough to me, Matt," Jimmy said, his freckled face turning red. "I wasn't starting anything. I just wanted to tell Billy I hope he enjoys his first week of junior high school."

Matt pushed the thoughts away and continued, "I'm supposed to believe that? You thought you could intimidate Billy. Well, that's not happening. And on that subject, tell Wayne *he* can find someone else to intimidate too. Now, can we move on?"

Jimmy stepped aside and extended his hand. "Sure, no problem. See you in school, Matt."

Matt shook his hand with a firm grip, but he felt uncomfortable. The situation with Jimmy at South Ward had ended in a superficial friendship. He'd had Jimmy's number since then, but today was different: the number seemed to hang around zero.

Matt detected a touch of nervousness in Jimmy's voice, and he sensed Jimmy was trying to regain his confidence. *Can't let that happen.* He put his arm around Billy's shoulder and smiled. "Well, Jimmy, we all need to get moving."

Jimmy nodded, turned and left without saying a word.

Billy looked at Matt. "I'm only twelve, but I'm smart enough to see when someone has an upper hand. Is there a story?"

"Yes, there's a story, but not today. Bob and John are outside waiting for us and the sidewalk is jammed with people waiting for a ride."

"What took so long?" John asked Matt. "We need to get to Frank's so Bob can get a shirt."

"I had to send Jimmy on his way."

"Where'd he go?" Bob asked.

"Walked toward Cleveland Street by himself, and that's strange 'cause he's not a loner."

"You know him better than I do," John said. "Think maybe he's up to something?"

"Maybe," Matt said. "Let's not make a big deal, but let's keep our eyes open."

"You're not worried about him, are you?" Bob said.

"No. He wouldn't try anything with me, but that wouldn't stop him from getting information for Wayne."

A car drove past and honked. The brake lights came on and the car pulled over to the side of the street. Dee, Bonnie and Elaine ran to the car and stuck their heads through the open car windows, then quickly stepped away as the car sped off.

"Was that your mom, Elaine?" Bob said. "Checking on you, huh?"

"Yes, Bob, but she wasn't checking on me. She's headed for the icehouse and then to the beach for a picnic. She wanted to know if I wanted to go. Is that okay?"

"Sure, Miss Priss," Bob said. "Just teasing you a little."

"Are you going?" asked John.

"Yes. She's picking me up on her way back."

"That's good," John said. A solid smile formed across his face. "You can, maybe, go out on the pier later with the adults in their lawn chairs and watch the sunset. Did I see a lawn chair in your mom's back seat?"

"Don't you get funny with me too, John. I still haven't totally forgiven you for that 'fatty on the beach' remark you made about Ann. But for your information, we're not going out on the pier. We're going to the south end where we can have a fire."

"Hot dogs?"

"And marshmallows."

Ten minutes later, two cars pulled up into the line of cars at the curb. "Elaine, there's your mom. Have fun at your beach picnic," Dee said. "Let's go, Bonnie, my mom is right behind her. Bye, boys. See you all at school on Tuesday."

Matt looked at Bonnie. "You should come fishing on Monday."

Bonnie didn't say anything but she smiled and gave him a slight nod as she walked away with Dee. The car drove past them with the windows down and the radio playing Ernie Ford's song "Sixteen Tons."

Matt snapped his fingers in time with the music, singing the words to himself.

Chapter 24

FRANK'S
DEPARTMENT STORE

BOB LOOKED AT HIS WATCH. "C'mon, guys. Gotta get to Frank's ... need a shirt for school."

"Here comes our answer," John said. "Hear that muffler? It's our old babysitter, Fraley. I'd know that sound anywhere. He'll take us to Frank's and give us a ride home, I bet."

John stuck out his hitchhiking thumb as a black '51 Ford coupe approached. "Going our way, Fraley?"

The highly polished black car whipped over and stopped as the DJ on the radio announced, "Okay boys and girls, it's time to Shake, Rattle and Roll with Joe Turner here on WTMP, former WIOK."

Lawrence Fraley leaned across the seat, pulled down the handle of the door on the passenger side and pushed hard. The door flew open, almost hitting the curb.

"Hi, Fraley. What's happening?" John said.

"Need a ride, you wannabe teenagers? You look like you're lost. Where to? Home?"

"Yes, thanks, Fraley. Shotgun," John yelled and shoved the passenger seat forward so the others could get in the back. "Why, Lawrence, I think I smell an attractor potion."

Bob climbed into the back seat and sniffed the air. "Canoe? Chanel

Number Five? I know where this car has been or is going. We hang out with the girls now too, you know."

Matt and Billy climbed in the back seat after Bob. "Hi, Billy. What's with the big Band-Aid, Matt?" Lawrence asked. "Problem on the camping trip?"

"Doc Haygood had to sew up a nasty little shark bite on his leg this morning," Bob said.

"I'm okay."

"True, but the escaped prisoner was really bad," Bob said.

"What? At Hog Island?" Lawrence said. "Get in the car, John. I need to hear the rest of this story later."

"Okay, two requests," Bob said. "Can you stop at Frank's so I can get a new shirt for the first day of school. Give me ten minutes?"

The hint of a smile appeared on Lawrence's face. "When have you ever been in Frank's for only ten minutes?"

"Today."

"Okay, now what's your second request, Bob?"

"Real rubber when you start, and more rubber when you pop second."

"Not here in downtown ... maybe later."

"Come on, Lawrence! Don't be a pooper. Floor it!" Bob said.

"Yeah, Lawrence, the ladies' man," John said. "You know you're driving the machine. This is one of the hottest cars in town and you always have the prettiest girls beside you. You drag it on Keene Road, don't you?"

"That's on a straight, quiet road, late at night," Lawrence answered. He pulled away from the curb, goosed the engine just enough to hear the glass pack sound then let it back down.

Matt listened to the rumbling backfire—pop ... pop ... pop—that beautiful sound he loved.

Lawrence threw the gear shift up into second, popped the clutch and gave it more power. The back tires squealed and the car lurched forward. He looked in the rearview mirror at Bob and smiled.

John stuck his head out the front window. "Oh my God. Please let me have a car like this someday."

As they pulled up in front of Frank's Department Store, Lawrence let the engine back down, glass packs popping. "I have an errand to run," he said. "Be back in ten minutes. Better be waiting outside for me or you're walking."

Bob pushed the back of the front seat. "Okay, the clock's moving, John. Hurry up." John opened the front door of the car and he and Bob bumped and shoved each other, then took off in a race to the front door of the store.

"Come on, Billy," Matt said. "Let's go in and see if the hooligans get themselves into trouble. You think they're ready for junior high?"

Billy shook his head. "I'm starting to have my doubts."

When they entered the store, a short man with glasses pushed down on his nose and wearing a white long-sleeve shirt and a brightly colored, red-and-blue-striped tie smiled at them. "Hello, Matt. Hello, Billy."

"Hi, Mr. Frank," they answered in unison.

"Matt, your mom has some clothes for you on layaway. You can add to them, if you want."

"Thank you, sir."

"And Billy, let me know if you see anything you want and I'll tell your mom when she comes in. She's a nice lady. She knows one of my cousins in Indiana."

Mr. Frank went to help another customer and Billy said in a whisper, "I think he knows everyone, like Mr. Black."

Matt said, "I think you're right. Your mom shops for you here?"

"Yes, but usually without me," Billy said.

"I don't know if you know this, but if your family was broke, he would still see that you got clothes," Matt said. "Between layaways and IOUs, no one leaves the store without a bag in their hands. My parents say he's one of a kind."

Ten minutes later, Lawrence opened the door of the store. "Hey, Mr. Frank. Kick 'em out, will you please? Get your shirt in a bag, Bob. It's time to go."

At the car, Matt stopped. "Oh man. I just remembered. I've got to pick up a package at Smith's Jewelers for my mom and she's going to pick me up there."

"Want me to drop you off there before I take these fellas home?"

"No, that's the opposite direction of the way you're going. I'll just walk. Thanks, Lawrence."

"I'm walking with you, Matt," John said. "I'll get a ride home with my mom when her shop closes."

"So, who's still riding with me?" Lawrence said.

"I am," said Bob.

"Me too. Thanks," Billy said.

"You're welcome, and on the ride, you two can tell me all about that escaped prisoner on Hog Island."

"Okay ... shotgun," Bob said and he frogged Billy on the arm.

The two boys hopped in the car and Lawrence goosed the engine as he pulled away from the curb.

"Keep an eye out for the boogie man," Bob yelled out the open car window.

"No worries," Matt answered.

PART 2

Chapter 25

THE ALLEY

THE LATE SATURDAY AFTERNOON lull had replaced the earlier bustling of the shopping district downtown. Stores were open, but the sidewalks and streets were mostly empty. Out over the Gulf, the sun shot its rays straight down Cleveland Street and the buildings on both sides made long shadows on the street.

"Just you and me, buddy. This town looks like a scene in *High Noon*. If you see a tumbleweed, then we're in trouble," Matt said with a serious look on his face.

"Maybe … It's definitely hot enough, but it's not that desolate yet," John said. "Quit trying to make me nervous. I'm already getting an eerie feeling in my belly. Should we be looking out for the boogie man?"

"You're not believing Bob, are you, John? Are you really afraid of seeing a boogie man?"

"Only if he's wearing a black leather jacket and answers to the name Wayne."

They passed the first alley way and John stopped to look down it. "Listen, Matt, I've really got a bad feeling going on right now. I'm serious. Yesterday morning at Brown Brothers, he affected us all—you included, right?"

"I think I scared you when I said 'High Noon.'"

"Maybe. The feeling's sure there."

They stopped for the red light at the next street corner—no cars, no buses, no pedestrians. John turned his head and looked down Garden Avenue. "Matt, look down the street about two blocks. I think I see three guys coming this way."

Matt looked to his left and saw them, but didn't say anything.

The light turned green and they walked across the street and continued on Cleveland.

"Did you see someone too?" John said.

"I'm not sure."

"I did see someone, didn't I?"

"Settle down, John. They're not paying any attention to us."

"How many did you see?"

"Three I think."

"You think?"

"Okay, John, I saw three. What are we getting into here? We're trying to help Billy. I'm ready for whatever comes our way, but I don't want to get ambushed. Let's cut over at Fort Harrison and get off Cleveland. We can walk up the back alley to your mom's shop, and they won't have any idea where we went."

"Maybe we should've gotten a ride home with Fraley instead of walking up here from Frank's. If those guys are following us, it's who we think, right?" John scratched his head. "What's the big deal with him and us? I woke up yesterday, brushed my teeth and Wayne Tyson lived on Mars. Okay, I said it."

Matt didn't smile. He thought for a minute. "You know, it's like someone pulled the plug in a bathtub full of water. First, you see a small swirl over the drain, but the water level along the side of the tub still looks the same. Then the swirl gets larger and you look at the sides and the water level has lowered. Justin pulled the plug two days ago, and all of a sudden, the water level is lower and something has happened for real. Wayne Tyson is the plug and he has started disturbing a lot of water. Am I making sense?"

"Are we the ones elected to stick the plug back into the tub?"

Matt smiled. "Sometimes you have to join the side you're on. Maybe today is the time for us, but I say we stay cautious and that means stay smart. We know we're no match for three of them physically, but they're not scaring me."

"If you saw three of them, I wonder who is with him? Two little midgets?"

"Hardly."

At the next intersection, the policeman was gone and they were alone. They crossed the street and turned left on Fort Harrison Avenue without waiting for the "All Walk" signal to blink on.

John looked behind them. "Don't see anyone yet."

"I'm waiting for a tumbleweed to roll down the street," Matt said.

"That's pretty eerie looking down there," John said as they stopped at the alley right before the bank. "Do you think they're on Cleveland yet?"

"Probably. Let's go down the alley and get off this street. They must still be behind us."

The sun blazed in the west but the alley felt damp. Saturday's trash of cardboard boxes and a few parked cars cluttered the space near the walls, and the bricks of the alley floor were wet, dirty.

John looked at the boxes stacked high beside the doors. "Should we run? This is a perfect place for an ambush. I'm not liking this."

Matt looked at him and walked into the alley. "We're fine."

A few yards in from the street, the alley became almost silent. A pipe hissed steam, and a compressor engine sounded its "pop-pop" one-cylinder noise beside a freezer that sat outside the back of a restaurant kitchen. A grease trap covered by a steel grate filled the air with a foul odor.

John pinched his nose. "Something's rotten in Denmark, Matt ..."

Matt stopped suddenly. "John?"

"What?"

"*You're* getting a bad smell—*I'm* getting a bad vibe. I think we ..."

Whoosh!

The sound behind them was almost inaudible. They turned in time to see a large, silver garbage can sail toward them. The lid separated in flight and the can crashed against the brick wall close behind them, sounding like a car in a head-on collision.

They jumped clear off the ground.

The noise reverberated through the alley. John yelled, "Oh God," and a chain reaction of noises began: sparrows dropped from under the eaves and pigeons bolted from the roof, leaving their nests and roosting spots.

On the other side of them, a second can landed on the bricks like a shotgun going off.

The lid flew off and hit on its edge with a tinny sound that got louder as the lid spun around on the bricks. The can lay on its side in the middle of the alley and the lid wobbled and hugged closer and closer to the alley floor with each complete rotation. The lid came to a halt and the scream of a black cat caught under the second can shattered the silence.

Matt looked around. "What next? Get ready!"

"You did it now, Ollie," John said in an attempt of a Stan Laurel imitation.

Matt looked at John with a faint smile and shook his head. John's confidence amazed him.

Behind them, something moved. They turned around. Two strangers emerged from a stack of cardboard boxes and stopped in the middle of the alleyway, one on each side of the tipped-over trash can.

"Holy smokes," John said. "The spinach guys."

"Not funny, John," Matt said.

"I know. They're real hoods. I'm starting to feel like the shrinking man."

"Stop it, John."

The strangers, legs apart and arms folded, blocked the exit. Their muscles bulged under their white T-shirts, and their Levi's sat low on their hips. Rolled-up cuffs revealed black boots. Both had greased down their hair and combed it back into ducktails. The sandy-haired stranger had blue eyes and smooth skin except for a v-shaped scar under his eye. The second stranger had brown eyes, dark hair and a stubble of whiskers on his face. They didn't speak.

A voice came from the other end. "So, how're the little wannabes when they don't have Mr. Brown around?"

Wayne stood in the middle of the alley, closing off the other route of escape. His boots rested on papers and mashed-down boxes that had fallen from the trash can. He had his jacket on, and like the two others, his arms were folded.

Matt and John backed into each other, Matt facing Wayne and John facing the two strangers. John closed his eyes for a moment. "That dark-haired guy looks cold and old. I wish we were still on Hog Island," he whispered.

"Me too."

Matt folded his arms like Wayne. "We're sure seeing a lot of you, Wayne. What's it about twelve-year-olds that intrigues you so much? And your support group here. Is that to give you courage?"

Wayne said nothing. The strangers remained silent. They looked up at the sky and then around the alley at the walls of the buildings.

"I have a question for you, Wayne, and hearing no response so far, I don't have a lot of confidence you've got an answer. Are you intimidated by me or by John? Or, are you afraid Justin is hiding in the shadows, ready to clean your clock a second time?"

Wayne didn't answer. He moved toward Matt and John. The two strangers moved forward and Matt saw that the hoods were much older and larger than he first thought. Their muscles rippled and veins as big as ropes bulged out on their biceps.

Matt stayed calm. He kept his eyes on Wayne, but from time to time turned his head enough to view the two intimidating enforcers. He knew John had also sized them up and hoped he'd concluded that under the circumstances, bowing to the two was a safe and prudent move.

The dark-haired stranger unfolded his arms and stuck his hands into his Levi's. "Wayne, this is embarrassing. The little one probably still remembers the taste of mother's milk. The fatty here has cheeks softer than a baby's ass."

Matt felt John's back tense up, but he didn't respond. His silence bothered Matt. A verbal comeback might blow off some of his built-up steam, but the silence told Matt a fist lay in wait.

Matt addressed the strangers. He wanted to embarrass them. "Are you here to take on twelve-year-olds and feel your oats? You guys look like you're headed to join the Navy. I hear Wayne's sixteen. You gotta be eighteen."

The sandy-haired one looked down. Matt saw it was working.

"They're here to watch me," Wayne said.

"Now that I see these babies, I don't want to watch anything," the sandy-haired stranger said. "The little one looks to me like Custer with a troop of one, and we're the Indians. And look at that bandage on his leg. You gotta be kidding me, Tyson."

Matt wanted to raise some hairs on the back of their necks. "You look like two guys hard-pressed to find a third," he said. "Where did you run into Wayne?"

"Shut up, you little turd," the dark-haired stranger said. "You're not in the best place here to mouth off with that kind of smart aleck talk. I could put you to sleep with a hard slap."

Wayne stepped toward Matt. "They're here to watch me take care of you," he said. "Quit your tough talk."

"You're a joke, Wayne. You're afraid to meet anyone by yourself. Your fight with Justin proved that."

Wayne's eyes almost closed.

Matt knew the comment about Justin affected him. He trusted his instincts. He pushed him. "So what are you going to do, Wayne? Talk, talk, talk?"

"I'm through talking."

"Then let's go," Matt said.

John moved forward. A hard hand grabbed his arm and yanked him back.

"You get to watch this with us. Don't make me have to hurt you."

John tried to pull away. The grip tightened. A hand grabbed his other arm. The second stranger held him too. Their grips tightened and all he could have done was kick. He didn't.

Matt saw John's predicament. "I'm okay, John. Rest easy."

John's face turned red.

Matt saw his face. "Another day, buddy. I'll be fine."

John relaxed. The two strangers lightened their grip but did not release him. "If you feel like getting a little scrappy, don't. You just keep listening to your wimp partner and watch him. Don't make me drop you to the ground," the dark-haired one said. "Save your fighting for the fairies. You might beat them—if they're sick."

John stood there, took the ridicule and relaxed like he'd been injected with a strong sedative. He let his arms go limp.

Matt moved in a circle and kept Wayne in front of him. Wayne moved in close to him. Matt watched what happened like everything was in slow motion. Something deep inside told him to hold back. He could see what just his verbal taunting accomplished.

Wayne's eyes narrowed and he gritted his teeth. His cheek muscles bulged.

In a strange way, Matt liked it, but he wasn't going to get careless. He needed to learn about Wayne so if Billy really needed him in the future, he could help him. He just wanted to survive the encounter without getting hurt. Fighting an opponent consumed with rage would be easy. If he ended up on the bricks, it was going to be because he planned to be there.

Matt backed up. Wayne moved forward.

Matt moved in a broad circle to his right. Wayne pursued.

Wayne lunged. Matt sidestepped. His leg almost gave way.

The dance continued.

Matt let Wayne get close—close enough to swing.

Wayne jabbed and Matt pulled in his stomach. A miss. His leg began to ache.

Wayne swung a haymaker, and Matt let the fist graze his forearm and slide off.

Matt countered with his own short jab and caught Wayne deep on the side by his kidney.

Wayne grimaced. Matt knew it stung. He eased away.

Matt backed into the dark-haired stranger standing next to John. The stranger pushed Matt back hard toward Wayne.

Matt faked a stumble and fell toward Wayne.

Wayne's hands struck Matt's chest and he pushed him to the side. Matt let his body go limp and fell onto a large cardboard box. He collapsed into it, rolled off and lay on the ground, facing up. He looked at Wayne and waited for him to jump on him.

The dark-haired stranger let go of John's arm and swung Wayne around. "That's enough. You got him. Let's go."

"I'm just getting started," Wayne said.

"I said, 'It's over.'"

Wayne stood over Matt and opened his fists.

Matt remained motionless on the ground, his eyes fixed on Wayne's face.

"You're easy, just like the rest," Wayne said. "Remember this at school. How can you help Billy? Shit, you can't even help yourself." He turned around and joined the other two hoods. "John, you teamed up with a fake. He's only tough in big groups."

The sandy-haired stranger turned. "Let's get out of here. I feel like we're in a baby crib. Let's go down to the bowling alley. Enough of this."

"Remember this on Tuesday," Wayne said.

John and Matt watched them walk down the alley.

Wayne kicked the tipped-over trash can as he walked past, and turned back. "Kicking this can was harder than kicking your ass."

The three hoods turned onto Fort Harrison Avenue and disappeared.

"Who were those guys?" John said. "Bet they carried knives— probably switchblades. Did you see the scar on that tall guy's face?"

Matt remained on the ground and didn't answer.

"They showed us who we are," John said. "Are we really little chickens?"

Matt pulled his knees up, touching his belly. Like a coiled snake, he shot his legs up toward the sky, and in an instant, he stood beside John. "We still have our feathers and our scalps. And my leg is feeling okay, thanks to Doc Haygood."

John picked up a loose rock and let it fly. It hit the trashcan. "Matt, you're too damn nice to take on a bully like Wayne. This was really scary. I have a question. You think you can help Billy? You haven't touched anyone since the fourth grade—and I'm thinking that knock-out was a fluke ... just some good luck."

"I'll have you re-think that thought—when I kick you on your butt. Ready for me to drop you right now?"

"You're itching for a lesson," John said.

"I'm scratching and I don't want to talk about this anymore. I've got to get to Smith's Jewelers," Matt said. "We live to fight another day."

John stopped at the door of his mom's dress shop. "This is serious. You know buddy, Wayne's not going away."

"I know. I'll see you tomorrow."

Matt whistled as he walked toward the jewelry store. John didn't understand what happened in the alley, and that was okay. It wasn't the time to prove anything. He wasn't sure how to handle the situation, but he knew where he could find the answer.

Chapter 26

FINDING ANSWERS

THUNDER RUMBLED FAR OFF in the east. A late afternoon thunderstorm was growing in its Tampa nursery.

Matt looked at the thunderheads forming in the distance. Would they stay away? He had a bike trip to make. He was glad on the drive home from Smith's Jewelers that his mom had been more interested in the bracelet that she'd gotten for Doreen's birthday gift than what he'd been doing that afternoon.

He got his bike out of the garage and shouted to her in the backyard, taking clothes off the line and putting them into the overflowing wicker laundry basket. "Got something to do, Mom. Be home by dark."

She looked up, waved and smiled.

He waved back, climbed on his bike and pedaled away.

The white sand trail beside the road was visible through scattered high grass, wildflowers and seed thistles a foot tall, but enough grew there to show his old path hadn't been used in a long time.

Matt pulled off the road and coasted about twenty feet before he stopped and dismounted. Behind a billboard about a hundred feet off the road, still on the soft sugar sand, he laid the bike on its side, out of view from the road.

The trail appeared to stop at a thicket of briars and elderberry trees, whose blue-colored berries, growing in full clusters, looked ripe. Bending down, he pushed a small limb out of his way and stepped onto the path he and Tom Jones had made the summer before fourth grade. Why had he waited so long to return?

The sound of something rustling in the thicket broke the silence.

He stopped. A dark brown swamp rabbit stood motionless twenty feet ahead, like a make-believe rabbit from Knowles Pottery. Only a slight wiggle of its nose indicated it was alive. Its big, black eye looked like polished granite. The rabbit held the pose for only a few seconds and then bolted through the briars.

Matt almost laughed out loud. Nature always taught him lessons: flight sometimes is the answer.

He searched the area and spotted small tufts of fur surrounding a small hole hidden from unsuspecting eyes under a bush. He lifted a small, leafy branch and looked into the hole. On the bottom of a fur-lined pouch lay at least four baby rabbits, still with no hair. He wanted to touch them but held back, replaced the branch and smiled.

On the other side of the thick growth of bushes, small minnows swam over the orange sand of a shallow creek, and big tadpoles disturbed the surface as they came up for air.

He walked along the edge of the creek until he reached a line of rocks that crossed to the other side. He stepped from one to the other and crossed the water easily. The last time he'd been there he'd had to jump to reach each rock.

In front of him towered a steep embankment of dirt, rocks and scattered weeds mixed with wildflowers. He climbed up on his hands and knees, following a crude path. An occasional rock slid back down, picking up speed and carrying others with it. Thirty feet up, he reached the top and stood on railroad tracks. Small granite rocks surrounded the wooden ties and a steel rail. He looked both ways down the train track. Nothing. The track disappeared into a sea of green trees in the distance. He almost stepped on a burnt flare. *Stay alert. Seaboard freight trains must still travel this track.*

He walked on top of the rails a short distance until he came to a second path etched into the embankment. The path led down to a concrete culvert that carried a slow-moving creek under the tracks. He looked closely and saw the fresh imprint of a large boot. *Be cautious. Might be a hobo around.*

He slid down the steep grade to a small sandbar at the edge of the creek, where raccoon footprints were visible.

Water fell from a six-foot circle of concrete into a waiting pool at least three feet deep. Dark wooden trestles supported the train tracks that crossed the water, and the strong smell of creosote filled the air.

He looked at "his" waterfall and sighed. He stood on the sand of the secret place that he and Tom Jones and some of the other boys in his neighborhood had enjoyed when they were much younger. They named it "Little Niagara Falls." They caught tadpoles, captured snakes and played in their own magical land, but their eyes had never strayed far from the tracks and their ears had always listened for voices, especially a call from a dad. If anyone found them on that side of the tracks, they would get a spanking.

An old railroad tie lay beside the basin where the water from the small falls collected before narrowing and again becoming a creek.

He sat on the wooden beam and looked into the water. He felt calm and ready to think the whole Wayne Tyson thing out with nothing to disturb his thoughts.

A crow called out to him.

Matt yelled up at him. "I'm not telling you anything."

He picked a yellow wildflower growing out of the rocks beside him and threw it into the moving water, watching it float away. An occasional minnow popped to the surface and tapped it, as it meandered down the creek. The flower floated out of sight.

He tossed another flower and the yellow-colored petals turned around and around like it was dancing, graceful and serene, before it, too, moved into the current and sailed away, one petal of the flower sticking up out of the water like a sail.

He sat on the beam for a long time. Finally, he smiled, stood up and stretched. Next to the railroad tie where he had been sitting, something caught his eye.

He leaned over and picked up a rusted three-inch metal ring attached to a small piece of old board with remnants of white paint.

The ring felt rough. The rust did not flake. It felt hard. A weird feeling overtook him. He had seen it before, but where? He closed his fingers around the ring and shut his eyes. His brain registered a blank, but his heart registered a double beat. He had to remember. His heart murmured, "Remember."

He put the metal ring back beside the railroad tie and walked along the creek until he reached the three rocks he'd put there many years before. Peering up out of the water, the rocks were almost dry, the tops a dull gray, but along the sides was a bright, deep green of live algae.

He hopped from one rock to the next across the creek to search for the hidden path to his secret of secrets, his special climbing tree. Only Tom Jones had been there with him.

He bent down and picked up a long stick as he approached an area he called "his" Okefenokee Swamp.

The oaks and occasional Sabal palms thinned. Small lagoons and cypress trees with pointed knees grew up out of the black cypress-stained water and green lichen moss covered the surrounding ground. The sour smell of stagnant water and the musky smell of damp peat replaced other strong smells and announced the beginning of the swamp.

A long narrow limb covered in thorny vines leaned against a larger limb and blocked the path.

He pushed aside the small limb, stomped down the larger limb and uncovered the trail to his destination.

The damp black peat trail meandered through the thick foliage. Dull rays of light pierced through small openings in the overhead canopy. A path crossed over the water following the high areas of debris from the swamp's forest.

A pileated woodpecker flew along under the thick cypress canopy and stuck on the side of one of the old palms. His distinctive call pierced the quietness.

He slowed to admire the woodpecker as it banged its beak into the old palm with a methodical tap-tap-tap, and tree debris fell into the water. He listened and watched, mesmerized. No fear now. He felt secure in his element.

He looked ahead and his eyes glimpsed a movement of something hidden in the firm black mud a few feet in front of him. Stretched across the trail in a lazy S position, a four-foot black-brown cotton-mouth water moccasin raised its triangular-shaped head, its mouth open, exposing a white puffy throat and huge fangs.

He stopped and stared at the snake and tried to regain his composure.

The snake didn't coil. Instead, it pulled its tail and moved forward a few inches with an easy slow tightening of its S-shaped body. It stopped with its head still raised.

Holding his long stick tightly in one hand, Matt bent over carefully and picked up a small broken piece of wood with the other.

The snake held its position.

"Move," he said, and he tossed the wood fragment at the snake's head.

The snake's head moved backward and it held its ground. It didn't strike.

He picked up a limestone rock the size of a ping-pong ball and tossed it toward the middle of the snake's body. The rock hit the ground and rolled into the snake, pushing into the snake's scales and making a shallow dimple in its side. The snake hissed and showed his fangs, but didn't move.

He reached out with his long stick and pushed on the snake's neck as it moved back and forth up off the ground. "I'm not afraid of you," he said. With beads of sweat forming on his forehead, he forced a chuckle. *Well, maybe a little.*

The snake struck the stick twice and then slithered off the path into the water and swam off. It stopped beside a cypress knee sticking out of the water and lay motionless on the water's surface, looking in Matt's direction, its back half submerged in the dark water.

Matt took a deep breath, thankful that he'd seen the moccasin in time to avoid getting bitten, and continued on the path out of the swamp and back into the hardwood trees.

His special tree stood all alone, growing on a large, elevated bare mound in a clearing. The ground around it was littered with leaves, broken limbs and small piles of gray Spanish moss, fallen down from the massive tree. The huge trunk looked like a redwood, but it was an ancient live oak that must have been there for hundreds of years.

The bark along the sides of the giant oak looked like individual wood slates with deep undercuts, and large limbs branched out high up in the tree and paralleled the ground. The tree topped out near a hundred feet or more, and some of the huge branches dropped down as they reached out, some low enough to mount like a horse.

A feeling of peace surrounded him. He hadn't been back since his family moved to another neighborhood two years earlier. As far as he knew, no one knew the tree was there except him and Tom Jones—and Tom had moved into town at the end of the summer before fourth grade.

He sat down on the ground, leaned against the base of the towering tree and remembered climbing and flying between tree limbs. It was the most magnificent tree he'd ever seen. The two boys had climbed and climbed and played and played.

Matt felt the rough bark touching him and jumped up. *How could I forget the bees?*

He walked around the tree and found the massive branch he was looking for—a large dark void in the trunk beside the branch was a hole that dropped down deep into the tree.

He looked at the opening. In and out of the hole flew small specks, reflecting a beam of sunlight that shot between the branches and the leaves and struck right on the hole. In that beam, the moving flecks looked like fireflies of the night. He smiled. The honeybees still lived there.

He didn't know why, but he felt at peace there. He sat on the ground, motionless, and prayed.

Something smacked him hard on the shoulder. It startled him. He didn't move. He turned his head and stared face to face into the eyes of a large gray squirrel.

"Missy, is that you?"

The squirrel crawled down his arm, jumped over to his jeans and stuck her nose into his pocket. He laughed. "It is you."

The spring of third grade, he had found a baby squirrel that had fallen out of its nest, eyes still closed and no fur. He took her home and fed her with an eyedropper, and she survived. Four months later, he brought her to the tree and released her back into the wild.

He touched her tail and she spun around. She bit his finger. She was gentle. She drew no blood. "Be good," he said to her. "You're my messenger. You tell me it's okay. I will draw no blood."

The light became dim. Out of nowhere, a flash lit up the forest. Instantaneously, a crash of thunder pounded in Matt's ears and shook the ground. Missy bolted up the tree.

"Wayne Tyson, you have met your match," he said out loud. "I have my answer. It's time to go home."

Another flash traveled through the trees, lighting up the forest like a strobe light. A sharp clap of thunder followed.

He covered his ears. *That was way too close.* He ran down the path out of the woods and picked up his bike.

The low black clouds rolling over on themselves looked like high surf at the beach. The temperature dropped and debris from the ground swirled in the air.

Matt shivered, crossed his arms and looked up at the scary sky. Did he wait too long?

Another crash of thunder banged at the same time the lightning flashed and hit a power pole along the road. Wind blew the trees, leaves sailed in the air, and a white sheet of rain blanketed the horizon to the south, a quarter mile away.

Big, isolated drops struck Matt, stinging his skin. He pushed his bike to the roadway, hopped on and peddled in the direction opposite the rain. He'd heard the thunder and decided it was made for him. The storm cell stayed to the east and he stayed dry.

Twenty minutes later, he turned onto his street and saw Mr. Weller, bare-chested with pumped-up biceps, trying to keep his wheelbarrow, loaded with dirt, from capsizing on his lawn.

He turned in the driveway, braked, hopped off and dropped his bike on the sidewalk. The front wheel, suspended above the concrete, continued to turn.

He ran to the old man, grabbed a handle of the wheelbarrow and helped keep it from tipping. Together they pulled it back up and set it down on the back braces.

Mr. Weller sat down on his garden stool and put his head down into his hands.

"Are you okay?" Matt asked.

Mr. Weller took his hands away from his face and lifted his head. "I'm okay. I'm still strong, but not like I used to be. Thank you, Matt Parker."

Those were the first kind words Matt had ever heard come out of the man's mouth.

"You're welcome. Where does this dirt go?"

"Behind the garage—I have a mulch pile."

"I bet you got fishin' worms in it."

Mr. Weller smiled. "Yep, they're in there."

"Can I help you?"

"Thanks but it looks to me like you have a new bandage on that leg. I'll finish this up tomorrow. I made myself a pitcher of fresh squeezed lemonade. Join me for a glass?"

"Yes, sir. Thanks."

They walked to the front porch. Matt sat down on the wooden steps and Mr. Weller went inside. He came back out holding a tray with two glasses full of ice, and a pitcher of lemonade. He set the tray on the wooden porch floor and sat down on the steps next to Matt. He poured the lemonade and handed Matt one of the glasses. "Now tell me where that bandage came from. Looks pretty serious to me."

"It's okay. Had a run-in with a small shark when we were camping last night on Hog Island and had to stop by the emergency room this morning and get a couple of stitches to close it. I'm fine. Are you okay, Mr. Weller? You seem fine now, but yesterday morning ..."

"I'm sorry for my behavior yesterday," Mr. Weller said.

"I know you lost your wife a little while ago."

"Yes, Matt. She was my sweetie. We were married over fifty years. But I wasn't fair with her."

"I'm *only* twelve," Matt said. "You don't *have* to tell me."

"Yesterday's date is a tragic one for us. On that day in 1944, we lost our son, our only child. He flew off the Lexington and was killed over Guam. We struggled after that. Young boys like you, loving life, made me angry. Yesterday morning I changed. I cleared my soul. Listening to that boy cry restored all that was missing. He was crying for my son. And now here you are, sitting on my porch. What are your struggles, Matt Parker?"

"You know I have struggles?"

"I suspect you do. I saw you with Billy—was that his name?—and I eavesdropped."

Matt finished his drink and set it back on the tray. "Yesterday, I doubted my half-hearted commitment to be there for Billy. And now, it's no longer only about Billy. This afternoon in an alley, it became very clear. It's also about me. And now I meet you. Thank you. Your sharing with me strengthens me."

"Remember, Matt Parker, when you think you're swallowed by that which you fight, kick hard, create the burp and you will fly out, ready to renew your struggle."

"Mr. Weller, what did you do for a living?"

"Sold hope."

"What do I owe you?"

"Weekly visits."

Matt walked to his bike and hopped on. He heeled the kickstand hard and locked it in the up position. The bike moved down the driveway. "That's a deal," he said, and with a wave, he peddled toward home, whistling.

Chapter 27

CHURCH BELLS RINGING

MATT OPENED HIS EYES and carefully rubbed his stitched-up leg. Too much bike riding, not to mention the fight with Wayne and the kip-up off the ground afterward to show John he wasn't hurt. Maybe he went a little over the limits Dr. Haygood gave him.

He looked at his watch. Dawn was still an hour away. The sweet sound of a familiar muffler filled the sleepy neighborhood street as Lawrence Fraley delivered the Sunday morning newspapers. Matt listened to the approaching car and smiled. As the glass packs beat on the house walls, the paper slid up on the porch and smacked the front door with a loud thud.

Three hours later, Matt met Bob on the steps of the Methodist Church in downtown Clearwater. The church bells rang and JB's dad stood by the large church doors, greeting people as they arrived at the church from three directions.

Dee walked up the steps with a big smile on her face, wearing a pair of white high-heeled shoes. She seemed at ease and steady on her feet. The three-inch heels remained vertical and never wavered, not like some girls who looked like they might fall.

"Hi, Bob. Hi, Matt. Isn't this exciting? Our last Sunday as sixth graders." She looked like she belonged in junior high, dressed in a suit with a string of pearls around her neck.

"Hi, Dee," Matt said. "I never got to talk to you yesterday at the movies. Did you girls have fun at your slumber party Friday night?"

"We had a blast. We started planning the dance party I'm going to have, and yesterday we went to the record shop after the movies and we all bought records. I know you have a big collection. Will you bring some? I know there's a worry they might get scratched or end up going home to the wrong house."

"I'll have my name on all of them."

"Then that's a yes?"

"Yes."

"Thank you," Dee said. "That will be wonderful. Oh, there's Maggie. I've got to go talk to her before church begins. See you in Sunday school. By the way, Matt, Bonnie thinks you're really cute."

Matt blushed and Bob laughed as they watched her walk away.

After the early church service, the boys went to the Sunday school classroom. "Our last time in this class, Bob," Matt said. "Next Sunday, it's into the junior high class."

He looked at Bob and then himself in the mirror in the Sunday school room and closed his eyes. They had a long way to go before they looked like teenagers. He looked over at Dee and thought how the older boys would look at her. He tried to understand how this was the same girl he'd seen there last Sunday. When was his body going to change?

"Boy, Bob, Dee has left us behind. She looks like a teenager, and we still look like part of 'Our Gang.'"

Bob laughed. "You're Alfalfa, I'm a skinny Spanky and John is Butch."

"You're right. Listen, Bob, I need to tell you something after class is over. Have you talked to John since we left you at Frank's yesterday?"

"No."

"Well, we had a problem after we left you and Billy. I'll tell you all about it after church."

The church bells rang.

"When does John get out of Mass?" Matt asked, as they stepped outside onto the church steps.

"Twelve o'clock, I think," Bob said. "He should be here any minute.

Something to share?"

Matt nodded his head. "Yes, but let's wait until John gets here so you can hear the whole story. I called Billy last night and told him about it."

Bob looked puzzled. "Give me a hint?"

"No, here's John. Let's go over there and sit on the grass."

Matt pulled a long stem of grass from the ground, seed pod at its top, and placed it in his mouth. He began chewing on its end and then rolling it around in his mouth like it was a toothpick. "Well, John and I saw Wayne one more time after you left with Lawrence yesterday."

"You saw him again?" Bob asked.

"That's what he said," John answered. "Listen to him so he doesn't have to repeat himself—it's not a story I want to hear twice."

"Aren't you a little touchy," Bob said. "Let me ask some questions. Right now, fog is covering the field."

"Sorry," John said, his voice serious and his expression solemn. "It was not a good ending for our team. Wayne is bad—real bad. I think we need to stay clear of him. And our buddy here—he couldn't fight his way out of a brown paper bag."

Matt spit the grass stem out of his mouth. "I think the good news is that maybe Wayne's attention has shifted to me because he wasn't able to intimidate me in Brown Brothers the other day. John doesn't agree, but I can handle Wayne, and I hope in time to win back John's confidence."

"Let's go, Bob," John said. "My dad's waiting on me at home. I'll fill you in as we walk."

"Okay," Bob said. "Have fun on the Miss Buckeye tomorrow, Matt. Sorry I can't go."

Chapter 28

THE HERMIT'S SHACK

THE MOON WAS STILL VISIBLE in the early morning sky above the Parker house. The sun broke through the cloud cover on the horizon, and its sparkling yellow rays created a silhouette of the clouds.

Matt secured his dad's saltwater fishing pole to his bike in the quiet of the early morning and headed toward the causeway. He hoped Billy had decided to go and wondered if he might see Bonnie. *Glad it's not a 'red sky at morning' sunrise. Rough seas might not be good. Don't want Billy getting seasick on his first offshore fishing trip.*

Thirty minutes later, the town dead quiet, he rode Nellie like he was in a barrel race straight west down Cleveland Street in between the town's storefronts, crossing three intersections and two sets of railroad tracks. From a distance, the street appeared to fall off the earth where it reached the bluff.

He kept his foot on the brakes and rode down the steep hill, not letting his coasting speed get up too fast. At the bottom, before he began his trek across the narrow two-lane bridge, he took his right hand off the handlebar and saluted the two bronze soldier statues as he rode by. He looked behind him—no cars yet. He'd ride across instead of walking his bike along the bridge railing where fishermen set up their tackle boxes. So far—all clear.

The crossing gates stood vertical ... no ding-ding sounds with red lights flashing. The bridge tender waved to him from inside his small room. Keep going.

As he crossed the metal grids of the drawbridge span, his handlebars vibrated and his bike tires began a soft roar. He slowed and looked down at the water below that was ripping as the strong outgoing tide pulled water through the navigable channel to the Gulf. Soon he'd be on the Miss Buckeye, headed along in the same direction—out to the Gulf of Mexico. Excitement raced through his body.

In his handlebar mirror, a car appeared in the single lane behind him. He pedaled faster.

Towering palm trees lined both sides of the causeway and on the north side, a wide, shallow body of water and an immense island of mangroves with intermittent water crossways extended north for several miles along St. Joseph's Sound.

He reached the end of the bridge and a soothing warmness heated his back as the sun peeked above the bluff and cast long shadows on the causeway. He pulled into the outside lane and let the car pass him, and then he swung into the center walkway, looked across the exposed flats, stopped pedaling and coasted to a stop. *I'm early. I've got time.* He folded his arms and relaxed with one foot still on the pedal and the other balancing him on the ground.

Looking at the bright green-leaved mangrove trees and their tangled roots brought back memories of the years he and BC Graham fished and explored the area in BC's old skiff powered by a ten horsepower Scott Atwater outboard engine. He was the tagalong eight-year-old. His teenage fishing partner BC—already known for his ability to find and catch fish—taught him the secrets of the mangroves and the bay, and where the bay waters held sought-after fish. They brought their fish to the dock threaded on a stringer and carried them in the baskets on their bikes from the boat slip to the back door of the Bay Drive In, a restaurant beside the bridge, where they sold their catch of speckled trout, mackerel, sheepshead and any other marketable fish they happened to reel in. The catch was a source for overhead costs, and a few bucks went to Matt. BC tucked the rest in his wallet.

Matt breathed in another deep and slow breath and savored the saltwater potpourri. He licked his lips and a broad smile appeared.

Look around—Smell it—See it—Feel the goose bumps—Touch them. He rubbed his chest with an open hand under his T-shirt. They were there.

Bonnie, are you coming to fish with us today? Be adventurous. I rammed you with my pram. You knew my motive. Forgive me? I'm different now. I saw myself. I wasn't a good person on the inside. I tried, but my need to win destroyed all my good intentions. I'll show you my mended ways. Come fish with us ... and one day I'll tell you this to your face.

Would she come? If so, maybe next he'd bring her here and share it with her—maybe as a girlfriend. Teenagers had girlfriends. His imagination kicked into gear. *Forget all the other stuff rattling inside you. Be happy. Erase Wayne Tyson and treasure off the chalkboard for today.*

The beauty of the moment etched a glowing picture in his mind. He stood there mesmerized by the action on the flats at the mangrove boundary. Small piles of dead, dark-colored seaweed wadded up in the shallow channel of water beside the causeway's edge, adding its sweet distinct aroma to the rest.

The picture spread across the water in front of him like a water-color of a mirrored bay. The riches of the bay showed itself and he felt part of it, an excitement he wanted to enjoy and share. A feeling of contentment spread over him. He loved where he lived. No wonder the beach town was growing. He sat still like the wading birds and listened to the recurring sounds of nature until a loud car horn jolted his world and took him out of his peaceful setting. Someone yelled out the window and waved. He waved back to the license plate of the car, already nearing the second small bridge.

He approached the "hermit's shack," a dilapidated old shack at the western end of the mangroves, visible to every car headed over the causeway toward the beach.

The spattering of gray peeling paint left the rusty tin-roofed old wood structure as living evidence of nature's decay over time. Mangrove limbs with green leaves, some turned yellow, grew over the peeled-up edges of the bent tin roof; others encroached against the back wall. Barnacle-laced pilings held up the floor. Some were so thin and eaten away they were non-supportive, and the side wall and floor, no longer level, dipped down toward the bay water underneath.

A short dock protruded from a screened wooden platform; the

remaining screen section lightly fluttered like a sail trying to find wind. The dock's walkway looked like a discarded piano with every other key missing and a sixteen-foot, two-by-ten board had been laid over the missing planks. The runners below the piling holding the dock above the water line looked like a skeleton stuck in the low tide muck.

A derelict white cabin cruiser moored beside the dock remained there with the question of "who held who?" Loose rope lines hung from the boat to two dock cleats, making a loose curve, the belly of the rope still out of the water and grass.

He had heard a gray-haired crabber spent time there, and his skiff already looked stuck on the turtle grass floor, but no one was visible. The skiff looked familiar.

He rested on his bike and turned his thinking elsewhere, back to his first home in the county—Dad's "Cracker Villa"—and the swamp sounds: the screech of a red-tailed hawk, the loud chatter of a pileated woodpecker, the low lion roar of a gator ... He smiled, pushed off on his bike and resumed his ride. *Let's go fishing.*

As the road curved into the second bridge on the causeway, he pictured the great schools of mullet that ran under the bridge in the fall and fishermen throwing long bamboo Burma poles with short lines and big snatch hooks into the moving sea of fish and flipping them from the water into the street. He loved his job of tossing them into the large round wooden fruit basket and hauling them off the road as his dad snatched them.

He had the same feeling when he looked at the bridge span, and in his fantasy, saw mullet flipping on the roadway. He dodged them, left and right, his front tire whooshing as its traction pulled it across the black asphalt. He crossed the bridge and saw the Miss Buckeye on the north side of the street where the bridge ended and the beach road began.

Chapter 29

THE MISS BUCKEYE

MATT PARKED HIS BIKE and walked down the gangplank of the Miss Buckeye. His friend Catfish Myers worked on the large fishing boat as the deckhand during the summer and on weekends during the school year. He was fifteen and the son of one of Matt's dad's sub-contractors. "I'll put that Harrington rod over there in the safe corner very carefully, Mattie boy," Catfish said, "and let's talk a few."

"You're working. I don't want to get you in trouble."

Catfish shrugged his shoulders. "We're fine. Sandy's the mate. I'm the gopher. My mom honked the horn and I waved at you on the causeway this morning. Did you see me?"

"No. Well, I saw a car and a hand, but that was all. I thought it might be you. I was looking at the old fishing shack. Does that crabber still use that skiff tied up there? It almost looked sunk."

"Nah, it's not sunk. He still fishes on it. Said it was missing on Friday—probably broke loose. He found it down near Hog Island. Tide took it way down there he suspected."

I bet that's not how it got there, Matt thought, but he changed the subject and didn't say anything to Catfish. "Who's in the galley today?"

"Miss Ellen," Catfish said. "Remember, she makes a real good hamburger on the grill."

"Yeah, I know, but I opened the fridge this morning and found a brown paper bag on the top shelf. Mom fixed me sandwiches."

"Did she throw in a banana?"

"No, she knows that's bad luck. There's an egg salad, ham and cheese, an orange and a cookie."

"Maybe I'll eat out of your bag or trade with you."

A sly grin appeared on Matt's face. "Trade for what?"

Catfish laughed. "A can of Spam, unopened, a dill pickle and four slices of white bread."

"Uh, no thanks," Matt said. "You tryin' to get the Yankees seasick watching you eat?"

A fisherman getting on the boat tripped and Catfish grabbed his pole and supported the older man with his free hand. "Okay? That's a nice pole. Don't want to booger it up."

The flustered man regained his composure and took the pole back from Catfish. "Thanks, son," he said.

Catfish lifted his shoulders and shook his head. "We gotta stay young, my boy."

"We've got to stay fit," Matt said.

"What's with the Band-Aid on your leg?"

"Encounter with a blacktip on Hog Island Friday. Needed a few stitches. I can still fish."

"Anyone else coming with you?"

"Maybe Billy. Herb Dudley's pitching for the Bombers today and John's going to the game with his dad and brother. Bob's at their family picnic at the horse barn property."

A voice yelled from the dock. "Hey, guys!"

Matt smiled. "Billy, you came," he said. "Come aboard." He looked at the American flag hanging limply above the marina across the street and smiled. "I told Billy I hoped it would be a beautiful, calm day with light seas."

"Hey, Billy," Catfish said. "I'll get you a rod. Ready to tackle some big fish?"

"Yes, I am. Never caught a grouper, but I have caught some big bass in Indiana."

Billy looked small standing next to Catfish, and the rods on the boat were six feet long with 4.0 Penn reels spooled with sixty-pound test line and heavy terminal tackle, but Matt knew Billy was strong and could handle them. Besides, he'd be right there to help him.

Matt wrapped a ragged red terry cloth hand towel around the metal railing of the area on the stern Catfish had saved for them, and secured it with a loose, overhand granny knot.

The boys propped their fishing poles beside it, put their tackle boxes in the corner and sat back on the fish box to watch the fishermen walk down the gangplank. The tourists stood out with either white or sunburned skin, and white lotion covering their ears and noses. And, they usually wore straw hats and sunglasses with plastic nose protectors attached. The local fishermen had tanned skin and wore regular clothes.

The first man down the gangplank had on an old plaid shirt over a T-shirt. A couple of buttons were missing. The man with him wore a T-shirt with Peck's Plumbing printed on the back. They both wore tan work pants and sported Philly baseball caps. "Locals," Matt whispered to Billy.

"Tourist," he said as a man appeared on the gangplank wearing a straw hat with a green visor sewn into the brim, a long-sleeved white shirt with a pelican embroidered on the top pocket and argyle socks with brown, laced-up leather shoes. His skin was as white as the sand on the beach, and he had Noxzema smeared all over his nose.

"Oh boy," Billy said. "My skin used to look like that, but now I've got a Florida tan."

Matt placed a hand over his mouth and covered up his smile.

Before Billy could comment, a girl's voice called out, "Hi, Matt!"

Matt looked at the dock and saw a girl in white shorts, a sleeveless blouse and tennis shoes coming toward the boat with a tall, good-looking man. It was Bonnie. They stopped at the gangplank and Bonnie gave him a kiss on the cheek. "Bye, Dad."

"Tell Captain Price I said 'Hi,' and don't show up the boys too bad."
Bonnie blushed. "Oh, Dad."

Matt watched her step onto the gangplank. Her tanned legs glistened. "What a surprise," he said, not knowing what to say. He looked at the man on the dock. "Hello, sir. I'm Matt and this is my friend Billy."

"Hi boys, I'm Mr. Curtis. You all have fun. It's a perfect day. Bonnie,

I'll be on the dock when the boat comes in."

"Okay, Dad." Her voice sent the message that her dad should leave.

Mr. Curtis waved and walked away, stopping a second to chat with the mate who was still busy on the dock.

Matt studied Bonnie's face, not believing she came there at his invitation. "Looks like your dad knows everyone who runs this boat."

Bonnie stepped off the gangplank, jumped, skipping the temporary steps and landed on the deck. A waist-length ponytail of light brown hair pushed through the back of her baseball cap and bounced as she landed.

"He fishes on this boat a lot. That's why he's letting me go. I think he talked to the captain on the phone last night." She looked over at Billy. "Hi Billy, I'm glad you came today too."

Billy grinned. "So am I, Bonnie. This is my first time on a boat like this."

"Want me to set up a place for you beside Billy and me?" Matt asked.

"Thanks, but I'm not planning on fishing today—even though I love to fish. Today I want to sit up on the top deck and enjoy watching all that's going on while getting some good sun ... But I might give some advice from time to time." Her eyes sparkled as she smiled. "Besides, I want to think."

"Think about what?"

"Think about being a teenager."

"Okay," Matt said. "But if you change your mind, I'll set up a pole for you."

"Thanks, but I'm sure there'll be no poles in my hands today. I'll see you later." She turned and disappeared into the cabin where seats lined the wall and a galley up in the front served fresh brewed coffee.

Two older men boxed in Matt and Billy's places on the stern. Matt knew the man beside him fished on the boat almost every day and was a good fisherman. The men tied their poles to the railing, put their tackle boxes on the floor and headed into the cabin to get a cup of coffee. The strong aroma floated through the door with the message it was brewed rich and strong.

Bonnie came out of the cabin and started climbing up on the rooftop.

"Are you allowed to go up there?" Matt said. "There aren't any seats—just the slippery roof."

"Captain Price said it was okay. I'm careful. I'll see you when he rings the bell."

The white water churned in back of the boat, and seagulls flew behind, occasionally dipping down to the white water and pulling something out. A tourist tossed the remnants of his sweet roll up in the air, and one of the seagulls caught it in midair and flew off.

Matt and Billy walked to the bow and looked down at the conchs visible in the brown-white sand twenty feet below. The sharp edge of the bow cutting through the water sounded like a wave turning on itself as it breaks on the sand. Matt looked up and saw Bonnie. She waved but remained up top.

Behind the boat, a wispy, dark smoke trail hovered over the propeller wake and the smell of diesel flowed out of the stacks. The fumes were strong in the back, but not noticeable up front on the bow, and Matt knew he should keep Billy on the bow at first. It was calm, but engine smells, coupled with the smell of frozen squid, frozen sardines and an octopus thawing on the rear fish-box, could still be bad on a queasy stomach.

"Come on, Billy, let's walk up to the front of the boat so we can see better. The island on the right is Hog Island."

"Boy, I didn't realize that island was so long. Are those pines on the south end the ones we camped under?"

"Yep. And down where the mangroves start is where I saw the giant's boat. I hope we never cross his path again."

"For sure. Boat's not there now. Guess they sent somebody back to tow it away."

The boat passed the last channel marker and steered out of Big Pass. The gulls stayed close behind them and followed the boat into the clear, green water of the Gulf of Mexico.

Behind them lay the barrier island of Clearwater Beach. In front of them, the water stretched out like a flat mirror, except for small, disturbed areas that announced bait just under the surface.

A black line of smoke started at the boat's smokestack and still could be seen a mile back. Matt saw the trail and wished for a little wind. With no wind, he knew when they stopped at the first dip, it would get hot fast. Wind—no wind. Nothing was ever perfect, but for Billy, if Matt had a choice, less wind was better.

The boat ran west. The trip out would take three hours.

Matt pointed out a small group of porpoises close to the beach that greeted the boat and put on a show, jumping all the way out of the water before they landed hard on their sides and made a big splash.

Offshore, the water turned from green to a deep blue. It wasn't black like the deep water, many fathoms down to the steep seafloor, but still a definite color change.

Billy pointed at something splashing far off in the distance. As they got closer, they could make out a group of spotted porpoises headed to the boat on a course perpendicular to the bow. The porpoises sailed gracefully out of the water and entered again headfirst as they sped alongside the boat.

"Those are 'spots,'" Matt said. "You find them offshore. Different variety than the ones we saw by the beach. They're deep water porpoises—maybe twenty or thirty of them in that group."

Matt and Billy lay on their bellies, flat on the deck, their heads over the bow. The porpoises played with the boat, dodging back and forth and keeping just under the bow. They came out of the water, blew water out their blowholes and shot back under the boat.

Matt felt someone beside him and turned to see Bonnie, flat on the deck with her head under the rail. "They're such beautiful animals. I never get tired of watching them, Matt. Do you?"

"No, me either," Matt said, still in awe that the girl beside him was speaking to *him*.

Sandy walked over beside Billy and leaned against the rail. He was barefoot and wore cutoff jeans. He was muscular and tan, and the faded tattoo on his right arm gave him a rugged look. Billy looked up at him. "How long do the dolphins stay with the boat?"

"I've been watching them for thirty years and it changes," Sandy said. "Sometimes we bore them right away and they head off for another adventure. Sometimes, they hang around for an hour."

He knelt down along the bow railing and slapped the side of the boat with the flat of his hand. He looked over at Bonnie with a smile. "Aren't you fishing today, girl?"

The RPMs of the engines had stayed the same for hours—in perfect synchrony, a droning sound that could put a baby to sleep—but the captain came off the throttles just a little bit, and that meant they were closing in on their destination. Before Bonnie could answer, Sandy stood back up and headed for the wheelhouse door.

"Let's head to the back, Billy," Matt said. "Time to get ready to fish."

"Bye," Bonnie said. "I'm going back up on top."

The boys reached the stern and the two local men already stood beside their poles, one on each side of Matt and Billy's poles.

The Miss Buckeye slowed to an idle and started a big circle. Catfish put the bait in small buckets and distributed them around the boat. "Ready to fish?" he asked Matt.

"I thought we were fishing over the wreck. I don't see another boat or a buoy."

"Last dip," Catfish said. "Captain said he and the other captains on the dock don't want to fish it out. They've already taken thousands of pounds."

"But are we going there?" Matt said.

"Last dip," Catfish said and he moved on.

"What were you talking about?" Billy asked.

"My dad said an old wreck was rediscovered and it held fish so thick the spike on the fish-finders filled the bottom and showed all the way up the water column."

The Miss Buckeye turned a little tighter, and out of the wheelhouse door a hand emerged holding a crumpled page of newspaper. The hand held the paper for a minute and then tossed it off the side of the boat. The only waves were shallow ones made by the boat. The rest of the Gulf was flat.

"What's the paper for?" Billy asked.

"Captain Price marked the spot he saw on the fish finder. The paper holds the position for a time."

Moving slowly, the captain pulled the boat on a straight course and made a complete turn, crossing over the floating paper. He leaned out the door and said to Sandy, "Drop it."

Sandy pulled the pin and the anchor dropped. The chain attached to it clanged as it passed through the eye and the anchor rope followed silently off the boat and into the water. Captain Price threw the gear into reverse on one engine and slowly backed up.

"This is when you'd like a little wind," Matt said to Billy.

"Why?"

"For a clear anchor heading."

"Oh," Billy said.

Matt couldn't tell if Billy understood or not, but decided he was so smart, he probably did. "Let's bait up and wait for the bell," Matt said. "You can't put a line in the water 'til Captain rings the bell."

Matt and Billy talked with the two men standing on either side of them, and Billy received some good instructions. The bell rang and the fishermen simultaneously dropped their lines into the clear blue water.

Matt watched his sinker drop and the bait twirl as it sank toward the bottom. At forty-feet it was still visible, but finally the white sardine disappeared into the depths.

"How deep are we?" Matt asked Catfish, who was helping a fisherman nearby.

"Between eighty and a hundred feet."

Matt's line went limp as the sinker hit the bottom. He reeled the line until the line was taut.

"Are you on the bottom, Billy?" Matt said.

"I think so."

"Hold on."

Billy grinned. "For what?"

"You know what. It might be a tap-tap first or it might be one bang."

At that moment, the pole of the man beside Billy slammed down on the railing, the tip near the water. He lifted up and the fish pulled the pole down. He lifted again and held it up. The rod bent and he started to strain. "Oh shit," he yelled. "I've got a big one."

The man standing on the other side of Matt shouted, "Keep him up! Don't let him get you down into the rocks!"

The poles of other fishermen around the boat bent over like willow branches.

"They're chewing," Sandy yelled.

The man beside Billy struggled and kept the fish off the bottom.

"Keep it coming," his friend said. "Let the pole do its work."

He pulled up, held and then wound in line as he lowered the rod. He had him coming up.

"Not too fast," his friend said. "Don't want him too green. He's up out of the rocks."

He pulled and he reeled. The boys looked into the blue water, searching for the fish. "Oh shit," the man said. "I see it."

Matt saw the fish swimming in circles, still deep in the water and trying to swim down. It was still down forty feet, but he could see its size. "Sandy," he yelled, "we need a gaff! Billy, better pull your line up so he doesn't get tangled with you. Reel it in fast."

Billy lifted his rod and began turning the handle of the reel as fast as he could. Suddenly, it almost jerked out of his hand and the pole tip headed for the water. He pulled back, but the rod continued its path toward the water. "Matt! Help!" he screamed.

Matt leaned his pole against the rail and grabbed Billy's belt between the back pockets. "I gotcha," he said. "Don't let go of that rod."

Billy looked around. "I won't."

"Quit looking at your neighbor and his fish. You got a big one too."

"I'm not."

Matt looked at Billy's arms. The muscles were flexed. His body was small, but his muscles were big. "You're doing good. Keep your pole up. Keep him out of the rocks."

A bead of sweat erupted above Billy's eyes and it wasn't hot yet. He held the pole up, but it started to bend. "I'm trying," Billy said. "Could this pole break?"

The man beside Billy continued to reel up his fish. It was slow, but the fish was coming. He pumped the rod and reeled faster, bringing a big grouper up to about ten feet. "Looks like a true black," his friend said. "Maybe a twenty pounder."

"Don't worry about his fish, Billy," Matt said. "You just worry about yours. Hold him up."

"I'm trying."

The man's fish was almost to the boat, but still had a lot of fight. It was swimming, belly down, near the surface. Sandy stood beside the rail. Catfish, too, but there was no talking. No one wanted to say anything that might bring bad luck.

"Keep him up. Go careful," Sandy said. He had the gaff in his hand. The fish made a short run but remained near the surface. The head was only inches under the water and its large fantail broke the surface.

"No slack. His head's about out of the water," Sandy said.

When its head broke the surface, the fish lay on his side. The hook was held by just a sliver of soft tissue at the corner of the mouth. "Oh God, go easy," the fisherman said.

"Ease him over to me," Sandy said. His voice was as quiet as if he were in church. "Back away from the rail. Keep him coming." The fish shook his head one last time and flipped his tail. The force put great tension on the hook set, and the hook sailed out of his mouth and onto the boat.

Sandy leaned over the side, holding the gaff with both hands—only his toes on the deck. He lunged and pulled. Water flew everywhere. "I got you, you son of a bitch." The gaff hook dug in beside the gill opening, and the fish threw a mountain of water in the air. In an instant, the fish lay in the corner of the aft deck. Sandy shook the hook on the gaff loose, and a large black grouper lay still on the deck. He grinned. "Next?" he said and he moved over beside Billy.

Matt had his hands tight around Billy's belt. Billy still held on to the rod, and it was bent even more. The line was no longer vertical. It moved away from the boat and whatever was on the other end appeared to be swimming off the bottom and away from the boat.

"What have you got on the end of that line?" Sandy said.

"This one might not be a grouper," Matt said. "What do you think, Sandy?"

"It's starting to fight more like a shark. I don't know, really big grouper do the same thing."

186

"A jewfish?

"I don't think so. They head for their hole."

Billy's line moved out more and started to shallow up. Whatever was fighting seemed to be headed to the surface.

Chapter 30

SOMETHING BIG ON BILLY'S LINE

"BILLY, MOVE AROUND the side of the boat and up to the bow," Sandy said. "And Matt, don't let go of that belt."

Sandy loosened the drag on Billy's reel just a little and line streamed out on the surface. "Jump, you sonofabitch, and show yourself," he yelled.

Matt got close to Billy's ear and whispered, "Remember, this is an old Marine. Be ready for some colorful language."

"I'm tired, Matt. Don't make me laugh."

Twenty minutes later, with the drag letting line out slowly, the spool was almost empty.

"Should we tighten?" Matt said.

"I don't know," Sandy said. "The line's coming to the surface. Let the pole do its job."

"What is it?"

"I don't know. Go easy, Billy. Go real easy."

"I am. My arm's numb. I'm that tired."

Captain Price came forward and looked at the direction of the line. "This is a head boat, not a sports fisherman. Reel that damn fish in, young man." He looked at Sandy and shook his head. "And don't ask me to pull the anchor."

Bonnie shouted down to them from up top. "You've got him, Billy, I think …"

Matt looked up at her. "Don't say that, Bonnie."

"I can see it. I'm coming down."

Billy stood out on the pulpit with Matt right behind him. The line stretched out over the Gulf's surface. One more pull and suddenly the tension on the line eased.

"Reel, Billy!" Matt yelled. "Reel."

Billy reeled. The line started filling the spool.

For the first time that day, the surface of the water changed to a light chop, not even one-foot waves, but the waves covered the line. Out of nowhere, the fish suddenly blasted into the air and water flew out of the hole it made on the surface.

"By God," Sandy shouted, "you got yourself a sailfish!"

Tail walking across the water, the sun shining behind and slightly above it, was one beautiful billfish.

Matt's heart leapt. "A sailfish. Oh my God, Billy. Go easy. It's a sailfish."

Bonnie joined them along the rail, her long ponytail bouncing from side to side as she shook her head. "This is so much fun. I could see him from up top. Oh, how I hope you catch him."

"Don't say that," Matt said again.

"Why?"

"If he gets off, you'll feel too bad."

"Sorry. I'll stay quiet, but Matt, this is so exciting!"

Billy fought the fish for another forty-five minutes while Captain Price and most of the other fishermen stood back and watched and enjoyed the youngster fight the fish of his lifetime.

After a final run and a show of acrobatics, the fish finally gave up and let itself be pulled slowly to the boat. Billy worked it beside the boat like a veteran.

"No gaff—let's take our chances, Sandy," Matt said. "Okay with you, Billy?"

"You bet."

"Get him, Sandy. I'll wrap up the leader near the sinker and you bill him," Matt said.

"Okay, boys," Sandy said. "You know how to wrap, right Matt?"

"Yes, sir. Outside wrap so I can release if necessary."

"Yep. You never want to give 'em a chance to take you down into the deep blue, if they take one last pull for freedom."

Matt leaned over the rail. "Walk back, Billy ... Now."

Billy backed away from the rail, keeping the line tight.

Matt grabbed the sinker and the grouper rig, wrapped the eighty-pound test leader the correct way and lifted the head out of the water.

Sandy grabbed the bill, and in one long swing, pulled the fish up and over the rail.

The fish was not green, but far from tired out. It lit up and its neon colors flashed in the sunlight.

"Oh my, he's beautiful," Bonnie said. "Look at those colors."

"Caught you, you son of a gun," Sandy said. He looked at Matt and gave him a big grin.

The sailfish lay on the deck. His big, black eye looked at all, yet seemed to look at nothing.

Matt felt a sadness fill his heart. The lump in his throat tightened as he looked at the magnificent fish.

Billy watched the fish quiver. Sandy removed the hook. The fish flipped and came off the deck twice and Matt pushed on its side and held it flat.

"What do you boys want to do?" Sandy asked.

"It's your fish, Billy," Matt said, "but I know what'd I'd do. "

"Is he okay?" Billy said.

"I think so ... right now," Sandy answered.

Billy stared at Matt. "You caught him. It's your decision," Matt said.

"Put him in the water, and let's watch him swim off," Billy said. "Get him back in the water ... quick!"

"You bet, boss."

They picked the fish up carefully, Matt grasping the tail section with one hand and the bottom stomach area near the pectoral with the other, while Sandy held the head and bill. Still holding the sailfish over the rail, Sandy lowered its head. "Drop him ... Now."

The fish slipped out of their hands, pierced the surface of the water and torpedoed down, his tail pushing water side to side. The big fish leveled out at six feet and slowly swam away from the boat, then sped up and sounded.

Billy and Matt took deep breaths and smiled at each other, and the crowd of fishermen standing by the rail cheered. A lady on the boat walked up, a camera in her hand. "I took some pictures of your sailfish, and you're in them too," she said. "I'll get your phone number later so I can get them to you."

Billy smiled with a look of contentment on his face. "Thank you, ma'am."

Bonnie leaned over the railing. "That was exciting. I can't wait to tell my dad about it. I'm so glad I came."

The fishermen on the boat returned their lines to the water and for the next hour, Sandy and Catfish were busy again, as the fishermen lifted grouper after grouper over the railing, some close to fifteen pounds. Billy and Matt just watched.

The boat moved a short distance and made another dip. After about thirty minutes, Captain Price rang the bell and leaned his head outside his door. "Lines up, this boat's headed for the barn. The wreck will have to be another day."

Catfish pulled the anchor and Captain Price pushed the throttles forward. The Miss Buckeye turned back to the east, and many of the fishermen headed to the cabin for the trip home. A few curled up on bench seats inside for a nap and some of the regulars sat around a table, dealt out the cards and put their change on the table, ready to win or lose a buck or two before they got to the pass. Most of the tourists stayed outside to enjoy the ride back to the dock.

Matt and Billy went up to the front of the boat, almost on the pulpit, and sat on the drying anchor line. The sea was still light. They could see a great distance, and they watched and waited. Flying fish exploded from under the bow, sailing just over the surface, and finally diving into the small waves and disappearing.

Bonnie hopped down on the deck beside Matt. "Hi. Can I join you? I love watching the flying fish."

"Sure," Matt said. "I never get tired of watching them. Looks like you got plenty of sun today."

She sat down. "I know. What a day and what a fish, Billy."

"Thanks, Bonnie. I still can't believe it. I'm glad that lady took pictures so I can show my dad and Justin when they get home."

"You caught that sailfish like an old salt, Billy," she said.

Matt stretched out across the rope and crossed his legs. He braced his head with his hands clasped behind his neck and relaxed. "Bonnie, I'm glad you came."

"I'm glad you came too," Billy said. He smiled, closed his eyes, and soon he was asleep.

Matt pointed at Billy. "Salt air and a running boat will do that to you."

Bonnie pulled her knees up and wrapped her arms around them. "I'm not sleepy."

Matt looked at her face. Her skin was smooth and her cheeks shiny like they were polished. Her tan was a bronze color. He couldn't believe she was sitting beside him. He wanted to say something, anything, but hoped it wouldn't sound corny. Instead, he'd just look out over the soft sea with its light chop and let her lead the way.

"My dad knows Mr. Myers, the owner of the boat, so that's the only way I got to go today. I'm sure Captain Price is looking out for me." She turned, looked into the wheelhouse and waved to the captain at the wheel.

"Well, I'm glad you came," Matt said.

"Me too."

He couldn't keep from staring at her. "I wonder if we have any classes together."

"I guess we'll find out tomorrow."

Neither one of them said anything else. They sat on the anchor rope watching the flying fish and the birds without a word until the boat slowed down as it entered the pass and Billy woke up.

The three of them walked to the wheelhouse to watch the captain dock the boat. A strong tide moved under the bridge close to the docks, and docking a boat like the Miss Buckeye was not a job for amateurs. As they approached, Captain Price pulled the throttles back and took the drive shafts out of gear. Matt leaned against the railing and smiled as he pictured himself someday docking a boat with the ease of Captain Price.

Bonnie waved at someone in the front row of the large crowd waiting for the boat. "I see my dad," she said, interrupting Matt's thoughts.

His smile disappeared as he spotted Bonnie's dad and a teenage boy standing next to him, both waving back. "I see him. You know the guy beside him?"

Yes, that's Jack Whiting. He's a ninth grader, but he goes to school in Tampa. He's a very good sailor. We sail together. I bet he wants to go sailing. The wind is ruffling up the bay. You don't sail anymore?"

Matt felt like she'd stabbed a dagger deep into his heart. He felt defeated. "No, I can't wait on the wind," he said.

"What a great day," she said, seemingly oblivious to Matt's inner turmoil. "I'm going to say goodbye to Captain Price, and after Catfish and Sandy get the lines tied and the gangplank in place, I'd better hurry."

He forced a smile. "Sure. It was fun fishing with you. Have a good time. Billy and I are going to get our gear and be on our way too."

Billy turned and looked at Matt after Bonnie walked away. "I caught a sailfish today," he said. "And I think you caught something else."

Matt blushed. "Your sailfish didn't get away."

Chapter 31

JACK WHITING

BONNIE SKIPPED UP THE GANGPLANK, greeting her dad with a peck on his cheek and Jack with a long, exaggerated handshake. The threesome stood talking and laughing on the dock.

A bolt of heat rushed through Matt's head and shot out his veins, carrying a touch of anger and a lot of hurt. His entire body turned a bright red. He couldn't see her face, but he wanted to grab Jack Whiting by the neck and squeeze him until he felt the same heat. A lump grew in his throat. He threw his Nehi soda against the side of a trash bucket and sent it spinning on the deck, scattering its contents on the stern floor. He grabbed a rag and wiped up the sticky mess. What a way to end the day. *Take it easy … You're okay … Make yourself okay.*

Billy collected his belongings. "I'm going to go over and sit down until my mom gets here. I'm still tired from fighting that beautiful sailfish. I'm so glad we let him go. Thanks for telling Sandy not to gaff him."

"Okay," Matt said. "I'm just going to stand here for a while."

Matt cooled down but remained fixated on Jack. He tried to tell himself no worries, but the scene on the sidewalk intimidated him. He watched as the three talked. Jack seemed nonchalant. He put his hands on his hips and shifted his body weight to one leg as he talked, and the stance projected "cool."

Matt couldn't make himself look away. He felt heat again in his head. "Aren't you cocky? Isn't it time for you to leave?" he said to Jack in an imaginary conversation in his head.

From the west, the afternoon sea breeze began to blow harder.

Jack patted his neatly combed hair, the part a perfect straight white line, and smiled at Bonnie. A paper cup moved back and forth on the grate of the storm drain beside his feet, but his hair never moved. He looked almost artificial to Matt.

Matt felt a hand touch his shoulder. He turned his head.

"You know you're staring at that guy?" Sandy said, leaving his hand on Matt's shoulder.

Matt saw the twinkle in Sandy's eyes. "I am? Can't help it, Sandy. He looks like a mannequin in the window of Short's Men's Wear. Look at the starched button-down, short-sleeved, blue Oxford shirt—it has to be a Gant shirt—tucked into those khaki slacks."

Sandy patted Matt's shoulder. "And how 'bout the sharp lines on his ironed shirt and the knife-like front seams of his pants? They'd make my ol' Marine drill sergeant proud. But Mattie, he farts and I bet he's got brown stains on his underwear."

"Sandy, look at him. Even the buckle of the red-and-blue-striped cloth belt lines up perfectly with the little white buttons on his shirt. And then there's the shiny Weejuns and navy blue socks—without a doubt, they're Gold Cups. I've seen him before. His dad has one of those big sailboats at the Yacht Club. Boy, I'm not in his class."

"No," Sandy said, his voice clear, low and emphatic. "He's not in your class. Remember, clothes and status do not make a man."

Sandy looked at the spectators now thick on the concrete sidewalk, staring down into the boat. He picked up a hose and began filling up a bucket with water, threw in some soap, tossed in a brush and walked to the transom to scrub off the dried fish blood still left on the gunnel. "Can't have this boat looking like a crime took place on it. Mattie boy, you just stay close to your dad's tree. It's been rubbing off on you pretty good."

"Do you think that's her boyfriend?"

"You think she's liking the yacht club boy, huh?"

"Maybe."

Matt looked back up on the dock and Bonnie was gone. Vanished. He looked into the parking lot. No sign of her. "Well, they're gone," he said. He turned and looked at Sandy. "I have a lot of friends whose parents belong to yacht clubs," he said. "It's just not for everybody."

"Think I could join?" Sandy said with a quizzical look.

"You wouldn't want to," Matt answered.

"Well, don't get tight with the Commodore's daughter."

"Why?"

"Paper napkins send her nose to the moon."

"What do you mean?"

"Only fine linens will do. That's what I'm talking about. There's a feeling with some of them that their birth dropped them into a special crib." He patted Matt on the head. "Your dad can belly up to the bar with any of them, but he stays away from that artificial stuff."

"Dad says he hasn't got the time."

"That's what I'm tellin' ya. He doesn't. He sees through that shit. Hell, your dad can be around someone only a short time and has them figured out. He sees through the fake Jap trinkets. He sees deep inside. I'm honored to be your dad's friend, and so is one of the richest men in Clearwater."

"Who's that?"

"None of your business. The point I'm making is friendships are made on character. Hell, look at Washington Masonry, you know, the colored man who lays block for your dad. That's his good buddy and this is a town like all the rest. People separated like water and oil. But not your dad."

"I know Mr. Washington's son," Matt said. "We're friends."

"You are?"

"He's been my friend since we were little."

"How's that?"

"Oh, I don't know. Started off when dad would go to Mr. Washington's house to pay him and I'd tag along. The dads would talk and Rudolph and I played. We understood."

"About segregation?"

"Yeah … different schools, different beaches, different everything."

"Well, that's good. Doesn't surprise me. Like I said, you're a shiny apple, and your apple didn't fall far from the tree."

Matt's mind drifted away from the boat and his issue with Jack, and a memory lit up within him. "They've got chickens in their back-yard," he said.

"So?"

"So, I've helped him collect eggs on Saturdays when I go over. We have fun. We make it work."

"I bet you do."

"Stringer number twenty-two," Catfish yelled.

"Ahhhhhhh." The spectators, now thick on the concrete, stared down into the boat and applauded.

Matt looked over at Catfish standing by the fish box, holding a large stringer of fish. Gathered around him, fishermen waited for their fish to be pulled from the fish box. He spotted Billy in the group.

A tanned old salt wearing only tennis shoes, shorts and a Phillies baseball cap stepped forward, and the deckhand handed him the stringer. He dragged the nice catch off the boat and walked through the crowd pulling the stringer across the concrete: three black grouper, one red grouper, two mangrove snapper and at least six nice-sized grunts.

"Are those grouper?"

"Some."

"Are they good to eat?"

"Yes."

"Want to sell them?"

"No."

Matt and Sandy walked over to the fish box.

"Number four," Catfish yelled. "Number ten ... Number three ..." One by one, each fisherman came forward and claimed his catch.

"And here's the big one ... Number sixteen," Catfish bellowed. With both arms, he pulled the largest grouper out of the box and it fell to the deck. "Thirty-two pounds," he boomed.

Another old fisherman walked up and waved the green bills he won in the "biggest fish pool," and with help, dragged his winning fish off the boat to the oohs and aahs of the bystanders. "Not a bad day," he said with a big grin.

"Was that the largest fish today?" a man on the dock yelled.

Sandy placed his hand on Billy's head. "No. This boy caught the biggest fish, a sailfish, unusual fish for a party boat. He did a good job."

"How much did it weigh?"

"Over forty-five pounds. We took pictures and released her," Catfish said.

The crowd clapped. Billy smiled and took a bow.

The lady who took the pictures of Billy and his fish walked up and handed him a piece of paper. "Here's my phone number. My name is Myrtle. Tell your mom to call me and give me your address so I can send her the picture. I need to run."

"Thanks," Billy said, slipping the paper into his pocket.

Sandy laid a nice stringer of fish at Matt's feet. "Here's yours, Mattie."

Matt set the stringer back into the ice. "Thanks, Sandy. You know my dad pretty well, don't you?"

"We went to school together. He's three years older than I am. When we were really young, he let me be his tagalong. I lived on the east side of the railroad tracks. Down near Belmont."

"I know you worked for Dad sometimes. He says you're a good carpenter."

"I've pounded a few nails. But the water draws me."

"Excuse me guys, but there's my mom," Billy said.

"Want me to come over later and help you clean fish?" Matt asked.

Billy gave Matt a blank stare. "I can clean fish."

"I know you can. Just asking."

"It was a great day, Matt. One of the best."

"What a fish you caught."

"Only because of you. See you in the morning at school."

"Yep. We'll make tomorrow another day to remember," Matt said, and somewhere deep in his head he questioned the statement.

With both hands, Billy dragged his catch up the gangplank and pulled it to his mom's waiting car. She honked her horn and Matt waved.

The box, full to the top with fish in the beginning, was now two-thirds empty. Only bloodstained, crushed ice filled the bottom third of the box. The crowd that had listened to Catfish's announcements dispersed.

Sandy and Catfish began the boat cleanup in earnest. Matt sat on one of the benches and watched. "Hey, Sandy, I found a picture in the attic from out of the paper a long time ago when Dad was still in high school. I wonder if you'd know any of the people in the picture."

"What's the picture about?"

"It's about my dad and some other kids looking for a treasure."

"I'd know 'em all."

Matt grinned. "You would? Really?"

"Yep."

"Last week in the paper, there was one of those 'Twenty Years Ago Today' articles about a robbery that took place and the gold treasure that was never recovered."

Sandy shook his head. "Yes, I saw it."

"Well, I remembered Dad showing me a map and a picture from the newspaper and it all revolved around that treasure. So, last Friday morning I went up in the attic and found the map and the picture."

Sandy sat down beside Matt. "Yeah, I remember all about that adventure."

"Well, listen to this, Sandy. My mom just found out that her mom and dad aren't going to be able to come and visit this year and she's really sad. If I could find that treasure, Dad could take off work and next summer we could all take a trip to Australia to see them. I'm not going to tell them I'm looking for it because I want it to be a surprise. I took the map with me Friday afternoon to Hog Island and we dug for it."

"Find it?"

"No, a shark bit my leg and we had to go home early."

"So, are there stitches under that Band-Aid?"

"Yep. I'm fine now, but then it was bleeding and we needed to leave. I'm not giving up, though."

Sandy chuckled quietly. "Why doesn't that surprise me?"

"And guess what?" Matt said. "While we were on the island, we were joined by an unexpected guest. It was the prisoner who escaped from the county jail Thursday."

"Go on."

"He walked right into our camp while we were sleeping."

Sandy beamed. "I've got a surprise for you, Matt. Want to hear it?"

"What?" Matt said.

"I know him too."

"Who? The prisoner? You know him?"

"Yeah, I know him well, just like I bet I'll know the people in your photo. I know them all."

"Oh my gosh, Sandy. I feel like I hit the jackpot. You know the giant?"

"He's a baby. Grew up near Belmont. Ol' Craig. Big, strong and sweet."

"His name is Jeremiah, not Craig, and that's not what the sheriff said about this guy. He said he broke a guy's neck."

"Probably needed to be broken."

"You really know him?"

"Yep, Jeremiah C. Rennolds. We called him Craig. He lived down the street from me."

"Go to school together?"

"No. He was six years younger. I don't know where he went to school. I do know he was a hell of an athlete."

"He must be fast. My dad heard that he broke away again at the dock Saturday morning. Threw two officers in the water and in the early light, bolted into the trees on the embankment behind the municipal auditorium."

"Dogs lost him?" Sandy said.

"At the corner of Pierce and Fort Harrison the scent disappeared, they said."

"Probably hopped a truck."

"That's what they thought, Sandy. Good thinkin'."

"So, he's on the loose again."

"Yep, how long are you going to be on the boat?"

"Couple of hours ... why?"

Matt clasped his hands together and looked right in Sandy's eyes. "You're my hope. You're my answer. You're my angel."

Sandy laughed. "I'm a lot of things, Mattie, but an angel is not one of them."

"If I ride home fast and get back before you're finished cleaning the boat, can we talk some more and look at the picture and you tell me who everyone is in the picture?"

200

"I'll be waiting."

"I'll go fast, but it still might be awhile."

"I'll be studying the moon."

"Okay, I'm on my way. I'll get my gear and fish on the second trip. I'll be right back."

"Okay. I'll be here."

Matt ran up the gangplank and jumped on his bike.

Chapter 32

THE BELMONT BOYS

THE LATE AFTERNOON SUN rested on the top of an oak tree across the street from Matt's house. Facing the street like a horse waiting for its rider, Nellie stood still and upright on her kickstand in the driveway.

Matt carefully tucked the folded newspaper articles in his front pocket. A shot of pure adrenaline blew into his heart. His hand slapped the wooden frame of the front door and the door opened wide to the limits of the hinges. He bolted onto the porch. The screen door slammed shut behind him.

He became a pony express rider, leaping into the air, arms and legs, for the moment free of gravity, touching nothing until he landed on the seat as he mounted his bike from the rear. When his hands touched the handlebars, his feet hit the pedals.

Nellie was old and slow in bike corrals, not streamlined like new Schwinn bikes, but Matt's strong thighs and his stamina made up for the bike's aerodynamic shortcomings, and soon he was almost on the causeway.

Answers to unanswered questions awaited him. The excitement within him exploded just thinking about it. Mysteries to solve and Sandy held the key. Matt felt giddy.

He pedaled harder and began singing Little Richard's song "Jenny

Jenny," using the name Bonnie instead of Jenny. "Bonnie, Bonnie, Bon ..." He repeated the words in cadence with his pedaling. It tickled him and he laughed out loud, repeating the verse over and over. The ride seemed quick. He topped the second bridge.

The parking lot looked desolate. Only a couple of cars remained. The Miss Buckeye looked like a boat asleep.

Where was Sandy? He stopped singing, pulled in the lot near the Miss Buckeye and dropped his bike. The front wheel tire continued to spin as he hurried toward the boat.

On a piling near the stern perched a pelican, his stomach filled, his head tucked up under his wing as he took his late afternoon nap. Sandy was nowhere to be seen.

Matt wiped his eyes. The quiet made his ears ring. The great joy that had filled him on his ride disappeared. "You said you'd wait," he said out loud to no one. His back collapsed on the boat's cabin wall and slowly he sank down, sliding down the wall like a slug on a window. He ended up sitting in a puddle of water, and he didn't care. He looked up into the pale blue, late afternoon sky, ready to cry.

The only noise inside the boat was the soft muffled sound of a generator engine. Outside, the water that kept the generator cool belched out on the surface, gurgling as it mixed with the bay water.

Matt sat on a ghost boat.

"Hey!" a familiar voice yelled.

He felt an immediate soaring relief like he'd felt the day he was lost in Sears when he was four and out of nowhere heard his dad call his name.

Sandy strolled across the street from the main marina. Still shirt-less, he held a Budweiser in one hand and the remainder of the six-pack cradled under his other arm.

With a burst of joy, Matt jumped up and shouted, "You had me worried. I was afraid you left."

Sandy stepped up on the curb. "Nah, I wouldn't leave you, Mattie. Needed something to keep my lips wet while we get into some serious talking. Cleaner than when you last saw her?"

"Yes sir," Matt said, still filled with elation.

He took a deep breath and pulled out the newspaper clippings.

One was old. The paper had turned yellow and brittle with age. The other was crisp and white with the black print in sharp contrast. "I brought back both articles. Are you ready to look at them and tell me who these people with my dad are and more about this robbery?"

Sandy walked across the gangplank and jumped onto the back deck with a thud. He downed the remaining beer in the bottle, cast it off into the trash bucket and stowed the rest of his six-pack in the ice in the fish box next to Matt's stringer of fish.

"That's a real nice grouper there," Sandy said as he pulled out another bottle, opened it with his teeth and spit the cap into the bucket.

"Aren't you afraid of breaking a tooth that way? I know where there's a church key."

Sandy grinned at Matt. "Too far to walk when I have an opener already."

Matt shook his head like an adult. "Whatever you say."

Sandy tilted his head back and raised the next beer high above his mouth. The beer poured out of the bottle into his mouth like a mountain waterfall into a pool below. He put the beer bottle down on the fish box. "This heat has given me a terrible thirst."

Sandy finished up the two inches of beer in the dark-colored bottle and grinned at Matt. "This sun is brutal. Think the moon will be the same?"

Matt laughed. "Hope not," he said, and waved the papers close to Sandy's face.

Sandy stretched out his hand. "Let me have a look."

He grabbed another beer, closed the box, walked around the back of the box and pulled out a bottle opener and popped off the cap. He smiled at Matt. "You got me kinda worried about my teeth. Watch this." He flicked the cork-lined bottle cap like he was snapping his fingers. The cap shot off his thumb, spun like a flying saucer out over the water and landed in the channel off the bow.

"Learned that trick in the Marines at the NCO club," he said.

"Wow, you need to teach me that—with Coke bottle caps, of course."

Sandy looked at Matt with a quick sly look, closing one eye to a slit. "Of course," he said. He turned over two buckets, sat down on one and rubbed his hands together. "Okay, Mattie. Have a seat. I'm ready."

Matt handed him the newspaper articles and sat down on the other bucket.

Sandy studied them both, his eyes moving back and forth between the two. He seemed to be deciding which one he would discuss first.

Matt touched the recent newspaper article. "Tell me about this one first."

"AUGUST 28, 1957... CLEARWATER SUN – TWENTY YEARS AGO this week, the largest unsolved robbery in Florida took place outside the First National Bank of St Petersburg. A Brinks armored truck was robbed in the middle of the day by three masked robbers, holding the driver and guard at bay with Tommy guns, reminiscent of Al Capone and the gangsters of that era. The truck was last seen heading north on 34th St. Heavy rains blanketed the area and the truck was thought to have been hidden in a warehouse in the nearby industrial area but was not located. One week later, the discarded truck was found, empty and burned on a dirt road off the Anclote River near Tarpon Springs. The amount stolen from the bank was never disclosed, but sources said it exceeded two million dollars in treasure, stored in the bank by R.A. Lipscomb, a treasure hunter who found a sunken Spanish galleon somewhere off the Keys. The stolen treasure was never recovered."

Sandy took a normal sip from the new bottle. "Okay. This bottle is only for keeping my lips moist because my lips will dry out telling you what you're about to hear. I remember the robbery. I was about your age and everybody talked about it. The intrigue came from the vision of what was stolen. Not hard cold greenbacks but pirate's treasure."

"Wow," Matt said. "Can't you see them? Gold coins dripping through their fingers as they scoop it up and watch it fall back into the box. Rubies, emeralds and diamonds worn by Cleopatra, glittering and sparkling as the sun's rays hit them. And there's Long John Silver, gloating over his fine bounty. Arrrrh."

Sandy laughed. "Your dad must have had the same vision, 'cause three years later, he grew his story."

"You think it was just a story?"

"Sure I do. Maybe not then, but knowing what I know now, I think your dad may have perpetrated the grand hoax of Pinellas County."

"You know what? Dad read *Treasure Island* by Robert Louis Stevenson to me as a nighttime story. He loved talking like a pirate."

"Well, he did himself proud. The Belmont Boys believed his story. Hell, I believed his story. All Clearwater believed his story. Ole Mr. Jones at the Army Navy store couldn't keep spades on his shelf."

Sandy handed Matt the recent article. "That's about it with that one. It pretty much gives you the background for this old picture." He became quiet and seemed somewhere deep in his thoughts. His eyes got glassy.

"You okay, Sandy?"

Sandy looked up at Matt and closed his eyes. He opened them back up and wiped them with his forearm. "Oh, what memories can do to you," he said.

Matt took a long breath and felt Sandy's feelings coming to the surface. The big strong muscular ex-Marine melted right in front of him. "Have another beer," Matt said.

"Believe I will."

"So, who are the Belmont Boys?" Matt said.

Sandy opened another beer. "There are a few of them in this picture. Several family trees are represented here," he said. He touched the tall boy on the far left with his fingertips. "These boys lived down in South Clearwater, down near Belleair Road. Still a lot of groves there, but when we were kids it was really rural and most of the roads were dirt. The railroad tracks ran through the area. An enclave of families lived there and they called it Belmont. I lived near there, and by the time we were in high school, they were known as the Belmont Boys. I called 'em the Backward Boys, but not to their faces."

"Why?" Matt asked. His eyes were wide open, and he was hanging on Sandy's every word.

"I didn't want my ass kicked."

"Oh."

"They were country boys. Hell, we were all country boys, but they lived two generations further back."

"Like, they were behind you?"

"They were the caboose before there were cabooses."

"How does this all fit in with this picture and who's the boy you're putting your finger on?"

Sandy studied the picture some more. "I'll get back to him."

Matt saw Sandy's nostalgia returning.

"Yeah, I remember those years," Sandy said. "They were rough. The depression had been hard on everyone, but these boys had it rougher. Their families, as I remember, didn't have regular work so they lived off the land, and their kids weren't raised with silver spoons in their mouths, as the old saying goes. The boys were always ready to scrap and they mixed it up with no holds barred. They got their learnin' by kickin' a yellowjacket nest."

"What do you mean by that?"

"School was only part of their education. Poetry by Walt Whitman didn't fill their plates at dinner or put a gallon of gas in their car. Their poetry was the smell of bacon grease popping out of the skillet or gas fumes flowing up out of the open cap. But school did put them in the limelight in one way and socialization helped some of them prosper. They were great athletes, especially in football, baseball and track. They either were big and mean, tough and fast or flat-ass bad, and they channeled that energy into sports." Sandy shook his head and smiled. "If there was a fight on the field, you could bet your last quarter one of them came from Belmont."

Sandy looked down and placed his finger again on the same boy. "That's Chuck Knox. We called him 'Red.' What a character: mean and tough, loyal and strong. Became a Marine too. Last time I saw him we were still in boot camp. Never saw him again. Killed down in the islands, the Solomons, I think. Not many know, but he was highly decorated. I'm sure he took a lot of Japs with him. If you see a redhead from south Clearwater, they are probably a Knox. Why am I telling you all this? Sports and war got some of these boys out of that circulating tornado wind down there, around and around, a no-escape circulation filled up with trash and debris. Because if they didn't escape it, they rolled in its mud."

Matt scooted his pail closer to Sandy and his head almost rested on Sandy's shoulder. "Who's that beside him?"

"That's his brother, Tom Knox, star linebacker, and his shot-put record maybe still stands."

"I have a Jimmy Knox in my class."

"Redhead?"

"Yes, sir."

"That's Tom's son. I can tell you stories about his dad."

"Not a friend?"

"Oh, we're friends, but there's drama."

"So, who's that?"

"Jeb Tyson and that's his brother Lem beside him. Lem married Sylvia Knox."

"Wayne's parents?"

"Yep, Lem was a good baseball player."

"So, that means that Wayne and Jimmy Knox are cousins."

"You got it. Wayne's dad was in the motor pool in the war and came back and was a heavy equipment operator for Cobb Construction before he worked for your dad. He died a few years ago."

"I know. Was he sick?"

"Alcohol sick. Alcoholism grew down there like mistletoe in an oak tree. Even if a tree looks healthy, mistletoe growing in it cuts off parts of the healthy tree in time, making a sick branch. Brown water does the same thing. Finally found Lem Tyson's liver—cirrhosis and death."

"So, he was an alcoholic?"

"Yep, turned his liver green. Died at Morton Plant Hospital. I'm afraid for his son. He's not on a good path. Got potential. Good young mechanic. But he's cocky and he's got that surly, bitter hatred."

"He's a hood."

"Well, stay clear of him. Right now, he's no good. Needed his dad."

"Too late. He's after Billy right now and I've already said I'd help Billy."

"Sorry to hear that."

"Tell me about the rest of them, Sandy, and see if I'm smart enough to sort it all out."

"Being a simple man, I'll try to keep it easy, you know, Dick and Jane."

Matt laughed. "You don't need to be that elementary."

Sandy smiled. "That's right. I forgot who I was talking to. Now, don't start off thinking I'm a Bible-pounding, box-standing evangelist who preaches in a revival tent that alcohol kills the world. Jesus took a sip of wine." Sandy winked at Matt. "Right?"

"Right."

"But I'm saying for some it does kill. Their firewater carries them down to where the demons ravage them. Now your dad and I enjoy a tall cold one, but we understand moderation. We don't allow it to become mistletoe. That's not to say I've never tied one on. A couple of weeks ago, celebrating at my niece's wedding, I ended that night hanging on the earth with both hands clutching the grass."

"The earth?" Matt said, a half smile building across his face.

"It was spinning so fast I thought if I let go, I'd fly off into the stars."

Matt giggled. "That taught you a lesson."

"The real lesson came the next day: a splitting headache and ralphing in the commode." He took a sip of beer. "Makes me feel sorry for the Yankees when they get sick on the boat. Me? That was self-inflicted." He laughed. "Back to your dad ... I've seen your dad on a Saturday at noon in ninety-degree heat leave the job site in his truck and come back with foamed top, ice cold beer in thick white paper cups for the crew. And everyone on the construction site raises their cups high and yells "Catfish!" before taking their first sips, making white foam mustaches along their upper lips. Now that's sweet, and that's okay in my book."

"I was there one time when he did that. I worked on Saturdays. He brought Rudolph and me root beer so we could do 'Catfish' with them."

"Catfish!" Sandy bellowed. "That was Freeman Collier's saying." Sandy thought a second. "He cut his thumb off with a table saw."

"I know," Matt said. "I remember when that happened. I looked for the thumb."

"Well, obviously you didn't find it, 'cause he ain't got one anymore on his left hand."

"Boy, he was tough. I remember he came back from the hospital, gauze wrapped all around his hand, and went right back to work like nothing ever happened."

"Another Marine."

"You guys are special,' Matt said, thinking about war movies and their heroes. "Freeman said he was on a battlewagon. He was a sailor."

"Yeah, you're right. Close enough anyway. These are the dads raising you young'uns."

"My mom says they're doing a good job."

"Hope so. Get you prepared in case we need to fight Khrushchev and the Russians."

"You going to build an underground atomic bomb shelter?"

"Only if I want to store potatoes," Sandy said. He looked back down at the newspaper picture. "Okay, we got sidetracked, Mattie. Look over here on the far right. That's Roscoe Tanner. He married Mildred Tyson, Lem Tyson's older sister. We called him 'Ace' in high school, but the mistletoe invaded him too. They divorced, and their son, Bruce, lives with her."

"So, Bruce is Wayne's cousin too?"

"Yep."

"And there's Dad and Bill Peart in the middle," Matt said proudly.

"Yeah, boy, that's them. Your dad was a funny guy. He was too smart to talk to most people about subjects he was interested in, so he got his laughs playing with his buddies' minds—especially the Belmont Boys on the football team with him. Bill Peart was his co-conspirator. The two of them messed with them all."

"What did they do?" Matt asked.

"They once put a horse turd on a pine cone and told one of them it was a Nutty Buddy, and someone in the group touched his tongue to its side before getting a good whiff of the horse fragrance, and he spit and spit and choked and gagged and coughed while your dad and Bill slapped their knees and laughed till they were out of breath."

Matt laughed. "That must have made the Belmont Boys mad."

"You'd think, but not with those two. Once he got the taste out, he and the others started laughing too. What stories, huh?"

Matt's face lit up. "Oh wow, Sandy. Thanks so much for telling me about all this."

"Well, the *coup de grâce* was when your dad planned the ultimate hoax about finding the treasure map. He tricked everyone. That's why they took this picture. Even the newspaper believed him. He and Bill claimed they found half of a treasure map and if they found the other half and taped them together it would lead to the mother lode. To add spice to the story, they said they would share the treasure with whomever found the second half of the map that was supposed to be buried with enticing rewards ..."

"Gems and gold?" Matt said.

"Yep, a little sugar before the apple pie. They told Lem Tyson he could be the one to lift it out of the ground and Ace Tanner could open the box."

"And they believed all they heard."

"Anyone would in the beginning, but it became a problem. In time, the story ran its course and no one ever found the second part of the map or any treasure. By that time, people had dug up half of Pinellas County and all of the northern beaches." Sandy tapped on the picture. "After this picture came out, your dad said he didn't think there was any treasure."

"So, he left them a ray of hope?" Matt said.

"I think he had to. He had to let it go down easy. Way too much hope became tied to that adventure. It finally faded, but for some of those boys, it never went away. Your dad was so convincing, some could never believe it wasn't true, and the myth soon turned into a legend."

"You mean some still believe there is a treasure?" Matt said.

"Yes, and they're not completely wrong. The treasure that was stolen from the bank was never recovered, so it could still be out there somewhere. The map was the hoax, not the existence of the treasure. I think Lem Tyson went to his grave still believing it was either still there or someone had found it. Some of the Belmont Boys couldn't let it go. It was their chance to escape."

"Wow," Matt said, overwhelmed by the story. He asked again. "Is that Lem Tyson, Wayne's dad?"

"That's him."

Matt pointed to the boy beside Wayne's dad. "Who's that again?"

"Robbie Tyson, his older brother. Distanced himself from the family after he got out of the army. Lives in St. Petersburg, I think."

He pointed to the boy on the far right. "And him? That's Roscoe Tanner? You called him Ace, right?"

"Yep, back in high school he was a hell of a pitcher … a lefty. Another Belmont sports celebrity, but now a functional alcoholic. I say that, but the last time I saw him at the Coral Bar he was beyond functional. He fell getting off his bar stool. I hear his master bedroom is in the fourth floor of the county jail. He resides there on weekends." Sandy stood up and placed his beer, still half-full, in the trash can. "Just can't lay down the gin."

Matt stood up. "Thanks, Sandy. I need to let you get home and I need to go home too."

"You're welcome Matt. That was fun bringing back all the old memories. Help me do one thing," Sandy said with a stern face.

"Sure, anything."

"Help me clean your fish."

"Really? I mean, thanks, but I can clean them at home."

"They won't fit in your basket. Filets will. We'll knock it out quick. I've got a sharp knife. Pull 'em out of the box and put 'em on the cleaning table. I gotta take a leak."

Chapter 33

THE FIRST DAY
OF SCHOOL

JOHN'S HOUSE

John sat at the table and slurped down the last spoonful of milk and cereal. He waited for the sports page, hoping to read about the Dodgers before he left for school. He leaned over the table and flicked the paper with his finger. The paper popped. Attention achieved.

His older brother looked up and gazed over the top. "What?"

"All I want to read is the box score. You've had the paper all morning, Bill."

John looked over at his dad. "Have you noticed your older son's reading skills compete with first graders'?"

Bill folded the paper, got up from the table and dropped it on John's lap. "Here—they lost. Snyder struck out in the ninth."

"Thanks a lot, brother," John said. He looked over at his dad. "Dad, did you hear Bill? That's as bad as telling someone the end of a movie." He pushed back his chair and got up from the table, reached for his glass of orange juice, swallowed what was left all in one gulp and slammed the glass back on the table.

"Don't get in a tizzy," Bill said, "or I won't drive you to school. If you're still riding with me better get your butt in gear. I'm leaving in ten minutes. By the way, I can't pick you up after school. I have football practice. You'll need to take the bus home."

"All right," John said. He headed for his bedroom. Bill still held the ace. He didn't want to ride the bus his first day in junior high.

"John, don't forget your gym bag," Mrs. Hollis said from the kitchen. "You've been waiting all summer to carry it to school today."

"Does he have a jockstrap?" Bill yelled from his bedroom.

"Don't embarrass your brother," she said.

"I'm just asking," Bill said. "Does he know how to put it on?"

She shook her head and suppressed a giggle. "That's enough, William."

"I hear you in there, Mom," John said. "You love having boys instead of girls, don't you? Instead of jock straps it would be bras and lipstick and crying in the bathroom because they don't like their hair. For us, it's protecting our giblets."

The giggle in the kitchen became a laugh. In the dining room, sitting alone at the table drinking his coffee, Mr. Hollis smiled. "You're okay, John. Your brother thought the first one we got him was either a nose protector or a slingshot."

"John, let's go," Bill shouted, running out the front door. "We don't want to be late the first day of school."

John followed Bill out the door. His mom watched from the kitchen door and shouted her instructions as the screen door slammed shut. "John, pull your jeans up and put your collar down."

"Okay," he said. "But I've gotta look tough for the hood at school who wants to give us a hard time."

Mr. Hollis walked out on the porch. "Just stay away from him, and be kind to your teachers so I can be kind to you."

John ran to the car and jumped in with an armful of books and a new gym bag over his shoulder. The engine was already running. "I will," he yelled through the open car window. "Catch you on the fly. Love you both."

"Bye. Love you too," Mr. Hollis said.

The baby blue, two-door '53 Ford with white caps and fender skirts backed out of the driveway and drove down the street, just under the speed limit, with the song "Let the Good Times Roll" drifting out the car windows.

"This is cool. Drive like you're on the beach at Daytona."

"Don't try to make me get a ticket, especially on the first day. Besides, you know Dad is still watching us."

★

BOB'S HOUSE

"Has anyone seen my new shirt?" Bob shouted out into the upstairs hallway. No one answered him.

Raised voices from the other bedrooms filled the air. "Where are my socks? ... You're wearing my blouse ... Susie, please help me ... The bathroom is free ... These socks are different colors ... Breakfast is ready."

He'd spent the better part of the early morning waiting his turn for a bathroom. He looked in his closet for an ironed shirt. No luck.

Danny, Bob's older brother, looked up from where he stood by the toaster, and frowned. "That shirt you have on has wrinkles," Danny said. "Mom's not going to let you in the car wearing a wrinkled shirt and we'll be more late this morning."

Bob poured some juice and sat down at the table. "Hey, big boy ... have you seen the new shirt I bought Saturday at Frank's? I can't find it anywhere, plus, I can't find any shirt that's ironed. I had to get this one from the ironing room ... Easy on the new, cool seventh grader. Dig?"

Danny ignored the comment. He buttered his toast and shook his head. "Why didn't you ask me about the shirt last night?"

"Did I see you last night?"

Danny took a bite of his toast and walked out of the kitchen. "Don't make me late for school today." He stopped at the base of the stairs. "Bob? Susie's upstairs ironing as we speak. If you don't think you can find that shirt, you better take that one you're wearing now and give it to her. I'm telling you, Mom won't like it."

"Okay. Let me throw down some food first."

Danny walked upstairs into the commotion: "Your school books are in the car ... You have to wear a belt ... Eat a banana on the way ... The raccoon goes outside ... Has Dad gone to work ... I need lunch money ..."

He walked into his bedroom and closed the door. "Tomorrow has got to be better," he said out loud. He looked at his watch. The car should be pulling out of the drive at seven thirty and it was already seven fifteen.

At seven thirty-five, five children and one adult sat in the family station wagon, everyone talking at once—Bob and Danny going to Clearwater Junior High and their younger brother and two sisters going to South Ward Elementary.

"Take a headcount, Danny ... Please back out of the drive slowly ... We'll make it on time ... I need to stay after school today ... Find a way home."

At seven thirty-eight, Mrs. Walton, white knuckles clutching the steering wheel, backed out of the driveway, looked in the rearview mirror, slammed on the brakes, put her hands beside her ears and screamed, "Bobby, your shirt is wrinkled!"

Bob lifted his hands with his palms up.

"Too bad, Mom. We've got to go. We're late," Danny said.

★

BILLY'S HOUSE

Billy's mother sat in a rocking chair on one side of the sprawling porch that wrapped around three sides of the old, white frame, two-story Cracker house with a tin roof, a hot cup of coffee in her hand and a napkin on her lap with a slice of toast lying on top. Early morning before daylight was her favorite time of day, and the quiet made her feel like her prayers were being heard.

She hadn't heard Billy yet, but she knew he was up and probably already showering. She looked out into the dark and wished Clint and Justin were home. The first day of junior high school should be an exciting day, but she knew on that morning, it was far from being that way. Billy usually shared a lot of things with his brother, but she was all he had today. Maybe she could help him.

The first light of dawn spread a red glow across the sky. The fragrance of the jasmine growing over the nearby arbor filled the porch. A rooster crowed. A dairy cow sounded a long moo on the other side of their fence and started her slow walk to the milking barn, and somewhere out in the pasture, the first meadowlark whistled. She waited to hear the ring of the telephone that would announce a surprise phone call from Indiana and the voices of dad and brother.

A light went on in the kitchen. A short time later, the door opened out onto the porch. "Good morning, Mom."

"Morning, Billy."

Billy stepped out on the porch and sat down on a second rocking chair beside the chair where his mom sat. He took a bite of a banana and stared out into the yard.

The sun moved above the flat horizon.

"You're very quiet this morning," Mrs. MacDonald said. "You're supposed to be excited. Are you feeling all right?"

"I'm okay. I just wish Justin was here today."

"I know, but you'll be fine. Just enjoy this new experience. Your dad and brother will be home sooner than you think."

She needed more light before she could sneak a peek at her watch and check the time. The long sleeve of her nightgown covered the watch, and Billy would notice. He'd ask why she needed to know the time because she always said at that time of morning, she didn't care what time it was. So she didn't look, and just then, the phone rang.

Billy looked at his mom with a puzzled look.

She looked back at him with the hint of a smile. "Who do you think that is?"

He sat there for a minute and all of a sudden, he jumped up from the chair like a light went on in his brain, and he ran to the phone in the living room. "Hello?"

After a pause, the operator connected the two parties. Static filled the phone line, but Billy could hear a voice on the other end. "Justin … is that you?"

Mrs. MacDonald entered the living room and stopped beside Billy. She rubbed his hand and tapped him gently on the shoulder. "I'm going to let you two talk," she whispered, and she walked to the bedroom, closing the door behind her.

Billy sat at the desk chair, and a happy tear ran down his cheek. "I miss you too … I know … Matt said that also … I know they will

… I know they do.

"Wayne had me scared … I know… I'll have some uncomfortable moments … Yes … Yes … Matt? … I'll tell him. I do believe that … He's going to do something … They can't protect me all the time … Yes, I believe that … Wayne?"

Billy wiped away another tear and laughed. "I think you're right … The three of them … Whatever he does to me … He's a bully … Thanks … I am … He'll be sorry … Regrets do, after the final lesson is delivered …You made my day … I'll tell them … I love you … Bye."

He hung up the phone and sat awhile. He tapped on his mom's bedroom door. "Dad and Justin sent their love. I'm getting ready for school. I feel great now."

Mrs. MacDonald opened the door and smiled. "I knew that phone call would perk you up."

"Well, it did. You know, Mom, I miss them both, but I'm going to be all right."

"Good."

"Oh, Justin said Dad will call you later and fill you in on what's going on up there. He'll keep it short."

"Well, he better. We can't afford too many of these long-distance calls."

Fifteen minutes later, Billy walked downstairs into the living room, dressed for his first day at junior high in a pair of Levi's and a short-sleeve, yellow-and-white-striped shirt over a white T-shirt.

Mrs. MacDonald looked at him. "You look nice," she said. "But to be safe, I think I'd unroll your shirt sleeves."

"Why?"

"Your white T-shirt shows."

Billy walked over and looked in the mirror and studied himself. "Maybe I should take the T-shirt off."

"Just unroll the sleeves of your shirt."

"Rolled up sleeves look cool."

"Then take off the T-shirt. Besides Billy, it's too hot anyway for that much clothing."

"It was going to be the Sal Mineo look."

"Well, Sal's mom would have given him the same suggestion I gave you."

Billy began unbuttoning his shirt. "I know. Justin wears his clothes better than I do. Justin's neat."

"So are you. You're just in between sizes now."

Billy sat back down on the chair in front of the desk, pulled the undershirt over his head and threw it onto the desktop.

His mom remained quiet and looked into his eyes.

He sat there staring at her. "How do you always know what I am going to say, Mom?"

"I'm not sure if I do, but I guess the best answer is that moms are supposed to know that."

Billy smiled, but his expression changed to a more serious look. "Is our family happy here? We've been here two years and I think we are, but right now this issue with Wayne has made me look at the family also, and I just wonder."

"What do you wonder?" She wanted all answers to come from him.

"Well, Dad and Justin are back at the farm, all the family is there, and they sounded happy. Mom, this is not about me. Justin set me straight on that this morning. It just made me think about the whole family and about everything. I'm just curious."

"What's everything?"

"I mean I've been thinking about making choices and how that works. Do you miss the farm?"

"I do, but I don't miss being sick."

"Well, I miss the farm and the rest of our family in Indiana, but I love it here. And Dad and Justin and I are most happy that you're well."

"Well, guess what?" Mrs. MacDonald said with a big smile. "Your dad and your brother love it here too. You're right. Making choices demands making conscious decisions and then living with them. If later a choice you made doesn't work, the world doesn't come to an end. You just make another choice and decide on another path. Your dad knows that very well. Good farmers live that way."

"I'm almost thirteen, and I already understand that principle," Billy said. "We made the choice to move to Florida because the doctors said the climate is better for you here. I'm glad we're here and I'm glad they were wrong and you don't have TB and you didn't have to go to Tampa to the sanatorium."

She smiled at him. "This is your dad's premature Florida retirement home, Billy. He found this little town and it appealed to us both. He knew you boys would love it. And he knew how to satisfy your mom. He found this old, make-believe farmhouse at the end of a dirt road, backed up against a dairy farm cow pasture with a few citrus trees in the yard, and until this town has a growth spurt, it will remain quiet and we'll enjoy country living. It's a perfect place for a transplanted Indiana farm family."

Billy tucked in his shirt again, minus the T-shirt. "Does this look better? I wish I didn't have this small, skinny body."

"You're not always going to be thin," his mom said. "You've got a major growth spurt coming, just like Justin."

"He wasn't as skinny as me."

"It would have been a close contest. Why do you think you could wear his hand-me-down clothes?" She reached over and squeezed his arm. "Nothing but muscle there, waiting to be unleashed."

They both laughed.

"No matter what you say, I'm still not eating spinach or liver," Billy said, and then he turned serious. "Mom, I need to show another side of me."

"Don't go crazy on me. I remember when you pulled the tail on the bull."

"Surprised Justin!"

"Surprised the bull."

"I think Justin wanted to protect me when we moved here, and I let it happen. Don't misunderstand. I liked it. And now Matt has taken his place and Bob and John are going to help him, but I want them all to see me in a different way, including Justin."

"You can," his mom said. "But remember, you are who you are. Justin hits baseballs—you hit piano keys. Justin reads comics—you read novels. Justin is smart—you are really smart. You're like Annie."

"She's my favorite cousin," Billy said. "I love her brothers too, but Annie and I seem to be alike. We don't mind getting black dirt under our fingernails, and we can slop the hogs with the best of them. Plus, we love to talk about things no one else wants to talk about. The boys want to know how the combine works. Annie and I want to know how an iron lung works. Just different applications, right? Maybe she's not a farm girl—and maybe it's okay for me not to be like Justin."

"That's right, Billy. I talked to Aunt Stella last week and she said for Annie it's all about becoming a doctor. My point is to just be you. It's okay. You don't need to change."

"Mom, you know who's really smart?"

"Who?"

"Matt Parker. He doesn't hide it, but he disguises his intelligence very carefully. You know, like not always raising his hand to answer a question or correcting someone if they're wrong. He's cool, Mom. I see why he became good friends with Justin."

"That's interesting," his mom answered. She patted Billy on the shoulder. "Your brother shared a similar insight with me regarding Matt's athletic abilities. He said he's a fierce competitor, always striving to help his team win, but handles his athletic prowess the same way you described he handles his intellectual abilities. Justin told me he just remains a regular boy."

"I'm so glad he's my friend now, and whatever happens at school, I know he's there to help me. Our differences are like day and night, and he seems to be showing me a bright sun on a moonless night."

Mrs. MacDonald rubbed Billy's head. "You're quite the poet."

"Thanks, but I need some Rocky Marciano. You know, become a little more 'all around.' That's Matt. He's an 'all around' guy."

"Don't cut yourself short," she said.

They walked back outside. His mom picked up the watering can and watered the Boston ferns that hung above the railing between the white wooden posts.

Billy put his things for school next to the railing and sat down in the rocking chair. He tried to digest all he had shared. He crossed his arms, lifted up his head and pushed out his chin. "But, Wayne's scary, Mom."

"Yes. I know a lot about Wayne. As Justin relayed it to me, Matt and the boys will help you, physically. I believe you will help yourself with your brains. Not that you're not strong."

Mrs. MacDonald walked to the next hanging plant. The leaves drooped. "This one really needs water ... Where was I?"

"It's okay for me to be me?" Billy said. "Remember, I boated a sailfish. That was scary."

She smiled and nodded. "That bull on the farm was scary too," his mom said. She put the watering can down and looked into Billy's eyes. "You pulled his tail. You did not pinch his nose." She sat back down beside him. "That bull finally got tired and just walked out into the pasture. You and Matt need to make Wayne feel tired and want to head for his pasture."

Billy got up and kissed his mom on the cheek. "Thanks, Mom. Between this talk and the phone call, I'm ready to face my day. I know when I see Wayne the first time, my heart is going to skip a beat or two, but I'll be okay."

Billy picked up his school stuff and headed for the bus stop. "Glad to hear about Annie. Hope we see them all during Christmas."

"I'm sure we will. Those plans are already in the works. Now, you 'shoo' off to school and I'm going to 'shoo' our resident cow away from my gardenia bush and off toward the barn."

She watched Billy walk down the driveway. He looked small. When he finally reached the hard white shells of the last unpaved segment of the county road, she sighed, turned around and opened the front screen door. "No," she said out loud to herself. "He is *not* Justin ... and that's okay."

*

MATT'S HOUSE

Matt sat at the table waiting for his poached egg to cook. The bread in the toaster popped up.

He jumped up from his chair and smacked the toast down onto the bare plate, buttered it and cut the crust off the edges, leaving a square-shaped piece of toast. Then he removed the egg from the hot water and placed it on top of the square. Perfect. The first cut would let the runny, yellow yolk spread out over the entire plate, and the sight made him happy. A hard yolk meant starting over again at his house, which made Mullet happy. Mullet liked table scraps, and cooking failures on the stove were success stories for him.

Mrs. Parker walked into the kitchen and watched Matt devouring his breakfast. "Why are you in such a big hurry?" she asked. "I'd have made breakfast for you. You have plenty of time to ride your bike to school."

"I'm not riding my bike today. I'm walking."

Sitting at the other end of the table, Mr. Parker looked up from his newspaper. "Why?"

"You know, Dad, I know this sounds silly, but at junior high today, guys will be riding to school on motorcycles."

"So?"

"So walking is okay. There's nothing wrong with riding a bike, but today I want to walk."

"Walking tells me there is still hope for you," Mr. Parker said. He picked up his coffee cup, lifted it high and tipped it toward Matt in acknowledgment. "Here's to an almost teenage boy who's getting smart." He looked over at Matt's mom, who had already started washing the dishes, and winked. "It's a guy thing."

Matt got up from the table and picked up a dish towel. "I'll dry, Mom."

With a light touch, his mom removed the towel from Matt's hand. "Thanks, Matt, but you're off the hook today. Have a great day. We'll be anxious to hear all about it after school."

She grabbed another plate off the table and carried it to the sink.

"You're off the hook too, Mom. No more homeroom mother for you. It's back to just being a housewife. Do you think you can stand it?"

"It might take me an hour or so."

"And then what?" Matt asked. He stopped at the door of the kitchen and waited for her answer. He knew it would be a doozy.

"Maybe I will have time to finish up the ironing, do a few loads of wash, and if I can locate the clothespins and the sun stays out, I'll hang the wash out to dry," Mrs. Parker said with a big smile. "But, I'm missing clothespins. Last year, I'd have been looking on your bicycle. Remember when you used all my clothespins to hook playing cards onto your spokes so it made the sound of a motorcycle?"

Matt couldn't resist. His dad had a known prejudice about what he called the "youngsters on motorbikes." He said in a serious tone, "That's probably the closest I'll ever get to owning a motorcycle, right Dad?"

Mr. Parker didn't look up from his newspaper. "That's the solution—clothespins and Bicycle playing cards."

Matt picked up his gym bag and his books and walked over to the mirror in the living room to check himself out. The butch wax made the wave in the front stand straight up and the sides above the ears stay combed back. Pretty short, but his dad would say still a touch too long. By the time his dad thought he needed a haircut, the length would be perfect. He knew he'd look cool wearing a DA, but he had to settle for the short version.

He climbed up on the sofa and looked closely at his face in the mirror. He couldn't find a whisker. Just one small pimple grew on the end of his chin. It wasn't on his chin the night before. He rubbed it and hoped no one would notice it.

He backed away so he had a full view of himself. The blue, orange and red madras shirt was neatly tucked into his new, washed and shrunk Levi's jeans, and he wore no belt. He looked cool, even though his new white tennis shoes stood out as "right out of the box." He hoped Bonnie liked how he looked. "Look out, Jack. You've met your match," he said out loud.

He yelled a last goodbye, walked out and closed the door of the house.

Chapter 34

THE BELL-SHAPED CURVE

MATT STARTED DOWN THE STREET whistling the theme song from *The High and the Mighty*. Junior high school—no more little kids playing around the playground, six teachers instead of one, a real gym class and old friends reunited. Sometime during the day, he'd see Bonnie. It was going to be a great day!

What was Billy thinking about this morning? Was he singing or was he thinking about Wayne Tyson? *Probably thinking about Wayne—I am. That guy worries me.* The reality hit him. Today he and Wayne Tyson would be at the same school. What was Wayne planning? When would he see him?

A few houses ahead of him, he spotted Tom Baker, one of his favorite neighbors, standing on the sidewalk outside his house, reading a book. A stack of books lay in a mound on the concrete beside his feet. He looked like a Norman Rockwell painting.

Matt whistled between his thumb and forefinger and the piercing shriek broke the quiet of the neighborhood. Tom looked up and waved.

Matt leapt over a crack on the sidewalk and hurried toward his neighbor. Walking to school on the first day with Tom, a ninth grader, seemed important. He was the basketball team's star player and had been nominated for Student Council President. Dad always said associate with people you look up to and don't walk with the turkeys. Tom fit that criteria.

"Tom, thanks for waiting," Matt yelled. "I thought maybe Mike grabbed you early and you both headed on."

Tom closed the paperback book he was reading and set it on the stack beside him. "No, we weren't leaving you. Slow down, Matt. It's already too hot to run. You'll be soaked. Mike is right behind you. Are you in some kind of hurry to get to school? Do you want those upperclassmen to tease you?"

"Yes and no," Matt answered. He tried to imitate Tom's soothing delivery, but his voice quivered.

Mike walked up, smiled and extended his right hand to Tom, ignoring Matt. "Good morning, Tom. Ready for our last year of junior high? Oh, good morning Matt. That's right. This is your first day of junior high."

"I've been kidding him too, Mike, preparing him for his first day," Tom said. "He'll do well."

"Thanks, Tom. You sure have a lot of books. Where's yours, Mike?" Matt said.

Mike folded his arms tightly and stared down at Matt's shoes. "Getting pretty cocky, pretty early, for an elementary school escapee."

"Get me now, Mike, 'cause this seventh grader grows fast."

"Guys," Tom said. "let's get going."

The three walked abreast with Matt in the middle. They bumped shoulders as Matt tried to force the bigger boys onto the grass, and the older boys held their positions.

"So, Matt, who's your homeroom teacher?" Mike said.

"Miss Jones."

Mike cupped his hands in front of his chest. "Va-va-voom ..."

"Does that mean she's good looking?" Matt said with a grin.

"That means she's stacked," Mike answered.

Tom blushed and put his hands up to his chest. "Big," he said.

"Oh, I get it," Matt said, and he blushed too.

"You'll be getting a lot of things this year," Mike said. "Got a girl-friend yet?"

Bonnie's face flashed in Matt's head. He wasn't ready to talk about that. "No, not yet. I've got Mr. North first period. What's he like?"

"Mr. North?" Tom said. "He's a one-of-a-kind, pretty much always serious. Some say he teeters on being mean. Don't get on his bad side. I had him. He's one of the best teachers though, right, Mike?"

Mike puckered up his face, stuck out his teeth and dropped them outside his lower lip, squinted his eyes and scrunched up his nose and said in his best Charlie Chan voice, "Teacher very hard, do not like sleepy student, wake him up with yell. Sometimes mean, but can be funny. Like title of Coaster song …'Yakety Yak.'"

Matt heard motorcycles in the distance and a chill went up his spine and down his legs. "You guys know any hoods?"

"Why do you want to know?" Mike asked. "Don't tell me they're your heroes."

"No way. Justin MacDonald's brother has a problem with one of them and Justin asked me to watch out for his brother until he gets back to town in a few weeks."

"Which one?" Mike asked.

Matt hesitated. "Wayne Tyson."

"Oh God—you stay away from me," Mike said. "I don't want that guy to even know my name."

Two motorcyclists roared up behind them and Tom turned around. "Those guys can answer your questions about hoods. Now's your chance—looks like we're going to have to stop here and wait for a red light."

Matt glanced over—no jackets or black boots—no one scary, just Buzz and Harry, classmates of Tom and Mike. He knew them already.

Both wore Levi's, white T-shirts and desert boots. They leaned on the handlebars of their Triumph Tiger Cubs, one painted gray, the other red, pulled over and stopped beside them at the light, goosing their throttles and revving their engines.

"So, what's going on? Helping the new 'tagalong'?" Buzz said.

Harry smiled. "Yeah, what are you 'footsters' up to? Babysitting the little one?"

Tom draped his hand over Matt's shoulder and patted it. "Yeah, we've been giving the neophyte a lesson in where he stands in the food chain."

Harry flicked his wrist on the throttle. His tight-fitting T-shirt with the sleeves rolled up emphasized his muscular body.

Mike stepped off the curb and tapped Harry's flexed bicep. His voice was almost drowned out by the loud mufflers. "Another summer in the gym pushing on barbells? When you're not riding, I bet you're walking with those pumped-up arms along the water's edge at the beach, smiling at the girls."

Harry lowered his head and blushed. He ran his fingers through his wavy blond hair and tapped one desert boot on the asphalt. "Come on, man. Stay cool."

The group waited for the light to change. "Where's Tippy?" Tom asked.

"Should be right behind us," Buzz said.

A Cushman Eagle with the fenders removed pulled up beside them. It looked like a seat on top of an engine with two wheels. Tippy gunned his engine twice, letting it backfire down to idle. He acknowledged the walkers with a nod of his head, revved the engine one more time and then said to Buzz and Harry, "Going up to Five Points to pick up a part from Tyson. Meet you at the lot."

When the light turned green, he popped the clutch and left a little rubber as he took off. They all laughed as the Cushman turned the corner and began weaving through the white lines in the center of Greenwood Avenue. He rode down the street with his madras shirt blowing up behind him, showing his tanned back.

Buzz and Harry signaled goodbye with an index finger held up from the handlebar and let their shoes skid along the asphalt as they also turned onto Greenwood Avenue, and gunned their engines. Their taillights came on quickly and they turned into the side street by the school.

Matt let his ears soak up the sound. He was ready for the fast cars, loud bikes and girls in junior high. He looked down at Five Points, the rendezvous where he knew the hoods gathered before the first bell. "Are Tippy and Wayne friends?" he asked Tom.

"I don't know, but when it comes to fixing cars and motorcycles, I've heard Wayne Tyson knows his stuff. Tippy is homogenous. He fits in with everybody. Yep, he's one cool dude. Let's get going. Time to get on the school grounds where ninth graders rule and seventh graders watch." He grinned and slapped Matt on the back.

A block away, the red brick two-story buildings of CJHS towered above the live oak trees that bordered the school on two sides. The tall oak trees with mottled gray trunks obscured the second-story windows and gave an antebellum graciousness to the school.

Matt thought about what he'd just witnessed: Tippy, a friendly, good-looking, good-natured guy just left them and headed to meet Wayne, the hood who threatened Billy. Wayne had brought Tippy something. Tippy went to pick it up. They planned on meeting—no big deal, no challenge—just a big lazy yawn thing. Matt couldn't grasp it. He was on his way to school, fearful of what might happen, and this cool guy, Tippy, headed off to Five Points to hang around with the cause of Matt's mounting tension.

Matt squinted and through the slits of his eyes he could see a red, white and blue barber pole and a group of about twenty kids on the sidewalk down the street at Five Points. A small white cloud of cigarette smoke hung in the air above them. He couldn't see faces but he imagined Wayne somewhere in the group.

Tippy sat on his Cushman next to the curb beside the hoods, his feet on the ground and his arms casually folded in front of him. A kid in a black jacket walked out of the wad of smokers and handed something to him and they stood there talking. The kid must be Wayne.

Matt watched them talk. It was a cool way to have a conversation. He knew Tippy didn't belong to the group, but there he was, sitting there so cool. The motorcycle, that's what made it right. Matt started to feel better. Maybe Wayne Tyson wasn't all bad.

"Hey, Mike? You ever walked down there before school?" he asked, pointing in the direction of the kids standing at Five Points.

Mike looked at Matt, then at Tom. The unspoken exchange between the ninth graders prepared Matt for the answer, and at that moment, he felt like a twelve-year-old. He braced himself for Mike's response.

"First you ask about Mr. North and now you ask about the hoods. What's it to you?" Mike said.

"Nothing. Just curious, I guess ..." Matt's voice tapered off at the end. He shouldn't have asked the question.

Mike smiled at Matt and his attitude seemed to change. "Most of those hoods are okay guys, I guess, but nothing down there for me.

They're not much into school. You'll see soon enough. There'll be guys in your class that will start hanging out there."

"Like who?" Matt said.

"Your buddy, John, pops into my mind. Clark Furlong's another."

"John?" Matt answered. "He likes to get grease around his finger-nails, and his attitude about school might be like the guys down there, but I don't think so. He'll be like Tippy. Who else? Me? I like motor-cycles. Clark? John says he's cool, he just likes wearing the clothes."

Mike hit Matt on the arm and laughed. "Oh for sure. Your white tennis shoes gave it away. Why, you'll have them exchanging their black boots for what you're wearing in a week. The dapper hood we'll call you."

"How about Jimmy Knox? Know him?" Matt asked.

"Is he a freckle-faced, red-haired kid?" Mike said. "He has poten-tial. Listen, it could be anyone. Unlike rebels without a cause like James Dean, I see them as rebels without a brain. That's who you find down there—no Einsteins down there."

"But maybe some diamonds in the rough," Matt said.

"What does that mean?"

"Oh, it's something my dad said. A diamond doesn't start off as a diamond. It's just a piece of coal, but given time and the right condi-tions, it becomes something very special."

Mike shook his head. "Well, I'd be hard-pressed to see a diamond come out of that group."

"My dad would say, 'Give it time.'"

Mike puckered up his face, squinted his eyes, stuck out his front teeth and resumed his Charlie Chan voice. "Maybe Dad right, but all clues now point to ... too much time needed. Only diamond Charlie see ... Joe Louis, fighter-in-the-rough, no Einstein-in-the-rough. Charlie say, put up your dukes."

"Now, that's the truth," Tom said. "Believe me ... a fight will come out of that group down there before the first week is up at school. Someone will leave the fray with a black eye or a bloody nose, and Mr. Luther, the assistant principal, will be giving someone three licks on the butt with the paddle."

"Does the assistant principal always give the spankings?" Matt asked.

"Usually. I saw Mr. Luther swing a bat one time during Phys Ed class, and you could tell he played baseball in college. They say he swings the paddle like he swings the bat for a home run. Some guys say it hurts as much as the black eye."

"Has Wayne Tyson ever gotten any licks?" Matt asked.

"Are you kidding me?" Mike said. "All the time. Not just for fighting either. Bad language ... talking back to teachers ... those can get you a lick or two. Wayne's had his share. When someone gets the paddle, the whole school knows about it. A story went around school last year that when Mr. Luther broke his paddle on Tyson's ass, the hood's expression never changed."

"Before Mike and I leave you, Matt," Tom said, "I want to tell you my thoughts about the group that has taken over our conversation the last five minutes. My aunt defends most of her arguments using the rationale of the "bell-shaped curve," and I want to use her philosophy here. You spoke of your dad and his teaching of finding the diamond in the rough. I want to connect that with the bell-shaped curve."

Tom cleared his throat. "The curve is a way of segregating groups. There's a top thirty percent, a lower thirty percent and a middle forty percent, and I'm sure you could take these three percentages and make new curves within them. That's not my point. The point is that in many different situations, we all fall somewhere on that bell-shaped curve."

"Math is not my strong subject," Mike said with a chuckle. "Keep the arithmetic simple."

"Okay," Tom said. "Just stay with me. Let's first look at the bell-shaped curve of IQ. On the very top of the curve lies the genius, and on the very bottom lies the imbecile and the moron. I believe this grouping is God's gift. It's our gray matter. It's our mental potential."

"Oh great. I have a feeling I know where I stand on that curve," Mike said. "Not with you and Einstein in the top thirty, my friend Tom. But at least I'm not with the dodos."

Tom just smiled. "Okay. Now let's talk about the bell-shaped curve of athletics, another of God's gifts. On the top is the professional athlete or the gold medal winner. At the bottom is the uncoordinated or physically handicapped person. It's our body, our physical potential. But the gold medal winner needs the desire and motivation to work hard and develop his gifts to achieve that gold medal."

"Yeah, like Willie Mays or Ty Cobb, right?" Matt said.

"Right, Matt. And now we come to the bell-shaped curve of life, which is a blend of all the innate human qualities and the desire and motivation that we incorporate into ourselves and use as we move through our lifetime. An oversimplified concept, but add to each of us descriptive words such as overachiever, underachiever, lazy, active—they all play a part in where we end up, and the conclusion is that we all have an influence on where we are on that curve."

Mike held up his hand for Tom to stop. "Whoa, Tom. This is getting a little heavy. Hurry it up. We've got things to do before school starts."

Tom looked at his watch. "Okay. So, Matt ... for all of us, including the group there on the corner, sometime in the future, we'll look back on our lives and either pat ourselves on the back, or wish, after it's too late, that we took another course. And if we're really honest with ourselves, our opportunities are starting now as teenagers, and we can see 'early on' where we are in life."

He looked down the street. "I know some of those boys down there don't share the need I feel right now for making good grades, and that's okay. The curve has a place for them. The most important point to understand about the curve is that there is no good luck or bad luck. We make our own luck. Remember, the guys on the corner are just kids like us and will hopefully end up somewhere on the curve of life in a place that brings them happiness."

Tom stopped across the street from the school building. "Okay, Matt, here we are. Welcome to Clearwater Junior High School ... a lot bigger than South Ward, but you'll learn your way around fast enough. I'll be going home right after school. We can walk home together, if you want."

"Thanks, Tom."

"How about you, Mike?" Tom said. "Want to walk home with us and hear all about the seventh grader's first day at school?"

"Maybe," Mike answered. "But I'm going to talk to Darlene before she gets on her bus."

"Okay. I'll be outside on the front steps by 3:15. Basketball practice starts tomorrow, so after today I'll be staying late. See you."

Matt grinned. "I know. I go to the other building. See you all later."

Chapter 35

SAM SCOTT

"HEY, MATT ... OVER HERE."

Matt looked around the crowded courtyard and saw John and Bob. Bob looked small. Even John looked small. Maybe he'd already seen too many ninth graders that morning.

Matt looked at Bob's shirt. "What's with the wrinkled shirt?"

"Hey, this shirt's clean. My house is always a little hectic before school, but today, the first day of school—it was crazy."

Matt knew the smile was sincere. Bob wasn't embarrassed. Criticism didn't affect him, especially the personal type. He brushed it off and moved on. Matt hoped that "Bob trait" would rub off on him someday.

A smile grew on Bob's face. "Tomorrow I'll wear an ironed one in honor of you and John."

"Guess John already made a comment," Matt said.

"Only after I said something about his weird shoes."

Matt looked down and tapped John's black shoes with his white tennis shoes. He'd seen pictures of them in a catalog. "Cool shoes, John. I like the snap closing instead of shoelaces."

"John's a fad setter," Bob said. "He's the style man."

"They're weird, but I think they're neat," Matt said. "Seriously, I tried to get my mom to let me have a pair."

"You're lying," Bob said. "I couldn't stand it if you both wore

Pinocchio shoes. John, they're more than weird. They're comical. Matt's mom has good taste."

John looked down at Matt's shoes. "What's with the clean white tennis shoes? Scuff 'em up now. Right Bob?"

"Yeah, and then take them home and pour Clorox over them."

Matt laughed and said, "Wrinkled shirts, weird shoes, clean tennis shoes … whatever. We stand here, almost teenagers, on the grounds of Clearwater Junior High, three cool cats."

John put his arms around their shoulders. "I don't know how cool we look, but we're cats ready to play in our new sandbox." He tightened his grip and his face turned crimson.

"Oooh," Matt said, crinkling up his nose.

"What?" John said.

"You know what," Bob said. "You farted."

John covered his mouth with his hand and laughed. "S.S.B.A.D."

"Oh, John," Matt said in disgust. "That stinks."

"Goat perfume," John said with a laugh. "Sometimes Silent, But Always Deadly."

The sound of motorcycles blasted and popped and echoed from the school's brick walls, shattering the tranquility of the side street that ran along the north side of the school as their riders converged on the street for a grand finale.

Matt and John looked at each other and smiled. John clapped his hands together. "Here they come. Hurry … let's go watch them park their bikes."

He ran ahead of Matt and Bob and stopped at the curb beside the basketball courts. The parade began. The rider on the first bike, a Harley 165—called a "Hummer"—goosed the throttle, lifted the front wheel off the pavement, let it drop and sped down the street. Next came Buzz and Harry on their Triumph Tiger Cubs, with Tippy close behind and catching up quickly. Tippy revved his "un-mufflerized" Cushman before braking and joining them.

In the next wave—a hundred yards behind—a group of larger bikes approached with a low, rumbling sound that shook the air. The riders downshifted their gears while their right hands continually goosed the throttle. The noise intensified.

Matt and Bob caught up with John. Matt tapped him on the shoulder to get his attention. Normal conversation was impossible. John turned his head. "Those big bikes—how old do you have to be to drive them?" Matt shouted.

"Probably sixteen," John yelled, as more loud engines passed by them. "Is this cool or what? Let's just stand here all day and watch them."

"Hey, those guys go to school too," Matt yelled back.

The riders parked their motorcycles and began walking in their direction as a red, 700 cc Indian Trailblazer with straight pipes turned onto the street. The big motorcycle slowed down and wove back and forth down the road and stopped. The rider pushed his bike backward into a parking spot, turned off the key and climbed off as if he were in a saddle. Most of the riders wore black leather jackets but he was wearing a denim jacket that matched his Levi's jeans.

"That guy looks like one of the precision Shriner motorcyclists twisting like a snake along the street in the Gasparilla parade on their big, beautiful Harleys," Matt said.

"Yep, only thing missing is a felt hat and a bright yellow jacket," Bob said.

"He looks familiar. I think I know him from somewhere," Matt thought.

"Boy, I'd love to park one of those bikes at my house," John said.

"Even Tippy's?" Bob asked.

"Heck yes," John said, looking like he'd just opened his main Christmas present. "Tippy's bike is the coolest. No fenders. That's my kind of bike—I *am* the coolest, you know. Sincerely, I am."

Bob laughed. "I see you on a moped like that tall, skinny guy with glasses that rode up a minute ago. Did you see him—a big kid on a girl's bicycle with a sewing machine engine? Yeah, there you go, John. You can tool up here on a moped."

Matt noticed four riders walking their way. Could that be some of Wayne's buddies? "Anyone seen Billy this morning?"

"You worried about him already?" Bob asked. "I could tell your mind was somewhere else."

John followed Matt's eyes. "Look at the guy in the front of that group. I can see his beard from here and he just shaved this morning.

My, my … I shave fuzz with a butter knife, just to learn how to do it. Matt, if those are Wayne's friends, I'm telling you, we're S.O.L. God, we're little tykes. We're in a different league. If something happens today, we'd better sweet-talk him. How did we get into this? Don't ask me to mess with any of those guys."

Two members of the group broke off and headed to the area between the two buildings. The other two walked past the boys and seemed not to notice them.

John pointed to the driver of the big Indian motorcycle. "Don't ask me to mess with that guy with the long blond hair, either. He must be over six feet tall."

The tall, muscular blond in the denim jacket was walking directly toward them. He pulled a comb from his back pocket and pulled it through his hair, gently patted it down with his other hand, returned the comb to his pocket and kept walking toward them.

Matt stared at him. He could be sixteen or seventeen. He was only thirty feet away and his Scandinavian blue eyes were looking straight at Matt.

"Matt," John whispered. "Quit staring."

"Why? It's a free country."

"He might not like seventh graders who stare at him," John said, his mouth barely moving.

The tall blond walked faster. Now was the time to run. They froze.

"Shit," John said under his breath. "We're doomed. Get ready. Oh … it's going to be bad. It's ready to turn ugly. But maybe the cavalry is coming," he added, nodding his head toward Tippy, Buzz and Harry who were walking their way.

The tall stranger stepped into their invisible circle and looked down at Matt. He towered over him. "Matt Parker?"

Matt stood looking up at him, trying to remember where he'd seen him before. "Yes. I'm Matt." He looked into the blue eyes and a wave of relief shot through his body like fresh, cool air. It was one of Justin's friends. The name came to him. "Sam Scott?"

Sam smiled and extended his hand. "Yes, I'm Sam Scott. Justin called me last night and I told him if I saw you today, I'd introduce myself to you."

Matt grasped Sam's hand with a strong, firm handshake. Tippy, Buzz and Harry walked by them and waved. "See you in homeroom, Sam," Tippy said.

Sam waved and looked back at Matt, folding his arms across his chest. "Just want you to know, I'll keep my ears open and if I hear anything you need to know, I'll find you. That's the best I can do here at school." He chuckled. "That's all I need—to get in trouble here."

Matt crossed his arms. "Thanks, Sam. Don't know what Wayne's up to, but I'm going to look out for Billy, and Bob and John here are going to help me."

Sam shook hands with Bob and John. "I'm glad Billy has friends like you. But I do have something to tell you youngsters. The grapevine says you boys entered school today already carrying baggage: dirty laundry, so to say. My advice is to lay low. I'll see you boys later."

John watched Sam move toward the upper-class building. He wiped his forehead. "Oh my God, was it only me who thought we were going to get our butts kicked? What the hell is a guy like that doing in junior high?"

"Maybe he missed a year of school when he had diphtheria, maybe he had his tonsils out. I don't know … but I do know if you don't change your language, it's not going to be fighting that gets you your first lick. It's going to be your cussing," Bob said.

"For saying 'hell'?"

"You said 'shit' too."

"I'd call a six-foot-two giant barreling toward us as justified 'shit in the pants' panic."

"Well, you're wrong. And as your buddy, I am giving you a warning. You can go to the office for that kind of talk. Better tone it down."

"Do you believe that guy?" John said. "Sam Scott—he looks twice my size and was heading straight for us. The words just came out my mouth."

"Not everyone talks like a construction worker," Matt said. "Miss Trott taught us last year that cussing is an excuse for not having a better vocabulary."

John started to laugh. "Poop wasn't forceful enough."

Bob looked at Matt. "Why does he always have to have the last word?"

"Because he's Big John. Let's find Billy. The buses should be lining up."

"I walked over here this morning after Bill dropped me off on the other side," John said. "You can go through a narrow brick area between the two buildings to get to the buses. One end smells sweet … the other end stinks. It should be called the 'Narrows of Many Smells.'"

Chapter 36

WAYNE AND HIS BUDDIES

BRUCE TANNER AND RICKY BOXER stepped between two stopped buses and crossed the street on the south side of the junior high to join Wayne, Cracker Jack and Skeeter. Bruce was Wayne's cousin. Ricky and Wayne had been friends since elementary school, and even though they argued often, Ricky kept Wayne out of serious trouble.

"Morning, Wayne," Ricky said. "You sure you want to do this? The word I'm getting from everyone is that the little twerp is already scared to death."

"Yeah, Wayne. You've accomplished what you wanted," Bruce said. "You've put the fear of bodily harm foremost in little brother's pea-brained skull and you've got Justin all in a tizzy up there in Indiana. Leave the pissant alone."

"No way. This is just a prank, but I also want it to be a warning that something else might happen. The plan remains."

Wayne stood up straight and placed the palm of his hand on one side of the post he'd been leaning against. He pushed. The pole did not move. "This will be perfect."

"What about his friends? They're too little to fight, right?" Cracker Jack asked.

"There won't be any fight," Wayne said. "I just want to see the little guy shake, and when Justin hears about it, I want him to think about what might happen later to his little brother. Plus, I don't want 'little brother' to feel safe. First we're going to make a fool of him and then I want to keep him worried … maybe forever."

Wayne played with the hook screwed into the post about five feet above the ground, curling a finger up and around it. He pulled. Nothing moved. "During school, this post holds the chain that closes the street to traffic. It's good and strong."

"What about the other three?" Skeeter asked. "They'll be with him."

"I told you already. That's how you and Bruce are going to help."

Bruce watched him. "Boy, you are riled up. What's going on? Is it Justin? Is Billy your answer? You're too tough to mess with that little kid. I think you should leave them alone."

"I think you should shut up," Wayne said. "If you don't like it, get your yellow ass out of here."

"Screw you, Wayne," Bruce said. He turned and headed back across the street and shot him a bird as he walked away. "You're making a mistake," he said loud and clear without turning his head.

"Fuck you," Wayne said. He flipped his hand in Bruce's direction. "You're a pitiful piece of shit."

Bruce stopped in the middle of the street and turned. "What did you call me?"

"You heard me."

Bruce turned and walked away, shaking his head.

"Quit arguing," Skeeter said. "I agree with you. Have some fun with the little one. The plan is cool. Nobody gets hurt. Why not?"

"Yeah," Cracker Jack said. "Good way to start the school year."

"I've got to get going," Ricky said. "Bruce will chill out. He's just staying cool. Dig? He made some sense."

Wayne spit on the ground. "Don't say another word using that asshole's name. Hear me? Maybe you should stick your brown nose up his ass and let him pull you along. You dig?"

Ricky walked past Skeeter and rolled his eyes at him as he headed to the Phys Ed locker room. "Going to class. See you guys later."

Chapter 37

DEE AND BONNIE

BESIDE THE STONE STEPS of the seventh grade building, a group of girls waited for the bell to ring, laughing and giggling. The girls' voices and a waving hand caught Matt's attention, but a waist-length ponytail that blew in the light breeze and reflected the sun's rays made him stare. The hand that waved belonged to Dee. The ponytail belonged to Bonnie.

Matt turned back to John, Bob, Billy and JB. "Hey, guys," he said. "Dee waved at me to come over there. I'm going to go see what she wants and I'll be right back."

Dee was his friend. He hoped Bonnie would be more than that. Excitement overwhelmed him. He walked toward the ponytail. As he neared it, his heart raced—*Slow down. Protect yourself. What about Jack Whiting?*

Dee waved at him and smiled. "Hi, Matt."

Bonnie turned her head and looked straight into his eyes. She looked surprised to see him. Matt saw an excitement in her expression that made any doubts he had on the dock disappear. Her eyes sparkled. "Hi, Matt."

He stared at her, but no words came out of his mouth. Her hair, held in a ponytail by a red ribbon, fell over a white blouse and reached down to a red, white and light green plaid skirt. A light green scarf tied around her neck matched the skirt, and black-and-white saddle shoes with white bobby socks completed her outfit. She looked beautiful. He felt awkward. He should have stayed with the boys.

"Hi, Dee. Hi, Bonnie. Ready for our first day of junior high?"

"It's going to be great," Dee said with a big smile on her face. "I've got to go right now. See you later."

Bonnie turned all the way around with her back to the other girls and smiled at him. "It was fun going fishing yesterday. How's your leg feeling?"

Matt smiled. She took away his fear. She broke the ice. She did it on purpose. "Hey, real good," he answered. "I'm top-notch. Can you believe summer vacation is over?" *No worries—your turn to sweat, Jack.*

"No, but I think I'm glad. How's Billy today? Is he okay? I know you're getting him through this."

"Not sure. Today he's acting like he can face anything, but Wayne isn't a very nice person. I think he enjoys preying on the most vulnerable."

"Why do you think he acts like that?"

"I don't know. I heard he was okay a long time ago, but when he got in sixth grade he started to change."

"I think that's when his father died. I know his sister, Nina. She's a nice girl and their mother is a very sweet lady."

"Losing your father is tragic, but that's no excuse for how he treats people. He needs to see the light and I'm going to help him see it, especially if he messes with Billy."

Bonnie wiped her eye.

"Did I say something wrong?"

"No, you said something right. I'm glad Billy has you to see him through this. Let me help too."

Matt wanted to touch her hand, but he just looked at her face. He liked her honesty. He wanted to know her better. "Can I walk you to class this morning?"

"Thanks, but you have more pressing concerns with Billy right now. How about another time?"

He hoped her answer wasn't an excuse. "Maybe I'll see you at the end of the day."

"Maybe so."

Matt's insecurity returned. Was she waffling? He turned and headed back to the boys. Under other circumstances, he would be whistling, but today was not the time.

The first bell rang.

He glanced back at Bonnie. She was gone.

"Matt, let's go. The rest of the guys have already gone. You're walking in the wrong direction," John said.

The two boys walked up the steps and through the south door of the seventh grade building into a hoard of screaming and laughing students.

The doors of the metal lockers that lined the walls between the classroom doors banged, and the sound of hundreds of shoes hitting the wood floor in the crowded corridor blended into one loud rumble that echoed off the hollow walls and ceiling.

"Geez," Matt said to John. "This is crazy. Are we in a dungeon? I think I might get sick. This is worse than deep down in an ocean liner. I need fresh air."

The stale air in the long hallway reeked of floor wax, and evenly spaced hanging light fixtures with domes of frosted glass hung from the high ceiling, casting a dim yellow light on the polished, dark brown oak floors.

"I know," John said, and he pinched his nose closed. "It stinks like dirty wet socks, the noise might break your eardrum and it's so dark, you need bat radar to find your locker."

"Give it a day, boys," a man's deep voice said. "The excitement will fade and so will the noise. Fresh air will quickly replace this locked up zestless smell and your new school will smell like a rose garden."

They turned to see a custodian leaning against his mop in an open classroom doorway close to where they'd stopped.

John laughed. "When you're not a custodian, do you sell cars at Dimmitt Chevrolet?"

"I wish. Only kidding. I was here when your dads roamed these halls. Been here thirty-five years. So, take it easy. After a week, the air turns sweet, the chatter turns to music and by ten o'clock the sun bursts through the live oaks, shoots through these doors and windows and lightens up this hall. Trust me. All you'll smell is the sweet aroma of baking bread and rolls."

Matt found his locker and threw his gym bag in it. He wanted to get to his homeroom class and get out of the confusion. He smacked John on the back. "I hope that man is right. Off to homeroom and then my first class with Mr. North—see you later, alligator. It all starts now."

Chapter 38

MR. NORTH

MR. NORTH STOOD IN FRONT of his desk studying a piece of paper. The smooth skin on his face made him look young, but his curly black hair, thinning on top with a few white speckles, suggested he might be older than he looked. He wore a short-sleeve plaid cotton shirt and navy blue pants with cuffs that touched the floor at his heel.

He glanced out at the room as it began to fill and then looked back at the paper and folded it. "Take any available seat, please," he said in a deep, quiet voice. "There are still some here up front."

Matt and Bob stood in the hallway by the door and listened. "Are you ready for this?" Bob whispered.

Matt nodded his head. "He looks pleasant—dresses out of the early fifties—I think the hour should be interesting. But be careful. The word is 'stay inconspicuous.'"

The two boys walked through the door and looked for a seat. The last two rows were filled. The first two rows were empty. Bob sat in the first row.

"First mistake, Bob," Matt thought. He spotted an open desk in one of the middle rows, right behind a girl he knew well from South Ward.

Lucy sat looking forward with her back straight and her chin up, and no movement except in her eyes. They followed Matt as he walked by her, and she rolled them once and then closed them when he was beside her.

He sat down behind her and looked at her long, sandy blond ponytail. Normally, he would have grabbed it and given it a little tug, but he only looked at her and remembered past days in sixth grade at South Ward.

The room remained quiet. The only sound came from a rotating fan in the front corner of the room. When the fan's transit passed over the edge of the teacher's desk, the papers held down by an ornamental rock fluttered.

Bob sat in front of the fan. Matt had a premonition as the fan lifted Bob's hair. *You're in trouble, buddy. Sorry.* Then he noticed Lucy's elbow moving. He cocked his head just enough to confirm what she was doing. A pencil was in her hand and she was writing fast. It was a note. It was headed for him. If Mr. North saw the transfer, it would not be a good way to start the class. She put down the pencil and folded the paper once on itself and then again.

The second bell rang and broke the silence.

Mr. North leaned against the front corner edge of his desk, folded his arms and crossed one leg in a casual stance. He didn't smile. He remained still and looked at his class.

Voices in the hallway interrupted the silence.

Mr. North unfolded his arms, put his hands on the desk and pushed himself up to a standing position. He walked deliberately and slowly to the door.

Lucy quickly turned and tossed her note on top of Matt's desk. He covered it with his hand. Mr. North stopped at the doorway and looked down the hall.

Matt took a chance. He unfolded the note. It read, "This is the way we start Junior High? Please tell me it's a dream. Save us, Matt. I need Oz."

Matt folded the note and slipped it into his folder. Mr. North's back was still facing them. Matt leaned up to Lucy's ear and said, "I think he's cool—no worries."

Mr. North closed the door, returned to his desk and resumed his previous stance. He still said nothing.

Matt looked at the teacher. *He's married and has children—two, maybe. He must be nice. He's a teacher, a real teacher. Let's get on with this class. Need to get my mind off Wayne Tyson.*

Another minute passed. Time seemed to stop. The induced tension filled the room like late night fog above gravestones, ready for ghosts to explode out of the crypts.

Pants with one pleat—a little baggy—lace-up shoes and argyle socks. Matt liked him.

Still silence. Mr. North's eyes scanned the students in the class.

Another long two minutes passed. Finally, after three or four minutes, the teacher's low resonating baritone voice broke the silence. "Good morning."

Silence.

"I said, 'Good morning.'"

"Good morning," the class murmured.

"My name is Mr. North, and if your first class is not history, then you are in the wrong room."

In the back of the room, a voice very softly asked, "This is not English?"

"No, young lady. I bet you need to be in the room across the hall."

A cute, dark-haired girl stood up.

Bob leaned over to the boy sitting beside him and whispered, "I'm happy Judy found her way to school."

The whisper sounded like it came through a megaphone. Judy was a pretty girl, a good tennis player and a good sport. She could take the ribbing and, when she needed to, give it back.

She walked by Bob and lightly pinched him on the arm. "I heard that." Her face blushed. She walked to the door, stopped, turned around and looked at Bob. "Don't forget you have 'home ec' with me next period, Bob."

The whole room laughed. Even Mr. North had a smile on his face.

The boy beside Bob whispered, "I guess Judy got the last laugh."

Bob's cheeks turned red. "She usually does," he said.

Mr. North walked away from his desk, carrying a slender piece of dark wood about three feet long and an inch in diameter with carving around it. It looked like the stem of an old tribal peace pipe.

He walked slowly up the middle aisle, swinging the stick back and forth, and made eye contact with each student he walked past. He said nothing. When he got to the back of the room on one aisle, he turned around, smacked the stick into his open palm and walked back up the second aisle.

He turned around at the front of the room and looked at the class. "Welcome to junior high school and welcome to history. I've heard by the grapevine that I am said to be strict. I don't think that's true. I only have a few rules, and I expect them to be followed. When they're not followed, there are consequences.

"My first rule is to always bring your textbook and homework assignment to class. You are here to learn history, so come prepared. Poor preparation will be reflected in your grade. Also reflected in your grade will be your conduct in my class. I have never had to send anyone to the principal's office. Any issues are handled in this room."

"My rule of conduct is quite simple: Show courtesy and respect for me and your fellow classmates. When I feel you're out of order here, I will ask you to spend special time with me here after school to get a special lesson in history. Am I understood?"

Silence.

"I said, 'Am I understood?'" he asked in a louder voice.

"Yes, sir," the class responded in unison.

"Very good."

He walked toward Bob, holding the stick in his right hand and slowly slapping it into the open palm of his left hand. He stopped short of Bob, pointed the stick at him and said, "So young man, if the young lady is correct, you must be the first boy to take home ec at this school."

"No, sir."

The room was silent. No one knew if they should laugh or not.

"How's that?" Mr. North continued. "I could have sworn I heard her say she would see you next period in home ec."

Bob blushed. "She was just kidding."

"Oh," Mr. North answered. "And what is your name?"

"Bob Walton, sir."

"I see. Do you like history, Mr. Walton?"

"Some."

Mr. North swung his stick back and forth with one hand like a baseball player in the batter circle. "Good. Can I ask you a history question, Mr. Walton?"

"I guess," Bob said.

"Do you know about the Civil War?"

"Yes, sir."

"In what year did it end?"

"I believe in 1865."

"1865. Are you sure?"

"Yes, sir."

"Are you really sure?"

"I think so."

"Are you really, really sure?"

Bob looked around the room. "Kind of ..."

Then in his lowest baritone voice, Mr. North said slowly, "Are you ... *dead* sure?"

"No sir."

The whole class laughed.

That's why you want to remain inconspicuous in this class, Matt told himself.

Mr. North looked at the class. "If you learn history in my class, I want you to learn with conviction. History shows us the way into the future. I want you all to learn it well. The Civil War did end in 1865. The American Revolution was a colonial revolt that started in 1765, one hundred years before that, and ended in 1783. Now open your books to page ten and let's get started learning about the history of our country."

The bell rang and Bob and Matt walked into the hall. "What a beginning for junior high," Matt said. "I have a question. Why in the world did you sit in the front row? Tell me, please, it was the fan."

"Yeah, it was the fan. Big mistake. I wish we had the other history teacher."

"I think Mr. North is going to be hard, but I kind of liked him. We'll be okay. Just always remember to come here prepared. Where do you go now?"

"English and then science."

Matt looked at his schedule card. "I have English with Miss Vernotzy right here, and look who's coming out the door. 'Hi, Judy.'"

"Hi, Matt. You're lucky if you're going into this classroom. She's fun."

"Hi, Judy," Bob said. "You got me good in Mr. North's class. Sorry, I didn't mean to embarrass you."

Judy smiled. "You did, a little, but that's all right, Bob. I'm just glad I'm not in that class. I have Miss V for English, and what a wonderful way to start the day."

"Okay. Just wanted to apologize. See you later. See you at lunch, Matt."

Chapter 39

SLOPPY JOES ON A TRAY

SOUNDS OF LAUGHTER and loud voices emerged from the open door of the junior high cafeteria. Students waited in line to have their trays filled by the cafeteria ladies. The room bustled. Pots and pans banged in the kitchen. Ceiling fans whirred on high speed. Chair legs grated on the wooden floor. Laughter and conversations created a pleasant hum.

Matt picked up his filled tray and walked over to Bob, who sat at a table close to a window. "This looks like a great spot for our first junior high lunch."

"Where's Billy?"

"He and John were behind me in line. We need to save a seat for them and one for JB."

"Okay," Bob said. "This lunch is great. I love sloppy Joes."

John walked up and sat down. "Saving a lot of chairs around you here today. Aren't you the popular one? Who are the rest of the honored guests?"

"JB and Billy."

John checked the saltshaker to be sure no one had loosened the top. He grinned at Matt and pushed it back into the center of the table. "Just helping you out, if you need salt. You can never trust some of these new seventh graders."

"Thanks, but I think I have my eyes on the main culprit."

JB walked up to the table. His pupils were dilated like he was in a dark room. He didn't smile.

Matt picked up his notebook and pushed the chair he'd been saving for JB away from the table. "Here, JB. Saved this for you. Have a seat."

JB set his tray on the table and sat down. "Thanks. Where's Billy?"

John looked over to the serving area. "He is just starting to put food on his tray. He'll be here in a few minutes."

"What I have to tell you is about Wayne," JB said. "Do you want me to wait on Billy or tell you before he gets here?"

"Tell us now," Matt said.

"Okay. In Phys Ed this morning, I overheard Wayne's friend Ricky Boxer telling one of his buddies what a jerk Wayne was and that he didn't approve of what he and some of the other guys have planned for sixth period Phys Ed today."

Matt looked up and saw Billy about to leave the serving area. "Well, that's the bad news, but there is good news."

"I can hardly wait to hear," John said.

"Now that we know, we'll be on the lookout and be ready for them."

John put his head in his hands. "That's good news?"

"Bingo," Matt said. "Come on, John, you love excitement."

"Oh yeah, it's exciting to get my ass kicked."

"More exciting to kick his butt," Matt answered.

Billy put his tray down on the table. He walked over behind John and put his hand on his shoulder and squeezed. "Am I worth it?"

John turned and saw Billy. He laughed. "You caught me. Hell yes, you're worth it. Pull up a chair, Ross Allen."

"Billy, JB just told us he overheard one of Wayne's buddies say that Wayne has something planned for Phys Ed this afternoon," Matt said.

Billy's eyes got glassy for a moment.

"You'll be fine, Billy," JB said. "You'll see. I just wanted to warn you all so you can be on the alert. I'll meet you after school and we'll get on the bus together."

"I don't like the way this is getting started," Bob said. "Do you, Matt?"

"Well, let's not let our minds start running too fast, too soon…"

"Yeah," John interrupted, "you've got two coaches right there the whole period. What could Wayne do?"

"I don't know," Matt said. "How do you get a sucker punch?"

"When you're not looking for it," Bob answered.

"Bingo!" Matt said. "So, we have to stay on our toes."

"You're right," Billy said. "Thanks for letting us know, JB."

"You've got red juice running down your chin, Billy," John said. "Who taught you how to eat?"

"Sorry. At least mine is still wet. Yours looks dry. Is it yolk from breakfast?" Billy asked.

John wiped across his mouth with his hand and looked into his palm. "Did I get it?"

"Yes."

Bob laughed. "Oh boy, did he get you, John. You didn't have anything on your face."

Matt loved it. *Billy's turning out to be pretty cool.*

"Hey, how was Home Ec, Bob?" John said. "Why don't you tell us all about Home Ec class?"

Bob's face flushed. "How did you hear about that?"

"I talked to Judy. She told me and the rest of the class all about you."

"Hey, she's the one that was in the wrong class. That girl—she must be related to Gracie Allen."

John looked at Bob and grinned. "You like her, don't you Bob? You can tell me. You know, maybe you'll see Judy at a party this year. You can slow dance. Maybe they will play Spin the Bottle."

"That's enough, John," Bob said.

Rocky walked up behind John. "Who are you going to play Spin the Bottle with, Mr. Hollis? One of your mom's dress shop mannequins?"

John turned around and looked up with a grin. "So, how come you and Porky left your campsite at Hog Island last weekend and why wasn't John Wolfington or Buzz Coop De-ville with you?"

"Well, Porky had to go home to help his mother," Rocky said. "Wolfington couldn't go because his sister, DeeDee, talked him into babysitting for her, and De-ville was out of town. From what I heard, we missed a lot of excitement. Wish we'd been there."

"Oh sure," John said. "You and Porky are just scaredy-cats."

"And you little twerps are so brave—I bet you soiled your pants when that escaped prisoner came into your camp."

"Okay, enough you two," Matt said.

"It's cool, Matt," Rocky said.

"Okay, Rocky," Matt said. "Sorry you weren't there to share in the fun. The sheriff and his deputies made quick work of rounding him up. Too bad they couldn't hold on to him when they got back to the mainland."

Rocky looked around the noisy room. "Listen, you two, I didn't come over here to talk about Hog Island. Let's go over by the wall. I want to tell you something."

"What's up, Rocky?" Matt asked.

"You guys had better be on the lookout for some trouble. I heard some rumors this morning. Billy needs to be really careful in sixth period Phys Ed class this afternoon."

"Thanks, Rocky," Matt said. "We heard that too. John, Bob and I are in that class with him. We'll be careful."

"Okay. Just want you to be on the lookout. Tyson's a bad dude."

The bell rang. "Thanks, Rocky," John said. "We'll help protect you on Hog Island next time."

Rocky frogged John hard on the arm. "I owed you that."

Matt picked up his food tray. "Let's go guys. We've got to get to our next class. Rocky was just warning us about Wayne in Phys Ed. Nothing we didn't already know."

"Good luck sixth period," JB said. "I hope Coach Smith and Coach Shank will protect you guys. Just watch out in the showers when they're not around."

Chapter 40

AT THE LOCKERS

THE BLUE SKIES, bright sunlight and high temperature created sharp shadows and sweaty brows. It was midafternoon, the end of fourth period.

Matt walked out of his first band class. He wondered if he could be good enough to be a drummer in one of the new teenage rock and roll bands like Doug Zollo, the ninth grade first-chair drummer he'd just met. *I can bang on the skins, but that boy's in a special league.*

Rock and roll music was becoming more popular than the crooners and big bands, and he wanted to be part of it. High school guys like Terry Minor and Ralph Stewart were forming new bands in the area. Maybe they'd become a new Buddy Holly and the Crickets —or a Ritchie Valens.

He had goose bumps when he went to watch Elvis onstage in St. Pete. Elvis tried to sing "Heartbreak Hotel," but the girls screamed so loudly that he finally gave up and just sang while they screamed.

Brad walked up behind him and interrupted his thoughts. "Band was pretty cool today, wasn't it? Heard about the potential problem in Phys Ed. Hope nothing serious happens."

"Thanks, Brad. I think John, Bob and I should be able to handle it."

One more period before Phys Ed. ... He climbed the steps and walked into the building. The long dark hallway provided relief from the sun and he welcomed the change. He removed his biology book

FRED HOSLEY

from his locker and turned the cover toward the dim light right above him to check the title.

Billy walked up behind him. "They need more lights in here."

Just as Billy made the comment, the lights went out. Screams and howls and one long shrill whistle filled the hall.

"I bet someone found the light switch," Matt said.

A minute later, the lights came on and Billy opened his locker. "I bet that person gets in trouble. See you here in an hour?"

"Yes," Matt said. "Have you seen Bob or John? We need to walk over to the gym together."

Bob arrived and stopped in front of his locker, just a few feet away. "Like the hallway with no lights?"

"It's dark enough with lights," Billy said.

"Oooooohhh ..." Bob let out a slow, low scary wail. "I thought maybe, when the lights were out, Wayne might jump out of a locker and attack us."

"Not funny."

"We've got to stay cool and calm," Bob said.

"I'm trying. Meet us here before Phys Ed."

"Okay. See you back here in an hour."

Matt closed his locker door and stared at it. He wanted the next period to be over. He had to be on guard and not get sucked into something that would get him in trouble with the coaches or the principal.

Billy looked at Matt. "Are we in a fix?"

Matt grinned. "No! It's not a fix ... It's a situation. Let's go find out what our biology teacher is like. I heard he's new, young and cool."

Billy walked beside him down the hall without speaking.

"I'll be honest, Billy, right there at the locker, I started thinking about the things that Wayne preys on—a feeling of being powerless. That feeling breeds insecurity. His type thrives on it. I lost my confidence for a minute, but I've got it back ... I'm pretty good at some things, you know." He smiled and winked at Billy.

"I'm glad, Matt. I get nervous when you don't seem strong."

"My dad says we have to fight through our own weaknesses. Weakness is what the Waynes of the world attack, but they lack what it takes to fight someone who is strong."

"Your dad has taught you well," Billy said with a smile.

257

Chapter 41

WHERE'S JOHN?

MATT AND BILLY LEFT biology class and hurried to their lockers in another stampede of students. They found Bob beside his locker with the door open. "Where's John?" Matt said.

Bob shrugged his shoulders and pointed to an open door a few feet past the row of lockers. "His class is right there. He should be here by now."

"Maybe he's still talking to the teacher," Billy said.

Bob pulled out his gym bag and tossed his books on the locker floor where his bag had been. "John talking to a teacher in English? That's not happening. Here he comes."

John walked toward them with a red face and a sheepish look. "Coming, guys."

Matt slung his gym bag over his shoulder. "We have to get going. You know the next period is important. Where have you been?"

"At the office."

"Let me guess. You're the one who turned off the light in the hallway before last period."

John reached in his locker and pulled out his bag. "Yep. Did it on a dare. JB showed me where it was."

Bob laughed. "That was you? Way to go—it's not taking you long to make a name for yourself here."

"What happened?" Matt asked.

"Just a warning, but guess what? I saw the paddle."

"Was there blood on it?" Bob said.

John pulled out his gym bag and snorted. "No, just some ripped-off flesh. And I met the principal. Told him all my ideas came from you guys. He pushed a piece of paper in front of me and told me to write down your names." John smiled and closed his locker. "You're going to like him."

"Bull," Bob said.

"Let's get going," Matt said. "I hear the coaches aren't very happy if you're not there before the second bell."

"Matt, we're okay. No need for your heebie-jeebies," Bob said. "Just cool it."

Outside, Matt looked down the street at four older boys crossing over to the Phys Ed building. One was Wayne. "Don't look now guys, but Wayne and some of his pals are headed where we're headed. Let's stop a minute so we don't get to the door at the same time. Billy, I don't see him taking any big risks in this class. Only thing I can imagine happening is him popping you with a towel in the shower."

"And trying to leave a big red welt on your butt," John said. "We can handle that, right? We're experts at towel fights and we're all in this together."

"I'm just going to tell the truth. I'm scared," Bob said. "Look at Wayne. He looks like a monster dressed in jeans. I'm afraid it's going to be something worse than towel popping. We need to prepare ourselves."

John pushed his finger into his thumb and pinched himself hard. "Ouch," he said, and then laughed out loud. "If we need to get physical to defend Billy, I'm ready. A little physical pain is no problem."

Matt looked over at Wayne again. "Man, he really does think he's cool."

Billy put his hand on his hips, separated his feet and flexed his upper body and arms. "How is this for my 'cool' stance? *I'm not afraid of no chicken hawks,*" he said in a cartoon voice.

John picked up on the routine and used his best Foghorn Leghorn voice. *"Ah … ah … ah say, boy, you gotta let me, ah say you gotta let me take care of the punk over there."*

He put one hand over his mouth, looked at Billy and whispered, *"He's ah … ah say, he's a pesky little fella."*

They all laughed.

The sharp shadows from the September afternoon sun disappeared and darkness spread over them. A large gray cloud directly above them blocked the sun and gave them a short reprieve from the heat.

Matt felt like he was sitting in the front seat of a roller coaster—going up, ready for something to happen. "Man, that shade feels good. It's hot. Let's go get this class over with."

"Too bad we didn't get morning Phys Ed," Bob said.

"That's no panacea, either," Billy said.

John smiled at Billy. "A pan of what? You can use those long words in the main building, but you're in 'jockland' now."

"I want you to learn new words. John. I'm giving you prodigious proportions on purpose."

"Whatever," John said. "So, why isn't morning gym good? I can hardly wait to hear your answer."

"In morning Phys Ed, you run around and then shower. You get back to class, you're still hot, the humidity is high and you sweat again," Billy said. "In the afternoon, you sweat, but you cool off after the shower and the day is almost over. You may go home a little sweaty, but at least you're not sweaty the whole day."

"Do you believe that, Matt?" John asked. "I think Billy's been hanging around those cold-blooded snakes of his too long."

"I'll answer you after this class."

"How about you, Bob?" John said.

"My vote is still morning," Bob said. "All I know right now is—it's hot and in about ten minutes we're going to be in Sam McGee's oven. The next time we have a campout, Matt, we have to get Brad to recite that poem around the fire."

Billy looked up into the sky again. "If it rains, will we still dress out?"

"Yep. We'll still dress out," John said.

"How about lightning?"

"Don't get under a tree."

"I hate lightning."

"I hate snakes."

Uneasiness suddenly overwhelmed Matt. He loved to set box traps, catch wild animals, take them home and after a short stay, release them where he caught them. One time he caught a very young raccoon and asked his dad if he could keep him as a pet. His dad said okay, but sometimes when he least expected, the raccoon would give him a bad bite. Whenever Matt handled the raccoon, he wondered if it was the time he'd get bitten.

He had the same feeling now. Wayne's threat was in a time frame with an end that was eerily open, and like the raccoon, he didn't know when Wayne was going to bite. When would Wayne show his teeth? It looked like it would be in the next hour during Phys Ed.

Chapter 42

COACH SMITH AND COACH SHANK

THE BOYS' PHYS ED building contained a small office for the two coaches, and a large changing room with showers. The girls' building was separated from the boys' building by sparse grass, three large oaks and a lot of gray sand filled with acorns and leaves. Bonnie would be over there with Dee, but he needed to concentrate on Wayne. He'd see her after school.

"Looks like a fire drill with everyone standing around waiting for the all-clear bell. Can this many people be taking Phys Ed at one time?" Bob said.

"Remember, shop and mechanical drawing classes are over here too," Matt said. "Not all these kids are going to Phys Ed."

Coach Smith and Coach Shank stood together talking by the door into the building. Both were tanned and athletic looking, but side by side, they presented a stark contrast. Coach Smith wasn't tall, maybe close to five feet ten inches. Coach Shank was an easy six feet four inches. He seemed rugged but still soft. His unruly blond hair made him look like the handsome Norwegians Matt had seen in pictures in *National Geographic* magazines.

Coach Smith's gray hair and shiny bald spot made him look older. He held a tan baseball cap by his side and smacked it on his leg as he chuckled without smiling at something Coach Shank had said.

The seventh graders, still holding their gym bags, stood outside waiting for instructions from the coaches. John leaned over to Matt and whispered, "My brother says when Coach Smith looks like that, he is really in a great mood."

"What does he say he looks like when he's in a really bad mood?" Matt asked.

"The same. I swear that was the beginning of a smile, but it left him in the blink of an eye."

Coach Smith walked over to the older boys, put his whistle up to his mouth and gave one short burst. "Listen up. My name is Coach Smith," he yelled. He pointed to his partner. "That is Coach Shank. This is gym class. If you are seventh graders, line up, single file, facing forward over there on the far end of the basketball court. You eighth and ninth graders line up right here." He pointed down at his feet. "We will begin roll call."

The older boys started moving around, and Coach Smith reached out and snagged the arm of a boy headed toward the back. "Buzz, you start the line here. Tippy, you fall in behind Buzz. I want you two up front where I can see you."

The seventh graders followed instructions and walked toward the basketball hoop.

"Did you catch the leather strap tied to his whistle that Coach Smith had wrapped around his hand?" John said.

"No," Matt answered, in a low voice just above a whisper, hoping John would get the message that he didn't think this was a good time to be talking.

"See, I knew you didn't. That's because you don't pick up on some of these important points that Bob and I see." John said in a normal voice. Either he didn't catch on that Matt's low voice was sending a message, or he didn't really care.

"Oh?" Matt said quietly. "You think it was important to point out the whistle was connected to a leather strap—a small leather strap, I might add."

"If you were an accomplished towel fighter in the showers, you would know Coach Smith's strap doubles as a whip, which he whacks across the bare bottoms of anyone he catches with a rattail towel, caught in the act of taking a piece of skin off or making a strawberry appear on the butt or leg," John continued.

"You know, I'm an AAU swimmer, so I've spent a lot of time carrying around a rattail towel," Matt said quietly. "But I see a leather strap and I conclude that is how the Coach carries his whistle. You see the strap and conclude that the strap is for making red stripes across white butts and the whistle is just there as a distraction."

John laughed and looked at Bob. "He's starting to understand."

Coach Shank looked right at Matt. "What's all that talk about over there? Form a line, girls. Now."

Matt fell into a momentary gloom. John had talked. He'd tried to let John know it wasn't a good time to be talking, and then he got caught talking. He glared at John.

"After all names are called, go inside and find a locker," Coach Shank said. "Your lockers are on the right side. The left side is for the eighth and ninth graders. Put on your gym clothes and then return to this area. And don't dilly-dally around. Okay, when your name is called, raise your hand and say here ... James Applewhite ..."

"Here ..."

Coach Shank looked to the end of the line where a hand was raised. "You Applewhite?"

"Yes, sir."

James Applewhite, the class clown in elementary school, was well liked by his classmates. He was small in height, but not in circumference. And the way he wore his clothes did not help his appearance. He had on a pair of jeans pulled at least four inches above his belly button, with an oversized madras shirt half tucked in. The belt was pulled too tight and created pleats in the area where he'd missed a loop. From the side, he looked like Humpty Dumpty.

Coach Shank looked at Appie and a smile slowly grew across his face. "Where's your gym bag, Applewhite?"

"At home," Appie said with a smile.

"That's a good place for it. What did you think we were going to do today, play board games?"

Everyone started to laugh.

"No, sir. J.C. Penney's downtown didn't have a pair of shorts that were the right color. Mom's still looking."

"Well, tomorrow have something. If you can't find shorts, just wear a bathing suit. Is there anyone else who is not prepared to dress out today?"

No one raised their hand.

"Okay, Applewhite, when you go in, find a locker and take off your shirt. You're still going to participate. At least you're wearing tennis shoes."

"Yes, sir."

After he'd completed the alphabet with Ralph Young, Coach Shank said, "Anyone whose name I didn't call? Okay, fall out and dress out."

The seventh graders filed into the locker room, picked a bench in the long row on the empty side of the room and started changing into their gym clothes.

Matt, John, Bob, Billy and Appie sat on a bench in the middle of a long row on the empty side of the room. "My brother says the first couple of weeks, stay out of the way of the ninth graders," Bob said. "They think they're cool and we're square ... especially taking showers."

"And Coach Smith takes no roughhousing," John said. "That leather strap. He will smack you right across the butt if you get out of line. Applewhite, you've got the biggest target, so watch your clowning in the shower."

"And the ninth graders will try to take you on," Bob said. "Just remember that."

"Okay boys, let's go," shouted Coach Shank. "Everybody outside now. Let's head across the street. We'll divide up into teams there."

Bob and Matt crossed the street together, walking right behind Billy and John. "Well, at least we aren't going to be around Wayne out here," Bob said.

"You're right. The only time we could be with the ninth graders is when we're showering," Matt said. "That's when we need to stay close to Billy."

At the courts, Coach Shank yelled, "Line up in a straight line."

He walked down the line to the middle and stopped in between John and Matt. "Everyone to my left plays volleyball and everyone to my right plays gator ball. Tomorrow, we'll change. Applewhite, I want you over here in the left line. You will be the volleyball scorer, so you don't get too sweaty."

"Yes, sir."

John slapped his leg and laughed. "Appie sweats just standing. He'd probably sweat inside the Atlantic Icehouse, Coach."

Coach Shank looked directly at him with a serious face that was almost a frown. "Are you Bill Hollis' brother?"

"Yes, sir."

"Well, at the end today when we run a lap around the basketball courts, you can give me two. I want to see *you* sweat for sure. I want no more lip from anyone. Now, let's team up and play."

Chapter 43

TOO LATE

FOUR STRAGGLERS DRESSED in gym shorts stepped under the chain stretched across the end of the street and walked toward the court where the ninth graders played basketball.

"You got it?" Wayne said to Cracker Jack.

"Tucked in my shorts by my underwear—held by the elastic."

"Good. We don't want it falling out early."

"It looks good."

"Real?"

"Like it could bite you."

Wayne smiled. "Listen up. Let's make this quick while Coach Smith's over there with his basketball players. For this to work, we have to separate Billy from the seventh graders. The wooden post looks good. You all just follow our plan. I'm getting that little shit."

"Think he suspects something today?" Bruce said.

A wicked smile spread across Wayne's face. "He knows some time, but not when. I'd like to go a couple of weeks just to make him sweat, but today works best."

"We're going to get some licks for this, you know," Bruce said, rubbing his butt. "The assistant principal gives some good ones."

"I'm not worried about licks. It'll be worth it."

"Only thing I don't understand is—why this little kid?" said Skeeter.

Wayne looked directly into his eyes and pursed his lips tightly. "Listen, it's not like I'm beating him up. I'm saying 'Welcome to junior high. Don't mess with me!' It's personal, okay? Let's just say I don't like the family."

"It's his older brother, isn't it?"

"Yeah, kind of. He's in Indiana and not here to protect his little brother. Let him cry in Indiana when he hears. If he were here, I'd kick his ass and push his nuts past his stomach with my boots."

"Okay, over there," Coach Smith yelled. "You do-nothing group— time to get your butts off the sideline and play some basketball. I know this is the first day, but you guys know what's expected. Tyson, pull your shorts up. You can wear your jeans down below your hips, but not your gym shorts."

The four ninth graders walked onto the court. "Everyone know what to do?" Wayne said.

"Yeah … we're cool," Cracker Jack said with a straight-lipped smile.

"Good. Should be easy to suck Billy in. Follow the plan. No mess-ups and this will be a riot."

Coach Smith gave a sharp whistle blast and the basketball game started again.

On the volleyball court a short distance away, Matt and Bob watched Wayne and his friends talking. "I wish Billy was in our group. John will be running extra laps and Billy will be unprotected," Matt said.

"Matt, if anything's going to happen it will be in the showers, not out here. No need to worry."

Coach Shank looked at them. "What is so important over there?" he said. "You boys get back into your own game."

Thirty minutes later, the two coaches blew their whistles.

Coach Shank pulled the whistle out of his mouth. "Okay boys, give me a lap around the field and head for the showers. Hollis, you give me three—do you hear me?" he yelled. "Two's not enough."

"Yes, sir."

On the other court, Coach Smith yelled, "Game over, one lap around the court and then head for the showers."

After the lap was completed, the groups blended together and headed back to the locker room. They were all hot and sweaty and tired, and most walked slowly, looking down at the ground.

Wayne stopped and tied his tennis shoes so he could walk behind the seventh graders and watch everything unfold. Skeeter walked up to Billy and another boy, and farther back, Bruce was talking to Matt and Bob. John was still running laps. The plan was working.

★

Matt scanned the area—no Wayne. Where's Billy? A hot pang seared his chest. "Bob, I don't see Billy!" he yelled and ran to catch up with him.

"He's up there with Appie in front of us," Bob said.

"I don't see Wayne, either."

"Relax, Matt. He's probably still running laps. Cool your jets."

A ninth grader with slicked back hair edged over beside Matt and Bob. "You guys look like you're really fitting in easily to the junior high style."

"It's going to be great," Matt said.

"So, how do you like it so far, Bob?"

"So far, it's pretty neat," Bob answered. "Do I know you?"

"Maybe … Name's Bruce Tanner. I know your brother, Danny. How'd you like Coach Shank?"

Matt recognized him, but from where? Bruce Tanner? Who was he? He knew that name. He searched his memory. *Who's this Bruce? Something's weird.*

Bob looked at Matt. "Something wrong?"

Matt shook his head. "I don't know."

"So, Matt, do you swim?" Bruce blurted out.

"Yes, I swim. Why?"

★

Skeeter walked up behind Billy and Appie. "Hey, you two seventh graders ready for the showers? I can feel that cold water soaking my head right now."

"Not me," Appie said. "I'm not even dressed out today."

Billy looked at the older boy and smiled. "I'm ready," he said. "It was hot out there."

As they got close to the street, a voice yelled, "Skeeter, come over here."

"Why?"

"There's something alive by this post, and I think it's a snake."

Skeeter looked at Billy and Appie. "A snake? How could it be a snake? Let's go have a look."

"Okay," Billy said. "I bet it's harmless. I know a little about snakes."

"Not me," said Appie. "I hate snakes. I'm not going."

Skeeter couldn't believe it. Wayne told him a snake would set the trap. "Yeah, let's go see it."

Billy and Skeeter walked up to the wooden post where the chain that closed off the street was hooked. "Where's the snake, Jack?"

Cracker Jack pointed down. "In the weeds next to the post. Be careful. It might be a coral snake. It's got the right colors."

Billy knelt beside the tall, brown-green weeds that hid the base of the wooden post. With an open hand, he carefully fanned the long stems to the side. "Something's down there near the bottom."

"I'm right. It's a snake, isn't it?" Cracker Jack said, standing over Billy. "Be careful."

Billy lowered his head closer to see through the vegetation and saw a small orange, red and black snake coiled. "I don't like the colors," he whispered. He moved the weeds carefully to get a better look. "And I still don't see the head."

★

Matt looked at Bruce—any connection to Wayne? A hot flash hit him. *Sandy told me—he's Wayne's cousin.* He froze and looked ahead of them for Billy. He couldn't see him. The feeling started in his head and went deep into his stomach. *Something bad is about to happen. Billy's in trouble. Find him, now!*

"Bob," Matt said abruptly. "Where's Billy? You said he was right in front of us."

Bruce turned away. "Hey, I'll talk to you guys later."

"I don't see him," Bob said. "Do you see Wayne?"

"No, I don't see either one," Matt answered. "Bob, that guy is

Wayne's cousin. We've been suckered. Something's going down."

Bruce had been sent to distract them. Maybe Billy was in the building and okay. Matt knew better. Wayne's plan must be in motion. A feeling of helplessness made his stomach sink.

★

Billy slowly moved his finger toward the back of the snake. It remained motionless and he carefully touched its back near the tail. "It's not real. It looks real, but it's just rubber. Is this a joke?"

Slap! A sharp blow hit each of his arms. A voice behind him said, "Yeah, it's a joke all right," and two strong hands grabbed him from behind. The hands tightened around his biceps. In one motion, the hands yanked Billy off the ground and lifted him in the air. The voice behind him snickered. "Where are your friends now?"

All of Billy's fears surfaced. "Help," he cried weakly.

The hidden face leaned around in front of him and grinned. "I'm your snake in the grass."

"Oh God, it's you," Billy said.

"Grab his right arm and I'll hold his left," Wayne told Cracker Jack. "We can lift him together."

Billy kicked the air. "Put me down!" he screamed.

★

Matt heard the scream and recognized Billy's voice. "Oh no, Bob! Wayne's got him!"

"Where is he?" Bob asked.

"Over by the street. Didn't you hear him scream?"

"No. What's he doing to him?"

"I don't know," Matt said. Nausea overtook him and a cold sweat replaced the beaded sweat on his forehead. How did he let this happen? Right out in plain sight, in front of everyone.

"Look Matt—by the post," Bob said.

He looked up the street and saw Wayne and someone else holding Billy with his feet off the ground. What was Billy doing way over there?

271

Matt watched Billy's legs thrashing. "We've got to get over there, Bob."

✶

Billy's screaming caught the attention of the girls playing volleyball across the street.

The server tucked the ball under her arm and stared at the commotion. One by one, the girls edged closer to the white sideline boundary.

"Oh no," Bonnie said. "It's Billy."

Dee covered her open mouth with her hands and shook her head. She closed her eyes and looked away. "I can't look, Bonnie."

Bonnie focused on Wayne. "Wayne—put him down, Wayne," she yelled. She repeated his name and pointed her finger toward him, jabbing it in short staccato movements. "He'll pay for this," she told Dee.

✶

Two of his tormenters held Billy high in the air. He flipped his head back and forth with spit shooting out in a stream, screaming, "Matt, help me! Help me! They've got me!"

"Help me put his waistband over the hook!" Wayne shouted to Cracker Jack and Skeeter. In five seconds it was done.

Billy's legs moved like he was in a race. His arms reached up toward the sky like he was trying to grab something. His red, cotton gym shorts were pulled up to his crotch and his feet dangled about a foot off the ground.

Bruce ran up and they all stepped back and laughed.

Billy kicked his legs and his shorts started ripping, but the elastic waistband held. He bounced up and down like a yo-yo. The more he kicked, the more he ripped his shorts, but the elastic band held firm. Finally, the red shorts ripped open, exposing his jockstrap.

Matt and Bob ran up. Bob couldn't keep a smile off his face. Matt didn't laugh. He wanted to cry. He'd failed. He'd let Billy and Justin down. He blinked away the tears.

Other boys in the class stopped to see what was happening.

John was the last one to arrive. When he realized Billy wasn't

272

hurt, his face slowly turned red and he began to laugh. "If you don't quit moving around, those girls over there are going to see your giblets."

Matt glanced around, seeing all eyes on Billy. He sensed Billy's feeling of shame and was suddenly overridden by a hot flash of anger. "Get him off that hook," Matt yelled. "Bob, John, stop laughing and help me get him down."

The boys were strong, but the elastic in Billy's waistband was twisted around the hook and they couldn't lift him and pull the elastic off the hook at the same time. "Settle down, Billy," Matt said. His voice was soft. "It's over. We've got you. You're okay."

Coach Shank arrived. The pupils of his eyes were small black dots. He gritted his teeth. "Stop running in place, son, and we'll get you down."

Billy stopped moving and Coach Shank lifted him while John pulled the elastic of his gym shorts off the hook. When his feet were back on the ground, Billy started to cry, but stopped when Matt put a hand on his shoulder.

"One of you boys get a towel so we can cover him up. You okay, son?" Coach Shank said.

"I think so."

"Where's Tyson? I saw him and two of his buddies holding this boy. I wonder if he'll think it was worth the licks he is going to get."

Matt looked at Coach Shank. "I don't know where he is, but there's no question—he'll think it was worth it."

Someone tossed a towel out of the crowd of boys. "Thanks," Coach Shank said. "Now let's get around him and walk back to the building. Time for you boys to hit the showers."

Wayne stood alone across the street by a tree, laughing.

Matt walked over and stepped up close to him, their bodies inches away from one another.

"You seventh graders are too easy," Wayne said, still laughing. "Think you're next? I do."

"No, I think you have that wrong. First will be the principal, three good licks from his paddle."

"Like I'm really going to feel them," Wayne said.

"Oh, you'll feel them okay, but I'm here to tell you that you hanged the wrong boy."

"Should have been you first?"

Matt moved closer. "Before this is all over, you'll wish it was someone else."

Before Wayne could react, Matt struck like a cobra. Both hands shot forward, and the heels of his hands clipped Wayne below his shoulders with a force that made him stagger backward and fall on the ground, looking clumsy and awkward. Matt turned his back to Wayne and walked away.

Bruce and Jack lifted Wayne and held him by the arms. He yanked his arms away and yelled, "You're next! Believe me, you little shithead, you're next!"

Matt turned back and looked at Wayne. "No," he said. "You're next—when you least expect."

Wayne lunged forward but Bruce held him back. "You and who?" he said.

"How about me?" said a man's voice. Coach Smith pushed his way through the watching boys. "Clear the way." He grabbed Wayne's upper arm.

"It was just a prank, Coach. Nobody got hurt," Wayne said.

Coach Smith grasped Wayne's arm tightly and started walking toward the building where the principal's office was located. "You don't do things like that in my class. You're coming with me."

Matt walked out of the seventh grade building in silence. Wayne won the first round, but there would be a second round. *Watch out, Wayne. You're going to hear—Checkmate!* He knew in his heart he was right.

"Billy, I'm sorry. I'm so sorry," Matt said. "I let you and Justin down. I should have seen it. I knew it was coming. I let it happen."

"I'm fine, Matt," Billy said. "I'm the one who was an idiot and followed that guy over to see a snake. I should have realized what they were doing."

"We thought it would happen in the shower room, Matt," Bob interrupted. "No one could have known he was going to hang Billy on a stupid post."

"I don't care, Bob. I should have been more alert," Matt said.

"Don't tear yourself up. It had to happen," Bob said.

"I know, but I told Billy I'd help him and I wasn't even there. Wayne got me so bad."

"He got us all," John said. "But now, at least, it's over."

Matt looked across the street in the direction of the post. "Oh no … It's far from over. No … for Wayne, it has just started."

John patted Matt on the back. "Sleep on that, Matt."

Matt's eyes flashed. "Wayne will be sorry he did this. In the end, the kids he assumes will back down like all the others he's tormented will teach him an important lesson."

John put his hand on Matt's shoulder. "You sound calm, Matt, but deep down, aren't you a little emotional right now? Like I said, let's sleep on it."

Matt pictured Wayne falling as he'd shoved him. He smiled and popped Billy on the back. "You know what? Wayne made a bad mistake. He chose the wrong seventh graders to pick on. I mean that. We'll get him. We're going to bring that scum bag down."

Billy took a deep breath. "Wow, Matt. Maybe we should let the day end before you start planning a reprisal toward Wayne."

"I am so sorry this happened, Billy. I've got to do something."

"Matt, he's bad," Billy said with a soft and deliberate voice. "Maybe we should leave him alone. Bob's right. He said he would do it and he did. It's over. I'm fine."

"It's never over with someone like Wayne," Matt said. "Someone's got to pull his plug. We can't be the 'let it go' guys."

JB walked up beside Billy. "Yeah," he said.

"Don't chime in like that JB," Matt said. "You're like the guy standing behind the poker player. It's not your wager, so keep quiet."

"Sorry, Matt," JB said. "I heard what happened. I'm worried about Billy and you. He's going to be after you next. You know that."

"We'll be okay, JB," Billy said. "Now let's go get on the bus before it leaves us."

"Yeah, get going," Matt said. "I'll check on you tonight, Billy. And JB … Thanks. Sorry I jumped on you."

JB smiled and nodded his head. "I get it, Matt. You're right. See you tomorrow."

A horn honked. "There's Lawrence Fraley," Bob said. "He's taking John and me home today. Want a ride, Matt?"

"No thanks. I'm going to walk home. I've got some serious thinking to do. Hey, Bob?"

"What?"

Matt grinned. "Don't wear a wrinkled shirt tomorrow." He turned and headed for the "Narrows."

"Matt?" John called.

Matt didn't turn around. He lifted his hand and kept walking. "I'll call you later tonight."

PART 3

Chapter 44

THE BOXING LESSON

NO CAR IN THE DRIVEWAY. No truck in the driveway. Mom not home—Dad still at work. Matt was alone. He needed to talk and no one was there. He walked in through the kitchen door and threw his books and gym bag on his bed.

Back in the kitchen, he poured cold water from the pitcher in the refrigerator into the free glass that came with a fill-up at the Spur gas station, gulped it down, grabbed an orange and walked back toward his bedroom. In the hall, he glanced up at the attic opening cover and for an instant thought about treasures and escaped prisoners, but the picture in his mind of Billy hanging from the post, legs flailing, while Wayne watched and laughed, pushed away all other thoughts.

He jumped on the bed and sat there with his feet still dangling off the side while he peeled the orange and ate it. After he finished the orange, he wiped his sticky fingers on his jeans, fell back on the bed and lay there looking at the ceiling with his hands clasped behind his head. He couldn't clear his mind.

Wayne got me. He got Billy, and he got me. I let Justin down. I taught Jimmy a lesson in fourth grade. I need to figure out how to teach Wayne a lesson.

Outside the bedroom window, a redheaded woodpecker worked the tall pine tree in the backyard, looking for food.

Thoughts buzzed through Matt's head as he watched the

woodpecker. *That woodpecker's going to find a bug; I'm going to find a solution. Can't let the 'Waynes' in the world have an upper hand. I'll get him, but I'm going to think of a way to take care of him without a fist fight.*

Smoky meowed. The sound was soft and quiet ... not like when she was hungry.

He bounced out of bed and checked his closet. Still no kittens. As he walked through the bedroom door, he passed her. "When are you going to have those kittens?" The cat hopped onto his bed near the pillows and curled up.

Mullet barked from behind the garage. Matt smiled. The barking proclaimed he wasn't really all alone. He walked outside to the kennel. Mullet stood on his hind legs, tail swinging back and forth in a wide arc.

"How's my boy? Are you excited to see me? I wish I were as excited right now as you are. Need more water?"

As he refilled Mullet's water bowl, it dawned on him. He could talk to Mr. Weller. His dad had told him, "I've known Vernon Weller a long time. His advice or mine is all you need."

He stuck his finger through the kennel fence and tickled the dog's ear. "I need to talk to Mr. Weller," he said. "Sorry, boy, got to go. I'll be home later."

In the kitchen, Matt scribbled a note: *Gone to visit Mr. Weller.*

He hopped on his bike, pulled his handlebars hard and lifted the front wheel off the ground, riding down the driveway and across the dip where it met the street on his rear wheel. He dropped the front wheel and picked up speed, removed his hands from the handlebars and continued fast with his hands hanging by his side.

At the intersection, he slowed, leaned the bike and turned onto Mr. Weller's street with still no hands on the bars. It was his personal way of reinforcing his physical abilities. He imagined he was one of the supernatural heroes that inhabited the night sky ... one of the images formed by connecting the star dots. He was Hercules as he headed along the street; his destination, Mr. Weller's house.

He stepped up on the wooden porch and the floor creaked like when he used a crowbar to pull nails from old wood. He knocked. A figure passed the living room window, and Mr. Weller appeared on the other side of the screen door.

"Come in, Matthew. I saw you walk by on your way home from school. I've been expecting you."

"Yes, sir."

Matt walked into the house. Unlike the cluttered garage, the house looked like the lawn—neat and clean. The living room appeared untouched, almost unlived in. A neatly folded newspaper sat on a corner table near a rocking chair.

The smell of old polished wood and a hint of mildew and mothballs filled the room. Not stale—just old. Matt thought about the smells and remembered the same odors in his grandparents' house on their farm. It must be the smell of old people's houses, lived in by their old people owners.

A grandfather clock tick-tocked in one corner of the living room and a grand piano sat in the other corner. Sheet music open, the piano looked ready for someone to sit down and play.

Matt knew he was staring but he didn't want to miss a thing. He couldn't help himself.

"Please have a seat anywhere," Mr. Weller said.

Matt sat down on a large tapestry couch with mahogany legs carved into sculpture-like feet. The wood was almost black and it looked very old. It could have graced a historic house like Monticello, but it still looked new, not a tear or stain on the multicolored red, gold and green fabric, and the wood was void of scratches. Most old wood furniture looked like his desk at school, scratched and furrowed, and the polish dull. Where else had the furniture lived?

On the polished mahogany end table, only inches away from where Matt sat, something unexpected stood on the table: a striking black-and-white photo inside a gold picture frame. He looked at a ghost and the ghost looked at him.

Without warning, he lost his breath. He could not pull in another. A sensation of lightheadedness overcame him. He felt like he might keel over onto the couch and slip into a total faint. He wasn't scared, but he didn't want to be embarrassed.

He stared into the eyes of the young man in the picture who

returned the stare. Matt studied him in awe and his eyes were bound to the eyes in the picture. He couldn't look away. The eyes that were fixed on him belonged to Mr. Weller's son. He really wasn't looking at Matt. He was looking at the lens of the camera for the picture to be taken, but Matt, startled by the pose, was now the camera.

The young man stood on the wing of his airplane with his hand on the canopy, ready to climb in. Matt recognized the plane as a Corsair and could see by the background that it rested on the deck of a carrier. The big radial engine engulfed the photo and bore witness to the power that pulled the plane through the air.

The twenty-two-year-old, trained and responsible for all that was asked of him, was dressed for flying. An aviator cap—pulled down, muffling his ears—fit tight to his head like a bathing cap. His leather jacket with a puffy fleece collar covered his neck and fit tight around his chest. Straps around his upper legs were part of the connection that held a parachute hanging down his backside.

Matt knew that soon after the photo was taken, this young man had climbed in, the prop had slowly turned and blue smoke and fire had blown out from the engine. It spit, sputtered and roared. The propeller turned into a blur and the engine sound was deafening. He taxied into position, saluted and left the aircraft carrier, disappearing for a second, falling into the sea, but re-emerging and racing up toward the plane in front and becoming part of the squadron's formation as they headed out on their mission.

Matt saw it all happening. Goose bumps covered his arms and he somehow felt proud and understood his feelings for Mr. Weller, but had no words to express them. He looked away and his eyes met Mr. Weller's. "Sir, I am so sorry," he said, his voice soft and gentle.

"He was quite a boy. You remind me of him."

"Thanks for saying that."

For the first time, Matt saw his dealings with Wayne and realized the insignificance of his problem. "Mr. Weller, did you fly?"

"I flew in World War I and instructed in World War II. My son was a good pilot. They all were."

"Dad never says a word about the war."

"He might never. But it will direct him."

"With me?"

"Yes, you ... and all."

After a long pause, Matt saw that was the end of *that* conversation, at least for that day, maybe forever.

"So you have a bully pushing Billy and bullying you too?" Mr. Weller said.

"Yes, sir. Today he played a dirty trick on Billy. Hung him from a hook out on the school grounds." Matt's eyes glazed and filled with water. "I'm probably next. I want to do what your son would have done when he was my age. Would he want to get Wayne first? I do."

"How old are you?" Mr. Weller asked, and sounded all business.

"Almost thirteen. I'm in junior high."

Mr. Weller walked in front of Matt. "Stand up."

Matt stood near him, only a couple of feet away. Mr. Weller opened his right hand wide and gestured like he was telling someone to halt. "Hit my hand. Hit it fast and hard."

"Now?"

"Whenever." Mr. Weller appeared to remain casual but Matt saw he was waiting for the swing.

"Are you going to try to make me miss?"

Mr. Weller didn't answer, but Matt saw a twinkle in his eye and an almost imperceptible smile.

Like a fast shutter of a camera, Matt struck. Equally fast, Mr. Weller moved his hand. It went down and away. Nevertheless, Matt's fist struck the soft palm of Mr. Weller's hand. As his hand moved, Matt's fist was already there.

"Let's go to the garage," Mr. Weller said. He rubbed the offended hand and watched as it turned red. "This lesson shouldn't take long."

In the back of the garage, obscured by paint cans, tools, garden supplies and other stored items hung a leather punching bag. Multiple pairs of boxing gloves, with their laces tied together, hung on nails driven into wall studs. The leather of the bag and the gloves was smooth, worn and looked as old as the couch in the house, but had fallen on rougher times.

Matt inspected the gloves. "Navy is stamped on some of this equipment," he said. "Dad said you taught boxing at the Naval Academy."

"I did," Mr. Weller said. He pulled a small set of gloves off the wall and tossed them toward Matt. "Try these on."

Matt put them on and Mr. Weller tied the laces tight. "They fit pretty well. How do they feel?"

"Okay … maybe a little big."

Mr. Weller spread out a mat over the concrete floor. "They'll work well for what I need to teach you." He looked up from the gloves and into Matt's eyes. "You know your skills are pretty special, don't you? How did you know where my hand was going when you hit it?"

"It seemed like the right place." Matt pushed the gloves in front of him and rubbed them back and forth on one another and then hit them together. "I don't want to hurt anyone."

"You might have to."

"I mean bad. I mean where someone really gets hurt."

"That might happen too."

"I'm really scared of that happening."

"Well, today, Matt, let's begin our lessons on how to win. For you, it won't take long."

"Really?"

"Really … I think you are going to be a fast learner." Mr. Weller laced up a pair of gloves on himself using one hand and his teeth while speaking. "Let's get started and let's see how you respond. We'll talk about 'between your ears' issues later, okay?"

"Yes, sir."

The lesson began. Matt was small and Mr. Weller was old. Matt didn't want to fight like their age difference made it equal. But after Mr. Weller hooked Matt under the chin and staggered him on the mat, causing him to drop on one knee, he understood with no doubt at all that being old was not a factor.

Mr. Weller showed Matt techniques that would help him. The more he learned, the more he wanted to learn. Mr. Weller obliged him. He could tell Mr. Weller enjoyed teaching him, and when it was over, the old man, gloves still on his hands, shot an arm over Matt's neck and patted the back of his head. "Come back tomorrow. By the end of the week, you will be ready," he said.

"Thank you, Mr. Weller."

He looked at Mr. Weller and stuck his gloved hands toward him. "Need some help?"

"I've made a knot."

"Knots require patience."

Matt nipped at the granny knot with his front teeth and slowly the tight lace started to loosen. He pulled on the end of the loosening knot and paused. "Mr. Weller, I get scared sometimes. Does confidence erase fear?"

The old man stared at him. "No, confidence lets you react to fear. But fear isn't a bad thing. Fear builds courage."

Mr. Weller looked at the clock on the garage wall. "Young man, it looks like it's getting close to dinner time. You better get home. I don't want Harry Parker mad at me."

"Okay, thanks for everything, Mr. Weller."

Chapter 45

CREST LAKE

THE SCREEN DOOR BANGED.

Matt walked into the kitchen and kissed his mom on the cheek as she stood in front of the sink with her garden gloves on, holding fresh-cut roses. He sat down at the table with a smile on his face. "Hi, Mom. I want to take a pole over to the lake and just fish and think a bit, okay? I've got some serious stuff to sort out. I can do my homework after dinner."

"Okay, son. You can tell your dad and me all about your first day of junior high tonight, but at least tell me about the girls right now." A sly smile crept across her face. "You know what I mean. As your Uncle Doug would say, 'Any good-looking sheilas?' I bet you had one or two flirting with you."

"Flirting with Brad, you mean, but I can tell you that I think junior high's going to be fun."

"Anything else to share with me?"

Matt's eyes filled with tears. "I'll tell you later. I need to think some more before I talk about it."

"Okay, sweetie."

"You Aussies know everything, don't you?" he said with a smile.

"We Aussies keep our hearts and eyes open."

"I know you do. Okay if I'm a little late?"

"I'll keep dinner warm in the oven."

"Thanks. Might stay and watch the ducks come in."

"Okay. See you when you get home. I know the ducks come in pretty late. Isn't it a little bit early? I mean, isn't it later in the fall when they start those fly-ins?"

"See, Mom, I've taught you well. How else would you know that?"

"Your dad?"

"Yep … he's the real teacher," Matt said with a grin. "He and Mr. Weller."

Matt leaned his bike against a large live oak tree that he'd climbed many times, grabbed his pole off the handlebars and his tackle box out of the bike basket and hurried toward the water. He loved Crest Lake. Even though they mowed the grass in the park and it had a sidewalk around it, the lake was still wild in some areas.

A young couple stood on the wooden dock on the western shore of the lake. The dock ran out a hundred feet with deep water at the end.

Matt walked in the other direction. He needed the serenity of the lake to open his mind—to clear the bad thoughts still banging around inside his head. Bass fishing and thinking went together well.

Swimming beside some cattails about ten feet away were a pair of coots and one gallinule. The coots were chasing one another, splashing water and making a ruckus. The gallinule voiced his opinion and sounded aggravated.

Across the water on the eastern side, where the shoreline was wild and swamp-like, the wail of a limpkin pierced the air. Two big white farm ducks swam up beside him. His dad said that farm ducks meant the days of the wild lake habitat were numbered.

He reached the water's edge in an area where grass grew a few inches above the surface of the water. He cut the shiner hook off the line, tied on a plastic worm and cast it right into the grass.

His first day of junior high turned out to be one of the worst days of his life. He needed to think and focus on things his dad had taught him about dealing with situations like this. His thoughts returned to Phys Ed class as he slowly retrieved the line. When he'd pushed Wayne, he'd crossed the point of no return. He would be Wayne's next target and he needed to do something. Wayne solved things with his fists. Matt needed to solve this with his brain.

When the worm was out of the water again and near the tip of his rod, he opened the bale of the Mitchell 300 reel and sailed the worm back into the grass. As soon as it hit the water and started to fall, he felt the bump. He let the line run off his reel, closed the bale, reeled the slack out and watched the line moving sideways through the water.

Thoughts of Billy disappeared. He lowered the rod tip slowly, felt the pull of the fish, yanked the pole back over his shoulder in one snapping motion and set the hook. The rod tip bent into the water.

He kept his pole up. A largemouth bass broke the surface of the water in the heavy grass, shook its head and returned to the water. He worked the fish slowly and after a couple of minutes, had it out of the heavy cover and in the open water.

His line was only eight-pound test and this bass appeared to be close to that. *Go slow.*

Once he had the bass coming his way, he walked backward and pulled it up over the mowed grass the same way he dragged a snook up onto the beach from the saltwater. He lifted it up by its lower jaw, held her out and felt her weight. Seven pounds—the size Dad catches at Lake Butler. He took the hook from its lip and examined the bass. Not one blemish—a healthy fish.

Returning to the water's edge, he released her in the shallows. The bass swam off with her tail still out of the water, snapped her tail on the surface, submerged into the deeper open water and disappeared.

The plastic worm was still intact and could be used again on another day. Matt reeled the worm up to the tip of the rod, walked back up and sat down on the grass. He set the pole beside him.

Catching the bass made him feel good. Thinking about Billy and Wayne made him feel bad. "If you catch Wayne like you caught that bass, you can feel the same satisfaction," he said out loud.

A single-engine plane flew over the lake.

Matt looked up and watched it heading for the Clearwater airport a few blocks away. Suddenly, it hit him. *Doolittle! That's the answer. We'll plan a Doolittle's Raid on Wayne just like Doolittle and the other pilots did on the Japs. Show Wayne we're not afraid of him and he'll go off in search of someone else who's easy and leave us alone.*

The sun was falling fast and the clouds in the western sky promised a pretty sunset on the beach, but in the east, thunderclouds reached high in the sky.

Matt felt the best he had felt all day. He'd found his solution: a Doolittle's Raid on Wayne's house. He'd call Billy when he got home.

The cattails bent with the breeze picking up over the lake, and the red-winged blackbirds playing in them rose up into the sky and did a loop in formation, then settled back into them.

The limpkin wailed from time to time as it waded along the shoreline, but the coots were now more interested in diving for plant life than talking to one another.

The clouds, the birds, the swaying cattails and catching and releasing the bass had cleared Matt's head. Now let a few ducks land on the water and that would complete his trip. It was getting late.

The first one came in high. It looked like a female mallard, but it was a Florida duck. Its wings made a high-pitched whistle. As it pulled them in, it fell like an F-86 tight on a target. It hit the water, its webbed feet stuck up and forward, and slid twenty feet before it stopped.

Only a few more of the Florida ducks landed. The teals, the woods and the pintails, his favorite flyers, hadn't started their migration yet, but in December and January he'd see them land at the lake again. Hundreds of them with wings sounding like the whirr of jet engines. *What would Wayne hear? Bombs?*

The sky began to turn gray. Time to leave.

Fifteen minutes later, Matt coasted up the driveway. As he passed his dad's work truck, his handlebars were so close to the truck the rubber handle almost touched it.

"I'm home," he yelled.

"I'm in the garage," Mr. Parker answered. "I'm making a box to put in your closet for Smoky."

Matt entered the side door of the garage and saw his dad standing over his workbench, with a power saw in his hand. "Did she have her kittens?"

Without looking up, his dad marked another piece of wood with his pencil and picked up the saw. "Yes, seven of them."

"Hooray! I'm going in to see them."

"Okay, Mom put dinner in the oven so we could all eat together. I'll be right in."

After dinner, Mrs. Parker got up from the table. "I'll clean up the table. It's late. You two talk and I'll listen. You'll both owe me. I baked a cake today. Would you like a slice?"

"Angel food cake?" Matt asked. "Got to have milk when I eat your cake, Mom."

"Yes, it's angel food and the milk is way in the back of the refrigerator. I bought groceries today. The cupboard was bare."

She poured two cups of coffee, wiped her hands on her apron and sat back down at the table. "Honey, I told Matt to wait and tell us both about his first day."

Matt's dad tapped his spoon on the side of his cup and a smile stretched across his mouth. "Attention, attention. Please hold all thought and hear the man of the hour, the one and only Matt Parker, our new seventh grader at the prestigious Clearwater Junior High School."

Matt placed his glass of milk on the table and bowed to all corners of the room. "My first day started off great. Saw old friends and met new ones. Liked all my teachers. Having more than one teacher for the whole day was neat."

He stopped and looked at his dad. His eyes watered. "But, Wayne Tyson ruined the party. After school, I went by Mr. Weller's house and we talked about it. Then after I saw Mom, I went over to Crest Lake to think about what happened and I decided I'm going to write another ending."

Wiping away a tickle on his cheek that he suspected was an early tear, he looked up at the ceiling. "Wayne showed everybody what whale shit he is."

"Matt!" Mrs. Parker said.

"In my eyes, he sunk to the bottom of the deep blue sea, and it gets no lower."

"What did he do?" Mrs. Parker asked.

"He hung Billy on a hook on a post beside the street with the help of some of his hood buddies in Phys Ed. They left him, his feet off the ground, flailing like a chicken held around the neck, flopping and kicking. That's what they did. And Dad, the girls' gym class was across the street where they could see it all. His jockstrap was showing, and even more. The girls and the boys in the gym classes were all laughing. John and I tried to get him off but couldn't. He had to hang there until the coach came and lifted him off. It was humiliating and embarrassing. Am I telling you how bad it was? And I didn't see it coming. What a help I was. I really let him down. I told him we'd be there for him, but in the end we weren't. Oh, Dad, Wayne got me. So, I sat there at Crest Lake and it became clear. This isn't going to be a one-round fight."

A smile spread across his dad's face. "I think you have a handle on it, son. Remember, Mr. Weller was one of my instructors at Drew Field. Taught me many skills. A special friend and mentor he is—for both of us."

Matt knew his dad understood and approved. No discussion necessary.

Sitting on the bed in his mom and dad's bedroom, Matt hung up the phone and thought about his plan and the phone conversation he'd just had with Billy. He picked up the receiver and dialed another number. "May I please speak to John? Tell him it's Matt."

He waited for John to come to the phone and listened carefully for the click of someone on their telephone party line, but didn't hear one.

"Do you spend your whole life at home on the pot?" he asked John, with a giggle in his voice. "I believe that, John ... Hey, my phone can be bugged ... You know, a party line. So don't say anything, just listen. I talked with Billy a few minutes ago. Let's meet in the cafeteria and talk before school ... Some things to clear the air ... Would you call Bob and tell him? Thanks ... See you in the morning. Tomorrow's a new day."

Back in his bedroom, Matt went in the closet and tickled the newborn kittens nursing on their mom in the box his dad had made. Then he slipped into bed, reached over and turned on the radio, making sure the volume was low, and turned off the light. Jimmy Clanton began to sing "Just a Dream."

Chapter 46

THE DOOLITTLE PLAN

MATT STEPPED UP ON THE CURB and onto the school grounds, ready to share his plan for retaliation with Bob and John, his stomach still tight but better than the day before.

The morning drizzle turned into a steady rain. Water covered the basketball courts, and the rusted metal nets directed rainwater to puddles beneath them.

Matt's yellow raincoat dripped water from the sleeves. The lights were on in the cafeteria. He entered the almost empty room and heard John's laugh.

John and Bob sat alone at a table back in the far corner, the rain pelting the window behind them.

"I thought you were the cafeteria workers back here," Matt said. He draped his rubber raincoat over a chair and stomped his soaked shoes on the floor. "Well, I got you guys moving early. Got some private talk to get the ball rolling on a payback for Wayne's sickening trick yesterday."

John pulled out a chair with his feet. "You got it, buddy. Have a seat and start talking."

Matt shook his head like a dog shaking himself dry, and water flew into the air. "Sorry," he said as he sat down in the chair. "Okay guys, yesterday Billy was the victim of a bully and that's a powerless feeling. We need to help him overcome it."

"I've never been bullied," John said in a quiet voice.

"Me either," Bob said, his voice soft too.

Matt thought about the ride on the bus in fourth grade and how he felt when Jimmy sat down beside him and pushed hard up against him. The memory still hurt. "Well, I have," he said. "So, I'm an authority on the subject. We need to keep this, or something worse, from happening to Billy or anyone again. Let's stop Wayne and let Billy be part of it."

"But Billy isn't strong enough or big enough," John said. "Agreed?"

Matt smiled. "Yes, he's small—but he has the brains. We'll be his fists. We need to show Wayne there's no honor in his kind of fighting. Let's make him pay and turn the tables so people will be laughing at him."

Matt's smile disappeared. "What happened yesterday filled me, consumed me. All I could think about last night was the terrible feeling I had watching Billy hanging from that post with everyone staring at him."

"Me too," John said. "I'm embarrassed that I laughed."

Bob dropped his head. "I bet those hoods over at Five Points are laughing it up right now and Wayne is the center of attention."

Matt's smile resurfaced. "Guess what? I talked to Billy last night and he's ready to move forward with an idea I have to get back at Wayne."

"What's the idea?" Bob said.

"First," Matt said, "we need to show Wayne who he's dealing with here. Let him begin to wonder what's happening and if maybe his reasoning has some flaws."

"Flaws?" John said. "You mean screwed up?"

"You got it, John," Matt said. "And the purpose of our plan will be to drive that home. We're going to be Doolittle Raiders."

"And ... Doolittle's Raid will be our code name for a counterattack against Wayne," said Billy, standing one table away with a big smile on his face. "Surprise!" He shook the rain off his umbrella and hooked it over a chair.

John pulled out another chair with his foot. His eyes opened wide and his jaw dropped. He motioned to Billy. "Sit down here beside me, Ross Allen, expert on snakes."

Billy slapped John on the back and sat down. His smile created dimples in his cheeks. "You're right, John. I can recognize a fake snake in a late second. I'm really cool—but today's a new day and I think a Doolittle's Raid is a great idea."

Matt knew from Billy's smile that he was going to be fine. "Okay," he said. "Remember the movie?"

"Sure," Bob said. "*Thirty Seconds Over Tokyo.* Spencer Tracy played Lieutenant Colonel Jimmy Doolittle and it took place right after the Japs bombed Pearl Harbor."

"Right," Matt said. "And a group of American flyboys under his command, all volunteers, I might add, planned a sneak attack on Japan to let them know what we were capable of accomplishing."

"I remember," John said. "It was so cool. They flew sixteen over-sized B-25 bombers off the carrier, Hornet, to bomb Tokyo."

Billy nodded his head. "Right, John, and they knew they didn't have enough fuel to make it back to a safe airfield after they made the raid. Some ended up prisoners of war, some were killed and some made it to the safe haven of China."

"So, if you're ready to volunteer, we can do the same thing. We'll carry out a sneak attack on Wayne when he's at home," Matt said. "Our raid will be a nuisance raid that will say, 'We can do it too.'"

"Okay, I'll volunteer, but let's include making it back to the safe haven of home," Bob said with a laugh.

John raised his clenched fist in the air. "Hip-hip-hooray. I'm ready. Bomb the shit out of him—with cherry bombs! I'm in."

"This is serious, John," Matt said. "Our mission is to teach Wayne that he's not dealing with cowards and his dirty deed will *not* be left unanswered."

"Matt's right," Billy said. "No more tears for yesterday. It's time for solutions."

Bob hit the table with an open hand. "That's the neatest idea, Matt. Give us the plan."

"Okay," Matt said. "Here's the short version. We go to Wayne's house in the dark of night and deposit a note on his bedroom pillow."

"That's all?" John said.

"That's all," Matt answered.

"Just a note on the pillow?" John asked. "Maybe a few cherry bombs?"

"Maybe," Matt answered. "Just like bombs on Tokyo. That's a good idea, John."

"I love it," Bob said. "When?"

"Friday night. John and I are already planning to spend the night at your house. We can leave from there after everyone's asleep. It will be perfect. And when the raid is over, Wayne will have some doubts spinning around inside his head about deciding to mess with us."

"Billy going with us?"

"No," Matt answered. "He doesn't know the area. We do. And we don't want anyone taken prisoner or getting lost if we get separated. He's going to be our Admiral Nimitz—the head of Planning and Operations. You're fine with that, right, Admiral?

"Right," Billy said. "And when the bomb bay doors are opened, my knapsack of armaments will rain over Wayne's abode. It will be spectacular and satisfying. Makes me think of a line from Ralph Waldo Emerson's poem, the 'Concord Hymn.' *Here once the embattled farmers stood, And fired the shot heard around the world.* We will awaken Wayne's mind to what he has unleashed. Carry on, airmen!"

John stood and clapped. "Those words shout out! Well done, Admiral—our little farmer, snake lover extraordinaire, Albert Einstein the Second and poet laureate. Hip! Hip! Hooray!"

Billy smiled and stood up and took a bow. "Kind words. Thank you, John."

"Okay," Matt said. "Admiral Nimitz, Colonel Hollis and Colonel Walton, we'll talk later about the details. Let's get on with this day."

Chapter 47

WAYNE'S MESSAGE

AT THE END OF HOMEROOM, Billy walked out the door of his class and bumped right into Jimmy Knox.

"Hi, Billy," Jimmy said. "Wayne said to tell you that you sure looked funny hanging from the post yesterday, and it was worth the three licks."

"See how you like Act Two, Jimmy," Billy said.

"I heard that, Jimmy," Matt said as he walked up beside them. "You can tell Wayne to watch his back. Oh wait, you'll have to tell him later, right? I hear he got suspended yesterday."

Jimmy's smug, round baby face lit up like a red traffic light, and he looked like a cookie stealer caught in the act. "Oh sure. He's really afraid of you seventh graders, you know. He thinks you're just 'twerps.'"

Matt looked Jimmy right in the eyes. "Well, he should be afraid. You know why? He picked the wrong seventh grade 'twerps' to mess with."

"I thought you were going to say Billy's brother's coming back."

"Guess what, Jimmy? A time's coming when Wayne will wish it *was* Billy's brother. Just so you know. We don't need Justin. You can tell your idol that."

Jimmy shrugged his shoulders and forced a smile. "I'll tell Wayne.

I'm sure he'll be shaking in his boots." He turned and started to walk down the hall.

"He should be," Matt said. "Jimmy?"

Jimmy paused at the door of Mr. Buchanan's seventh grade math class and turned around to face Matt. "What?"

"You are on the wrong ship."

"What does that mean?"

"Your ship is going to sink. See you later."

Jimmy turned and walked into the class without an answer.

"Way to go, Matt," Billy said. "They just don't know what we have in store for them, do they?"

Matt squeezed the back of Billy's neck. "Nope ... but they're going to find out." I'm sure right now Jimmy thinks I'm blowing air up his butt. Soon they'll see the first squall line. See ya later, Billy."

Chapter 48

A NOTE FOR BONNIE

JOHN ENTERED THE CAFETERIA right before Matt and was in line just a few people in front of him. "Hey, John, wait up. We can go sit over there with Billy and the girls," Matt said.

In his pocket, he had a note he'd written Bonnie, asking her to meet him after fourth period. He hoped he'd be able to slip it to her without anyone noticing.

Elaine, Maggie and Bonnie were sitting on one end of a long table. John put his tray down on the table and Matt sat down beside Billy.

Bob walked up carrying a tray full of food. "Where are you sitting, John?"

"Right here. How'd you get them to give you that much food?"

"I just said, 'Fill it up, please,' and they did."

John pointed at the chair across the table from him. "Sit there, Bob. Holy smokes, if I ate that much food, *I'd* look like a fatty on the beach."

Dee walked up to the table and sat down beside Bonnie. "Oh my gosh," she whispered. "There's Mr. North, and I think he's coming this way." She looked at Matt. "Why is he here in the cafeteria?"

"He probably has cafeteria duty today. He's strict—but he's okay."

"Oh no—here he comes," Dee said. Her voice was barely audible. "You do the talking, Matt."

Mr. North approached the table and stopped behind Bob's chair.

Everyone except Bob stopped talking. Bob laughed. "And then we could call you 'fatty on the beach' and see how you like it, right Elaine?"

Matt looked up at the teacher standing behind Bob. "I think you should ask Mr. North that question instead of Elaine."

Bob turned his head and looked up, "Oh hello, Mr. North. I didn't know you were back there."

Mr. North looked up and down the table, slowly swinging the "peace pipe" he always carried. "Hello, Mr. Walton. Go ahead and eat. I just came over to see what the laughing was about."

Mr. North looked at John. "I don't recognize you, young man. Are you in my class?"

"No, sir," John said.

"Are you glad?"

John's face turned red. "Kind of. I mean, not really."

Mr. North swished the peace pipe back and forth. "That sounds like two different answers to me."

John cleared his throat. "Well sir, the word is you're pretty hard and Mr. Kimery is pretty easy."

"Oh, so you have Mr. Kimery then?"

"Yes, sir."

"Now, Matt here and young Bob have me for history, right, boys?" They both nodded.

"Am I hard?"

"No," Bob said. "And I'm really, really sure."

Mr. North's lips stretched just enough to show the start of a smile. "Good answer," he said, and he turned and walked away.

Maggie watched him until she knew he was out of hearing range. "Oh my gosh, I'm so glad I don't have him. I'm sure he's a good history teacher, but he makes me too nervous. I could never be relaxed in his class."

Dee stood up and walked to the end of the table, where she could look down the entire length. She clapped her hands for attention. "Okay, listen up," she said. "Mr. North has left the area, and I have important news.

"I'm having a party a week from Friday night from eight until eleven. It's going to get cranked up early and don't cut out till it's over.

You boys wear your dancing shoes, and girls do the same. My mom is mailing the invites tomorrow."

"How about food?" John said. "I won't dance much, but I sure can eat."

"You know how to dance, John," Dee said.

Matt started to laugh. "You must have seen him on an ant bed."

"Matt, will you bring some of your record collection?"

"Sure. I'll bring some good dancing songs for the real dancers and love songs for the beginning dancers like John."

John got up and started moving his feet. "I'm a dancing fool."

Elaine looked at Dee and shook her head. "What do you call that, John?"

"I call it the Number Two Jig. It's my new rendition of the Bop."

The more John moved his feet, the more he seemed to get into his dance with no music. The girls clapped their hands, trying to keep beat with his out-of-rhythm steps.

"Am I cool or what?" John said.

The girls giggled at the other end of the table.

"Matt, do you like to dance?" Bonnie said.

"Yes. I love music and I have a cool record collection."

She looked at Matt and blushed. "I think the party sounds like fun."

"We're going downtown to the record shop after school," Dee said to the boys. "And then we're going to Brown Brothers. Any of you want to come with us?"

"John, Bob and I are going downtown too," Matt said. "Maybe we can meet after school and walk together." He looked at Bonnie. "You going?"

"Yes. I don't live very far from the record shop."

"Maybe I can walk with you," Matt said.

"That would be nice."

Matt noticed Dee kick Bonnie's leg under the table.

Bob leaned over to Bonnie. "Bonnie, can I walk with you too?"

Bonnie looked at him and smiled. "Sure you can."

Dee looked at Bob and giggled. "I'm going downtown too. How about walking with me instead, Bob?"

"Sure, Dee. But don't you like Brad?"

Dee blushed. "Maybe."

"I thought so ... I don't want him getting mad at me."

Matt laughed. "How about me?"

Bob smiled. "You can't get mad at me. Brad can."

Matt saw Brad at another table. "Brad," he yelled. "Come over here."

Brad made his way over, looked at everyone at the table and winked at Dee.

"We're all walking downtown after school. Want to join us?" Matt said.

"Sure."

"Good," Dee said. "Let's meet at the front of the school. You coming, Billy?"

"Sure."

"Great," Dee said. "Hey everybody, we've got a plan. We're walking downtown after school. It's going to be lots of fun. I love being in junior high."

The table emptied and Matt walked over beside Bonnie, slipped the note on her tray and said quietly, "See you later."

Bonnie blushed, picked up the folded paper and slipped it into her purse. "Okay."

Chapter 49

MEETING ON THE STEPS

BONNIE STOOD ON THE STEPS of the seventh grade building. Matt's note asked her to meet him between fifth and sixth periods, so she slipped out of Home Economics class early. He said the talk was confidential. She knew it had to be about Billy and that meant it was about Wayne. The situation worried her. Why must Matt be so involved?

Her first cake had turned out all right, maybe a little too firm and dark on the bottom, but Miss Briggs said it tasted really good and she liked the orange juice flavor and aroma. She had cleaned up her mess in the classroom and left the other girls finishing up.

The bell rang. The building door opened and she looked for Matt. He came out in the second wave. Seventh grade boy-girl meetings attracted attention and she didn't want to become part of the girls' gossip. "I'm over here, Matt," she said softly.

Matt saw her and worked his way through the congestion. He stopped beside her along the side rail. "Hi, Bonnie. Thanks for coming. Let's walk over there by the big oak—too many big ears here."

She nodded and followed him.

"I have a big favor to ask," he said.

Bonnie smiled at him. "Will I end up in the principal's office and be the first seventh grade girl in the history of the school to get three licks? Will this be the next episode of *Bonnie and Clyde*?"

"No, they don't spank girls and it's not about school. Besides, who could ever spank you?" Matt grinned. "And I'm not Clyde."

"Is it about Billy and Wayne?"

"Can I talk first?"

"Why? Because you want to ease into the story and make it sound tame?"

"Bonnie ..."

"Before you say another word, Matt, I want you to know I'm worried about you. I saw Billy on the post. Please don't do anything, Matt. Please? Wayne got his licks. Can't it be over?"

"No."

"Why not?"

"Because he expected the licks. There were no lessons learned there."

"And you?"

"We're going to give him the real lesson, a real consequence. Bonnie, please let me talk. The bell's going to ring."

"Go ahead, but don't ask me to do something where you get hurt or in trouble."

"I'm not going to lie. There are some possible backfires, but if you help me, we eliminate one of them, maybe both."

"Okay ..." Bonnie said. Her voice trailed off like the volume was turned down all the way. "Go ahead with your story."

"We want to show Wayne we're not afraid of him. We're going to show him we can get him if we want to."

"What are you going to do?"

"We're going to Wayne's house and I'm just going to pin a note on his bedroom pillow. That's all."

"Isn't that breaking in?"

"Not if the doors and windows are unlocked."

"You're bending stuff, Matt."

"No one will be hurt and no damage done. We just want to show Wayne he's vulnerable. His sister is your friend, right?"

"I told you already—yes," Bonnie said with a different tone in her voice.

"This is a big favor, and it doesn't put you in any jeopardy. Would you go over to Nina's house and find out if their front door can be locked from the inside without a key and if Wayne's window is unlocked? And I also need to know where his bedroom is located."

Bonnie softened. "All right, I'll do it only because it's you, but I have one last word about the whole thing: I am strongly against it all. Be careful."

"Thank you," Matt said.

"Who else is in on this?"

"John and Bob."

Bonnie shook her head. "That's scary. Not them—it's you three together. Please be careful. When do you need this information?"

"Doolittle's Raid is Friday night. I need to know by Friday, but tomorrow would be best."

"Doolittle's what?"

"Doolittle's Raid—that's what I'm calling it."

"You're not going to get in trouble? Be honest."

"We're on the fringe."

The bell rang.

"I've got to go. I'm going to be late," Bonnie said, but then she smiled. "I'll see what I can do. But remember, I think this is dangerous. You don't know Wayne, Matt—I do."

"Oh, one more question, Bonnie. Is their dog friendly?"

"I think so. Bye. See you after school."

Matt watched her walk back up the steps. *Friendly dog? Owned by Wayne? Fat chance.*

Chapter 50

AFTER SCHOOL
WITH THE GIRLS

"LET'S GO, MATT," John yelled.

Matt quickened his pace. "Sorry, I just had to put some things in my locker. Ready to get started?"

Dee looked over at Bonnie and winked. "We thought maybe you changed your plans and ducked out on us like Billy did. Let's split."

John and Bob led the way.

Dee, Bonnie, Margaret and Elaine picked up their books and followed them. "Get out your radio, Dee," Margaret said.

Matt joined Brad. "I'm glad you're going. Walking with girls is all new to me."

"You know me. I'm always ready to walk with the girls. And I'm glad this afternoon I don't have to walk downtown alone," Brad said.

A breeze met their faces as they left the school property and headed downtown.

Dee turned on her mint green Emerson portable radio and the music set the cadence. Everyone walked in beat as Chuck Willis sang "C.C. Rider."

"Hey Dee, I've got a question for you. Wait up," Brad said.

Matt walked up behind Bonnie, Margaret and Elaine. "May I join you?" He directed the question to all three, but his eyes ended on

Bonnie.

Bonnie didn't say anything, but she grinned at Matt and dropped back to walk beside him. Matt felt his heart beating.

In the front of the group, John stopped and stuck his nose up near his armpit. "Mmmm, Panther Poo 102."

Dee smacked him across the back. "John, that's gross."

"Hey, it's hot. I wish the breeze would pick up. You know what Matt's Aussie mom would say: 'The Queen of England would smell a little dicey today.'"

Like a wish granted, the breeze blew harder and an isolated, dark cloud covered them with a shadow.

John looked up. "Relief on command. You girls might use your umbrellas yet."

At the next intersection Bob stopped. "Okay, here's where we say *adios.* John and I have some business down the street at the Army Navy store. We'll see you boys and girls tomorrow."

"Okay, boys," Dee said. "Glad you came with us today."

The shadow had taken away the reality of the hot September afternoon, but the sun poked out again and the heat reemerged.

"My house is on the next street," Bonnie said to Matt. "I promised Mom I'd go straight home."

"Okay," Matt said. "Hey everybody, Bonnie has to go home so I'm going to walk with her. I'll meet you at the record shop."

Dee looked at Bonnie, squinted her eyes and smiled. "See you tomorrow, Bonnie. Call me tonight after you finish your homework."

Matt knew what that smile meant. His heart started beating a little faster and he walked right through a puddle.

"C'mon girls," Brad said. "I'll walk you to the record shop. We'll see you there, Matt."

Matt and Bonnie turned and walked down a tree-lined side street. "I only live about five minutes from here, so you won't be very long getting back to them."

"That's okay. I've waited all afternoon to walk you home … and it's not because of the information I asked you to get me."

"You mean it's not because you want to see if I might become a Ma Barker?"

"Who?"

"Ma Barker—the old gangster lady who terrorized the South back in the twenties and thirties with her four sons."

"How do you know about her?"

"They killed her and her son Fred in 1935 over on Lake Weir in Ocklawaha where my grandparents live," Bonnie said.

"Who killed them?"

"The FBI in a shootout right at the Barker household."

"Do you think her crime sprees began by checking to see if a house was unlocked?" Matt smiled. "I'm not worried about you."

"You never know," Bonnie said with a smile. "Behaviors sometimes begin very innocently."

"Listen," Matt said and the smile left his face. "Know for sure, I'd never ask you to do something that would get you in trouble. I know our house is always unlocked, and Wayne's probably is too. Are there any houses locked up in this town while someone is home?"

"Not very many," Bonnie said, "and guess what?"

"What?"

"I saw Nina after I talked to you this afternoon and I'm going over to her house tomorrow after school. I'll check out the locks and the dog and tell you on Friday."

"Thanks, Bonnie. I just need to be sure."

"What if he catches you?"

Matt grinned. "He won't. I'm too good—really. Good planning results in success, you know."

Bonnie didn't smile. "I'd be so nervous. And don't forget, their dog is big."

"That's okay. I'm good with animals. That dog will probably want to walk home with me."

Bonnie stared for a moment into Matt's eyes. "Well, thanks for walking home with me."

He looked down at his tennis shoes. He couldn't think of anything to say. He liked this girl and he was walking her home from school.

They walked on and the quiet started to make Matt a little nervous.

Bonnie stopped and looked right in his eyes. "I was on the volleyball courts in Phys Ed yesterday, Matt. It was so sad. I know Wayne got a spanking from the principal so at least he was punished, but I don't think a spanking was enough."

"I know. I was sad, too, but my sadness turned into anger."

"Matt, every girl on that volleyball court was angry. My friends Peggy McDaniel and Dorothy Hagan were there with me and they said they wished they could punch Wayne in the nose. I wish you could do something."

Matt's eyes twinkled. "We'll see."

"I know Wayne's a lot older and bigger than you, but I heard a lot about you today at school," Bonnie said. "Billy's lucky to have you for a friend."

"Thank you."

Bonnie pointed across the street to a yellow-and-white frame house with flowering allamanda bushes along the fence. "Guess what? That's my house."

They crossed the street and Matt walked with her up to the front door. She held out her hand. "Thank you for walking me home."

Matt smiled, took her hand and gave her a firm handshake. "You're welcome and thank you so much for getting that information for me. See you tomorrow at school?"

"Yes," Bonnie said. She opened her front door, turned around and wiggled her fingers in a little wave. "Bye, Matt."

Matt raised his hand and held it straight. "See you in the morning."

He turned and ran back across the street, trying not to skip, and when he reached the sidewalk he began singing "Since I Met You Baby." He sang the whole song and then smiled and said out loud, "That's my song—thank you, Ivory Joe Hunter."

He looked at his watch and started to run. His thoughts were going a thousand miles per hour and so were his feet.

Chapter 51

DOOLITTLE'S RAID

BOB, JOHN AND MATT lay quietly under the sheets in Bob and Danny's dark bedroom, dressed in their camouflage shirts, waiting to leave on the Doolittle's Raid.

Bob pulled his pillow over his head and began to giggle.

"S.S.B.A.D.?" John whispered. He started to laugh and the white sheet pulled over his body fluttered like an awakened ghost.

"No," Bob answered. "Want to hear a secret?" His giggle intensified. "It can't leave this room."

"Promise. God is my witness. Tell us," John begged. "We're waiting, right, Matt?"

"It should be good," Matt said quietly.

"It is," Bob said. "Ready?"

John sat up in bed. "Come on, Bob. Tell us!"

"Tell us quick, Bob. Our mission starts soon. We're listening," Matt said.

"Okay, the little kids are all asleep, Danny's spending the night with Buzz and Mom and Dad are probably still at the Park Terrace with their Friday night square dance group. I've got something to show you. Get your flashlight, John."

Matt sat up and shook his head. "I can see that look on your face in the dark, Bob, and I don't like it. We've got to be careful. No screw-ups.

Not tonight."

John handed the flashlight to Bob. "Easy, Matt, go with the flow."

They went down the hall and entered the parents' bedroom.

"Why are we in here?" Matt said.

"Hold the light, Matt, and I'll show you," Bob said. "John, help me lift dad's side of the mattress."

The two boys separated the mattress from the bed springs and Matt pointed the light into the opening. The beam shone directly on a circular package with Trojan printed on the face.

John smacked his lips. "Oh my God … rubbers!"

"Can you believe it?" Bob said. "Danny found them."

"Let's get out of here," Matt said. He'd never seen one, but he knew what they were. The package looked just like the picture in the bathroom at the Spur filling station on Fort Harrison Avenue.

John snickered with his hand over his mouth. "Your dad's the man, Bob."

Bob held up his hand. "Quiet. I think I just heard the front door."

John dropped the mattress and grabbed the flashlight from Matt. "Oh shit! Let's get out of here."

Back in the bedroom with the covers up to their chins, they waited and listened for footsteps on the stairs.

Just as Matt said, "I hope they get up here quickly," the floor outside the bedroom door creaked, they heard some muffled laughter and then a door close. "Whew," he said. "That was too close."

Bob and John started to laugh. "Well, Matt, you finally saw one," John said.

The very personal secret caught Matt flat-footed and made him pull in a fast breath. He didn't say a word.

"So, rubbers do exist, and in an hour, Wayne's going to get surprised like you did," Bob said. "But you guys have got to keep my secret, right?"

"Yes," Matt said. "And same for you too, John?"

"Yessiree," John said. "That's a good one, Bob."

"Ready for me to check the hallway?" Bob said.

"Yes," Matt said. "Time to get this mission started."

Bob slipped out of bed and turned the glass doorknob of the

bedroom door. He opened the door slowly and peeked into the dark hallway, then carefully closed the door, letting the latch re-engage, again with no sound. "All clear on the western front."

Matt looked at the phosphorus hands of his watch. "Eleven-thirty. Time to go, men," he whispered. "Be quieter than a mouse. This is a little scary, but it's going to work. Ready?"

"I'm cool," Bob said.

"John?"

"Hell, yes."

"Let's go. No talking until we're across the street."

"Are we forgetting anything?" Bob asked.

"No," Matt whispered. "You sure everyone is in bed?"

"The little ones are asleep. Mom's in bed. Dad's watching TV downstairs," Bob said. "When he turns the TV off, it's a straight shot to the bed after a pit stop at the toilet. He won't open our door."

"Any hanky-panky?" John whispered, covering his mouth and holding his nose. A little fart broke the silence.

"Not funny, John," Matt said.

Bob raised the window as slowly as he had opened the door. The silicone he'd rubbed on the runners earlier helped it slide up easily. "I'll go first," he whispered.

Matt slipped through the window and onto the tree right behind Bob. "Doolittle's Raid, here we go," he said in an almost inaudible whisper.

"Last, fast, ready to kick Wayne's ass," John said. "Here I come. Can I leave the window open?"

"No, slide it down. Don't want to come home and have a room full of raccoons," Bob said quietly from halfway down the tree.

"For no talking, we're sure doing some," John said, closing the window.

The three boys dropped to the ground and Bob picked up the things he'd hidden earlier that evening deep in the ligustrum hedge growing beside the house.

They crossed to the other side of the street. "Okay," Matt said, "hand me Billy's list and let's double-check the supplies he put in the knapsack."

"Steak bones with fresh meat on them? Wow, he didn't forget anything," Matt said.

Bob opened the sack and peered inside. "Check."

"Firecrackers, cherry bombs and two aerial flash bombs ... where did he find them?"

"Check."

"Probably in South Carolina. Can't get 'em here," John said.

"Matches?"

"Check."

"Flashlight for emergency use only?"

"How do you think I'm seeing this stuff?"

"Note paper with message for Wayne?"

"Yes."

"Candle and holder?"

"Check."

"Ribbon?"

"Check."

"Anything else?" Matt said.

"Binoculars and a bazooka," Bob laughed. "Only kidding about the binoculars."

"Good," Matt said quietly. "Doolittle's Raiders ready to head for Wayne's house, and our reconnaissance report says that his window looks out on the backyard and is unlocked. Thank you, Bonnie. Let's go."

Matt and John followed Bob on a well-used path through a hedge between the Waltons' house and Mrs. Cunningham's house, and around the goldfish pond. A bullfrog croaked as it jumped from the bank and plopped into the pond with a loud splash.

John jumped. "God! Is that a bad omen? Maybe we should turn around."

"Shhhh, John! No more negative thoughts. Always fly the plane," Matt said.

Bob giggled. "And keep the wings level."

A streetlight lit up Mrs. Cunningham's front yard.

"We can be seen now," Matt said softly. "Follow the shadows, Bob."

They reached Fort Harrison Avenue and backtracked by the Little Big Market with its bins of fruit behind the closed screen fence.

"I could eat one of those oranges right now," John said as they walked by the vegetable stand.

Matt looked down Fort Harrison in both directions. "We're vulnerable now. If you see any headlights, jump off the sidewalk and hide. Might be Jap fighters."

They turned left on Lotus Path and soon reached the railroad tracks of the Seaboard line. Darkness and a heavy junkyard stench engulfed them.

"Did we have to start walking on the tracks here?" John moaned.

"Just hold your nose," Matt told him. "No more complaining."

"Yeah, John ... you're a raider tonight," Bob added with a snicker.

"We're supposed to be in airplanes flying over this junk. How much longer, Matt? That smell's killing me."

"Bad question, John," Matt said.

"Oh God, reminds me of needing to pee on a vacation trip."

They left the tracks at the Lakeview intersection and headed down a path that skirted a fence next to a field. A cow mooed.

"You know, I don't think my dad has any rubbers," John said.

"Probably not," Matt said.

"That was a quick answer," John said.

"I mean you guys are Catholic, right?"

"So?"

"Well, maybe he doesn't need them. Now let's get our minds back on this mission." He checked his watch again. "Okay, men ... it's midnight ... 2400 hours. Let's start our roll and get this B-25 off the deck of the USS Hornet. We have our armament on board?"

"Yes, sir ... ready to hit Tokyo, Colonel Parker, and go on to land in China," Bob answered. "Let's teach that Jap he's not safe from us and all the brave airmen flying this mission."

"The bombardier is ready, sir," John added. "Push the throttles forward."

"Okay ... over the fence and off we go into the wild blue yonder," Matt whispered.

"Matt, why here with all these cows? And why so quiet?" John asked.

"We're getting close."

"I don't know if I like these cows," John said. "Do they have horns to go after us? I wish we were flying in a B-25."

"No, they're all milk cows like Elsie, the talking cow. They're not going to chase you. Your only issue will be stepping in a cow pie."

"I know," John said. "I wish we had a moon so I could see them."

"Darkness is what we need."

The boys reached the other side of the pasture. The cows grazing by the fence made a quiet, eerie sound as their tails swished, softly hitting their sides. The cows lifted their heads. Only a dim silhouette of them was visible. The boys heard a low moo and then another sound, almost like a warning with a snort of air.

"Are you sure they won't charge?" John said in a soft voice. "The one in front of me is hoofing the ground like he thinks I'm a matador. Anyone besides me scared?"

"Okay, I'm at the fence," Matt said. "Keep coming. They'll move out of the way."

Twenty feet down the fence line, something bolted out of the woods, ran a short distance and stopped.

"What was that?" John said.

"Probably a rabbit," Bob said. "Or maybe it was a pasture monster."

"Stop the kidding, Bob," John said. "That wasn't funny."

"Quit sounding like a baby."

"I hope it's a bobcat and it nails your ass, Bob."

"No more cussing."

"Okay," Matt said. "Let's get over this fence. This is Wayne's road."

"I can't see anything," Bob said.

A dog barked.

"Quiet! We've got to be stealthy," Matt whispered.

"Stealthy?"

"Yes, and invisible. Let's follow the fence and walk in the high grass instead of on the road."

They walked another five minutes in the darkness.

Matt stopped and held up his hand. "I think we're there."

"Think?" said John.

Matt knelt down in the grass on one knee. "We're there."

The other two dropped to their knees, and Bob opened the knapsack.

Matt sat back and pulled his knees up in front of him. "Okay, Bonnie said the backyard's fenced and the dog's friendly. Nina won't be there tonight. She's spending the night with a girlfriend. His mom goes to bed early and Wayne has a twelve o'clock curfew so he'll be there."

"Curfew?" John said. "I'm not believing that."

"Way to go, Mom," Bob said.

"Let's check our watches," Matt said. "Mine says twelve forty-five."

"I can't read mine," Bob said.

"Mine says the same," John said.

"Use yours, John. You guys set up in the front yard. Put the flash bombs right in front of the gate so they go off right above the house. Billy said he put long fuses on the ends. Light them one at a time. While they're burning, set off the firecrackers and a couple of cherry bombs. That should get Wayne onto the front porch. When he tries to get back in the house, hightail it back here. Wait for me and we head for the cows for safety. If I'm not here in two minutes, go on your own. Got it?"

"Got it," Bob and John answered together.

"We're over Tokyo ... there's still time to cancel," Matt said. "But this is going to work."

"See you in China, boys," Bob said.

"Affirmative," John said.

Matt looked at Wayne's house through the binoculars. "I see someone in the kitchen. It's Wayne. Oh boy, the lights went out. Give me five minutes to get ready and then set them off. If all goes well, Wayne should come out on the front porch in his skivvies."

John snorted and blew air out of his nose. "Or his birthday suit. Meet you back here at the fence, and then let's get our tails out of here."

Matt pulled the bag of steak bones, the note and the candle and matches out of the knapsack. "See you in China. Mark your watch now, John. Five minutes and the show starts." He crouched down and crawled away into the darkness.

A white figure lay in the dirt in front of the doghouse across the grass in the opposite corner of the backyard. Matt knew not to climb and jump. He lifted one leg over the fence, put the toe of his sneaker into the fence on the other side and swung his other foot over without as much as a crack of a stick. He turned to the doghouse. "Molly. Here, Molly," he said quietly.

A white shadow came across the lawn. The dog gave a muffled whine, her tail wagged like windshield wipers and Matt rubbed her head. "Good girl, Molly." He pulled out the steak bones and put them on the ground in front of her. She dropped on the ground and began to lick them.

He crawled to the window on his knees and without a sound, lifted his head just enough to take a peek. Wayne was lying on the bed.

Matt's heart began to beat so fast he was afraid that Wayne might hear the sound. He looked at his watch. Come on boys, now is the time.

"BOOM ... the first cherry bomb exploded. Then another. BOOM ... flashes lit up the surrounding trees and the top edge of the rooftop. Then off went the first round of firecrackers.

Matt lifted his head and peeked again.

Wayne sat up. Another round of firecrackers exploded and Wayne jumped out of the bed and ran through his bedroom door.

Matt could hear the latch of the front door through the open window. He carefully pulled open the bottom of the screen, lifted his leg over the windowsill and was in the bedroom. He stuck the note on the pillow and pulled out the candle and holder and placed it on the nightstand. Firecrackers continued to explode.

He struggled to get the matches out of his pocket. His hands shook. He struck the match and it didn't light.

He hit his hand hard and the hand stopped shaking. He struck the match again and placed the flame against the candle wick. The room came alive with the light and jumped like it lived along the bedroom walls and ceiling.

BOOM ... the house shook. Wayne stood in his white underwear on the porch.

Matt ran to the front door. In the dark, he felt for the dead bolt. He pushed it and flipped up the light switch beside the door.

A voice yelled from the other bedroom. "What's that?"

Matt turned and ran back into Wayne's bedroom.

In the doorway of the other bedroom, a woman in a nightgown stood looking at the front door. "Where are you, Wayne?" she yelled.

Wayne stood on the front porch clad only in his white Fruit of the Loom underwear. "I know who's out there," he yelled. "It's you seventh grade pricks. I heard your voices. Come on over here, John "The Pussy" Hollis."

Crouching behind a hibiscus bush on the other side of the fence across the front yard, John shouted, "Meow! You're the pussy ... where'd you get the nylon underwear?"

"Dance for us, queer-beer," Bob yelled.

"What did you call me?"

"Hey, queer-beer ... put on your tall high heels so you don't look like a midget on the midway," Bob answered.

"Where's your little shit-ass leader. Hiding under his mommy's skirt? Come out here and say that!"

"Meow. Tyson, you're a pussy," John yelled.

The first fuse reached its big flash bomb. KABOOM!

"Suck that up your tight scared ass," John bellowed.

FLASH! Daylight replaced the blackness of the night.

"You're a freakin' joke. You've been had." John stomped his feet and his deep loud laughter sounded like a lion roaring. "Change your tighty-whities. I see a brown circle on your pooper."

Bob reached over and slapped hands with John. "Go find your litter box, pussycat," he yelled.

Wayne bolted down the front porch steps and stopped just as Bob lit the fuse for the finale of fireworks.

"Bite me," John shouted.

BOOM! BOOM! SWISH! KA-BOOM!

Windows rattled. The sky lit up, and John and Bob disappeared into the darkness of the trees on the other side of the street.

Wayne ran back up to the front door and tried to open it. "Shit!" he yelled, and started pounding on the door. "Mom, let me in!"

Matt ran to the window, jumped out and ran across the backyard. He turned and watched Wayne rush into his bedroom in his white underwear.

Wayne's hands closed into fists and he yelled, "Where are you, you little turd?"

"Wayne, your bedroom is on fire," Matt heard Mrs. Tyson say.

The bedroom light went on. Wayne picked up the note. "Kilroy was here," Matt said aloud, as if he was reading the note. He stood at the fence and hugged the dog who growled softly as if protecting her new bones. He gave her one last pat on the head, bounded over the fence, this time not worried about sound, and bolted back to their meeting place. He could hear sirens.

John ran up. "Let's get out of here."

Matt rooted around in his sack. "One second." He pulled out a small container. "Ta-da."

"What's that?" Bob asked.

"Pepper."

Matt opened the lid and sprinkled it on the ground. "Just in case they try to follow us with dogs."

"Are you a bad guy, Matt? How do you know all this stuff?" said John. "Have you been fooling us all of these years?"

"Books—I read books."

He finished sprinkling the pepper and threw the can in the sack. "Let's go. Those sirens are close."

The three boys climbed over the fence and started back. The only light in the pasture was from the stars. The cows had moved away from the fence.

"Mission completed, boys," Matt said. "Good job. Let's get to China."

A heavy mist grew in the shallow sky a hundred feet over the boys' heads and the stars disappeared. They stayed close together, John sometimes holding on to Matt's shoulder so he didn't become separated.

"Stop," John said, his voice quivering.

Matt felt the vibration that John couldn't control. "What's going on?"

"I can't see."

"I know, but we can't take a chance on the flashlight. The mist is probably just in the pasture."

"Anything could be lurking out there in this blackness, maybe a stretched-out snake. Oh God, that's all I need … a wet, cold, scale-covered skin slithering under my feet. And what about the railroad tracks, walking over those wooden trestles."

"Trestles?" Matt said. "They're only some concrete culverts."

"Trestles, culverts, whatever. You're pissing me off, Matt. Shit, little trolls might live in them, or big things ready to pull us down into their lairs. It's too dark to walk safely."

"So, what's your answer?" Matt said. "Wait 'til morning?"

"I don't know," said John. "But right now, this is giving me bad vibes."

"John, our eyes are going to adjust," Bob said calmly. "Just give it a few seconds more."

"I know what 'blind as a bat' means now. Anybody scared?" John asked.

"Not like I was when we were going the other direction," Bob whispered. "This time I know we're going home. We're going to make it to China!"

"Good job, men. Doolittle would be proud," Matt said.

"Mission accomplished!" Bob said.

"Yeah, Matt," John said. "We got his ass!"

Matt could barely make out the pattern of a fence ahead. In the distance, a faint light that looked like a street light shone through the trees.

"Shit," John said.

"What?"

"I just stepped in a paddy of cow poop. All this walking through a poop mine and just before we get to the end, I step in the stuff." John reached down to feel his shoe. "It's hot and wet as chocolate pudding before Mom puts it in the icebox. Can you believe this?"

Bob snickered. "Smell it? The aroma of grass fricassee. Not bad actually. Sincerely, not bad."

"It's not funny, Bob," John said. "It's in my shoelaces. Oh God, it's in my socks. A sick cow made this pie."

Matt started to laugh. "Well, squish and walk, John."

They climbed over the fence and walked down a dirt road, with John still mumbling about his misfortune. Down the road, a car had stopped in the center where the dirt road ended and the pavement began.

"Oh no!" Matt whispered.

"What now?" Bob said.

"It's a police car."

Chapter 52

LIGHTS IN THE LIVING ROOM

THE STREETLIGHT ON THE CORNER cast a dim light down the residential street, and the Waltons' house was visible tucked in among the live oaks.

Bob stopped. "Oh God, we're in trouble," he said. "Look."

"Shit," John said. "The living room lights are on."

"Yep …we're in trouble," Matt said.

"I see two men sitting in the chairs beside the fireplace. My dad's in one," Bob said.

Tears welled in Matt's eyes. "The other one is my dad. That's his truck."

"Want to climb back in the house through the tree limb?" Bob said.

"No, I say let's go in the front door and face the music," Matt said.

"We're screwed," John said. "What do we say?"

"The truth," Matt said. "What else? The cookie jar's open. Where's your hand, John?"

"Damn … right beside yours."

"What time is it now, Matt?" Bob said.

"Three forty-five."

"That's a nice time for a hanging."

They stopped in the driveway. "We're here," Matt said. "We might as well go face our next fireworks for the night."

"Yep," Bob said. "Standing here won't make it go away."

"Maybe I'll just stand out here," John said.

"No, you get to walk in first," Bob said. "You're lucky. Your dad's not here."

"Okay, let's go," Matt said.

They walked up the front walkway, and Matt ran into John's back. "Quit pushing me, Matt."

"You're slower than a turtle."

"Are you the rabbit?"

"A very, very sick rabbit," Matt whispered.

John touched the doorknob and held it. He looked back at Matt and Bob.

"Turn the knob, John."

John's mood changed. He covered his mouth with his free hand and air forced its way out of his nose. "Are they praying in there?"

"Hardly," Bob said. "Open the door, John. Let's get this over with."

"Here we go," John said. He turned the knob and pushed the door open.

Mr. Walton and Mr. Parker sat across from one another in the overstuffed leather chairs beside the fireplace. They looked at the boys nonchalantly.

"Sorry," John said.

"Finally decided to hit the bed?" Mr. Walton said. "Come on in."

The three boys filed in and stood in a straight line facing the dads like a police station lineup. Bob was on one end, Matt in the middle, and John on the other end.

"We've been taking care of a bully," Matt said. "And we caught him with his pants down."

"Before you say anymore," Mr. Walton said in a quiet baritone voice. "I will protect you all from making fools of yourselves trying to get out of this by making statements on the edge of being outright untruths. Mr. Parker, Mr. Hollis and I know where you've been, what you've been up to and some of the outcomes of your night on the town."

Mr. Walton's eyes moved down the line—stopping at each face and staring a moment before moving to the next. He ended with John.

His stare remained fixed and long. John started to move around like nature called him.

"John," Mr. Walton said. "Do you need to pee?"

"A little."

"Well, tighten it up, son, because you aren't going anywhere. Your dad was here earlier and is in agreement with what I have to tell the three of you. He'll pick you up tomorrow morning at seven-thirty."

"Yes, sir."

Mr. Parker remained stoic on the couch, his arms folded and one leg crossed over the other, allowing Mr. Walton to be their spokesman.

"Let's see if I'm close. A little after midnight, you shimmied down the oak and made your way to the other side of town. Someone entered a house—maybe breaking and entering. At the same time, fireworks were set off in the front yard—illegal inside the city limits. The house inhabitant was locked outside and an intruder seen in the house—criminal mischief. Note left in a bedroom—menacing. Crossing a fence into property—criminal trespass. Which all adds up to possible time in the pokey. One of you wants to go to a service academy? Scratch that off your list. Your rap sheet follows you a lifetime."

"Now the good news," he continued. "You stayed enough in the gray zone that you're okay with the police chief. But with Mr. Parker and me, and Mr. Hollis, you're in trouble. First of all, your plans for tomorrow are canceled. Instead of the road gang, it's our gang. And I don't mean the little rascals. You're too old for spankings. Hell, you're almost thirteen. But this time last year, I'd have heated up your bum."

"Starting tomorrow, on Saturdays when your buddies are camping or sitting at the beach on blankets with what would have been your girlfriends, you three will be at my grove pulling nails out of the timber from the warehouse that was just torn down and stacking the wood in piles. Once the job is started, you three are there until there is not one nail still stuck in a board. And then Mr. Parker has a job for you. If you have a free Saturday before January, I'll be surprised."

Mr. Walton sat down in the chair. The boys stood quietly.

"Was it worth it, boys?" Mr. Parker said without changing his pose.

"Yes, it was, Dad. I'll pull out each rusty nail with a smile," Matt said.

"And I'll bandage every blister with a grin," Bob said.

"I'll pull the wood splinters out of my fingers, hoping I get another one," John said. "It was worth it, Mr. Parker … That kid's poison and he needed Raid shot in his face."

"Dad," Matt said, "seeing Billy hanging on that hook is branded into our brains. We're sorry, but we gave the bully a taste of the reality that we're around and he can't do things like that without consequences. We'll take the punishment."

The dads listened to the exploits of the night. John had them all laughing, and Bob shared the scary moments. Matt mostly listened.

When Mr. Parker stood up from his chair and stretched his back, the message was clear—it was late and time to end the conversation. Equating themselves with Colonel Doolittle was a wise move and proved to keep them safe from other disciplinary actions.

John had to ask one last question. "Did the police chief say who saw us?"

Mr. Walton pushed his cigarette butt into the ashtray and squished it around. He looked up and smiled. "I don't remember."

Mr. Parker walked outside, Mr. Walton followed him and the two dads talked on the front porch.

The boys ran up the stairs to Bob's bedroom. Bob closed the door hard. The sound reverberated in the bedroom but then silence ruled the room.

John started to giggle and broke the silence. "Well, at least we can still eat ice cream."

"I'm sorry, guys," Matt said. "I thought we'd be able to sneak back home and nobody would know we'd left the house."

Bob found a baseball under the covers and tossed it up into the dark air and caught it. "It's not your fault, Matt," he said. "And the plan worked. Doolittle's Raid was cool."

"You didn't see it, Matt," John said, "but Wayne stood out there in his skivvies, and when the flash bombs went off, I swear I saw a potato load fill up the bottoms."

John farted. They all laughed out loud.

"So," Matt said, "you're okay we did it?"

"Hell, yes," John said, still laughing. "I'll never ever forget this night. At least there wasn't a snake in the pasture. Snakes … I hate 'em."

Bob tossed the ball up again. It hit the ceiling and fell into his hand. "Well, there's one thing I know," he said, "we can expect a hot Wayne on Monday. You know … flames shooting out his wazoo."

"I can't wait," John said. "We need to tell him in the showers that if he's going to keep messing with us, white underwear might not be his best color choice."

"I don't know," Matt said. "I've got some hard thinking to do. At school on Monday, I think it should be 'mum's the word.' We need to stay silent and listen to all the talk."

"What if Wayne doesn't say anything?" John said.

"Fat chance," Matt said. "He'll sing like a canary with a cat on his cage. Let's get to sleep. We've got a busy day pulling nails at the old barn tomorrow."

Chapter 53

PULLING NAILS

MATT HAMMERED THE POINTED END of the last nail in the board resting between two sawhorses, flipped the board over and yanked the nails out with the claw of his hammer.

Nearby, off to the side of the barn, two old rusted-up grove trucks rested, and knee-high weeds grew around the tires. Half of the barn's tin roof lay on the ground, stacked sheet over sheet. The remaining tin on the old wood trusses was splotched with large rusty brown patches and somehow looked historic.

He looked out into the orange grove. In the distance, the dull yellow color of the maturing fruit and the dark green leaves of the trees blended into a mosaic of yellow specks in a sea of green. "That's one beautiful view … don't you think, John?"

"I'm glad I'm not an orange picker," John said. "That's what I think."

The expansive orange grove ran to the east, dipping down into a large shallow bowl that exposed the tops of hundreds of trees. The long rows of trees—separated by gray lines of dry, sandy ground—stood like soldiers in formation, climbing out the distant edge of the rim onto a small hill and dropping off the back, appearing endless.

A large green farm tractor pulled a wagon up a row of orange trees and disappeared over the top of the hill. "Look, we're not the only ones working on a hot Saturday afternoon," he said.

FRED HOSLEY

He pushed the board back to John and pulled a red-and-white cotton paisley handkerchief from his back jeans pocket to wipe his face. "Give me another board, John. Do you two still think Doolittle was worth it?"

"Definitely," Bob said.

"Worth every splinter," John said. "Hey, we're a team." He grabbed another board off the pile of lumber that looked like a poor spread of pick-up sticks and placed it on Matt's sawhorses beside the broken-down barn. "Wonder why they want these old boards? They look like bonfire wood to me."

"It's heart pine, John," Matt said. "Mr. Walton is going to use it for a cabin on Lake Butler. This is special lumber. They didn't know that when they were building this barn; it was just what was available."

"And Dad's going to reuse most of the tin roof too," Bob said. "It's going to be a cool cabin."

Matt picked up a broken piece of board to toss it on the burning trash pile. A rusted large sixteen-penny nail that had been curved by a crow bar stuck out the end. He looked at the nail and held it still while he studied it.

"Find a diamond?" John asked.

"I knew it ... I got it!" Matt said.

"Got what?" John asked.

"I saw something last week, was stumped and I now know what it is."

"That's a nail, genius."

"This is, but not what I saw at Hog Island. Mind if I leave a little early today?"

"Better be a good reason," John said.

"It's about that giant that was in our camp at Hog Island."

Bob put a nail head between the claw of his hammer, torqued the nail, and it came out with a loud squeak. "I'm trying to forget him. That was scarier than the scariest movie we've ever seen. He made 'The Thing' look tame."

"That wasn't a reason. Give us a clue," John said.

"Okay, I think I know who he is, and he's not like he appeared."

"And?"

"And, I want to meet him."

"What?"

"You know. Shake hands."

"You're known as a little brainy," John said, "but this is a lot of brainlessness."

"I know what I'm doing. I'm putting two and two together."

"Well, you're not getting four as the answer."

"Seriously, I think I know who this guy is … and he has answers."

Bob dropped another nail into the rusty coffee can beside him. "About what? Scaring twelve-year-olds to death?"

"Do you need a posse?" John asked.

"No."

John dropped another board on the sawhorses. "Why not? You want to die alone?"

Matt chuckled. "Trust me, John. I'm pretty sure this is not going to be scary."

"I heard that nervous laugh," John said, smiling. "Drop whatever stupid thing you're thinking. Just keep pounding nails. That's what you're good at today. Okay?"

Matt smiled like he was on the front cover of one of his mom's Hollywood movie star magazines. "I'll be careful. If I'm going to do this, now is the time. You want to find that treasure?"

"Hell, yes," John answered.

Matt threw his hammer into the tool crate and headed for his bike. He turned back and looked at John and Bob. "It's near quitting time. Cover for me?"

"Sure," Bob said.

"Should we look for you at Moss Funeral Home," John asked, "or the emergency room again?"

"Neither."

"Then where?" John said.

"Home. I'll call you later."

"Hope you'll have 'jeep in the box' news."

Matt zigzagged his bike through the deep soft sand and rode toward the city limit sign. When he reached the pavement, he waved without turning around.

"Good luck," John yelled.

Chapter 54

ANOTHER VISIT
WITH SANDY

THE SATURDAY AFTERNOON bumper-to-bumper traffic in the eastbound lane of the causeway moved slowly getting off the beach.

Matt pedaled down the middle in the other direction, frequently checking his handlebar mirror for any cars speeding up behind him.

When he reached the second bridge, he could see Sandy on the Miss Buckeye spraying down the boat with a hose. He lifted both hands off the handlebars and shook his fists high above his head like the conductor of an orchestra. "Hallelujah," he shouted.

He leaned his bike against a piling and walked down the plank onto the boat. "Hi, Sandy. I was hoping you'd be here."

"Where else would I be? Sittin' under a coconut tree, sippin' on a cold beer, serenaded by a beautiful Hawaiian girl strumming on a ukulele and doing the hula?"

They both laughed.

"Should have been with us today, Mattie."

"You had a good catch?"

"They were jumping in the boat. What brings you over here?"

"Can we talk while you work?"

"Did our last talk create more questions?"

"Yes, sir."

"Okay, but keep 'em easy."

Sandy looked at Matt's dirty jeans and black hands. "What have you been doing to look like a common laborer?"

"Pulling nails out of boards from an old barn in Mr. Walton's orange grove."

"On a Saturday afternoon? Must be a story there."

"You're like my dad. You always know."

"A black sheep stands out."

"Well, me and my buddies John and Bob ... you know them ... got in trouble last night and pulling nails was our reward."

"Must have done something bad to get them that upset."

"Yes, sir. We might be pulling nails into next summer."

"What did you boys do?"

"Did you hear any fireworks late last night?"

"I was sawing logs."

"Well, we lit up the sky at Wayne Tyson's house and then made our escape. But ... our dads were waiting for us when we got home."

"Is that why you're now here to see me?"

A grin began on Matt's face. "No, that's over and we're paying the price. I'm here because I hope you can help me with something else. I now know for sure that Dad's map was a hoax, but ..."

"You still want to try and find that treasure."

Matt stared into Sandy's eyes. "Oh my gosh, Sandy, you know everything."

"You give good descriptions. What's red, has a ladder on top and blows a siren and is headed toward black smoke? A fire engine, right?"

"Right. So, the escaped prisoner was digging on Hog Island that night and he may have some clues about other places to look for the lost treasure."

"And now you want to meet him. Am I warm?"

"You're amazing."

"No, you just ask easy sixty-four-thousand-dollar questions."

Matt turned over an empty bucket and sat down.

Sandy rolled up the hose. "Excuse me a second." He walked into the boat cabin and returned with a Budweiser and a Nehi Grape soda. He popped the Budweiser and handed Matt the soda. "Like grape?"

"Yes, sir."

Sandy turned up the bottle, poured beer down his throat and set the half-empty bottle on the flat railing. "How can I help you?"

"Answers."

"I'm listening," Sandy said.

"Is that guy, Craig, really friendly like you said?"

"Life can sometimes scar us up, but under the skin of that man lives gentleness and sweetness."

"I want to go meet him. If what you say is true, I'm okay. Right?"

"My only reservation is if I'm wrong and he harms you, it would screw with my mind and my mind's screwed-up enough."

"Does that mean I might not be okay?"

"Yep."

"How about you writing a note and I give it to him. That would be my evidence that you know me, I'm okay and you promised me I'd be okay."

Sandy scratched his head. "Are you pressuring me?"

"No, I'm begging you."

"Let me go get some paper."

"Thank you, Sandy."

"I haven't written anything, but you've got me thinking."

Sandy took a quick swig of his beer and went into the boat again. He returned with a yellow legal pad and a pencil and started writing. He folded the paper and pushed it toward Matt. "Here, take this."

"Thank you, Sandy. Thank you so very much."

"Read it."

"Now?"

Sandy folded his arms and his large biceps popped out. "Now."

Matt read the note and looked up. "This says the man Craig hurt is better and confessed the fight was his fault? Does this mean Craig might get out of jail after his breakout is settled?"

Sandy smiled and nodded. Then he chuckled. "You need to get this note to him fast and first ... is that clear?"

"Clearer than a marine's spit-shined boots before an inspection."

"That's the answer."

Matt got up from the bucket, downed the rest of the Nehi and stuck out his hand to shake Sandy's. "Thanks for the note."

"Matt, do you know where he is?"

"I think he may be under a trestle with a large concrete culvert, east of town. I was there last Saturday after we got back from the island. I saw a fresh boot footprint and a metal ring attached to an old piece of wood that looked familiar. This afternoon, it came to me. I'd seen a ring like that when we were following the map to find where to dig. There was part of an old boat buried in the sand, and I'm pretty sure it had a metal ring attached to it. He could have picked it up."

"You going now?"

"Yes, sir."

Sandy scribbled on another piece of paper and handed it to Matt. "My number ... I'll be home. If I don't hear from you in one hour, I'm calling the police."

"Okay. Thanks. I'm gone."

Matt leapt off the boat, pushed Nellie up to the street and hopped on, his heart pounding.

Chapter 55

JEREMIAH CRAIG RENNOLDS

MATT SKIDDED TO A STOP by the front door of the A & P Grocery, slammed down the kickstand and ran in. "Almost ready to close?" he asked the white-haired lady standing behind the cash register.

She smiled and nodded her head.

In the back of the store, he grabbed a pack of Lykes bologna and a small bottle of French's mustard, and then hurried down the bread aisle where he picked up a loaf of "batter whipped" Sunbeam bread. At the front of the store, he dropped the items on the checkout counter and pulled out a dollar bill. "Barely made it," he said as he handed the cashier his money.

"You're okay," she said, "but we close early on Saturdays."

"I know," Matt said.

Back on his bike, he headed for the railroad tracks and the culvert, his groceries in a brown paper sack in the basket. He'd go in the back way.

The immense live oak tree shook lightly as a soft breeze meandered through its leaves.

Matt stopped, smiled and gazed up through the branches of the tree—his destination now a short walk away. "Keep me safe and keep me strong," he said to the presence he felt there.

He walked toward the railroad embankment through the swampy

area of the forest. When he reached the cleared area, he stepped on the path leading up to the tracks. This time, he would follow the small creek. He stayed still and listened. Nothing—no sound of any kind.

He walked carefully along the creek and approached the trestle. The water trickled from the culvert into the waiting pool. He nudged a large loose rock and it rolled down three feet to the base of the embankment and splashed into the water.

Matt closed his eyes, squeezed his teeth together and froze. Nothing.

He walked to the culvert. The metal ring still sat where he had seen it the week before. Beside the ring, large boots sat on a flat stone. They looked clean and damp. A pair of socks lay in the sunlight on another stone. He detected no odor.

It was all coming together in his mind—the ring from the wooden plank on Hog Island, the reeking boot beside him as he lay in his sleeping bag—he understood it all. A sharp tingle ran through him.

A large arm grabbed him around the chest and lifted him high off the ground. It tightened and a musky smell filled the air.

Matt held the bag of food in a tight grip. "I can't breathe. You're hurting me, Craig."

He felt an immediate relaxation of the massive arm holding him. His fear began to fade. He was right. It had to be the giant from Hog Island. "I have a note for you from a friend of yours named Sandy."

The grip relaxed more. "Who are you?" said the huge man holding him loosely off the ground.

"My name's Matt Parker and Sandy is a friend of mine too."

The man dropped Matt to the ground. "What are you doing here?"

Matt turned around and held out the brown bag. "Here, I brought you some food."

The huge man with curly blond hair and a full beard opened the bag and looked down into it. "Thanks."

Matt took a normal breath and settled down. "And here's the note from Sandy. He wanted you to read it before I leave."

Craig gazed at the note with squinted eyes and then folded it up and pushed it into his back pocket. "What did you say your name was?"

"Matt Parker, sir."

"I knew a Parker once."

"I think it's my dad. About six years older than you, named Harry?"

The first hint of a smile crossed the man's face. "About like that," he said. "If he's your pappy, you got good blood."

"Thanks," Matt said. "Sandy said you were cleared of any wrong-doing except escaping."

"I guess I can turn myself in and face the music."

"We'll find you a good attorney."

"How old are you, boy?"

"Almost thirteen."

"Yep, you're Harry Parker's son, all right." He pulled the note back out from his pocket and read it again. "Is this why you came out here? To hand-deliver a note?" He half closed his eyes. "Or something else? You're some kind of smart kid."

"I think you have answers to some very important questions that I have."

"So you took a chance on me?"

"Sandy told me you were a nice man."

The giant laughed. "And you believed that crazy fisherman, sometime philosopher?"

"Yes. I know him and I know his friends."

"I'm his friend," the giant said.

"And I am here," Matt said.

He cocked his head and looked at Matt. "And you're thirteen?"

"Almost," Matt said.

The giant carried the bag over to a broken concrete block that looked like a river rock but was actually part of the riprap foundation under the railroad tracks waterway. He pulled out the contents and opened the package of sliced bologna and the cellophane wrapper of the loaf of bread. He unscrewed the lid of the mustard jar, threw a couple slices of meat on a slice of bread, picked up a knife lying on the rock and spread mustard everywhere, and then dropped a second slice of bread on top. "Want some?"

"No sir. I brought that for you."

"Thanks."

"It's no Dagwood," Matt said with a smile.

The giant engulfed half the sandwich in one bite. He wiped the mustard off the corner of his mouth with the back of his hand and rubbed it on his pants. "It's mighty fine," he said. "So, what are your questions?" He took a second bite and tossed the remaining crust in the pool of water. Minnows swarmed to the bread. "They're as hungry as me," he said. He made a second sandwich.

Matt tried to look serious so Jeremiah Craig Rennolds would understand why he took the chance to come there. "Did you dig in our hole over on the island? And if you did, why?"

"Yes, it was me," the giant said. He took a bite of the second sandwich, covered his mouth while he chewed and answered, "I was looking for buried treasure."

"How did you know about the treasure?"

"A cellmate while I was in jail."

"He knew?"

"Only that it was on Hog Island. I was hiding in the palmettos; I heard you talking. I searched after you were asleep."

The giant pushed the last corner of the sandwich into his mouth and slapped his enormous paw-like hands together, scattering crumbs from his fingers into the air. "That tasted as good as a sandwich from Sipple's Garden Seat restaurant."

"Ever been there?" Matt said.

"After a wedding one time. Not my kind of dining—a little too high class for this Belmont boy. I still like Thomas' Milk Bar."

"So, who was this guy who told you there might be a treasure?" Matt asked.

"Ace Tanner. Almost didn't know him. Pretty much skin and bones. Don't get much nourishment from alcohol. His face was hard—tan, wrinkled skin, tight to the bone. His cheekbone could perch a bird."

"Wow. That's sad."

"And when he was your age, he was growing into a star athlete. Now he's a drunk … an angry, sad drunk. While we were in jail, he told me a story." The giant's blue eyes sparkled and he moved around in his seat. "And that's why you're here.

"He held up an article he'd cut out of the newspaper and popped

334

it hard with his finger. 'I'm going to find this,' he said to me."

"Was it that 'Twenty Years Ago Today' story?"

"You read it?"

"Yes, sir."

"Well, he was all worked up about it. 'It belongs to me,' he yelled, 'and my dead ex-brother-in-law, Lem Tyson, who will never reap its rewards, may he rest in peace. But I will.' Then he kicked the metal pole of the bunk bed hard with his shoe."

"What do you think he was saying?" Matt asked.

"I was about your age when this all went down, but I was into it like everybody … the great 'search for the second map.' It was never found and in time interest in it petered away. But ole Ace, I guess, never let it go. The article must have detonated a time bomb within him."

"So, Mr. Rennolds, how did you find yourself on Hog Island?"

"Ace was getting out of jail on Wednesday and he lit a match under me. Told me he'd share the money with me. I was supposed to meet him on Hog Island Friday night, but he never showed. I remember saying, 'Let's go to Cuba.' When they led him from our cell, I thought 'I got to get out of here.' I got an opportunity the next day and took it. After dark, found a boat and headed your way. Once on the island, I followed Ace's directions from his mental map. And guess what? Ace's directions led right to where you were digging. Then I listened to you boys talk. I left the hole disappointed and returned to your camp, starving.

"Boy, you sure did smell. It woke me up."

"I know. I stank from slipping and rolling in some spoiled food while I was looking for food behind the Bay Drive Inn. I'm sorry."

Matt listened to the giant's soft voice and understood Sandy's description. "Well, I'm glad to meet you again."

"And I don't stink."

"No, sir."

"Tomorrow I will turn myself in at the jail."

"They'll like that," Matt said, relieved. "And Sandy and I will visit you."

"I'd like that."

"You know, the sheriff said you were crazy."

"That's another story. Let's just say I didn't like the way they

335

handled me after the trouble I was in. Rearranged some furniture. Enough said?"

Matt nodded his head. "Mr. Rennolds, do you think there's really treasure to be found?"

The giant smiled. "The real truth is 'no,' but dreams let you say 'yes.'"

Matt leaned back with his arms straight and his hands spread out on the sand. "Some dreams come true."

They both sat in silence for a moment and then the giant stood up. He towered over Matt. He looked almost unreal and for an instant, Matt felt scared. He thought of Sandy and the feeling passed.

"Matt Parker," the giant said, looking down at him, "you're a brave boy, coming here. What led you here must be strong within you. I hope I've helped in some way."

"You have, Mr. Rennolds."

"Well, time for you to skedaddle," the giant said. "Thank you, young man. Call Sandy when you get home and tell him I'll turn myself in tomorrow morning, and tell your dad you met a nice man. Will you?"

Matt stood up. "Yes, sir ... a special 'nice man.' And I'll call Sandy and give him your message."

"Bye, and thank you for the food," the giant said, his voice melancholy.

"Bye, and thanks for the help," Matt said. "I'm not giving up on finding that treasure. Who knows? I may get lucky and find it."

"That wouldn't surprise me one bit."

Chapter 56

TROUBLE BEGINS AS FUN

MATT SAT DOWN ACROSS from his dad's opened newspaper. "Morning, Dad," he said to the face hidden behind the paper.

His dad folded the paper and set it beside him. "And a top of the morning to you, son. You had a busy weekend. Ready for your second week of junior high?"

Matt pointed to the cherry red blister between his thumb and forefinger. "Think this will remind me of my weekend?"

"Trouble begins as fun …"

"Yes, sir. Blisters now—maybe a black eye by tonight."

"Possible, I guess. Wayne probably didn't like the whole neighborhood seeing him in his skivvies on his front porch." His dad chuckled. "The life and times of Matt Parker …"

"I could use some advice."

"Good … advice I can give, but this is *not* a sympathy pow-wow. Your blisters came because of bad choices. You meant to show him you weren't afraid of him, but you boys took the prank too far and the law only left you alone because your actions fell in a gray zone."

A hint of a dimple showed on Matt's cheek. "I'll get sympathy from the 'sheila' down the hall in the bedroom. I need advice from you, Dad."

"Your path right now has become a real crooked road, son. I see some deep potholes. You'll figure it out—or you won't. This is my advice: Handle this like you handled the Knox boy in fourth grade. Make Wayne learn his lesson. Teach him. I'll be waiting to hear how your day goes. You are strong and smart. I think the prank you and the boys played on Wayne was successful in letting him know you weren't going to let him intimidate you. That's over. Now think about your payback—your real lesson for Wayne. You can handle whatever the day brings. If you have to—hit him hard!"

"Thanks, Dad."

Mr. Parker stood up, walked around the table and squeezed Matt's shoulder. "You're welcome, son. And ... I have one more suggestion ..."

"Yes, sir?"

"Cover the blister with salve," he said with a grin.

Matt walked through the Narrows. The marble steps of the building where the seventh graders gathered looked empty. Already in the eighties, the air felt sticky and heavy. Only a few small clouds were visible in the dull blue sky.

Damp sweat cooled his scalp, but he knew the throbbing rush of heat behind his eyes did not come from the early heat of the day. His day of reckoning had started and it might become a full-fledged storm by the end of the day.

When he reached the seventh grade building, he set his books on the white stone wall and noticed a lone student with a paunchy stomach and high-waist pants standing up near the front entrance, gazing down at him through thick glasses. He was bigger and older looking, and Matt guessed he was an upperclassman.

Their eyes locked.

"Hi," Matt said from the bottom step.

The boy came down the steps and stopped directly in front of him. "You're still alive, Matt Parker. Scuttlebutt says you and your 'fear no evil' followers gave Wayne Tyson his consequences for last week's prank with one of your own, an early fireworks surprise, and Wayne's ready to make you eat dirt mixed with blood."

"Is that so?"

"That's what I'm hearing."

"At the barber shop?"

"No. I get around. You scared?"

"Should I be?" Matt answered.

"I'd be shaking in my boots."

"Who are you and how do you know my name?"

I'm in your Phys Ed class. Name's Clifford."

"Ninth grader?"

"Yep."

"Well, Clifford, I've heard enough of your predictions. I think you should move on—now!" Matt turned and watched JB walking toward him.

"Hey, Matt, who was that guy?" JB said.

"Hi, JB. I don't know … a ninth grader named Clifford … a guy who likes to be first to raise his hand."

"Put him in front of the Fort Harrison Hotel in a doorman's uniform, shouting, 'Call for Phillip Morrr-issssss!'"

"Clifford needs to lose some weight for that part."

JB slapped his hands on his knees and laughed. "Well, you are the news of the day," he said. The smile on his face disappeared.

"That's what Clifford said."

"You three sure got Wayne. Bob told me all about it. Hope this day stays calm."

"It was pretty cool at the time."

The stairs had filled with laughing and talking students, and somewhere a squeaky witch voice cried out, *"I'll get you, my pretty."*

"The thrill of blood," Bob uttered in his Bela Lugosi impersonation as he walked up to Matt and JB. He smacked Matt on the back. "Wow, we're the main talk."

"I know."

"Well, watch your back today. You're the new Billy."

"And who are you, *Kemo Sabe*?"

"The new spectator," Bob said.

Under a nearby oak, Bonnie stood, her eyes glued on him.

Matt saw her. She looked sad; her eyes were shining with unshed tears. He knew he was the cause. Tears nearly flowed from the eyes of the girl who had awakened his strange new feelings. His shyness said, "What to do?"

Rather than see Bonnie cry, he'd reach his arm deep into a hole and blindly search for a stone crab, knowing full well a snap meant pain.

He sighed and stepped off the steps, casually stooped and picked up a fallen acorn and tossed it, and stalled before he sauntered her way. As he reached her, he hesitated and tried gathering thoughts. "Hi," he said.

Bonnie dabbed her eyes with a Kleenex. "I helped you for what—this?"

The loaded verbal punch jabbed Matt hard in his heart. He recoiled. "What do you mean?"

She blew her nose in the tissue. "All you did was take kindling and start a forest fire."

"I'm sorry, Bonnie, but sometimes a forest fire is a good thing. You know, you're as pretty as Grace Kelly this morning. You're not getting on the *High Noon* train are you?"

"Of course not, Matt. I'm just worried about you. You do amaze me."

Matt patted her hand. "Sorry you're crying. It'll be okay. Remember, the purpose of all of this is to stop a bully. Don't forget what he did to Billy. I knew he'd be mad and I'm prepared to deal with him. I promised Justin I'd watch out for Billy, and I'm doing it … to the end."

"I talked to Wayne's sister. She said Wayne's mad, really mad, and he's not coming to school today." Bonnie squeezed the hand that patted hers. "It's not over, Matt. Not yet. Far from it. Nina told me. She and her mom are worried about him and he has no dad to straighten him out."

"We'll see," Matt said. "Doolittle's Raid was a prank just like his. He knows it was a payback. I'm sorry he lost his dad."

Matt looked back at the steps where he saw many eyes on them. "I don't like this attention. Are you ready to move on past this?"

"Okay."

"Good. See you at lunch."

Bonnie's tears vanished. "One last thing—watch out for Lynn, Wayne's girlfriend. She's cold and scary. Be careful. I hear she's looking for you. She's not a nice girl."

The first bell rang and kids scattered like a rush to a fallout shelter.

Matt smiled at Bonnie and they headed to opposite buildings. With Wayne not coming to school, maybe he'd get through the day with no mishaps or theatrics.

He detoured around the building to give himself more time to think and less time to have to answer questions about Doolittle's Raid. As he walked along the back of the building, he noticed a girl headed his way. He appeared to be her target.

His heart skipped a beat, and a worrisome signal overtook his body—the tingling reached his fingertips. It was her. Walking up to him in a white cotton blouse sheer enough for her bra to show through was Wayne's girlfriend, Lynn. A yellowish peroxide streak in her black hair rose from her forehead into a teased beehive hairdo, and her dark red lipstick, heavy rouge and thick coat of mascara on her eyelashes was overdone.

He remembered Bonnie's warning. He had never been slapped by a girl. He prepared himself for the expected assault. He felt vulnerable. He waited.

No eyes closed to slits, no expression of anger ... that's a surprise. She walked up to him and with her eyes close to his and her blouse touching his shirt, she said in a soft, sexy voice, "Hello, good lookin'... My, my ... you're on your way to becoming a hunk. I'm hearing you have a fancy for Bonnie."

His throat felt tight. "Maybe," he said. He hoped his voice hadn't quavered.

"Well, I hate to see that pretty face of yours get messed up. I just wanted to warn you to stay away from Wayne. I hope he cools off soon, but there's no predicting what he'll do at this point. I'm glad he didn't come to school today. See you around, handsome. Maybe we'll run into each other at the beach—or somewhere else—one of these days. I'll be looking for you."

He watched her walk up the stairs, the side slits in her tight black skirt revealing pale skin above her knees. *What was that all about? Her legs aren't tanned. She doesn't go to the beach. Watch out for her. Don't take the bait.*

Chapter 57

A POP QUIZ

MATT PUT HIS GYM bag in his locker but his encounter with Wayne's girlfriend still clung to his sweaty skin.

Bob and Billy walked toward him.

"Hi, guys. Let's get to class," he said in a voice as upbeat as he could muster. "Wayne's not coming to school. He may be mad but he's not showing his face. Maybe he's going to back off a little. Let's make it a good Monday. Maybe he's not as tough as he pretends to be."

He wrapped one arm around Bob's neck, the other around Billy's, and they wove down the hall singing "The Great Pretender."

Billy laughed. "Bob, you need to spend more time in music class so we can sound like The Platters."

"I don't care," Bob said. "I just like this song. The question is … am I loud enough?"

Billy grinned and his eyes flashed. "Oh yeah … sincerely. Wish I didn't have to leave, but my classroom is right here. See you all later."

Matt and Bob kept singing, other students joined them, and when they stopped outside Mr. North's room, everyone clapped. Matt and Bob took a quick bow, and just like they were onstage, slipping through the curtain to make an exit, they opened Mr. North's door and walked in.

Matt sat down in his seat, thinking of Lynn and Wayne. He looked up at the assignment written on the top left corner of the blackboard, still there from Friday: *Read the second chapter of the history textbook.* He'd gone to bed the night before without reading any of it. He'd been so wrapped up in the entire Doolittle escapade that he'd forgotten all about the assignment.

He opened the book and turned to Chapter Two. The second bell rang.

He looked up and saw Bob watching him with a satisfied smile growing across his face. He could tell Bob saw he wasn't prepared and the smile told him that Bob was prepared. He and Bob competed academically, and history was Bob's favorite subject.

Mr. North picked up a stack of papers neatly placed on his desk. "Good morning. Place all your notes and books on the floor. All you should have is a sharp pencil in your hand." He paused and looked around the room. "Let's see who read their assignment over the weekend. Did I tell you I like pop quizzes?"

Mr. North walked up and down the aisles placing a test on each student's desk.

If Matt had a chance, the test needed to be multiple choice. It was fill in the blank. He looked down at the paper and the realization he'd been caught overwhelmed him. He signed his name, wrote "unprepared" across the top, folded the paper in half and looked blankly at the blackboard. *It happened, Justin—I completely forgot about this assignment. I'm going to get a big fat zero on this quiz! Get home so I can get my life back to normal!*

After class, he waited by the door. Bob milled around the room and Matt stayed at the door. "What makes you do that?" Matt said as Bob finally walked up to him.

"Do what?" Bob said in a cocky voice.

"You know."

"Because I was prepared?" Bob said.

"No. Because I wasn't," Matt said.

"What does that mean?"

"It means you're happy I failed. Why is that, Bob?"

"Do you really want to hear my answer? I'm in the mood to tell you."

"Maybe I won't believe you."

"Maybe you won't want to believe me. Believe the truth, that is. I'm sorry, Matt. We all fail at some time."

"That's right, Bob. I accept that."

"Sometimes with difficulty."

"I accept that too."

"Do you really?" Bob said.

Matt broke out with a hint of a smile. "With difficulty." The smile left him. "The problem, Bob, is you cherished my shortcomings. I usually suck it up, but I can't today. I'm at the end of my rope. We got Wayne for Billy on Friday night. It was great. I knew I was going to have to face Wayne. My turn in the bucket. I don't need your smugness right now. Don't celebrate at my expense."

"Matt, I'm sorry. Sometimes you drive me crazy. You compete too. Hey, you can't always sit on the top of the mountain like a king."

"You think that's what I do?"

"Sometimes."

Matt thought about himself. Hard to accept that side of the argument. "I'm sorry too. Maybe we both need to reflect on our motives."

"Where's John?" Bob said, smiling. "He needs to hear this."

"I'm that bad?"

"Sometimes."

Matt smiled and threw his arm around Bob's neck. "You know you and John are my best friends, and John and I hate to lose—at anything."

"Sometimes humility is good," Bob said.

"I know. Forgive me?"

"Always."

Chapter 58

MR. CANTOR

THE CLOCKS IN THE CLASSROOMS had moved into the afternoon hours and the rumor of Wayne Tyson not coming to school remained true. As the bell rang for the end of fourth period, his ghost had even disappeared.

The door to the biology room was wide open—a wooden shim pressed in tight at the bottom. A number of students had gathered outside the classroom: a total of twelve—almost half the class.

Billy held his finger and thumb tight to his nose. "Wish I had a clothespin. I know why the biology door is open."

"I smell it too," JB said. "Formaldehyde?"

"Yep."

"Mr. Cantor is letting the room breathe," Matt said.

"It's not that bad," Mr. Cantor said from deep inside the room. "Come on in. Between the open door and windows, the sweet perfume of laboratory education should soon dissipate."

"I can stand the odor, but not what it does to my eyes. They are already starting to water. I wonder what's dead on the slab," JB said.

"Whatever it is, it will be neat," Matt said.

Billy rubbed his hands together in a sinister gesture. "Or maybe the scientist in there is hooking up an electrode and creating his own Frankenstein toad."

"Toad?" Matt said.

"Frog actually. I think he's demonstrating pithing today"

JB grinned. "I already know how to go to the bathroom."

"Really? What's the dark spot between your legs?" Matt said, laughing. "Just kidding, JB. Let's go in."

Mr. Cantor sat on the edge of his desk in tan slacks, his feet crossed at the ankles. He jiggled his upper foot and his Weejuns loafer—polished to a high luster with cordovan wax—looked like it might fall off. His navy blue sports coat lay neatly folded across the top of his desk with a red handkerchief partially sticking out of the breast pocket. The knot of his red-and-blue paisley tie, held in place with a tie tack, had been loosened to the level of the second button of his white dress shirt. He smiled at the students entering his classroom.

Henry R. Gregory, a student who'd moved to town over the summer, entered the room just as the bell rang. He stopped and looked at the class, at the laboratory table and then the teacher. "It fucking stinks in here. What's the lesson today ... how to make a fart from a dead frog?"

Mr. Cantor crossed his arms and his rolled-up sleeves revealed muscular forearms and a watch with a leather band around his thick wrist. "Take a seat, Mr. Gregory, and cease that language now. It's not my assignment to teach you proper manners in my class, but it is my duty to see that bad manners are disciplined so they don't continue in my class. Students in my classes are here to learn, and it is my responsibility to give them a classroom setting conducive for learning. Your comments today reflect a willing consciousness to dwarf this philosophy. Manners begin in the home, and I look forward to discussing your continuous obstruction of teaching in my class with your parents."

Henry R. Gregory stuck out his lower lip and blew air upward, flipping the long black wave covering his right eye out of his way. It fell back over his eye. He left it there and didn't move. "I'm really worried."

"You should be, but for now, let's you and I take a quick walk to the principal's office."

"Why ... and what for?"

Mr. Cantor stood up. "Why? This whole class and its teacher have had enough of your disruption. What for? Let him decide on the discipline you deserve. Not me. I'm now prejudiced. You're a smart aleck with a flair for words not suitable for females or me to hear, and I feel I can't be fair. I don't care if you ever step foot in this class again."

"I'm sorry."

"I'm not. Let's go," Mr. Cantor said, and gave him a push toward the door. The boy stumbled but stayed on his feet.

"I'll be right back, class. Stay in your seats, please. And no loud talking."

"That boy got his," Billy whispered to Matt.

"You knew it was coming. I thought it was going to happen last Friday when he started to argue with Mr. Cantor. Remember?"

"Who is he? Is he from around here?"

"He's new. I introduced myself to him on the first day. Came from New York. Picked up from him that school right now is not a priority," Matt said. "I told him he'd better watch out in this class."

"Well, he didn't listen—and I think this is the neatest class," Billy said. "We have a mule named Molly up at the farm. Henry is like Molly. She has lapses in her thinking, and when that happens, she needs to be retrained. She won't pull a wagon or a plow straight. Dad said she was just being a mule—obstinate. She liked loose reins and she tried to make us believe the tight bit hurt her mouth. But he got her thinking right again and now she loves to be in front of the wagon.

"When Henry gets enough training and gets tired of dealing with it, he'll rethink what's important, learn how to plow straight and keep the wagon on the road. Right now, Henry doesn't even know what a plow does or that he is off the road. He's got to feel those reins and understand what they're telling him."

Matt smiled and said softly, "You might be a teacher someday."

"I want to be a scientist."

"Keep learning from Molly," Matt said, and they both laughed.

Five minutes later, Mr. Cantor reentered the room. Like an afterthought, he turned and kicked the shim down the vacant hall like a hockey puck sent the entire length of the ice. It stopped at the other end with a dull bang. He shut the door, put his hands in his front pockets and walked over to his desk.

Everyone sat quietly in their seats.

Mr. Cantor leaned back against the corner of his desk and looked around the class. "I am here at this school to teach you biology. And that I am going to do. But before I do, I need you to understand me and what I believe. I need to know you, too, so I understand you.

"What I am going to tell you is not from a textbook. It is from me. It is what I feel. It's about education. It is about you. It is about the generations before you. It's about what they wanted for you, that which they did not have but yet worked and sacrificed for you so you could have.

"When I started college, the war was just over. The husbands and fathers came home. They were proud and yet most were quiet. They did not need to tell us their individual tales of war. Their hearts were full and their optimism for our country was great. What they won, they wanted to share.

"I was the first in my family to get a college degree. It was so important, so really, really important. For boys and girls, the schools expressed the need for both skilled curriculums to learn trades yet expand general knowledge. We all had a lot to learn: biology ... not to be biologists, but biology to learn more about why the knowledge of living things is fulfilling. Math ... not to all be mathematicians, but maybe just to expand the wonder of numbers and how they fit into understanding our universe. And maybe most important, the need to read, write and express ourselves.

"This is why you are here and why I am here. My parents, grandparents and great grandparents have let me know why I am here in this school now. Learn. Learn for life and learn for happiness. Let me help you. Let me here in biology teach you what I know. Grasp the fun of learning. Grasp the work of learning. Grasp the challenge. Grasp the wonders. Study and smile. We're not all geniuses, but we're all God's children. Approach school each day wondering not where this knowledge leads you, rather how you lead your life with it. Salute our forefathers and praise our Maker ... Now, let's learn some biology."

He pushed away from the desk and walked to the table.

At the end of the hour, Matt looked over at Billy. Wayne needed to hit the skids ... for Billy and for the rest of them. Mr. Cantor dealt with the disruption Henry was causing in his class. They needed to deal with the disruption Wayne was causing in their lives in the same way—grab him and cast him out of their lives.

Mr. Cantor's words interrupted Matt's thoughts. "There is one overriding lesson I want you to take with you today. For knowledge and understanding there needs to be sacrifices. Pithing is, and must be, humane. Never lose track of this. We strive for understanding and to accomplish this, there must be always a humane reason for euthanizing. This frog today felt no pain. He was sacrificed so we can learn. It's always a fine line. I hope today you can feel the incredible responsibility we have to handle this part of studying the living model. Class dismissed."

The students got up from their seats and slowly headed for the door. No one talked. Mr. Cantor covered the frog with moist cheese-cloth and gave a final nod to the retreating class.

Billy leaned over to Matt and said quietly, "Well, this hour should spark some talk in the hallways. And it won't be about pithing a frog."

Matt looked straight ahead like he was in a daze. "Yeah, that's for sure."

"Ready to go? You all right?"

"Go ahead. I want to talk to Mr. Cantor. I'll catch up with you. I'll only be a minute."

"Want me to wait?"

"No."

Matt patted Billy on the shoulder as he walked down the aisle of empty desks toward Mr. Cantor, who was sorting through a stack of papers on his desk. Matt coughed and the teacher looked up. "Hello, Matt—is it?"

"Yes, sir. Matt Parker. Have you got a moment?"

"Sure. Tidying up my desk and heading for the teachers' lounge for a cup of coffee. This hour gave me a headache. I need some caffeine to get my brain straight again."

"Yes, sir. I understand."

"What can I do for you? Frog issues?"

"No, sir ... bully issues."

"Ahh ... bully issues. You need to know how to pith him?"

SORRY YOU MISSED IT...

Matt smiled. "I could maybe be talked into it, but I came to ask your advice."

"I've been told I'm a good listener."

"I don't know why, but I'm a little nervous."

"You're okay."

"Last week a friend of mine that a group of us had vowed to protect was humiliated at school by a boy who is older, larger and sinister; his threats became actions. He got three licks from the principal. That was good, but not enough, and it hasn't stopped his threats. We're younger and smaller, but we're not afraid of him. We tried something over the weekend ..." Matt started to smile but he wiped it away and looked at the teacher with a straight face.

"I heard about that in the teachers' lounge," Mr. Cantor said with his own hint of a smile.

"Well, sir ... he didn't come to school today. We're not sure if we accomplished our goal, but if he continues, I have another plan we can put into action that will teach him the lesson, for sure. There are some potential bad outcomes, but I think it's worth the gamble, and when I saw how you handled Henry R. Gregory today, I needed to speak with you. You handled that situation logically and methodically and satisfied all of us who were there watching. Your solution could remedy our problem. Do you have any advice for me?"

"Do you think my answer is—or might be—leave it to the adults, at school or at home?"

"Yes," Matt said.

Mr. Cantor stood up, placed his sports coat over his arm and put his hand on Matt's shoulder. "Matt, I'm a teacher and I'm a man. As a teacher, I'd say ... consider letting this bully feel the wrath of someone in authority. Let him learn his consequences by rules of fairness, rules of morality and rules of expectations. As a man, I feel an emotional tugging within me. I listen and hear your courage. I will never say anything to discourage that strength." He slipped on his sports coat. "Does that help?"

"More than you know. Thank you, sir."

Mr. Cantor smiled. "You're welcome, Matt. Good luck with the bully."

Chapter 59

THE SHOWERS

THE SEPTEMBER SUN in the cloudless blue sky bore down over the brown patches of weeds and crisp burned grass.

John joined Matt on the steps in front of the seventh grade building. He wiped his forehead, removing the sweat already beading on the surface. The wax holding his flattop firm ran onto his skin above his eyes and cast an oily sheen that reflected the bright sunlight.

"A little hot?" Matt said.

"Yeah," John said. "You don't look so bad ... no 'Waynster' today did the trick. You've recovered."

"Yeah, the day didn't start off so good with Mr. North's pop quiz."

"Tests don't mean anything to me, but I understand. If I struck out in a big game because of not studying, I'd have felt like you did this morning."

"I'm better now, but I'm not sure what to expect from Wayne. That guy doesn't react like us. At least we won't have to deal with him in Phys Ed today."

"He's a bad SOB, isn't he?"

"Yep."

"Remember, whatever happens because of Doolittle, Wayne standing on the porch with only those tighty-whities covering his giblets makes it all worthwhile. We got him and we're probably going to have to pay the price," John said.

Bob and Billy walked up and Bob gave Matt a long look. "You okay?"

"Pretty good."

"Damn good," John said.

Bob grinned at Matt. "We pissed Wayne off. He didn't even come to school today. That says something. When he finally shows up, he'll probably just give us the evil eye and then cuss us all out."

"I guess," Matt said, shaking his head. "I hope we're rid of him. Let's get going ... don't want to have the coaches mad at us for being late."

Billy nodded his head. "Today's a new day. He learned there's consequences with us and he'll find another person to bully ... or maybe not be a bully at all. When Justin gets home, things will change."

"Maybe for you," John said. "But Matt and Bob and I have pissed him off now. Doolittle's Raid could have been a warm-up and we might have to think of something else."

The boys walked past the office where both coaches sat at their desks, and into the locker room. Whistles, catcalls and occasional screams rose to a high volume and echoed off the cement walls. The ceiling lights cast shadows around the room and the room smelled like a moldy dungeon.

"This is the place to be, right, Appie?" John yelled. "Who would want to be under an umbrella at the beach when this oasis is a choice?"

Appie threw a laced shoe into his locker and shot John a bird.

Coach Smith walked into the locker room, blew his whistle and yelled, "Listen up! Every year I have one trouble class. ... This year it's this one. You're testing me." He walked around the room, swinging his whistle around his wrist. "Today, everyone takes a shower—not a wet cloth under an armpit like you're bedridden in a hospital. I want soap and water in every crevice. No one leaves this room smelly. Is that clear? I let it go last week. Not this week."

He walked over to the ninth grade bench. "And, if I see a towel folded into a rattail or see anyone pop someone on the butt with it, I promise you'll feel this leather strap on your butt instead. That's not a threat, men. You want to test me, Cracker Jack?"

"No, sir."

"Skeeter?"

"Definitely not, Coach."

"Good. And Bruce—I don't want to see any more of that behavior I saw last week with you and your cousin and these two friends of yours." He took two steps and turned. "Fall outside in five minutes in your regular groups." Without another word, he put the whistle around his neck and went back toward his office.

"I told you. That whistle is his rattle," John whispered. "I'm glad he focused on the ninth graders today. When he started talking about crevices, I could only think of Applewhite trying to clean all of his."

Matt tried not to laugh, but he wanted to laugh for any reason to clear the tension he'd felt all day. He began to laugh and couldn't stop. He laughed until his tears flowed.

Outside, Coach Shank yelled at the seventh graders, "Okay, boys. Single file for roll call and then we're picking gator ball teams."

"Why do I always get picked on a team that Applewhite is on? He's going to just stand around, sweat and complain," John said as the boys walked across the street to the fields.

"Maybe because you're both so alike," Bob said. "Besides, what do you care? Today's game is just for fun and exercise."

"Fun is winning," John said, "and Appie couldn't care less. See Robbie over there? He tries out for all the teams and never makes them. He's not good enough, but I like him on my team here. He tries and has fun. Fatso over there just picks his belly button looking for lint." He laughed. "Hey Bob, am I a belly button picker like Applewhite?"

"No," Bob said, "but you both sweat a lot."

Coach Smith blew his whistle and yelled to both groups. "Hit the showers. We're letting you off easy today so you'll have plenty of time in the showers, and remember, I better not see a dry head among you."

"Why can't math class go this fast?" John said.

"You know the old saying," Matt said. "'Time stops when you're having fun.'"

"I hope it stays fun," John said. "When we hit the shower, I plan on popping that eighth grader over there with the red hair. He's a friend of Danny's and I owe him one, but if Coach Smith sees me, the fun might stop real fast."

Bob, John, Matt and Billy took off their gym clothes, wrapped towels around their waists and hurried into the crowded shower rooms.

John hung his towel on a hook, waved his hand through the fine mist and started to cough. "No one in here has the croup. You guys must be trying to fog it up so no one can see your privates. Why take a hot shower in the summer in the middle of the afternoon? It'll be cold water for me and the soap will work just as well."

Matt hung up his towel beside John's. "Hang your towel over here, Billy. I've been on the swim team since I was eight so I'm used to showering in a group, but the first few times, I think I felt just like you probably do now. Actually, I still feel that way ... a little. Let's go in. Just face the wall, and we can talk as we shower off."

He picked up two bars of soap off the tray suspended from the pale green concrete block wall, pulled them apart and gave one to Billy. "Don't get this soap in your eyes or you will cry for an hour."

"Thanks," Billy said.

Matt rubbed the soap in his hands and spread the lather over his face and up into his hair. He began to talk with his eyes closed. "There are two words that describe the public shower experience for boys: modesty and pride. You listening, Billy?"

"Yes."

"Good. So, those words define two types of normal behavior that I call the postulate of the public shower. You still listening?"

"Yes."

"Me too," said John from the foggy room.

"Me too," said Bob standing on the other side of Matt.

Matt rinsed his face off with the water from the shower. "The postulate states: all teenage boys taking a public shower always take a peek at everyone's privates. And if we are modest, we like to face the wall when we shower and cover ourselves with a towel the minute we exit, or if we are proud, we face outward when we shower and are not in a big hurry."

Billy started to laugh and covered his mouth with his hand. "I know what category I'm in."

Matt laughed too. "I think modesty fits most seventh graders, and pride fits most ninth graders, especially the ones that could get into the Navy. The bottom line is we're all normal. It's just where we fit in that postulate."

"That's why, in the middle of the summer, we modest kids still like hot showers," Bob said. "We don't need cold on this. It's bad enough as it is."

John filled his cupped hand with cold water and threw it on Bob, then another on Billy, and finally, one on Matt. "Does that remind you guys of *The Wizard of Oz*?"

"You've turned us all into turtles," Bob screamed.

John washed away the rest of the soap on his face and his face turned red. "We can't all be a Charlie Niven or a Mr. Chapman," he said, blowing water out of his mouth.

Bob and Matt laughed out loud at John's statement. "Who are they?" Billy said.

"Charlie's a ninth grader and if there was a contest, he'd win the blue ribbon."

"He's big?" Billy said.

"Oh yes," Bob answered.

John started to laugh. "He might embarrass our dads."

"And Mr. Chapman was the custodian at South Ward," Bob said. "John and JB saw him peeing in the urinal. Ever since, John always talks about Chapman's Dick."

"Enough shower talk," Matt said. "Just remember, we're not a Charlie yet and that's all right."

John wrapped his towel around his waist and laughed. "We might never be a Charlie. We take what we get. I'm still waiting for hair down there."

"Let's get out of here and get dressed," Bob said.

John suddenly froze like a pointer on a covey of quail, removed his towel, folded it quickly and stared at an eighth grader walking out of the other shower room, rubbing his head with his towel. "Watch this, Billy," he said. He twisted his towel and flipped it into a tight tail, pulled the towel back and sent it forward. Just before it completely uncoiled, he snapped the towel and hit the unsuspecting eighth grader on his bare butt.

A scream followed the snap, but the eighth grader kept on walking.

"We're even, buddy," John said.

"Lucky for you there's enough noise in here that Coach Smith probably didn't notice that scream," Bob said. "Let's go, John."

"What's your hurry, Bob? Your mom's not picking us up. We're walking downtown today, right?"

"Yeah, and I'm hungry. I've got a vision of myself sitting in Brown Brothers sucking the straw in a chocolate ice cream soda."

While the other boys dressed and clowned around, Matt sat alone on the end of the seventh grade bench and thought about the day as he laced his desert boots. Flunking the pop quiz, seeing Bonnie's tears, experiencing Lynn's unexpected flirtation with him and wondering if Wayne would show up had made the day an emotional one. He shook his head in disbelief that it was time to go home and he'd gotten through it all.

As he prepared to stand up, a stiff finger poked him hard in his back.

He jumped up and whipped around. Jimmy Knox stood eye to eye with him. He leaned toward Jimmy, their faces inches apart. "What's up, Jimmy? Lost? This isn't your Phys Ed period."

"I've got a message for you," Jimmy said with a smirk on his face.

"Let me guess," Matt said. "It's a message from Wayne. So, hurry up. Tell me and get out of here."

"Wayne's outside under the big tree by the girls' volleyball court. He's waiting to tell you about his plans."

Chapter 60

A CHALLENGE
FROM WAYNE

THE LIVE OAK TREE stood alone in a strip of sparse, trampled grass and flowering wild weeds between the girls' volleyball court and the street used by the buses. Its root system protruded through the gray sand and its huge trunk stretched high in the air before large branches spread out with a thick foliage of shiny green leaves and scattered clumps of mistletoe that created a wide circle of shade on the ground.

Matt's eyes focused on the trunk of the tree. He could see Wayne casually leaning against the trunk, leg bent and boot pushed against the bark, looking the other direction. Matt's stomach churned, but he kept walking. It was time to face the inevitable.

As Matt approached the tree, Wayne straightened his leg and stepped out into the open. He folded his arms and his biceps filled the sleeves of his grease-stained white T-shirt.

"Well, I sure expected you earlier," Matt said. "Why did you miss school today? Didn't you get enough rest this weekend?"

Wayne stepped closer, reeking of cigarette smoke, engine oil and gasoline fumes. "Shut up, prick. Are you ready for an ass kicking? I'll be waiting for you on the dirt road after the bell rings—if you've got the balls to show up."

"You don't have to worry about that. I'll be there."

Wayne hooked his finger into the denim jacket on the ground, slung it over his shoulder and stepped into the street. "You know where to meet me, and don't be too long. I've got some important things to take care of—after I take care of you."

Matt watched Wayne cross the street and then turned to walk back to the Phys Ed building. He was ready. John and Bob would be there. Now was the time to end this.

He walked past Jimmy who'd been standing within hearing distance. "You're on the wrong team, buddy," he said.

John walked out of the lavatory with a comb in his hand.

"Going to go down and watch the fight after school, pretty boy?" Bruce hollered to him from the ninth grade side of the room.

John looked over at Bruce. "What fight?"

"The fight between your buddy and Wayne this afternoon," Cracker Jack said.

"Wayne's not even at school today," John said.

"He is now. He's outside at this very moment talkin' to the little pain in the ass," Bruce said.

"Good," John said. "It's about time we get this over. I can't wait to see him kick Wayne's ass."

"You're dreamin' boy," Bruce said.

"Yeah? You just wait and see." John looked at the door just as Matt walked into the room. "Do you know you're fighting Wayne?"

Matt sat down on the bench. "Yep, got the invitation. Just heard it myself."

"Damn," John said. "So he showed?"

"Outside the gym."

"Somehow you look bigger to me right now. A yardstick wouldn't show it, but I like it. You sound okay too. Alley fight, round two? Maybe I can help this time."

"I'm fine," Matt said. "I knew this was coming when Justin called. It was just a matter of time."

"You're growing taller as we talk, but maybe I should take your place. The alley ending has me worried."

Matt shrugged. "No worries. Thanks though."

"I like your confidence. Stay positive, right?" John said with a touch of skepticism in his voice.

Matt picked up his books and gym bag. "Right. Here come Bob and Billy. Let's change the subject."

"Just heard," Bob said. "I guess Wayne's not happy with the leader of the Doolittle's Raiders."

Billy sat down on the bench and put his head in his hands. "He's outside bragging about how he's going to beat you up. And it's all because of me."

Matt popped him on the arm. "I've already told you. This is no longer about you. Wayne's an asshole always looking for some way to make himself seem bigger and better than he thinks he is. It's just my turn in the bucket. Don't worry. I can take him and I'm ready to do it. Let's get over there and get it over with."

Outside, the bell rang and a stream of students from the Phys Ed class headed for the dirt road that ran through a wooded lot across the street from the western edge of the school property.

At cheerleading practice, Bonnie stopped doing cartwheels and watched Matt leaving the gym building with Billy, Bob and John. "Why are Billy and Matt walking that way?" she asked Dee and Elaine. "I thought Billy was riding the bus home."

"I just heard that a lot of the boys are going over to the dirt road to watch a fist fight," Elaine said.

Bonnie covered her mouth with open hands, gasped and closed her eyes. "Who?"

"I don't know," Dee said, "but I heard Mrs. D say she saw Wayne Tyson standing under this tree while we were in the showers, and she was ready to send him away when he walked over to the boys' area and started talking to someone. He's probably involved in it some way."

"Oh no!" Bonnie said. "Wayne wasn't at school today. If he was talking to one of his friends, they might be planning something."

Dee wrapped her arm around Bonnie's neck and squeezed. "Don't worry. It's going to be all right. We'll check on them when practice is over."

A group of eighth and ninth graders in the Phys Ed class headed for the dirt road across the street from the school property, talking and laughing as they walked to watch another fight.

Matt, John, Bob and Billy followed the group, and Matt suddenly realized there would be lots of spectators at the fight ... maybe forty or fifty. They were coming from everywhere, not just Phys Ed class. His heart fluttered and shyness overwhelmed him. He wanted to bolt.

John stopped. "Man, how did all these kids find out about this so fast?"

"Danny says news travels fast when there's a fight over there," Bob said.

"I'm a little scared," Billy said. "Justin's told me about these, but I never expected to be at one. I just see high weeds and trash plants over there. Where's the dirt road?"

"It's about twenty feet back from the street," Bob said. "The trees thin out and the road opens up into a sandy area in the middle of some trees. It's perfect because you can't see it from the street."

A solitary red Indian motorcycle made its way down the street by the school, weaving slowly back and forth. The eyes of the blond-haired driver searched the group of students walking across the street, and his bike slowed to a crawl. He steered to the nearby curb and stopped. He casually folded his arms together and nodded toward Matt with a 'come here' jerk of his head.

Matt walked up and rested a hand on the vibrating polished chrome handlebar. "Hi, Sam," he said in a clear and confident voice over the sputtering of the loud engine.

"Matt, you know Wayne will be throwing more than words. He'll be throwing hard fists. I heard on the grapevine that you entered school today carrying some baggage. My advice is to hold up, lay low and let the stinky dead seaweed go out with the tide."

Matt stepped back. "Thanks, Sam, but my blood is hot. It's moving on that tide—and its ripping. This time my anchor is in the boat."

"Okay, buddy. Then give him hell!" Sam goosed the throttle, lifted his boots off the pavement and screamed away.

"Not taking his advice?" John asked.

Matt looked straight ahead. He didn't answer.

Chapter 61

THE DIRT ROAD FIGHT

WAYNE STOPPED OUTSIDE the group of students who'd gathered to watch the fight. He took a long drag off his cigarette, flicked it to the ground and smudged it deep into the soft dirt with his boot.

Matt stood in the middle of a group of kids, in his blue jeans, plaid shirt and desert boots, his hair still wet from the shower, talking to John, Bob and Billy.

"Give 'em room," Cracker Jack yelled.

The kids who'd come to watch clasped hands and spread out to form a large circle around Matt. Wayne handed his jacket to Bruce, pushed his way through the crowd and dipped under the outstretched arms into the circle.

He gave Matt the once-over. Matt appeared muscular, but was smaller than most others he'd faced, and he seemed casual and relaxed. Wayne found that a little worrisome. He shook his head. "Look what we have here. I feel like a babysitter." He stepped closer to Matt. "Rules?"

Matt didn't flinch. "Your call."

Wayne scuffed the dirt with his boot. "Since you're a nice guy and only the guys who love to see a little blood are here to watch this ass-kicking, I suggest we keep it refined."

"Should we have worn ties?" Matt said with a smile.

"Don't screw with me, prick."

"I like the word 'fair.' Stay away from the balls, the eyes and the Adam's apple. Can you fight for honor?" Matt said.

"I'll try my best, asshole."

"Bending arms 'til they break?" Matt said.

Wayne grinned. "Of course. If you want it to end, try to spit out an 'I give.'"

Matt nodded.

Wayne spotted something he didn't like. Matt's face showed no sign of tension. He looked like a kid who was ready to sit down to a game of checkers. It was the same look he'd had in the alley. The little twerp might not be the Aussie mommy's boy that he thought, or he might not realize the difference between fighting in grade school and junior high. Either way, this was his chance to teach the kid a lesson and get some respect from the guys at Five Points at the same time.

As he scanned the circle to see who was in the crowd, he came up with another possibility. Justin chose him to protect his baby brother—Billy, the nerd. The kid might actually have the equipment. *Pinned that note on my pillow. Had the balls that night. Should have thought of that sooner … too late to worry about it.* In three years, he'd never lost a fight on the dirt road. Make this another notch on the gun.

He moved toward Matt and stopped three feet away. "Ready when you are, twerp. Feeling tough?"

Matt remembered Mr. Weller's lesson—a raging lunatic is the fighter that gives you the best chance. "Is Kilroy here?" he said, a cocky smile on his face.

Wayne's fists tightened, his knuckles blanched above his grease-filled fingernails and the smell of gasoline rose from his sweaty skin.

Matt raised his fists and made a slow move to the left.

Wayne slid to the right and looked for an opening. Matt faked with his head, giving Wayne a good idea of what to look for next. Get it over quickly. Make the twerp feel some real pain, maybe crack a rib or two. He anticipated the punch and lunged in to deliver a blow to Matt's midsection, realizing as he delivered the blow that something wasn't right. The kid was a lot quicker than he'd anticipated. The little shit had doubled back on his own obvious fake and was two feet to the right of where he should be.

The crowd started to cheer.

"Way to go, Matt, baby," John yelled.

Wayne had been suckered and was out of position, but he wasn't worried. He pulled back his fist and got ready to go back in again on a different plane. He started to deliver his second strike. Something was wrong. He sensed Matt's fist bearing down on his face. The crushing blow landed just above his right eye. It hit him so squarely that he went down on one knee for a second. As the next one headed his way, Matt stopped his fist. Why did he stop? If that blow had landed, he'd have been knocked out. He hadn't been hit that hard in a long time. He'd better launch a counterattack fast or he was going to get his ass kicked. This boy was lightning fast. He sent two more jabs.

Matt pivoted on his back foot and kept out of range. He countered. The white knuckles of his tight fist struck Wayne's upper lip, split it and stopped as it banged into an upper tooth.

Blood gushed from Wayne's lip and he could feel that his tooth was out of line. The follow-up punch hit his right eye at the upper brow. His eye began to swell. He was in trouble. The last punch struck him under the chin. The uppercut jarred him and he saw stars. He collapsed on all fours and then hit the ground.

Matt's feet were close beside him. He could feel the blood running down his neck. He had one chance. He struggled to his hands and feet in the soft dirt, grasped a handful of the dirt and flung it into Matt's eyes, blinding him.

As Matt staggered back, trying to wipe his eyes, Wayne kicked him hard in the groin. Matt buckled at the knees and held his crotch. Wayne kicked him again. He had him now. He struck him straight in the left eye. Matt collapsed.

Before Wayne could kick him again, an arm came out of the crowd, caught him around his neck and spun him around. Sam Scott stood staring at him. "It's over, Tyson. Get out of here. You don't have a clue what the word honor means. You're an SOB, and we all know who the real winner was."

Sam pulled Matt to his feet. "You let him sucker you. Never, ever fight fair in this kind of a fight. There are no trophies here." He patted Matt on the back. "Go home. This fight is over."

He looked over at Wayne. "You heard me. This fight is over. Get outta here and go clean up your bloody mess of a face."

Wayne walked away, wiping his nose, lip and chin with his bloody T-shirt. Bruce walked beside him with the jacket still in his hand. Sam followed three steps behind.

Most of the crowd moved back across the street onto school grounds, but a few of the hoods hung around talking and laughing with exaggerated arm movements replaying the fight and Wayne's groin kick that ended it.

Jimmy Knox stood alone at the edge of the area and watched the group light their cigarettes and scatter.

Matt stood next to John, silently patting his swollen eye with his dirt-filled handkerchief. A glistening web of road maps filled the pink whites of his eyes.

"That's strange," John said. "Looks like Jimmy might be on the fence."

Billy picked up Matt's books and gym bag and wiped a tear rolling down his face. "What does that mean?"

"He knows the right side, but family blood is tugging on him," Bob said. "Right, John?"

John nodded and his eyes looked over at Matt.

Matt remained silent, patting his swollen eye with his bloodied handkerchief.

"I know where there's a quiet restroom," John said. "Follow me buddy. We gotta clean you up."

Chapter 62

CLEANING UP

JOHN LED THE GROUP to a lone door at the end of the main building of the school. He turned the knob. "It's unlocked."

He pulled the door open and revealed the school auditorium— quiet, unlit, filled with long curved rows of connected dark folding chairs, a purple curtain partially enclosing the stage, a lectern along its edge and in the shadows at the back, a trampoline, ladders and stored equipment.

"Last time we sat in here, it was noisy," Bob whispered, "but now it's only inhabited by us and sad lonely ghosts showing Matt respect."

"And so they should," John said. "I'm proud of you buddy. Sam said it best. You beat the SOB. You were destroying him until the end when he kicked you in the balls." "Yeah, Matt, you looked like Sugar Ray Robinson. Wayne's just a dirty fighter with a black heart," Bob said.

John shut the door behind them and darkness filled the area. "Up the incline on this side is a large boys' bathroom. It should be quiet and private." His voice echoed, bouncing off the dark walls and high ceilings.

"Lead the way, John," Bob said.

John pushed the bathroom door open and swept his free hand across the open doorway. "Enter my private study," he said, and a smile wrinkled his cheek. "This is where we need to be."

Billy turned on a faucet and the whooshing sound of water filled the room like a waterfall in a forest. "Here you go, Matt. Use your handkerchief like a washcloth and I'll get some paper towels."

The water in the bowl of the white sink turned dark as dirt ran off Matt's forearms, hands and face, and blood from the handkerchief dissolved.

John walked behind Matt who was bent over the sink and studied himself over Matt's shoulder. "Victory was yours. What made you hold back? You were kicking his ass and you could have finished him off."

"You were so close. I thought you had him," Bob said from across the room, struggling to button his jeans. He pulled down the lever on the urinal and stared blankly ahead at the wall. Another loud whoosh joined the water sounds in the room.

Matt lifted his head and looked at John in the mirror. "I don't know, John. I was ready to nail him, but for an instant I saw the possibility I might hurt him bad."

"Yeah, and he nailed you before you could say 'Jack Shit.'" John splashed water on his face and yanked a paper towel from the dispenser, dried his face and balled up the towel and threw it into the basket, tightening his mouth. "And I got more to say."

Matt stared at him without smiling. "So, say it."

"I remember the stories Lawrence Fraley told about you when you lived out in the country when you were six or seven. He said you were tough at the so-called bullpen and you'd wrestle anyone. And how about Justin? He picked you to watch out for Billy here, against Wayne, but something happened in the alley with Wayne when this all started. I saw it. You laid down then ... and now, the same thing today. You're too kind and thoughtful. Gentleness doesn't fit the likes of Wayne. That dirty SOB doesn't know etiquette. Chivalry is dead with him. So take off the scarf, you old World War I biplane pilot. You found that out. Matt, you've got something going on in your head and you'd better figure it out or hand it off to adults. Thank God for Sam Scott."

Matt took the paper towels Billy had stacked beside him and began drying off. All he wanted to do was get away from everyone. His groin ached, but his heart felt like it might burst. A heavy concrete block pressed on his chest. He held back his tears, but they wanted to erupt and blow out like a water balloon hitting a sidewalk. He held the emotion inside. His inner self knew … now *he* knew. "You're right, John. Something's going on. I need to figure it out and I know who can help me do it."

"Mr. Weller?"

"That's where I'm headed first."

"You already know how to fight," Bob said.

"I need to learn how to finish."

John patted Matt on the back. "And you need to learn it fast."

Matt nodded. "Thanks, John."

"Sorry," Billy said.

"Don't be. I'll be fine. I'm going to get moving and I'll see you all in the morning."

At the corner of Drew Street, Matt stood waiting for the light to change.

"Matt," a familiar voice yelled.

He turned his head toward the voice. "What?"

"Wait up."

Jimmy Knox walked up and stopped nose to nose with him. "Am I still your friend?"

"Not the best time to ask … but sure."

"He's bad, but he's my cousin."

Matt put one hand in his pocket. "And …"

"Blood is thick."

"And …?"

"You were the winner, and I wanted you to win."

"Thanks."

"That's all I wanted you to know," Jimmy said, and he turned and walked in the other direction.

Chapter 63

TALK WITH MR. WELLER

MATT TURNED ONTO Mr. Weller's street and his heart started to pound. *Please be there, Mr. Weller. I need to talk to you.*

Mr. Weller stood on his front porch, a dull tin sprinkling can in his hand, methodically tipping the end into a flower container, pouring in water walking to the next plant, and repeating the process. He looked up and set the can down on the porch railing as Matt walked up to the porch. "What happened to you?"

"Got in a fight."

Mr. Weller shook his head. "I hope your opponent looks worse."

"He did … for a while."

Mr. Weller looked like a trainer sorrowed by a look of defeat he saw as his fighter walked back to his corner at the bell ending a round. "Need to talk?"

"Yes, sir."

"I'm listening."

Matt walked up the steps and looked into Mr. Weller's perceptive eyes. "Mr. Weller, it was Wayne and I had him, but when it came time for the knockout punch, I stopped. He was on the ground, threw dirt in my eyes, and then he kicked me in the groin and nailed me when I wiped my eyes. You know I need help. I should have finished him off when he fell, but I didn't."

"Do you know why?"

"I'm not sure, but I think so."

"I'll be right back. Have a seat in the rocker. It's my confession chair."

Mr. Weller opened the screen door, smiled and winked. "Setbacks are restart buttons. Let me get us some tea."

The screen door banged shut.

Two minutes later, Mr. Weller returned and handed Matt a cold glass filled to the brim with iced tea. "Truth serum."

"Thank you," Matt said.

He moved a chair close to Matt and sat down.

"Settle yourself. Take your time." He pointed to the glass. "Sip away. It will be good for you. Cleanse your soul."

The glass jiggled in Matt's hand and tea spilled over the rim and ran down the glass, dripping into his lap. He pushed the glass hard into his lips and stopped the shaking. He hoped he could settle his nervousness and talk. He drank and hoped the cold liquid would clear his throat and allow his voice box to work. He swallowed, his developing Adam's apple pushed out, and he wiped his dry lips with his wet tongue.

"Talk to me. I'm ready if you are," Mr. Weller said.

"This isn't easy."

"I know."

Matt coughed and cleared his throat. "Three years ago ... it's so hard to even think about, but I know I need to tell you." He took another sip of his tea and pulled in a deep, fresh breath. "Have you got time for me to tell you about it?"

"All day ... all night."

"It might be long?"

"I'm listening."

"It was awful and it was sad. My mother dropped John, Bob and me at the beach one summer morning right before school started. We planned to spend the day there like we always did, just swimming and messing around with the other kids. After lunch, we were tired of the water so we decided to walk to the north end of the beach and see if Jonathan, a friend of ours who lived up there, could play. We saw a crowd gathered on the sand, and we ran up to see if another old person had a heart attack while swimming, something we had seen before. They wouldn't let us get close. They were working on a little boy ..."

The '53 blue and white Buick pulled in the parking lot at four o'clock and parked on the shell-paved area in the shade of the Australian pines. Blue skies surrounded the white sun and not one cloud competed for competition. The skies touched the Gulf waters to the west and Clearwater's small skyline to the east.

June Parker opened the door and got out of the car. Dressed in white shorts and a blue halter top, she looked more like a high school student than the mother who was picking up the nine-year–old boys she dropped off there at ten that morning.

Matt walked toward the car, a towel over his shoulder and a black inner tube hooked under his arm. The smile that usually filled out the dimples of his cheeks was missing. "Hi, Mom."

"You look sad," his mom said.

John ran past Matt. "Mrs. Parker, Jonathan Wolfington's little brother Timmy just drowned!"

Mrs. Parker threw her hands up against her cheeks. "What?"

"Oh, Mom," Matt said, covering his face with his hands. "It's true. He drowned."

Bob walked up and put his arm around Matt's shoulders. "We ran way up the beach and we saw him."

"Yes, but we didn't see it happen," John said, an excitement in his voice.

"Son, do you know how it happened?" Mrs. Parker said.

"Little Timmy, along with some older kids, were on the north beach near their home," Matt said. "You know, where the water goes up to the seawall at high tide."

"Today, the tide was low," Bob said. "He was picking up shells by the edge in the small rolling waves and they looked over and saw him face down in the water with the waves moving his body back and forth. His sister pulled him back out on the sand and screamed for help."

"A lady started giving him artificial respiration," John said, "but they said his blue face and purple lips never changed."

"Finally, the ambulance arrived," Matt said, "and the men tried to revive him, but they couldn't. After a long time, they put his body on the stretcher and

covered his head with a blanket, and then they carried him out over the hard, wet-packed sand to the ambulance parked on the street. It left the beach quiet and slow, and the red light on the car's roof changed from a flashing, rotating, bright Christmas red to a dull red glass dome. Everybody was crying."

Matt wrapped his arms around his mom's waist and sunk his head deep into her stomach, pulling very tight. "Mom, he was such a happy little boy and there he was … lying on his back, in red swimming trunks … his blond curls caked stiff with sand and saltwater, not moving … with his eyes closed."

All three boys began to cry and Mrs. Parker silently opened the trunk for their inner tubes, and got them into the car. The Buick engine started and the trip home was slow and quiet.

The night of the visitation, a hushed silence persisted around the dinner table after Matt's dad said the grace. His prayer reflected on the terrible loss and blessings on the family. It compounded the sadness and created an anticipation of what awaited them later in the evening.

Matt felt a sorrowful urge to cry again like he did in his bedroom before being called to the table for supper. The sadness hung over the table like a cold, foggy mist. It soaked into everything that it touched.

His mom pulled a Kleenex from her apron and dabbed her eyes. She placed dinner items on the center of the table beside a single lit candle. Its flame jumped and moved. Matt watched it. Tragically, he wanted the candle flame to be the toddler, who they would later see at the funeral home, whose living moments were snatched away.

"Matt," his dad said, "times like this reveal the finality of life. Even a young emperor could not be shielded from its presence." He looked into Matt's eyes. "But you do not need to go."

"It hurts so bad," Matt said, through his sobs.

"I know," his dad said.

Matt pulled his forearm all the way across his nose. He looked at his mom and then back at his dad.

"I want to go."

"Okay," his dad said. "Matt, remember when you look in the casket, all that is there now is a vacant house. The occupant has left. He sits with the angels, is maybe already an angel himself."

372

Mr. Parker pulled into the parking lot of Wilder Funeral Home and turned off the car's headlights. They all got out of the car and Matt stretched out his arms, reaching into the night for an invisible object beyond his reach. It relieved some tension.

The three pulled each other together in a tight embrace and walked to the door, hand in hand.

Outside, a man in a black suit and tie with polished black shoes that reflected the outdoor light above the door reached for the handle and opened the door for them. Matt hesitated an instant, had maybe a second thought, then signaled with his hand for his mom to go first. He and his dad followed.

"Good evening," the gentleman said, his voice soft, restrained and clear. "Please sign the registry."

Once in, Matt looked around the room. It resembled a formal living room with beautiful, soft elegant furnishings. Comfortable upholstered chairs lined the wall along with a large blue upholstered couch, which was bounded on each side with highly polished end tables holding tissues in small boxes. Exquisite lamps sat on the tables and floor lamps stood on the floor carefully spaced by a decorator just in the correct positions. The lampshades were white and their low-wattage bulbs cast a soft light around the room.

Down at the end of the room, two large wood panel doors stood open, and beyond them, the lighting appeared dim.

A flutter awakened in Matt's chest. He stopped, for he knew what lay within the room. Soft music played. It was an organ. It played a Methodist hymn.

Matt's stomach churned. This time, the churn elicited a beautiful feeling. He almost wanted to sing the verse.

The next song was soft and sad. Sobs from the visitors were intermingled with the melody. The sobs were muffled but audible and real.

Matt took a deep breath. The three walked into the room through the entrance, and when they did, everything seemed to stop ...

The beautiful scent of roses filled the air and the clean outdoor smell of jasmine mixed with the scent of the roses.

Matt inhaled the fragrance deeply. He would never forget it. He took a deep breath because the strong floral scent took his breath away. He started to cry. At that instant, he lost control. "Breathe," he said to himself.

Down in front, a small white casket had been placed on a special stand; its cloth covering was spread with red rose petals. Flower arrangements crowded the floor, all squeezed together, no room to place another.

The small chapel setting with pews placed on each side of a center aisle directed the attention to the casket at the front. From where they stood, the vision of the casket was clear. Matt could not see him, but knew Timmy was there.

Matt whispered, "Dad, can I go up there by myself?"

A large, strong hand grasped his shoulder followed by a long gentle squeeze. Matt's jitters returned but emotionally he felt the power to control them. He looked at his dad. His dad said nothing. He closed his eyes a moment, reopened them, and a twitch of a nod signaled the answer. Mom and Dad slid into a pew and sat.

Matt heard his mom say, "Harry, he's only nine."

Matt strained to hear the answer.

"Not between the ears and not inside his heart."

He walked down the aisle. There were other adults sitting along the way, but he never glanced toward any of them. As he got closer, the profile of a face appeared. Soon, he stood in front of the casket. There right before him, close enough to touch, lay four-year-old Timmy Wolfington. His closed eyes looked peaceful. His hands crossed one another and rested on a gray-and-white seer-sucker suit. He wore a red bow tie, and alongside him, a plastic yellow bucket with its matching shovel inside rested on a satin fluffy pillow and sheet. Two shells lay in the bottom of the bucket.

Matt looked at the statue-like face, as smooth as marble, and through the light dusting of powder a tinge of a blue cast appeared from deep inside his skin. Matt waited for him to move, but he didn't. He listened for a word spoken, but the lips remained sealed. He wanted him to climb out, but nothing happened.

Matt felt an urge. He cast it aside. He gazed at the little boy. The urge resurfaced with more urgency. He reacted. He took his hand and placed it on Timmy's hands. He felt the hard stiff texture of the skin with no naturalness. A coldness, like ice, ran from the hand into Matt's. He left his hand there. The finality reached Matt's heart. He touched death.

In the front row, Timmy's mom cried. The agony of the sound he would never forget. He prayed there for Lazarus' good fortune. The little boy remained unchanged.

Matt began to cry. He listened to his heart. He walked over and hugged the whole family and tightly hugged Timmy's mom.

"I'm so sorry," Matt said.

Matt put the glass on the table and stared out over the railing of Mr. Weller's porch. "Four days after the funeral, I started fourth grade, Mr. Weller," Matt said. "And the first week of school, Jimmy Knox and I had a fight on the playground. I knocked him out, but I thought I'd killed him."

"Is my scholarly student discovering something?" Mr. Weller asked.

"Mr. Weller, it's clear. As I looked at Jimmy on the ground, I saw Timmy's face in the casket, and then my feeling of doom was reinforced when our teacher walked up and one of the girls asked if he was dead. But I was saved— Jimmy moved and the whites of his eyes disappeared and his pupils returned."

"And?"

"And now I realize that's why I stop when I'm about to win a fight. I cannot take that chance ever again."

Mr. Weller smiled at Matt and grasped him in a tight bear hug. "A lesson of life, Matt: Warriors sometimes have to fight, even when death looms." He released his grip and patted Matt on the shoulder. "Time for you to get home, young man. I'm proud of you."

Chapter 64

THE PUZZLE IS SOLVED

MATT SAILED OVER Mr. Weller's front porch steps and landed on the pebbled walkway like a broad jumper trying to surpass the world record. "I can do it, Mr. Weller. Thank you for your help."

He would share his discovery with his dad. The ache inside him had been erased and he felt grown up. He whistled the song from *The High and the Mighty*, a movie he'd watched three times with his dad, and his inspiration grew as he pictured John Wayne flying the distressed plane.

He sensed an awakening inside. He was ready for Wayne Tyson. *I'll bring my plane in too. My handcuffs are off. Please, Lord, help me with the 'how-to's.'*

He lifted his books and gym bag high over his head and in quick thrusts, jabbed them toward the sky. "Yippee," he cheered in an excited, child-like yell. "Yippee, the puzzle is solved!"

As he got close to his house, the fragrance of his mom's roses filled the air. His dad's truck was in the driveway. Good! Usually he drove in between five fifteen and five thirty—you could count on it—and it wasn't even four o'clock. He'd rinse off with the hose and then talk with his dad.

He turned on the water hose and drenched himself from head to toe. Black remnants of the dirt road ran into the grass like sandcastle sludge dripping off his fingers at the beach, and flakes of dried blood floated away in the muddy stream.

He looked at his reflection in his bedroom window. A new Matt Parker greeted him. The old imposter washed away. He had much to share with his dad.

He walked into the garage. "Hi, Dad. You're home early. Got a few minutes to talk?"

His dad looked up and put the box he was carrying on a shelf. "Looks like you've had an encounter with Wayne Tyson."

"Yes, sir."

His dad picked up a skill saw from the concrete garage floor and put it on a shelf. "I was just dropping off some stuff in the garage and then going back to the job site, but I have time to talk."

"Want to sit on the porch?"

"Sure."

His dad walked over to the door to the kitchen. "Hi, honey. Matt and I are going to have a chat on the front porch. What's for dinner? I can smell something good."

Mrs. Parker came to the screen door with her apron on, holding a head of lettuce in one hand and two small tomatoes in the other. "Hi, dear. I have a pot roast in the oven ... and an apple pie for dessert that I baked this afternoon. Hi, Matt—Oh no! What's happened?"

"I'm okay, Mom. It's just a shiner and some bruises. I'll tell you all about it after Dad and I talk."

Mr. Parker opened the door just enough to put his head inside, leaned in and gave her a quick kiss and closed the door before the cat could get out. "After Matt and I talk, I need to go back out and see one of my subs, but I'll be home on time."

A blue jay flew into the pine tree just off the side of the garage, and then a second one arrived. They began bobbing their heads and screeching.

Matt and his dad walked down the pebble walkway that ran through a manicured flower garden and ended at the front porch. Flower bushes lined both sides of the walkway. Only the hibiscus bushes were blooming. The azaleas and gardenias would not show their flowers again until spring.

Matt climbed the stairs and sat down on the porch swing. The springs squeaked and it sank down a few inches.

Mr. Parker chuckled. "After hearing that sound, I think I'll sit here on the steps."

"Oh, it can hold us both. Last week three of us sat on it—and one was John."

Mr. Parker smiled, and then sat on the porch floor and leaned back against a wood column. "So, what happened?"

"Well, I was beating him today, Dad, and then when he was down on the ground, I stopped again. He threw dirt in my eyes and then got up and nailed me in the crotch with his boot. I fell down. Lucky for me, Sam Scott stopped him before he could do anything else."

The swing had been moving slowly back and forth and Matt realized his legs were now really pumping the swing. He slowly brought the swing to a halt.

"Lucky for him I wasn't there," Mr. Parker said. "I might have killed him. I thought you had Wayne's number. How'd you get yourself in that position?"

"I was beating him good, Dad, but then I held back and quit. I couldn't finish him off." Matt's eyes filled with tears. "I stopped and talked with Mr. Weller on the way home this afternoon and I figured it out. When I fought Jimmy on the playground in fourth grade, I'd just been to Timmy's funeral and I remembered Timmy's face in that casket ... the face of death. I thought I'd killed Jimmy when he didn't move. Today, I think I was afraid Wayne might die if I hit him again. I've been reading *The Red Badge of Courage* and how Henry went from coward to hero. I feel like I've been acting like a coward—but I'm not a coward. Does that make sense?"

"You're a very bright boy, Matt. Fear sometimes protects us, but a warrior sidesteps that barrier."

"Did you sidestep your fear in the war?"

"Maybe a better way to say it would be I pushed through it."

"How did you do that?"

"By believing in the cause. Strength comes from an inner pull in your heart."

Mr. Parker leaned forward and touched Matt's shoe with his hand, tapping it softly. "Sounds to me like you've found your answer. You won't stop the next time."

Matt waited for his dad to say something else, but his dad stood up and placed his hand on Matt's shoulder as he walked by the swing. "I've got some work to finish."

"Any advice, Dad?"

"Matt, with bravery and conviction comes a hard truth—in a battle you must be prepared to beat your enemy. You know the costs … it's you or your foe. Fight to the end!"

"Thanks, Dad. Next time I will!"

Mr. Parker walked to the truck, started it up, leaned over to the passenger side and rolled down the window. "I'm proud of you, son." He threw the gearshift into reverse and backed out of the driveway. As he drove away, they waved at each other.

Matt got off the swing and picked up his things. In other father-son talks, he'd been told why he should not have chased his mom down the hill carrying baby mice in his hand and not stopping at her cries, but continuing to chase her until he was caught by Grandpa; or why painting the kitchen and appliances a pretty pink from a can of paint from the garage that was earmarked for an outside wooden fence in the garden was not a good idea; or why a spanking was required even though you were just late for dinner, but no one could find you because you were catching tadpoles down by the creek, beside the railroad tracks, two miles from home with the older boys.

His dad's reasoning always seemed just and the discipline always seemed appropriate to him. Once again, his dad's reasoning seemed right on target. He breathed a sigh of relief. A great weight had just been removed from his shoulders. Next time—and he knew eventually there would be a next time with Wayne—he would sidestep that feeling if it reappeared, and kick Wayne's ass!

He laughed and started to whistle as he walked back to his bedroom.

PART 4

Chapter 65

PHYS ED IN THE CAFETERIA

THE RAIN HADN'T STOPPED all day, which meant instead of Phys Ed, seventh graders would have study hall in the cafeteria and the eighth and ninth graders would be in the auditorium. Wayne had skipped school again and the day had been peaceful.

Students filled the hallway after fifth period, and the sound of voices became a loud hum, like mosquitoes in the woods on quiet nights in the summer.

Matt stared into his locker. Last period coming up. His talks with Mr. Weller and his dad after the fight had cleared his mind and his heart. He knew what he had to do. He was ready. Time to put this baby to bed. He'd have plenty of time to go over his new plan with John, Bob and Billy.

He felt a light tap on his back.

"Hi, Matt. You coming to my party Friday night?"

He turned around and smiled at Dee. "Yes, for sure. Still want me to bring records?"

"That would be great. We need plenty of cool music for dancing at our first junior high party. Wow, I hadn't seen your black eye."

"It's okay. It's starting to turn yellow. Should be gone by Friday."

Dee turned her head as Maggie walked by. "Hey, wait just a

minute, Maggie. I need to talk to you about the party. See you later, Matt." She fluttered her eyelashes at him. "Don't worry. You'll be looking good for Bonnie by then."

Matt looked down the hall. No sign of Bonnie. He closed his locker and started walking to class, softly singing "Party Doll."

Coach Shank stood by a table in the front of the cafeteria. "Find a chair and take a seat. After roll call, you can study or talk quietly among yourselves."

"This table is perfect," Matt said. "We can talk without sending up any red flags. No one's close enough to listen to us, but let's still talk quietly. No need to take any chances."

"Give us the skinny, Lenny," John said.

"Okay, I talked this over with my dad last night. That fight yesterday isn't going to put a stop to Wayne going after us. He's not at school today. Who knows what he's cooking up. It's time to go on the real offensive and we need to hit it quickly. I have a plan that will make him believe it's time to start looking elsewhere for his fun and games. Interested?"

"Hell, yes," John said.

Matt looked at Billy. "What do you think?"

"I'm ready, Matt. We're already in this pretty deep and I agree that he's not stopping now. I'm with you."

"Did you have a chance to call your mom, Bob?"

"Yes, she can take us."

"Okay, the next step is a big one. You know that big snake we saw at the horse barn last week? We've got to catch it, and we need to do it today. My plan will take time to set up, and it all revolves around having that snake. Mrs. Walton can take us out there this afternoon."

"Well, shit," John said. "Why not an alligator. Rub his belly and put him to sleep. I hate snakes."

"We know that John," Bob said. "Chicken?"

"Careful, Bob, or I'm going to pop you the minute we get out of this class. I'm tired of you saying that. You didn't let me finish. I hate snakes, but I'll be right there with you. I'm ready to get Wayne back for that dirty fighting yesterday, and if it means catching a snake, I'm with you. Just don't expect me to hold it."

Matt smiled. "Okay, team ... let's meet at Bob's house today after school."

"Okay ... I'm sure my mom will let me go," Billy said. "I'll bring all my stuff to catch it. Sounds like a great way to spend the afternoon. Just hope this rain stops and the sun comes out."

Coach Shank approached the table. "A lot of quiet talk going on here."

"Sir, Billy passed gas in front of his new girlfriend and he's embarrassed," Bob said. "We're trying to help him. What would you say?"

The bell rang and Coach Shank looked around the table with a big smile on his face. "You boys get out of here. And Parker, that eye looks a little swollen. Run into a door?"

Chapter 66

THE HORSE BARN

"YUMMY COOKIES. THANKS," John yelled to Susie, who was standing behind the screen door at the side entrance to the Waltons' house.

"You're welcome, John," Susie said. "I've got to get back to fixin' dinner. You boys be good now. No foolin' around. Mrs. Walton will be here in just a minute."

As Susie disappeared into the house, Bob punched John on the shoulder and ran past him. "Tag, you're it."

John ran after him, yelling, "You dirty dog. You made me drop my cookie."

Suddenly, Bob stopped in his tracks, turned toward John and yelled, "Shotgun."

John looked at Bob, his mouth open in total disbelief. "How can you yell shotgun? Your mom hasn't even gotten back yet. There's not even a car here."

"So?"

"Not fair. That's not the rule. Before long, Bob, you'll be yelling shotgun the night before."

"What a crybaby."

"Then I say shotgun for the ride home."

"You can't do that, John. You have to be out of the car first before you can call it again."

"Then you can't say it now. Listen, Bob, you win everything because you change the rules." John grinned. "I think I'll pop you."

"You pop me and you'll regret it."

"Hey guys, back me up. Bob is making all the rules."

"What's the big deal, John? Bob is just too quick for you," Matt said.

"You're siding with Bob."

"No, I'm not. He just beat you. That's all."

Just then, Mrs. Walton's station wagon barreled down the quiet street and turned sharply into the driveway with the horn honking and the tires squealing. She slammed on the brakes, the front dipped and the station wagon came to a screeching halt.

The radiator hissed and the engine crackled.

"The race car lady from Daytona has arrived," John said with two thumbs up.

Mrs. Walton stuck her head out the window. "Let's go, boys, I'm already late. Pile in."

John jumped in the front seat but before he could close the door, Bob was right beside him. "Move over, John."

"I got here first."

"I called shotgun."

"So?"

"So, move over."

Mrs. Walton looked at John. "Move, John, I have no cooties. You two can settle this later." She looked at her watch. "We need to leave now, if you boys want to go to the barn."

John moved over. Bob squeezed in beside him and closed the door. His hip rested on the armrest of the door. "Move over, John."

Matt and Billy hopped in the back seat.

"John, you sure you don't want to sit in the back? It might be more comfortable," Mrs. Walton said.

"No thanks. I'll run the radio."

Mrs. Walton backed the station wagon out of the driveway and pulled forward slowly. She looked in the rearview mirror at Billy. "Bob says you're going to try and catch a big black snake in the tack room of our horse farm. Don't you hurt that snake."

"No, ma'am. I love snakes. I'd never hurt one."

"What are you going to do with it if you catch it?" she asked with her eyes still focused on Billy.

John leaned over and put his arm around her neck and gave her a tight hug. "If we told you, we would have to kill you. It's a secret … but we promise, we won't hurt the snake."

"Okay, I will ask no more questions, but I have a favor to ask."

"What is it?" John asked.

"I want you to name the snake. It needs a name—you give it a name and it will become more than just 'the' snake."

She finished talking and Little Richard began singing "Lucille" on the radio.

"That's it. Let's call it Lucille," Bob said. "Today Lucille will come out and we will catch her."

"I like the name, Bob," Matt said. "A snake named Lucille. I move that will be the name. Is there a second?"

"Second," Billy said.

Matt looked at John.

"Yeah, that's okay."

"Okay, that's it. Lucille! How's that for a name, Mrs. Walton?" Matt said.

"Good! I'm glad you named her fast before John had a chance to think of one."

John started to laugh. "I would name it 'BB' for Butt Biter."

Mrs. Walton grabbed him around the neck, put a knuckle on his scalp and gave him a hard 'Dutch rub.' "John, you're bad!"

"Watch your driving, Mrs. Walton," John said with a grin.

Mrs. Walton put her foot on the brake and slammed it down. The car skidded and began to slide. She pulled John's head closer to her again and repeated the Dutch rub. "Say you're sorry, John."

"Quit! Ouch! Stop!" John said, snorting and laughing. "I'm sorry."

"Okay, John. Let this be a lesson to you. That snake deserves a good name! And don't forget I do have soap in this car."

Ten minutes later, just beyond the city limits, she turned onto the rough gravel road that led to the family's horse barn and began fish-tailing down the road, pebbles striking hard against the fenders like guns shooting plastic yellow ducks at the county fair arcade.

Dust whipped up into the air behind the station wagon and covered the weeds and tall grass beside the fence with a brown dry powder. "Quick! Roll up your windows everybody," she said.

A dense white cloud of dust chased a pickup truck coming down the road toward them. "Hey, Mrs. Walton," John said. "You're not the only dust producer on this road today."

The truck drove by; the driver honked his horn and waved. Mrs. Walton waved back. "Boy, it's dry," she said. "We need a hurricane."

On the right, several live oak trees and a stand of small pines grew in a pasture. Cattle lay in the shade of the large oaks, seeking a reprieve from the hot sun. On the left side of the road, a citrus grove spread far in the distance. A man on a tractor pulling a bush hog worked between the edge of the grove and the fence, but the dust he threw in the air didn't compare to the dust from the station wagon.

Mrs. Walton sped down the road, braked late, skidded long and turned just in time to fishtail over the culvert and stop in front of the gate to the Walton property.

Beyond the gate on the dirt road, two horses stood motionless in the pasture, their heads high in the air. Damon, Mr. Walton's palomino stallion, was the larger of the two. He lowered his head and slowly walked toward them. After a few steps, he stopped and began to graze. The last time the boys played at the horse barn, Damon was frisky and chased them into the pond.

Bob jumped out of the car to open the gate. Matt rolled down his window. "Keep an eye on Damon, Bob. He's keeping an eye on you."

In the pasture dotted with a dozen cows and five other horses, Jippo the billy goat stood watching them. "And, don't turn your back on Jippo," John said as he rolled down his window.

Mrs. Walton moved slowly down the tire ruts sparsely filled with gravel. Bob jumped on the hood of the station wagon for the short ride to the trailer on the property, and the horses fell in behind the car and followed.

"I say we play it safe today and leave Damon alone," Matt said. "That's Mr. Walton's horse to ride. Let's face it. He's the ruler of this pasture."

John looked over at Billy. "What about Jippo?" he said. "You know he looks for total strangers, Matt."

"Be honest, John," Mrs. Walton said. "If Jippo has an eye on anyone, it'll be you. No worries for you, Billy."

Billy smiled. "I had to deal with a bull at our farm in Indiana, John. I'm not too worried about a goat. Is there a bull around here?"

"He's in a separate pasture, Billy. No worries about him," Matt said.

"Slow down, Mom. Stop!" Bob yelled from outside the car. He pointed to a line of quail crossing in front of them. The last two ran across and disappeared into the higher grass. Another covey emerged from the cover and began their run. The lead quail stopped in the middle of the road and looked at the car. More came out of the weeds, stopped in a group behind him and flushed along with the other covey already in the nearby pines.

Thirty birds scattered. Some flew to the corner fence. Some dropped into a small farm equipment graveyard, and the rest flew into a thick bay of trees along the fence beside the outside road.

Matt watched the coveys spread out. "I bet we'll hear them talking to one another trying to reconnect this afternoon," he said. "Is Mr. Walton ready to hit the field with his dogs and shotgun?"

"Yes, but not here. These quail are protected from you hunters. I call them my pets. Now you boys get out. I'll be back in two hours. Hope you catch Lucille. Good luck and be careful!"

They climbed out of the car and Mrs. Walton moved slowly down the dirt road. Bob closed the gate. She looked out the window, accelerated and waved. Pebbles and gravel flew out from under the car, and dust rose from behind it in a thick brown cloud like she was part of an army convoy.

Bob waved and blew her a kiss. "Let's go catch a snake," he said.

Above the trail through the tall pine trees, white puffy clouds floated in the blue sky, and from time to time blocked the bright sun and created a pattern of shadows and bright spots on the ground.

Billy pointed to a sunny area on the trail. "The rain clouds are gone and rattlers come out of the palmettos and lay in sunny places like that on days like today. Keep your eyes open."

"I'm keeping my eye out for Jippo," Bob said. "You know our goat. Anyone seen him?"

"Yeah," John said. "I saw him out in the pasture with the horses when we drove up."

"Well, he knows we're here, so keep an eye out," Bob said.

"Thanks for reminding us about rattlers, Billy," Matt said. "When Jippo is on our mind, even rattlers are on the back burner, right, John?"

John rubbed his butt. "Last time we were here, that goat got my back burner. You know ... right on my blue flame burner." He laughed and snorted.

"I understand, but there's a big difference between two horns nailing you and two fangs embedded in your leg."

John nodded in agreement. "You're right, Billy. The heck with the goat, let's focus on snakes."

They rounded a curve in the path and the barn came into sight. Shiny reflections from the barn's tin roof looked like shots from a Flash Gordon ray gun.

Billy put up his hand, "Let's stop and talk about what we're going to do."

Beside the path, welding arc flashes of sun shot between a stand of tall, narrow-trunked pines with a canopy of green-needled leaves. Puffy white clouds periodically moved under the sun, creating patterns on the ground that changed like a twisting kaleidoscope.

Matt pointed to a shaded area circled by dense palmettos and padded with a carpet of fallen brown pine needles. "Let's stop there. Billy's right, we need to gather our thoughts before we get to the barn. We can't mess up. If Lucille slips us and gets away, my plan will have to take a long hiatus."

"Quit the long words," John said.

"Make it 'take a long sleep' then."

"Better."

The four boys plopped down in the shade of the small clearing.

The cloud above continued moving shade across the ground, pulling its shadow along at a fast clip. The shade disappeared and the bright hot sun emerged.

John leaned back on his hands in the dark-colored pine needles. "I like it here."

Matt looked at John as he spoke. In the mosaic of brown, gray and white behind his outstretched hand, he saw something move. He focused his eyes on the area just as a huge diamondback rattlesnake raised its head. *Oh God …*

"John, don't move. Don't anybody move or say another word," he said quietly. "A diamondback rattler is close to John's hand, coiled and ready to strike. John, don't flex a muscle. Don't even blink. His tail is raised, ready to rattle. He's ready to strike. I see his fangs."

John's face turned white.

"A rattler?" Bob mouthed. "Where?"

"Shhh. Stay calm," Matt said.

The snake's tongue started to whip out and back, but the rattle remained still.

"Be patient," Matt whispered. "The rattle is quiet. That's good. Nobody move. He might settle down and sneak away."

Out of the quiet, the rattle began—a slow quiet hum.

"It must sense heat and is waiting for movement. Don't move, John—Don't move! I'm afraid he'll strike."

John closed his eyes. Beads of sweat gathered on his forehead. Droplets ran down his nose, onto his chin and dripped on the collar of his white cotton T-shirt and soaked it. His tanned skin showed through like the shirt wasn't there.

The hum changed to the clicking sound of castanets in a Spanish troupe. The snake's tail stood erect and moved in a blur. Its head dropped into the tight coil and the coil almost magically started to disappear. The clicking stopped and it became a lazy S on the ground.

"Hold still, buddy," Matt said. "It's uncoiled. And it's quiet."

"Don't move yet, John," Billy said in a quiet voice. "They don't need to wrap themselves to strike."

Behind Matt, something crashed into the small brush and palmetto bushes on the other side of the path.

"Oh my God," Bob whispered. "It's Jippo. He's headed toward us."

The goat broke out of the bushes into clear view. The snake remained still and lazily stretched out in its loose position.

"Get ready, John," Matt said. "We gotta make a move."

"I've got the snake stick in my hand. Can I turn my head?" Billy said.

"No! Not yet!" Matt said.

Jippo began to meander their way, chewing things he found on the ground and glancing periodically toward the boys.

The snake's tail rose into the air and its rattle began to shake again, louder than ever.

"John, that rattler isn't happy. When I say 'Now,' lunge forward and roll like a tire coming off a race car traveling at 100 mph. Bob, at the same time, you get the goat out of here and be careful to stay out of the snake's strike range. Billy, use your snake stick as soon as Bob is out of the way."

The goat walked into the clearing. The snake coiled up into a tight circle and the sound of the rattles came to a new crescendo. Jippo froze.

Matt yelled, "Now!"

John lunged and rolled. Bob grabbed the goat by the horns and pushed him toward the trail. The snake flew into the air, its long diamond scales almost gyrating for gravity to keep it floating to its target. Its yellow fangs appeared and the snake missed John by inches. It struck again, falling just short of Matt's foot.

"Catch!" Billy threw the snake stick to Matt and Matt pushed it under the snake's body. The snake contorted into loose knots, twisting on the stick. Matt pushed hard behind the head of the snake. It squirmed and tried to strike again. He released the pressure on its body and with both hands and all his strength, he lifted the snake off the ground and balanced it on the stick.

"Heave it, Matt," John yelled.

Matt juggled the snake on the stick and tossed it as high as he could. All six feet of the snake stretched out, flew into the air like a diver performing a full one-and-a-half reverse somersault in the layout position and crashed into the middle of the palmettos on the far side of the stand of pine trees.

Matt collapsed to the ground. He wiped his face with his sleeve and felt emotionally dead. "He's gone ... I'm gone."

John dropped down beside him.

"That was truly close, buddy," Matt said, "and you were super brave. There's no other words to say. I'm serious."

Billy walked along the edge of the palmettos, scanning its perimeter, and Bob stood out by the path and kept his eye on Jippo, who continued to graze, his head down, paying no attention to the boys.

John took off his T-shirt, wrung it out and used it as a towel to wipe the perspiration still forming on his head and body. He pushed his face into the shirt and didn't move. "I'm done," he said.

"No, you're not!" Matt said.

"The hell I'm not! I'm ready to go cool off in the lake. I'm not going in that barn. No more snakes for me today. Just give me the goat ... I can't step into that barn."

"We need you, John," Matt said. "We need to catch that snake today. You don't have to touch it. Just help us keep it in the barn."

John stood up and put his T-shirt on. "Okay. Let's get on with it. What's next, Billy?"

"I think, looking at the afternoon's weather, we have a good shot at finding our snake. She might be out."

"Outside?" John asked.

"No, inside the barn, probably near the tack room where we saw her the last time, but she might be coiled in a corner or stretched out on the floor. I meant 'out' in a place where we can see her. As I remember, Bob, the door inside to the tack room is open. So, if we walk through the stalls, we don't need to open the main door. Right?"

"Right," Bob said. "Do we turn on a light? It's still pretty dark in there."

"No, let's leave the light off initially. We need to keep quiet, walk very softly and let our eyes adjust."

John shook his whole body. "I don't want to step on Lucille in the dark. That is one big snake. If I step on her tail, she can bite me anywhere, and you know where she'll probably aim." His face turned red again, and he snorted. "Snakes love me ... they love to bite me."

"You've got on jeans, John. She can't bite you," Bob said, grinning. "Might strangle you though, or maybe give you a little snake kiss on the neck."

John quivered. "I hate snakes. Hate 'em! Hate 'em! Hate 'em!" He stopped and looked at the other three boys. "Why am I here?"

Matt smiled. He walked over to John and rested his hand on his shoulder. "Because we're a team and it will take all of us to pull this off—that includes you, John. You a baby?"

John's expression changed the minute Matt said "baby." "Listen, Matt," he said, looking deep into Matt eyes. "I'll go into the bull pasture, walk up to him, spit in his eye and hit his balls, but I don't like snakes. I hate them, but I am not a baby!"

Matt patted John on his shoulder. "I hope Wayne feels the same way about snakes. And after we catch this snake, I can't wait to see you in the bull pasture."

John looked at Matt, Bob and Billy. "Poor Wayne, if this works."

"It'll work, but we first have to catch her … and we have the guy to do it," Matt said. "So, what's the plan, Ross Allen?"

"I'll go in first and you all follow," Billy said. "If she's out, I'll pen down her head with my snake stick, grab her behind the head and secure her. Then we put her in the bag. Done deal."

"What if she isn't out?" John asked.

"Then we look for her," Billy said.

"All of us, or just you?"

"All of us."

John rolled his eyes and sighed. "Please, Lucille, just be stretched out on the floor and roll over on your back when you see us."

They all laughed as they started toward the barn, but there was tension in the air. Billy was good, but this was a big snake, and cornered snakes were not friendly, even black snakes.

"Another adventure," Bob said. "Let's go for it."

Chapter 67

THE TACK ROOM

"OKAY, TIME TO GET SERIOUS," Billy whispered as they reached the barn.

"Tell us what you want us to do," Matt said.

"Follow me to the tack room, but start looking the minute you step in the barn. She could be out anywhere." Billy's confidence showed. "Okay ... let's go slowly and let our eyes adjust."

In the middle of the room, he lifted his hand. "Stop ... don't move. I heard something."

"It's a mouse," John said. "I see him ... he's on the rail."

Matt could make out a saddle and bridle and a closed bin of oats with a small metal bucket hanging on a nail above it.

The mouse on the rail moved again, jumped off the rail and onto a wall stud then ran up to the ceiling and disappeared. Another mouse darted across the bin and also headed up the wall.

"Anyone see anything besides mice?" Bob said.

"No. Be patient," Billy said. "If Lucille is here, she's doing just what we are doing. She's remaining still. She's a hunter."

Matt saw something about four feet long lying along the wall. It moved. "What's that?"

John jumped. "Oh shit! It's a snake."

"Shhh. Be still. It's a snake, but not a big black. It's a corn snake.

Stay still."

"Should we catch it?" Bob asked.

"No. We want the black. I have a good feeling she's here, also."

The corn snake stopped, still stretched out, and lifted its head just off the floor. Its tongue moved in and out.

"I'm glad you're here, Billy, 'cause this is giving me the creeps," John said. "From now on, I'm calling this place the 'Snake Motel' and the outside will be named 'Rattlers' Paradise.'"

"Don't you start laughing, John. This is serious," Matt said.

Billy pointed to a saddle lying on the floor in the corner next to the feed bin, and said, "Matt, walk over there where she was last time. She might be there again. I'll walk along the other wall."

Matt walked carefully over to the saddle on the floor. "I see something black, about three inches long, sticking out from under the saddle."

"That's got to be her tail," Billy said, coming up the other side. "Bob, any big cracks or holes in this area?"

"None. Maybe a crack that a mouse can get through, but not a big snake."

"Then let's say it's her and we have her cornered."

John took a step backward. "Cornered? Snakes don't like to be cornered."

"That's right, John, but that's how we can catch her."

Matt looked down at the tail and the hair on his arms stood up. "What's the plan, Billy?"

"You need to lift the saddle."

"And then what?"

"Get ready for the action. If we are lucky, she'll coil up, and I can get my stick on her head and secure her to the floor. I'll get hold of her behind the head and we'll have her. But … if she decides she wants to run, it's a matter of not letting her get past us and get outside."

"She hasn't moved yet," Matt said.

"She probably doesn't feel threatened yet. But when you lift that saddle, that will all change."

Billy looked around the room. Sweat beaded on his forehead. "Bob, you and John stand there in the opening at the last stall. Stomp your feet and make noise. Don't let the snake get past you. Hopefully, she'll stop and coil, but she'll be fast—lightning fast—if her belly gets traction on the pine floor. These are not aggressive snakes, but they will bite when they can't get away. You both okay to do that?"

Bob and John looked at one another and nodded.

"Okay Matt, you lift the saddle. If the snake stays there, I'll get her. If she moves, we play it by ear. Ready?"

"Ready as I'm ever going to be."

Matt stepped forward. The tail moved. He put his hand on the saddle horn. "Her tail's gone."

Billy moved closer to Matt. "She's still there. Ready to lift the saddle?"

"Yes … On three … Ready? … One …"

John sucked in a deep, loud breath. "Hold it!"

"Two."

"Hold it, Matt—Stop! You got to start over. Give me one more breath."

"Okay, here I go. One … Two …"

Everyone watched the saddle.

"Three." Matt took a deep breath and in one motion lifted the saddle off the floor and tossed it to the other side of the room. It hit the wall with a force that shook the whole tack room.

Exposed on the floor at Matt's feet was a huge black snake over six feet long—not coiled, just folded back on itself.

"It's a monster black snake," Billy said. "Be careful."

The snake began to move. It lifted its head at least two feet off the ground with its mouth open.

"She's not happy," Matt said.

"Hold your ground, boys," Billy whispered.

"Oh God! Please, snake … don't come this way," John said.

Billy moved toward the snake, but before he could touch it with his stick, the snake lunged at him, stopped just short of his chest and recoiled. He jumped back. "That's the biggest black snake I've ever seen. Don't let her get past us. They're very fast."

John yelled, "Please don't let her get to me."

"If she does, try to stop her."

"My butt," John retorted.

The snake struck again, this time in the direction of Matt, then straightened out and started zigzagging toward John and Bob.

"Why me?" John screamed.

"Kick her back, John, before she gets traction on the floor," Billy yelled. "But don't hurt her."

"You kick her!" John said. "I'm out of here."

"No, John—don't you dare. Hold your ground," Matt yelled through clinched teeth.

The snake darted between John's legs.

"Oh God …what's that nasty smell?" John said.

"It's just the snake," Billy said. "They do that when they're cornered."

Matt put his foot in the snake's path, slid his foot under it about a foot from its head and lifted it off the ground. He kicked his foot. The snake came off his foot, but his foot continued up and caught John in the crotch.

Between John's legs were a flying snake and a moving foot. The snake latched on to John's pants leg near the inner thigh. "Oh God. Get this thing off me," he screamed. "No more!"

Billy grabbed the snake with his left hand just behind its head, and about three feet further down he supported the middle of its body. Still, almost three feet of the snake was writhing on the ground. "I got her," Billy said.

"She's still got me," said John.

"Just hold still. She'll let go. She's got your jeans, John, not you."

"Easy for you to say. This snake is biting me."

"Bob, get the burlap bag. Matt, help him hold it open. John, when the snake lets go of your pants, help us get this big girl into the bag."

"I'm not touching that snake."

The snake suddenly released John's pants leg and Billy was holding six-plus feet of one upset snake. "Matt, help me support her. John, she won't hurt you. Help us and let's drop her into the bag. Easy. Keep the opening as big as you can, Bob."

"Done," Matt said as they carefully slid Lucille into the bag. "Way to go, Billy."

With the snake in the bag, the four boys began cheering and yelling like they were on the rocket ride at the fair.

John's smile returned. "What a snake! Lucille, we can't wait to introduce you to Wayne!"

"That's the biggest snake I've ever caught," Billy said. "We need to tie the top closed. Don't want her getting out."

They walked out of the barn holding the bag and sat down in the pine needles under the pine trees beside the barn.

Sweat dripped through the dirt on John's face and down his arms. "That cool breeze feels good. Did you do a rattlesnake check here, Matt?"

"Yes … all clear, John, and you're right … that breeze is nice. And no wonder. We're all dirty and sweaty. We need to get cleaned up. Bob's mom won't let us in the car like this, but let's just rest here a while and gloat about what we did."

The boys stretched out on the pine needle floor, looking up through the tall trees. The sound of the soft wind moving through the pines was like a mom singing a lullaby to her babies.

"This is making me want to sleep," Billy said.

"Let's not do that," Bob said. "We can rest, but we need to talk."

He looked at Matt and pointed to the bag, "What's next?"

"We have the snake, the main ingredient for the plan. Now, we need to take our time and carefully set the trap."

"What's the trap?" Bob asked.

"I will tell you—all in good time, but just little bits at first. Too much information, too quickly, can cause a leak, and then the surprise is ruined."

Billy sat looking up at the trees. "I feel so satisfied. Do you realize what we just did? We caught one big snake, and now somehow we are going to introduce it—excuse me—somehow we are going to introduce *Lucille* to Wayne. We have the snake and Matt will be the mastermind of the plan to set Wayne up and put an end to his fun. So keep going, Matt …"

"I was saying … I don't think the whole plan should be divulged at once—too much risk of Wayne finding out. I'm still working on the plan and I'll set it up like spies would do it, a little information given out at a time. When we know the rabbit took the carrot, we reach for the next carrot. And in the end, the final carrot is given and it will taste the best. That means into the snare!"

Bob wiped his forehead. "I'm finally cooled off. I know this feels good here, but we should start walking to the front gate."

"Yeah, let's get going," John said. "I have homework to do."

Matt laughed. "What subject?"

"How to Catch Serpents, by Ross Allen, aka William MacDonald."

In the distance, Mrs. Walton honked her car horn.

"See ... here she is. She's at the gate. Hey, John?"

"What, Bob?"

"Shotgun."

Chapter 68

A PIPELINE TO WAYNE

THE NEXT MORNING before school, John, Bob and Matt stood talking next to one of the green benches under a tree outside the school. "Hey, here comes Ross Allen," John said.

"Hi, Billy," Bob said. "How's Lucille?"

"She's fine. Wow, what a monster snake."

"We're ready to begin the first episode of 'Lucille Loves Wayne,'" Matt said. "Who knows you have her?"

"No one—except my mom, Bob's mom and us."

Matt smiled, "That's good."

"You sure you've got Lucille in a safe place?" John said.

"She's fine. I have her in a large covered aquarium. She's almost seven feet long. I thought there was a chance she was an indigo, but this snake is too skinny. She'll love to run. She's a huge black racer. Not much of a biter, but she is gigantic."

"So, what are we doing, Matt—and when?" Bob asked.

Matt rubbed his hands together. "This plan requires secrecy. We're in this together and I'll tell you everything, if you want. But I think we have the best chance of succeeding if each of you only knows a part of the plan. That way, as information is leaked and questions are asked, you'll answer no differently than anyone else. You'll have no pressure, and when the end comes, you'll be there, watching it all happen."

"I can only speak for myself," Bob said, "but just knowing that something's going on will give me goose bumps. I can keep a secret, but I know I could let something out carelessly. I'd die if I did that. Just tell me what you want me to know."

John nodded his head. "Me too."

Billy's lips turned down and his eyes lost their sparkle. "I agree on sharing only parts of it with each of us, but as much as I want to get Wayne, the most important thing is that we don't hurt this snake."

"Keeping her safe will be part of the plan, I promise," Matt said. "And I'll be sharing that part with you. There's always a risk, but if we plan this right, Lucille is going to do fine."

"Okay, Matt. Just tell me what you want me to do."

"Right now, I just want you to keep her safe, Billy. Now, for my plan to work, we need to get information to Wayne. I think my neighbor Kathy will be our pipeline."

"Can you trust her?" Bob asked.

"Actually, no, I don't trust her and that's why I think this will work."

"She talks a lot, I know that," Bob said.

Matt smiled. "That's why she is going to be important. First, she's a busybody, and that works right into our hands. Second, she's my neighbor and she's on my party line. And third, she's friends with Wayne's girlfriend, Lynn, and I'm sure she will tell her anything she hears me saying about Wayne."

"So?" John said.

"So, if I entice her properly, she'll be listening to my conversations at every opportunity."

"How will we know?" Bob asked.

"Good question, Bob. I want you to call me tonight at eight o'clock. If she's on the line, I'll give you some information that I want her to pass on to Lynn."

"Can you tell?"

"Usually, I can. My party line has everyone on our side of the street connected, and if someone picks up their phone to make a call when I'm talking, I can hear a click on my line."

"I'm confused," Billy said.

John slapped him on the back and laughed. "Just don't get

confused between what's the tail and what's the head of our seven-foot black snake."

Matt looked at his watch. "We don't have much time. The first bell will ring soon and I've got a lot to tell you. First, John, there's something I want you to do next weekend, and I need to know if you'll be able to go downtown with me Saturday afternoon. I need your help for this plan to work."

"Sure. Will you at least tell me what we're going to do?"

"Not now. I'll give you more information later, and don't say anything about this to anyone else, okay? Keeping this plan between the four of us is critical."

"Okay, Matt."

"And Bob, I need you to do something before the bell rings that will set this plan in motion, okay?"

"Sure."

"Kathy is standing over by the steps. Walk over near her, and when the bell rings, I'll yell to you to wait because I've got to talk to you. You answer that you can't and you'll call me tonight. Okay?"

"Okay," Bob said. "And then I'll call you at eight o'clock tonight."

"Yes, and I'll tell you a long story I made up about the treasure to make Wayne angry. I hope she'll relay it to Lynn. I'll tell you to call again tomorrow night at eight o'clock, and these calls are top secret. Then I'll say something about Robin that Kathy, the gossip, should pass on to Dee and Lynn in Home Ec class. If we hear about it tomorrow at school, we'll know for sure she was listening, and we can be pretty sure she'll listen for Bob's call to me tomorrow night. That's our first carrot. You with me?"

Everyone nodded.

"And remember, Bob, we are trying to get Wayne. The plan involves the treasure hoax, but none of the story I'll tell you is true. Just play along with me and pretend it's true." Matt looked at his watch. "Okay, the bell's about to ring. Bob, go over close to Kathy so she can hear us. Billy, you stay here with me."

Bob reached Kathy just as the bell rang.

"Bob," Matt yelled.

"What?"

"I need to tell you something important. Wait up."

"Too late. I've got to go. I'll call you tonight."

"Okay, call me at eight o'clock. This is really important."

Bob stopped on the first step. "All right," Bob said. "Eight o'clock—on the dot."

Matt glanced at Kathy. Her eyes were on Bob. "Perfect timing," he said to Billy.

Chapter 69

WALK HOME WITH KATHY

AFTER THE LAST PERIOD BELL, Matt stopped to talk to Dee and Bonnie and then went to his locker and picked up his books. The day had been uneventful and his mind was on the phone call he'd get from Bob that night. He walked behind the school, waved at the eighth and ninth graders at basketball practice and started his walk home. Most of the motorcycles were gone, walkers were scarce and the area was quiet.

He stopped at the corner of the school to wait for the stoplight at the intersection and heard a girl's voice. "Matt, wait up."

He turned around.

"Can we walk home together this afternoon?" Kathy said.

"Sure."

"Great! You know Dee's party is this weekend, and I want to ask you some questions."

"Questions?"

"Yes. First, who's driving you there?"

He watched Kathy for a reaction. "Maybe Bob's mom or mine—all boys, though."

She folded her arms tightly and frowned. "It is not about riding with you. It's about getting my records to the party, okay? And since you live just down the street, I thought I'd ask you."

"Oh, I thought you were looking for a ride."

"No, I might not be able to go because one of my cousins is coming to town, and I told Dee that if I can't go, maybe I could give you some of my records to take. I thought if we walked home together, we could talk about which records you have—it's certainly not just to walk home with you. Don't you go getting conceited on me," she said with a smile.

"Sorry. I was just playing with you. It'll be fun to talk about music on the way home."

Fifteen minutes later, Matt waved to Kathy and walked down the sidewalk, his house only minutes away.

He looked down at the roses Kathy's mom had given him for his mom, and he felt bad. He'd had fun walking home with her. They had talked and laughed. They had a lot in common, but something wasn't right. That had to be more than a coincidence.

He liked Kathy. Her mom was so nice. They were both nice. Was he nice? He knew he was nice. Kathy had listened to some of his phone conversations. He'd told her not to do it, but now he wanted her to listen. It was part of the plan. Was that bad?

Matt's pace slowed. He'd discovered why he'd been trying to stay out of fights—that was his secret. What made others the way they were? That was their secret. Maybe as he grew up, he'd figure it all out.

He stopped, closed his eyes and saw Billy hanging on the post. He let his feelings come out—embarrassment, sadness and finally anger.

"Listen tonight, Kathy. I want you to. I will not feel guilty! Wayne needs this! Billy needs this! We all need this!" He looked around the quiet street and realized he had said all of that aloud. He had actually shouted the last three sentences.

He finally felt better. The guilty feeling that grew inside him the whole walk home with Kathy was gone. It escaped from him with his shouts. Matt laughed to himself and a warm sensation spread through his body.

He started to walk again and began humming Chuck Berry's song "School Days." Was he going too far with all the planning and how involved it was becoming? The answer popped into his head and he started singing "That'll Be the Day."

A block down the street, he put the roses, his books and his school bag on the ground and pulled his Duncan yo-yo out of the bag like a magician pulling a rabbit out of a hat. He waved the yo-yo around as if he had an audience. At that moment, the sun came out from behind a cloud, and its rays reflected the sparkles of the diamonds embedded along the sides of the yo-yo, four of them in a line on each side.

He stuck his finger through the loop at the end of two lines of string, and in one motion let it sail to the ground, stop just short of the sidewalk pavement and return back up to his hand. He "walked the dog" and thought about the "Duncan Man" who came to the Saturday movies and put on demonstrations. Matt wasn't as good as the "Duncan Man," but he was good.

Throwing the yo-yo away from him and watching it return to his hand seemed to remove the tension that had built up inside of him. He completed a few more loops, shooting the yo-yo straight out, and as it came back to him, instead of catching it, he allowed it to loop around his hand, not touching it and sending it out away from him again. After about a dozen times, he let it stop in his hand and had to pick at the tight knot around his finger to remove it. Dropping the yo-yo back in his bag, he looked up into the sky and said, "Thank you."

He slung the bag over his shoulder, picked up his books and walked down the sidewalk, carefully holding the roses for his mom.

Chapter 70

THE FIRST PHONE CALL

THE CLOCK ON MATT'S DESK said four-thirty. Eight o'clock would come fast. He closed his eyes and went over his plan. Dad home by five-thirty, dinner between five-thirty and five-forty-five, after-dinner chores finished by six-thirty and an hour and a half to complete all his homework. Eight o'clock would be clear to talk on the phone.

Forty-five minutes later, with his history read and his sentences diagrammed, he went into the kitchen. "Mom, Bob's calling me at eight o'clock tonight. May I close your bedroom door to talk?"

She smiled. "Talking about girlfriends already?"

"Not tonight, Mom. Tonight, the phone call is about another try at teaching Wayne a lesson. Dad said Wayne would get his full consequences someday. We're going to see that he gets his 'someday' very soon."

"Does your dad know what you're planning?"

Matt smiled. "Not yet, but don't worry, he'll approve."

"Okay. Close the door. Don't forget we're on a party line and you know what that means."

Matt gave her his biggest smile. "That's what we're hoping for."

Mrs. Parker looked out the window. "Your dad's here. Dinner will be served in fifteen minutes. I'll get him moving to get cleaned up."

"Thanks, Mom."

The cuckoo clock in the living room sounded off, and on the fourth 'cuckoo,' the phone began to ring. The clock in his room said eight o'clock. Bob was right on time.

Matt jumped up from the desk in his bedroom. "I got it," he said as he zipped across the hall into his parents' room and lifted the receiver. "Hello?"

"Hello, snake in the grass."

"Hi, Bob."

Matt didn't hear the click that indicated someone else picked up the line, but he hoped Kathy was already listening. He knew he needed to say everything right. The story he'd concocted to tell Bob had to make sense to Wayne, and just as importantly, it had to make sense to Kathy who would pass along the information, and she needed to get it right.

"So, what did you want to tell me?"

"First and foremost, this is top secret and you've got to promise me you won't tell a soul."

"You know I won't tell anyone. I promise on a stack of Bibles."

"Okay, here it is. After school yesterday, I talked to a friend of mine named Philip. That's a name I made up because I need to keep his identity secret."

"Okay, that's cool. Keep going."

"Philip's dad was one of my dad's friends in high school and was one of the two boys who spent the summer looking for the missing half of the treasure map with my dad. His dad always believed if they found the second part of the map, it would lead them to a pirate's fortune of gold and gems.

"When Philip heard about the escaped prisoner and us on Hog Island before Labor Day weekend, he decided the missing treasure might be involved, so last weekend he took his dad's boat there to check out the area. He was supposed to be going to the fuel dock and then home, but before he fueled the boat, he decided to ride over to Hog Island. He knew our Boy Scout troop camped in the same place as his troop, so he beached his boat near there and looked around. Ready for this?"

"Ready."

"Philip saw where someone had dug a hole and filled it back up, so using the stem of a palmetto, he dug in the same place and guess what he found?"

"Turtle eggs?" Bob said with a giggle.

"Don't laugh, Bob, this is serious. He found a rusty tin box. In the box was a small cloth bag, like a marble bag. Inside were four gold coins. He said they were still shiny gold, like they had been polished. In the box, he also found the other half of the map inside a white envelope with yellow blotches all over the surface. Guess what he did?"

"I bet he took them. I would have."

"Right! He took them out, buried the empty tin box back in the same hole and ran back to his boat with the loot."

Matt paused. "So, what do you think?"

"It's almost unbelievable. Why did he tell you about all this?"

Matt stood up and stretched the tangled phone cord so he could close the door completely. He needed privacy and closing the door added suspense. He was ready to connect the dots. *Listen closely, Kathy. This is for you.*

"He told me because he wants to get the map and the gold coins to his dad without him finding out he went to Hog Island, and he wants me to help him."

"So why doesn't Philip just give the map to his dad and they go find the treasure?"

"Because he had explicit rules not to be on the island. His dad had given him—for the very first time—the opportunity to take the boat by himself and gas it up at the fuel dock at the marina. An admission that he went farther means severe punishment. Trust is everything for his dad. There would be no hands on the throttle and steering wheel or adventures on Hog Island for a very long time for my friend Philip if his dad found out.

"Boy, if I took the boat over to the island secretly and my dad found out, it would be a butt warmer and no island camping for a long while—that's for sure—even if the treasure had a thousand gold coins worth a million dollars."

Matt transferred the phone to the other ear. His heart started to race in his chest. He knew he had the right girl listening. When you have "aces full," you are confident to spread them out over the table.

Matt liked his hand. He was ready to spread it out and show the whole table, and he knew Kathy was sitting at the table. "Ready for the rest of the story?"

"I'm ready."

Matt paused. "Guess who the other person was who looked for the treasure with Philip's dad? You're not going to believe this."

"Who?"

Matt whispered, "Lem Tyson, Wayne's father."

"Wayne Tyson's dad?"

Matt cleared his throat, silently swallowed and licked his dry lips with his tongue. He was ready to let it go. He'd repeated the lines to himself over and over, like a person learning a speech, and the moment had arrived. He was ready to begin.

"Yes. Wayne's father died a few years ago—may he rest in peace. Philip doesn't know if Mr. Tyson ever said anything about the map to his wife or children, but his dad and Wayne's dad had a falling out after high school and hadn't spoken in years."

Matt paused to catch his breath and slow down. *I'm telling this story, Kathy, and you better be listening.* He looked up to the ceiling and put his free hand on his cheek. A smile built around his lips. *Here comes the line.* "Philip is worried that if Wayne's dad ever said anything about the treasure map to him, Wayne will think he should get part of it even though Philip found the rest of the map. So Wayne *cannot* know anything about this—just in case."

"Okay."

Matt paused. "And, here's the best part. If I help him, he'll make sure my dad gets half of the treasure, and that means you guys will get a share of it too, if you help us. He needs to transfer the gold coins and the map secretly to his dad. Will you help?"

"You bet. And I know John will help too, if we need him."

"Thanks, Bob. Don't mention a word of this at school. I'll talk to Philip tomorrow and find out what we need to do. Call me at eight o'clock tomorrow night and I'll give you the details."

"Great," Bob said.

Matt smiled again. *Time for the dummy information.* "By the way, have you talked to Robin this week?"

"Not really. Why?"

"I think he really likes Linda. My mom saw him buying a girl's necklace at Smith's Jewelers yesterday and he said it wasn't for his mom ... Hey, Mom said I've got to get off the phone. Sorry. See you in the cafeteria in the morning ... Mum's the word."

"Okay," Bob said. "Bye."

Matt held the phone and listened. Click. The sound he'd hoped to hear.

In the living room, his mom and dad were watching "Peter Gunn" on television. He walked out of the bedroom with a big smile and gave them a "thumbs up" sign. "First, I'm going to the fridge, and then I will say thank you and goodnight."

Chapter 71

A NECKLACE FOR LINDA

THE EARLY MORNING sun penetrated the glass panes of the school cafeteria windows and fell onto the open page of Robin's magazine.

Matt walked directly to him and tapped him on the shoulder. "Morning, Robin. Good article?"

Robin jumped. "Oh! Hi, Matt. Yes. It's a fishing story in *Field and Stream* and I'm at a good part. Hey, when are we going back to Hog Island to look for that treasure?"

"Not sure. Maybe Sunday afternoon. Listen, we have a new top-secret plan to get Wayne Tyson and I need a little help from you, okay?"

"Sure, Matt. I'll do whatever I can to help you."

"Okay, I know you have home room with my neighbor, Kathy. If she asks you if you bought a necklace, play along with her and say yes, you bought it for your mom or something. Last night I think she was listening when Bob and I were on the phone; I told him you bought one and I thought it was for Linda. If she asks you about a necklace, please tell me. Okay?"

"Okay. Is this part of the new plan?"

"It is. Mum's the word. Thanks."

The next person Matt needed to talk to was Dee. He spotted her at a table of girls and walked over. Dee, Maggie and Bonnie sat next to each other with their purses open. He grabbed an empty chair, turned it around backward and sat down. "Sure smells good at this table. Smelling perfume and talking about boys, I bet. May I join you?"

"Sure," they all said at the same time.

"Okay, I'm taking a guess—I smell 'Jean Nate,' right? But I have no idea what boy you were talking about. John?"

"No," Dee said. "We like John, but let's face it. He can be hard on everyone. When it comes to teasing, everyone is fair game for him. If you aren't the victim, he can be funny, but sometimes he crosses the line and goes too far."

As loud as the room noise was, John's laugh stood out. Matt shook his head and smiled. "There he is."

Dee smiled too. "John's in a good mood today."

"Well, was I correct on the perfume?"

"You got one almost right, but there are two," Maggie answered. "The other one is 'Joy' and it's a perfume. 'Jean Nate' is a body wash—right, girls?"

Matt leaned over to Dee, close enough to smell her neck. "Well, who has got on 'Joy,' so I can smell them both?"

"I have on 'Joy,'" Dee said. "Bonnie has on the 'Jean Nate.'"

Bonnie blushed.

When Bonnie's cheeks turned red, so did Matt's. That seemed like the perfect time for him to talk with Dee. Everyone at the table would think he was using that to change the subject and no one would be suspicious. He looked back at Dee. "Can I talk to you for a second in private? It's about Brad."

Dee looked puzzled, but she stood up. "Sure, I guess."

Matt got up, pushed the chair under the table and he and Dee walked over to the wall. "This isn't about Brad. I have a favor to ask and I didn't want everyone at the table to hear."

Dee smiled at him. "That's too bad. I was hoping it was about Brad."

He looked around the cafeteria one more time and heard or saw nothing alarming. "Maybe next time, Dee, but this is so important. Didn't you tell me that Wayne's girlfriend Lynn is in Home Ec with you and my neighbor Kathy?"

"Yes. Why?"

"Because I want you to listen and see if she and Kathy have any kind of a conversation about Wayne or me today. And I'd also be interested to know if she says anything about Robin and Linda."

"I can do that, but I don't know what that does for you."

Matt smiled. "A lot. Please don't say anything to anyone else, but whatever you hear, will you share it with me?"

"Sure."

"Thanks. I've got to go. When can I talk to you again privately?"

"After school at cheerleader tryouts."

Matt patted her on the shoulder. "Good. I'll find you. Mum's the word?"

"Mum's the word. When am I going to find out what this is all about?"

"Saturday. I promise. Thanks for your help."

They returned to the girls' table, and Matt said with a voice loud enough for them all to hear, "I'll tell Brad I spoke with you."

"Okay, Matt."

"See you later." He looked at Bonnie and smiled. "That means you too. I'll see you after school at cheerleading practice."

John's laugh boomed from a distant corner in the large room.

Matt looked over and saw him hitting his leg with a slap of his hand in perfect cadence with each laugh that bellowed from his open mouth. Bob and another boy grabbed him around the waist and a third held his arms behind his back.

In one move, John spun around and threw all three off him like cowboys coming off a bull at a rodeo. The biggest of the three sailed over the table, landing on the floor between two chairs that broke his fall.

Matt laughed to himself as he turned to leave the room. No worries. John would be able to handle the job Matt had for him Saturday.

Chapter 72

CHEERLEADER TRYOUTS

THE FINAL BELL RANG and within ten minutes, the school grounds had emptied except for a few stragglers and people who remained for sports and other after-school activities like cheerleading. Mrs. D stood outside the door of the office, talking to another coach. The girls, dressed in shorts, blouses and tennis shoes with white socks, waited on the courts, milling around or practicing their acrobatic moves.

Matt almost danced across the street to the cheerleading tryout area on the volleyball court outside the girls' locker room to talk to Dee before tryouts began.

Dee was doing a cartwheel, and Bonnie stood nearby, arms crossed, watching the other girls.

The sight of Bonnie made his heart race. This new feeling was exciting. He'd first felt it the week before when he walked her home from downtown, but right then he had the strongest feeling yet. She was the cutest girl he'd ever met, and he wanted her to be his girlfriend.

He stepped up on the curb and headed toward Dee, both hands in his jeans pockets, trying to look cool, even though inside he was tense and nervous. He never knew a girl could do that to him. He told himself to relax. Dee held the information he needed. She finished another cartwheel and walked back toward Bonnie.

Bonnie still hadn't seen him. Her eyes were fixed on Dee.

A big smile spread across Dee's face. "Hi, Matt."

The smile made him optimistic.

Bonnie turned, and in the surprise and the sparkle in her eyes, he could see what he'd been hoping for. *She likes me—she really likes me.* His heart beat fast and his throat tightened up. Was this the "puppy love" he'd heard about? He felt wonderful. It was an "Oh my golly" experience, and he relaxed and let it happen, but the feeling took a back seat at that moment to the anticipation of Dee's information.

"Hello, you two," he said, letting his eyes move back and forth between the girls. "Thank goodness for oak trees. This is still a place to get out of the heat. I need to ask Dee some questions, Bonnie—about Billy and Wayne. You can listen, if you want."

Bonnie smiled. "I can be quiet as a mouse."

"I know you only have a minute, Dee," Matt said, "so let's get right to it. Did you see Lynn in Home Ec today?"

A broad smile spread across Dee's face and he knew he was going to like the answer. He closed his eyes and said a quick prayer.

Dee's smile got bigger and wrinkled her nose. "I did."

"And?" Matt said.

"And, she and Kathy spent a lot of time whispering. I heard Lynn say to call her tonight."

"And?"

"And Kathy asked me if I heard Robin bought a necklace for someone and it might be Linda."

"And?" Matt said again.

"And that was all. Did I do good?"

"Did you do good? You did great! Saturday I will tell both of you what this all means."

"I can't wait to find out," Dee said. "Be back in a minute. I've got to go talk to Mrs. D."

Bonnie's eyes sparkled again. "And you're finished with Wayne and fighting, right?"

"Listen, Bonnie," Matt said quietly, "we're trying to get Wayne to leave us alone. Sometimes you have to stand up to a guy like him to make that happen. We're planning to teach him a lesson and the outcome is not predictable, but I promise another fight is not in our plan. Your support means more to me than you know. I won't let you down."

She patted his hand. "Okay. Stay safe."

"I'm working on it. Good luck on your tryouts."

Matt waved to Dee. "I'll see you both tomorrow."

Chapter 73

THE SECOND
PHONE CALL

MATT SAT ON HIS BED with his bedroom door open, watching the clock. Across the hall, the black phone rested dormant on the desk. It was almost time. His heart fluttered and goose bumps covered his arms. *No screw-ups … I'm ready.*

The phone rang at eight o'clock on the dot.

He took a long breath and exhaled slowly before he jumped off the bed and ran to the phone. *Here we go!* He lifted the receiver. Click. Kathy was there. The direct line to Wayne was open.

"Hello?"

"Hi, Matt. What's the plan?"

"Hi, Bob. Philip and I have it all figured out."

"Believe me, I'm all ears."

Matt paused. Bob sounded calm and confident. "Okay, Bob, but before I tell you the plan, I've got to tell you what else Philip told me. Remember last week when we camped on Hog Island and that gigantic prisoner came into our camp? And after the sheriff's team caught him, we discovered someone had dug in the same hole where we were digging for the gold coins and half of a treasure map?"

"I do."

"Guess what? What Philip told me confirms that the prisoner was

SORRY YOU MISSED IT…

the one digging in our hole. And you know what else?"

"What?"

"This is so cool … Our hole turned out to be very close to the map and the gold coins. Philip told me he found the treasure buried by some palmettos in another stand of pines just one dune away. And we think the giant must have planned to hide on the island until after dark that night and then retrieve his bounty. Yep, Philip stole the real treasure just in time. and like I told you, we're still getting our part of the loot for my dad and for us."

Matt paused. *Go slow. This is a complicated story, and you want Kathy to believe it and be able to remember it—so Wayne gets all the details.*

"Holy moly, Matt," Bob said. "That's so cool. We were lucky the sheriff showed up."

"You're right, Bob. Wait 'til we tell the guys all of this. But that's got to be a long way down the road. First, we've got to get the gold coins and map back to Philip's dad without him knowing his son was on Hog Island with their boat. And then the treasure has to be found. Can you keep the secret that long?"

"I can. No problem."

"Okay, so here's the plan to get the map and the gold coins to Philip's dad and keep Philip out of trouble. Ready?"

"Ready."

"Philip mailed his dad an anonymous letter on Monday that said the sender had found some gold coins and the other half of the old treasure map that he'd seen framed at the Marlowes' house. The letter explained that he'd had an opportunity to study the framed map with a magnifying glass and discovered a number error caused by a smudge in the crayon drawing. The letter said he'd exchange the coins and the missing part of the map for a promise to be given half of the treasure and not be asked to identify himself, so no one would know.

"Mr. Marlowe told Philip about the letter yesterday and Philip said he seemed more enthralled with getting the treasure than how the map was found or who the sender was. And he was glad he wouldn't have to share any of it with Lem Tyson, his partner in the treasure hunt in high school, because he had died a few years ago."

"Wayne's dad? Too bad for Wayne, right?" Bob said.

"Right. Mr. Marlowe told Philip that when this is over and the loot is shared with the anonymous letter-writer, he's not telling anyone about finding the treasure, because a bunch of other people searched for the treasure, and he doesn't want to have to deal with them."

"And you said Phillip will give you the half that's supposed to go to the anonymous letter-writer, right?"

"Right."

"And you're going to share part of it with us for helping you, right?"

"Right. The letter gave Mr. Marlowe directions for picking up the gold coins and the other half of the map. That's where we come in."

"Cool."

"The first part of our transfer of the map and gold to Philip's dad will be handled by John at the Atlantic Coastline train station this Saturday night at six-forty-five. Philip's dad doesn't know John. He only knows to look for someone wearing a Dodger baseball cap. John will give Philip's dad an envelope with directions to the place to pick up the map and gold coins. And you and I and Philip Marlowe will be waiting at the second location with a briefcase containing the map and coins. We'll set the briefcase out close to the street so Philip's dad can pick it up easily and not see any of us. Got it?"

"Yes! That's brilliant, Matt! John will be at the Atlantic Coastline station Saturday night with directions to the pickup location. What time did you say? Six-forty-five?"

"Yes. The Atlantic Coastline station at six-forty-five on Saturday night. Philip's dad already has half of the map, and when he gets the second half, he'll know where to go to find the treasure that he, my dad and Wayne's dad, and lots of other people hoped to find many years ago. I'll tell you later who Philip Marlowe really is and where you need to meet us. Just keep Saturday afternoon open.

"Okay, Bob. That's it—the secret of secrets. You must *not* tell John about this phone call. I'll tell him Saturday morning about his role in the transfer at the train station. It'll be just you and me and Philip Marlowe with the gold coins and the map."

"Just you and me and Philip. Okay, see you tomorrow morning in the cafeteria, Matt."

"Okay, Bob. Zip up the lips."

"Consider them zipped," Bob said, and he hung up the phone.

Matt sat there quietly holding the phone up to his ear with a sweaty hand, waiting to confirm once again that Kathy was on the line. ... Click. ... He hung up and fell back on the bed with his hands clasped behind his head. *I hope you got all that, Kathy.*

Chapter 74

CONFRONTATION IN THE CAFETERIA

DEE GOT UP from the table of girls in the back of the cafeteria and walked over to the table where John, Bob, Matt, Billy and Brad were sitting. She put her hands on her hips. "Good morning, boys. Anybody at this table going to the football game tonight instead of my party?"

"It's an away game, Dee," Bob said. "That lets you girls have your party without a conflict."

"I know, but John, I bet you're going. Your brother is a senior and he's the quarterback."

"I got a better deal," John said with a wink.

"And what's a better deal?"

"I'm going to a dance party tonight to watch the gyrations on the dance floor. I hear there's going to be a dance contest. Hope I'm a judge."

Dee laughed. "Why should someone who can't dance be a judge?"

John stood up, tensed his right leg and then moved his left leg around real slow, pressing his foot on the floor like someone putting out a cigarette butt on the ground. "I got style, and I got rhythm."

"You're no Elvis," Brad said.

"No, Brad—Elvis is no John," John said, smiling.

Matt glanced over to the other side of the cafeteria where a group of ninth graders sat, and he could see Kathy talking with Lynn. He nudged Bob in the chair beside him. "I bet we know what that conversation is about. Things are heating up to the boiling point."

Bob followed Matt's eyes. "Yep."

Wayne walked up to the table and Kathy moved over to another table.

"Look what the wind blew in," Matt said.

"I've never seen Wayne in the cafeteria before," Bob whispered.

"That's because he's always over at Five Points before school starts. He must have been looking for Lynn."

Wayne turned his head and his eyes met Matt's. He looked away and began talking to Lynn. After a minute or two, he looked back at Matt.

Matt continued to stare at him and he looked away again. "I think I'm making him uncomfortable, Bob."

"Why?"

"I think *he* knows—that *I* know—that *he* knows." He looked at Wayne and grinned.

Wayne responded with a grin.

Bob turned his head so Wayne couldn't see his face. "It feels like you two are having a duel—a staring duel. You're making me nervous, Matt. The fight at the dirt road is a recent memory."

"We're okay. He won't start anything in the cafeteria ... but then ... I might be wrong," he said as Wayne took a step toward him.

Wayne pointed a finger toward Matt and motioned for him to come closer.

"Matt, why are you doing this?" Bob whispered.

Wayne took another step.

Matt got up and took a step toward Wayne.

John kept talking at the other end of the table, seemingly unaware of what was happening.

Wayne started to move forward, but Lynn grabbed his T-shirt and pulled him back. He yanked away from Lynn and turned to face Matt. "I'm going to get what's mine," he said to Matt in a loud voice.

The cafeteria got quiet. John turned around and saw Wayne and Matt facing each other. He jumped up, and he and Bob moved on both sides of Matt.

Matt smiled. *I was wrong. He knows—but he doesn't know that I know that he knows. I'm loving it.* Satisfaction surged through his body. Wayne had taken the bait. "Sounds like you're hearing a lot of rumors, Wayne." His voice reverberated through the quiet cafeteria.

Lynn grabbed Wayne again, and Wayne pushed her hand away. "Come here, Parker," he said, slowly closing his fists, "and bring your two twerps with you."

In his best Laurel and Hardy voice, Bob said softly, "Ollie, look at the predicament you have got me in."

The deep voice of Coach Smith broke the silence in the cafeteria. "That's enough, Tyson. Say goodbye to your lady friend and leave the cafeteria, unless you want to go to the office."

"I'm not doing anything, Coach ... just talking to the little seventh grader."

Coach Smith walked past the three seventh graders and right up to Wayne. "Well, your conversation is over, so get out of here!"

Wayne started toward the door and as he walked past Matt, he brushed against him and said quietly, "I know some things."

"Like how easy ninth grade is the third time around?" John said with a grin.

Coach Smith looked at John. "Son, do you want to go to the office?"

"No, sir."

"Then keep quiet."

The bell rang and Bob picked up his books. "I dig Coach Smith. He's pretty cool. He takes no guff."

"It's all coming together," Matt said. "Wayne's taken another bite of the carrot. He just doesn't know for sure."

John looked at Matt. "He doesn't know *what* for sure?"

"Stuff, John ... just stuff. ... Right now, *you* not knowing helps the cause. Tomorrow it will get real clear."

"Well, I'm ready to find out. Let this day go by fast."

Chapter 75

GETTING READY
FOR THE PARTY

MATT WALKED ONTO HIS DRIVEWAY with a sigh of relief. He'd walked home alone after school, keeping a lookout for Wayne, and now he could think about Dee's party and seeing Bonnie and forget about everything else.

"I'm home, Mom," he said as he walked through the front door.

"I'm in the kitchen. I'll have a lemon cake ready in a little while."

Matt gave her a kiss on the cheek, dipped his finger into the mixer, thrust it into his mouth and said, "Mmmm … off to a great start."

She covered the bowl with her hand. "Batter isn't ready yet," she said. She turned on the mixer and poured another ingredient into the bowl. "By the way, Dad's not having dinner with us tonight."

"I know what that means … he and Bill have gone fishing, right?"

"Right. He said to tell you to have fun tonight, say hello to Dee's mom and dad for him and most importantly, teach a good lesson tomorrow."

Matt's eyes lit up at the word "lesson," and he whistled as he went to his bedroom to figure out what he was going to wear to the party.

Thirty minutes later, he was back in the kitchen. "So what's for dinner, Mom?"

"Leftovers. Easy cleanup."

"Sounds great. You wash and I'll dry?"

"Yes," she said. She reached under the sink and pulled out a big bag. "Feed the dog, please, and when you come back in, dinner will be ready."

Matt poured the dog food into the food dish. "Here you go, boy. I'll walk you after dinner."

Mullet plunged his head into the bowl, and Matt turned and headed back inside.

"So, Mom, what should I wear tonight—blue jeans, Bermudas or slacks?"

"Pretty warm. I say wear Bermudas for the party and take jeans for tomorrow. You going to the horse barn?"

"No, ma'am," he said, giving her a smile. His mom always seemed to know everything ... but not this time. She smiled back.

"You knew I wasn't going to the horse barn, didn't you?"

She didn't answer. She just continued to smile.

"I know you're right about wearing shorts, but I think I'd rather wear slacks, my madras shirt and the new Weejuns you bought me. I think Bermudas look corny on me."

"Please wear socks."

"Oh, Mom, 'no socks' is cool. You don't want me to be square, do you?"

"Okay, no socks, but if your dad were here, there would be a discussion."

Matt smiled. "It's the new style, Mom. Dad is not with it. He still wears pleated pants. This is the fifties ... rock 'n' roll and all that jazz."

"I'm sure he could give you a good argument."

"If it was how to dress for hunting, fishing or working, I'd listen. But Mom, if Dad dressed me to go to this party, it would be all over—and you know who would be the first to get me?"

"John?"

"For sure."

They laughed and continued to talk. After supper, they cleaned off the table. "You left a lot of food, Matt."

"I know. I have a nervous stomach, I think."

"Excited?"

"I think so."

Mrs. Parker grabbed a pan and dropped it into the water. "So, you think you're nervous about the party, or is it more about something tomorrow?"

Matt looked at the plate he was drying and rubbed it with the dishtowel in continuous circular movements.

"Are you drying that plate or polishing it?"

"Sorry," he said and set the dry plate on the counter.

"You go ahead and get ready for the party. I'll finish up this kitchen."

"Thanks, Mom. And Mom—I'm ready for tomorrow."

Matt finished dressing and was putting the records he'd already sorted in his carrying case when his mom knocked on his open bedroom door.

"You look very nice. Must be some pretty girls coming to the party."

Matt blushed. "First-ever teenage party."

"Are you taking all those records? That is a big investment of yours."

"I'll be careful. My name is on every label."

"Don't cry to me if they get scratched or broken. I know how you are about your collection."

"I'll be careful. At least I don't have to bring Kathy's records. She's going to be able to go after all."

Matt looked at the clock on his nightstand. "Mom, can we pick up Brad and Billy? It's on our way. I told them I thought it would be okay."

"Sure."

"Brad and I are good buddies again *and*—as you know—the girls love him."

"Must be like his dad. That apple landed right under the tree." She let out a quiet but audible giggle.

"What?"

"Nothing."

"Inside joke?"

"Fair dinkum. I'm ready when you are."

"Dee asked if we could get there a little early to set up the music. The party starts at eight o'clock. I said we'd be there by seven forty-five. Okay?"

"Yes. If we need to pick up Brad and Billy, we should leave in fifteen minutes. You know I am a slow driver. I'm not like Mrs. Walton."

Matt laughed. "No, you sure are not, but it's okay, Mom. All the boys still love you. I'll call Brad and Billy and tell them when to expect us."

Mrs. Parker sat behind the wheel with the engine running and Perry Como singing "Hot Diggity (Dog Ziggity Boom)."

Matt climbed in the front seat. "Took me three trips, but I have it all. And I won't be playing that song that you've got playing on WSUN," he said with a grin.

"Look closely, because when I pull out of this driveway, I'm not turning around and coming back for something you forgot."

"We're cool. I've got it all."

Mrs. Parker put the car in reverse and eased out the clutch. "My next car will be automatic, and it will have power steering." Her hands turned white from her tight grip on the steering wheel as she changed from first to second gear.

"Oh, Mom, our car's cool. Automatic is for old people. You're doing good."

"Thank you for the vote of confidence, but just keep me on the flat roads."

As they drove into Brad's driveway, Matt said, "Honk the horn, Mom."

"No, you go up to the front door and ring the doorbell."

"Mrs. Walton would have whipped into the drive, and Bob would have reached over, regardless of what seat he was in, and laid on the horn."

"Well, I'm not Mrs. Walton—and you're not Bob."

"She's cool."

"I know."

Before Matt could get out of the car, Brad ran out onto the front porch and, in one jump, cleared the three steps and landed on the sidewalk. Matt opened the door and Brad slid into the front seat beside him. "Hi, Mrs. P. Mom and Dad said 'hello.' They're inside getting ready to go out."

"Hello, Brad. Looking more like your dad every day, but I still see your mom." She opened the corner vent window and backed out of the driveway. "Open the one on your side, please, Brad, so we can get a nice flow of air through here. Will it be too chilly? I know it won't rearrange your hair. I don't think a hurricane would move one hair with all that butch wax you two have on."

"You think we have on a lot—you should see John. Right, Brad?"

"For sure. John looks like a porcupine that's been scared by a bear. He has it everywhere, Mrs. P, even on the sides. Matt and I just have it on the front."

"Bet you're glad John's not in the car to hear this conversation," Mrs. Parker said, laughing. "You boys can be so cruel."

"All in fun," Matt said, pinching his mom's arm. "Can't be thin-skinned around us."

She responded with her own pinch. "That's for sure. Now, let's pick up Billy and get you boys to the party."

"Mrs. Parker, would it be rude to ask to change the radio station?"

"Matt's already been pleading. Go ahead."

"WALT, Matt?"

"For sure."

Chapter 76

DEE'S PARTY

MRS. KIRKPATRICK STOOD at the front door and waved at Matt's mom. Dee ran out to the car. "Hi, Mrs. Parker, isn't this exciting? Matt, have you got the records? I'll show you where to set up by the record player. Hi, Brad. Hi, Billy." She gave Brad a big smile and a wink, and said, "Do I get your first dance? I've got to go. Bye, Mrs. Parker," she said, and she was off to greet the people in the car behind them.

Matt pulled three record cases out of the trunk.

"Think you brought enough?" Mrs. Parker said, shaking her head.

"Can't talk now, Mom. I love you."

"Love you too. Call me in the morning."

"Thanks for the ride, Mrs. P," Brad and Billy said together.

"Open the door, Richard," Matt said.

"I'm not Richard, but come in, boys," Dee's mom said with a big smile. "The record player is in the Florida room down the hall. Kathy brought records too."

"Thank you, Mrs. Kirkpatrick."

The French doors of the spacious Florida room opened onto a large outdoor patio. Strings of white lights hung from hooks in the large oak trees and lit up the backyard, and spotlights at the bottom of the trees illuminated the higher branches and their leaves.

Matt looked up. It was a beautiful night to have an outdoor party. Now, he understood why Dee had said at school, "Please, Lord, don't let it rain."

"Bring the records over here, Matt," Brad said. "The record player is here, and the food table is close by. Change a record and eat some food. Are you coming?"

Matt came out of his daze and walked over and put his record cases beside the record player.

"Hey guys," John said, laughing as he walked past Matt, Brad and Billy. He headed for the food table, one step behind Bob.

Matt grabbed John's neck and squeezed. "Remember, there are about forty people coming, so don't eat it all."

John swallowed a mouthful of potato chips and moaned. "Don't make me choke. You should be telling Bob that. He's the one with the hollow leg."

"What was all the laughing about?" Matt asked.

"Have you seen BB the Bat, also known as the Pirate, tonight?" John said, before laughing again. "Where does he get these outfits? He has on a pair of new pants called calypsos, and a square-neck pullover T-shirt. The pants are white and the pullover T-shirt has red and white stripes."

"Hey, John, calypso pants are in," Bob said. "I've got a pair the same as BB's."

Dee walked up to Matt. "You boys are having too much fun over here. Remember, this is a dance party. Let's turn on the music, Matt. And John, straighten up."

Bob walked away, carrying a plate of food. "Need to fill up my spare leg before I dance."

Dee frowned at him. "Thanks for all your help, Bob."

Matt put a stack of his forty-fives on the Kirkpatricks' record player. The first record dropped on the turntable and Bill Haley and the

Comets began singing "Rock Around the Clock." He snapped his fingers to the beat. "Now that should make everybody want to dance," he said. He looked down at more of the records he had spread out, reading the labels, selecting more songs.

Maggie and JB stepped onto the smooth concrete patio. JB took her right hand with his left hand, wrapped it around her head, spun her around and the dancing began.

Dee pulled Brad out to dance with her, and Bob and Judy joined them.

Dee's parents and two other chaperones watched the couples dancing. They clapped to the beat and encouraged more couples to get on the dance floor.

From the side of the dance floor, John pointed to Bob's feet. "Bob, you missed that roach over there."

"What?"

"You look like you're stomping on roaches—oh, that's right, you're dancing. American Bandstand ... eat your heart out."

"Why don't you try it, John," Judy said.

"Because he knows he can't," Bob said. He moved his feet out of step with the beat. "This is what he'd look like."

John jumped on the dance floor. "Watch this." He fell on his back, kicked his legs wildly in the air and started shaking his arms.

A new song started: Gene Vincent singing "Be-Bop-a-Lula."

John stopped and extended a hand to Kathy who'd been laughing the hardest. She grabbed his hand and he pulled her up against him. He placed one hand on her back and stuck the other hand holding hers straight out, and walked forward, Kathy trying to follow him.

"That's sure not the bop," Bob said. "Is that the tango?"

John abruptly reversed his direction and started the other way. "It's my version of 'the stroll.' I call it 'the monster glide.' Dig it, Bob?"

Dr. Kirkpatrick laughed. "That boy's got talent, but it's not dancing."

John was out of control. Kathy was too. She was as crazy as John, but unlike John, she could dance. She slowly developed a rhythm and started to give John's awkward movement some style. When it ended, the pair got a loud, clapping ovation. John gave a slow bow, turned, bowed again and turned again, repeating the bow a third time.

"A show stealer," Mrs. Kirkpatrick said. "John has gotten this party hopping."

Matt watched it all and then moved back to the record player.

"Oh, Matt," Dee said. "This is so much fun. Thanks for bringing your records."

"Dick Clark has nothing on us," Matt said.

The last record dropped onto the turntable. He could see the yellow label and knew it was Jerry Lee Lewis. The needle touched the record, a piano started pounding and "A Whole Lotta Shaking" began.

Matt pulled Elaine to the dance floor before he asked, "Wanna dance?" with a big smile.

Moving bodies packed the dance floor, and no one judged anyone.

Matt studied his records and selected the next group of songs he would play. "Put on some slow songs," Brad said. "The Platters, maybe?"

The first record dropped. "I'm Sorry" began.

"Come on, Billy," Bob said. "It's easy. You just shuffle your feet back and forth to the music, and try to keep the girl's hair from getting in your mouth."

Billy laughed. "I'm game—but the girls are all taller than I am."

Bob looked around. "Hey, they're all taller than you *and* me. So what? Let's try it."

"I think I'll ask Dorothy again," Billy said. "Maybe she'll say yes twice."

"Heck yes, she will," Bob said. "Who's that older girl beside Kathy?"

"Her cousin, I think—she's too old for me."

"Me too," Bob said. "She sure is pretty."

John walked up to the two of them. "Looking at the high school girl, are you?"

"Maybe."

"No falsies in her bra."

Billy shook his head. "Let's go, Bob. Leave the older one for Brad."

Matt lifted the needle before another record dropped onto the turntable. "Attention," he yelled. "This song is dedicated to Wayne from Billy."

A piano intro began and "Lucille" by Little Richard blasted from the speakers.

After the song ended, Billy walked over to Matt, grinning. "I've sung that song and never thought much about the words. It definitely fits our new short-term pet."

Matt continued to sort through records. "Yes, it does. Have you put a picture of Wayne in Lucille's cage so she knows him?"

"Yes, I show her Wayne's picture then pinch her tail. She's a smart snake. Yesterday I showed her the picture, and she hid her tail."

"I think she's ready," Matt said.

"Oh, she's ready all right,"

Matt smiled. *But are we ready? You bet your life … Hurry up, Saturday night.*

Dee walked up. "Okay you two … what's the Wayne dedication about?"

"Private joke—can't tell you now but someday soon it might be made public."

At the drink box, Dr. Kirkpatrick chiseled big chunks off a new ice block with an ice pick and tossed them into the cold water.

Matt, Billy, Bob and John pulled out a Royal Crown Cola, a Coke and two Nehi Grapes from the large assortment of drinks in the icy water, dried the bottles and their hands with a towel and used the opener on the side of the box to pop off the caps.

"That water is cold, sir," Matt said. "Guess that's why the drinks taste so good."

"It's cold, but it needs more ice to keep them that way," Dr. Kirkpatrick said. "You boys be sure to close the lid after you get your sodas, please."

Matt handed him the towel. "Yes, sir."

"Thanks, Matt," Dr. Kirkpatrick said. "You know, I still prefer block ice, but I don't know how many more years we can get it."

"Why, sir?" Matt asked.

"Our refrigerators are electric. Not many iceboxes left in homes. With electric refrigerators, people can make their own ice cubes and don't need to buy ice for refrigeration like they used to. Train boxcars are following the same path. Ice is starting to be used only for picnics and outdoor activities, and most people now prefer to buy it in a bag, but I'll buy it by the block as long as I can get it."

When Dr. Kirkpatrick walked away, Bob said, "Do you think we'll be tested on that?"

"I don't know, but now I know why Atlantic Ice sits beside the railroad tracks," John said.

Matt walked over to the food table and reached for a potato chip. He felt a light tap-tap on his shoulder and turned around to see Kathy smiling at him. "Hi, Matt, I want you to meet my cousin, Susan."

Susan's hair was long and blonde and reached all the way down her back. Kathy forgot to tell him she was beautiful. Matt swallowed. "Nice to meet you, Susan. Kathy told me a lot about you—all good, I might add."

John pushed Matt aside. "Hi, Susan, I'm Kathy's friend, John, and this is Bob and Billy, two young neighbor boys who climbed over the fence just to get a look at the party going on. Music was the bait. Speaking of music ... would you like to dance? ... Only kidding."

John looked at Kathy. His face turned red. "Hi, Kathy. Would you like to dance?"

Before Kathy could answer, Susan grabbed John's hand and pulled him on the dance floor. "You asked me first," she said.

"Come on, Bob," Kathy said. "Let's dance."

"Okay. Let's step on John's toes while we're out there."

Matt looked at Billy. "You learn a lesson every day."

"What's the lesson today?" Billy asked

"Never expect anything and assume everything," he said with a laugh.

Susan moved her feet in a rock-and-roll dance step to the fast song playing, but pulled John in close like you would with a slow song. She was a good dancer. Once again a circle formed around John, but this time, all eyes were on his partner.

"This was a favorite song of mine last year," Susan said. The song ended and she pulled him by the hand back to Matt, smiling. "I was just checking to see if John came over the fence too."

"And what's your verdict?" Kathy said.

"John's *not* a fence climber."

"We're not either," Billy said, looking at John with a little contempt.

"I know you're not," Susan said. "Would you like to dance?"

"Okay, but I'm not … but I'm just learning," Billy said.

"I remember when I was learning," Susan said. "You know what's important?"

"What?"

"Have fun! That's what dancing is about. And rock 'n' roll makes it happen."

Chapter 77

FIRST DANCE

MATT FELT A HAND on his shoulder. He turned around and smiled. "Hey, Bonnie. When did you get here?"

"Just now. Are you the DJ tonight?" Bonnie asked.

"Not really, but I just put on a new stack of records. Would you like to dance?"

"Sure."

"Like Lloyd Price?"

Bonnie nodded, and "Just Because" began to play.

He had a little experience slow dancing, but he'd never asked a girl to dance that he had feelings for. His heart began to pound. He took her hand, and they walked to the dance floor.

He gently placed his right arm around her waist and then pulled away and looked at her. "I'm glad you're here," he said.

"Me too."

"I'm pretty new at this, Matt," Bonnie said with a smile. "I can tell this is 'old hat' to you."

Matt moved his face a little closer to hers. "What do you mean?"

"I feel clumsy and you aren't. You seem to know how. Who taught you to dance?"

"John ... no, only kidding ... actually, an older girl named Linda Anderson, a neighbor when I was in elementary school. She was in ninth grade and I was in fifth. She said some girls held onto doorknobs and practiced dancing with the door, but she wanted a real partner. So I became her 'door,' and she taught me how to dance while she practiced."

They didn't talk, and the song playing seemed to help, but there was still the silence between them. Matt felt awkward, so he whispered, "Have I stepped on your feet yet?"

"Only once," Bonnie said, not moving her head, "and that was my fault. I'm not good at following."

"I think we're both doing good and who cares, right? We're having fun, and you're fun to dance with."

"Thank you … me too."

Matt knew Bonnie liked him when he felt her head slowly rest on his shoulder. When the song ended, he walked her over to the girls. "Can I have the next slow dance?" he asked her.

Bonnie smiled. "Yes, you can."

He let go of her hand and headed toward the record player. "I'll be right back."

The next song had started, and it was skipping, hopefully not from a scratch because it was his favorite record in his collection. The needle slid over the record, instead of staying in the groove.

Matt stopped the player, removed all the records, used a cloth to wipe the record that was skipping and put it back onto the turntable. He lifted the needle, carefully set it on the outside edge and held his breath.

The instrumental began—first the slow rhythmic sound of a guitar, followed by the beat of the drum and cymbal—then the sax—and finally Bill Doggett in the background playing the organ. "Honky Tonk" filled the air. Not a hint of a scratch. His favorite record was fine.

He looked up and saw John and Bob walking toward him. The looks on their faces told him what was coming.

"We saw you dancing with Bonnie," Bob said. "We saw you—our new Hootchie-Cootchie lover boy."

"Yeah, in the darkest part of the dance floor," John said.

"I didn't know there was a dark part."

"Oh, there was one, before the chaperone turned the lights up," Bob said.

"Did we see you kiss Bonnie?" John said.

"No! I did *not* kiss Bonnie."

"We saw her head snuggled up into your neck and we heard her cooing," John said, laughing.

"You did not, John. We were just dancing. Maybe I saw you kiss Susan. Wow—our new Burt Lancaster. Next you'll be on the beach ... rolling in the surf."

John laughed. "I wish you had."

"I bet you tried and she pushed you away and said, 'I don't kiss boys who shoot blue flames.' You know, John, if your blue flames ever take you to the sideshows on the midway, one of the carnie's daughters might kiss you—probably one who's eating good, to replace her mom as the fat lady on the midway."

Bob laughed. "Okay, Matt won that round. I bet Shirley would kiss you, John. I don't think she's danced with anyone yet. Ask her to dance to the next slow song."

"Don't make fun of Shirley," John said. "She's a friend of ours. You're trying to get me ... and innocent Shirley became the victim. Just because she's a little plump, you singled her out, Bob. How low can you go?"

"I know what you're trying to do John, and it's not working," Bob said. "I didn't know how sensitive you were. Sorry, I was only kidding. You know I wouldn't hurt your feelings on purpose like you would mine."

"Ouch," John said. "Matt, let me find a record. I want to dance with someone."

He carefully picked through the stacks and pulled out one with a yellow label.

Matt smiled when he saw the title, "Boney Maroney." He pulled off the other records, set John's record on the bottom and replaced the stack on the record player. The record dropped and the needle found the groove.

John walked over and asked Shirley to dance. Before she could answer, he took her by the hand and pulled her out to the dance floor. Shirley had rhythm, and she was good.

John twirled her around. "You're no stick of macaroni."

Shirley laughed. "Nope, I'm the noodle variety."

Matt watched from the distance. John could be hard—and John could be soft.

While John and Shirley danced, Dee turned on a lamp at the edge of the patio where Bob and Judy were sitting. She looked at Matt and winked. "Mom said we have to keep the lamp on." She rolled her eyes. "She's afraid spin the bottle might start over here."

Judy put her hand up to her mouth and stood up. "I'm not a kisser."

"Don't look at us. We're not kissing," Bob said.

Judy stood up and walked away. Bob walked over to the table next to the record player, picked up a *Look* magazine and showed a picture of Elvis to Matt. "Put on an Elvis song next, Matt."

"You got it. How about "Heartbreak Hotel"?

"Way to go, Daddy-O," Bob said. That's just what I had in mind." He stood up and assumed an Elvis pose, pretending to hold a stand microphone in one hand with his other hand straight out, pointing to the floor. As the song began, he stood with one leg firm and straight while the other gyrated around with only the toe of his shoe on the floor.

The other boys joined in and gave their own renditions of Elvis.

"Who are you?" John said, looking at JB, who moved his feet like he was standing on hot coals.

"Elvis?"

"Hardly. You look more like a boy who stepped in a bed of red ants that are working their way up his leg, getting close to the privates," John said. "You're hopeless, JB, but so is everyone else, including me. At least I'm cool, right Matt? Come on, Shirley, let's show them how to do it."

More couples joined them on the dance floor, and when the song ended, the patio filled with laughter. "If I wasn't watching the record player, I'd have been out there too, Bob," Matt said. "I could make a bigger fool of myself than you, JB *or* John."

"Why do boys always tease each other, Matt?" Dee asked.

Matt smiled as he gazed out over the dance floor. "Boys are boys, Dee … teasing tames your own insecurity. Plus, boys, pretty much, have skin as tough as leather. What we have here is our first experience at a party with girls. I bet the next one will be easier."

"I bet you're right, Matt," Dee said. "Keep the music rockin'. I'll be right back."

Billy walked up as Dee left. "What are you smiling about? How awkward we all look trying to dance?"

"Well," Matt said, letting out a big sigh, "I don't see the makings of a dancing pair like Fred Astaire and Ginger Rogers, but I see a lot of them out there enjoying themselves. Who knows, maybe Fred and Ginger started the same way."

"You're being way too optimistic," Billy said. "And I should know. I think I'm the worst."

"It's all about the music, Billy. You've got to love the music. The dancing is secondary. Just enjoy the music ... rock 'n' roll is here to stay!"

"I am," Billy said. "Guess what? Your neighbor Kathy just came up and asked what Lucille meant and what was the joke with Wayne?"

"What did you say?"

"I told her it had to do with Wayne, a girl's name and showering in gym class." Billy gave a confident smile and nodded his head. "That shut her up."

Matt wiped his forehead. "Sorry! I knew I shouldn't have said that. I forgot about Kathy." He squeezed Billy on the shoulder. "Quick thinking. Sounds like no harm was done, thanks to you."

"And then she asked what rumors were going around."

Matt felt his heart skip a beat. "And you said?"

Billy grinned. "I said I was hearing that the way Wayne started the year, he might be the first student in the history of the school to be a ninth grader for four years. I laughed, but she didn't. I couldn't wait to tell you, Matt. We're a 'go.'"

"Yes, we are! Way to go, Billy. You did well."

The next record dropped on the turntable. The song began with a loud, repetitive guitar, and Sanford Clark began singing "The Fool."

"This is the Lucille encore. You might sing this song tomorrow night at the Carib when you tell Lucille goodbye," he whispered to Billy.

Chapter 78

TAKE A CHANCE

MATT SEARCHED HIS COLLECTION and found the song he wanted to play next. He slipped it on the bottom of the stack and headed toward Bonnie. The record dropped, and "Since I Met You Baby" by Ivory Joe Hunter began.

He walked over to Bonnie and Dee who were talking to Judy beside the food table and tapped Bonnie on the shoulder. "Can I have this dance?"

She nodded and smiled, and he led her by the hand to the dance floor.

He pulled her to him like the couples he'd seen dance on television, his right hand secure around her waist and his left hand holding her hand up and away from their bodies. *Don't step on her feet.*

They began to dance and Bonnie gently settled her head on his shoulder.

He let his cheek come into contact with hers and closed his eyes. Her perfume was subtle yet strong, and her hair smelled clean and fresh. He couldn't believe how he felt. He pulled his head away and looked into her eyes.

She smiled just enough to show the beginning of a dimple and gently stroked the back of his neck with her hand. He felt like he might faint.

"You okay?" she asked.

"I'm fine."

"You're a great dancer."

"So are you."

"You nervous?"

"A bit."

"Why?"

"I'm afraid I might step on your feet."

She laughed.

"Don't you believe me?"

"Maybe a little ... I think you like me."

He laughed with relief. "That's an understatement."

She settled her head again on Matt's shoulder, and they stayed almost stationary on the dance floor.

When the song ended, Matt looked down at her, and she looked up. He leaned down, and his lips met hers. He kissed her fast—quickly, yet gently.

He couldn't believe it. He just kissed a girl! He squeezed her hand and smiled at her. She smiled. He knew it was their secret. They walked off the dance floor, Matt still holding her hand.

The record player dropped the next record—back to rock 'n' roll. The perfect harmony of the Everly Brothers began as they sang "Wake Up Little Susie."

Twenty minutes later, parents started arriving.

Chapter 79

IT'S THE MUSIC!

MATT STARED OUT the rear window of the station wagon and looked at the house they'd just left, thinking about Bonnie—dancing—his record collection—Lucille—but not really focusing on anything. He had a warm feeling within him, a feeling he couldn't describe. He knew the next day was a day of reprisal, but now was a time of awakening. The party seemed to be the beginning of the next plateau in the events of his life.

Mrs. Walton started the car and pulled out of the Kirkpatricks' driveway. "How was the party, boys?"

"Fun, fun," John said, sitting in the shotgun seat that he had once again managed to secure. "Your son is the new teenage boys' inspiration. He turned off the light in the corner of the patio and started kissing with Judy."

"That's right, Mrs. Walton," Billy said. "Dee's mom would turn the light back on, and in ten minutes, he'd turn the light off, and they'd start kissing again."

"They're lying, Mom."

"We are *not*, Mrs. Walton," Billy said. "It was like the love scene on the beach in *From Here to Eternity*." Mrs. Walton turned around with a surprised look on her face. "Bobby! You're too young."

John reached into the back seat and messed up Bob's hair. "We're proud of you, Bob. You are *the man*."

"I didn't kiss anybody, Mom," Bob said.

Her expression changed to a knowing grin and John started to laugh. "I'm telling you, Mrs. Walton, he's a blossoming Casanova."

John turned up the radio and Buddy Holly's voice filled the car, singing "Peggy Sue."

Alone in the third row seat of the station wagon, Matt smiled. He'd kissed Bonnie, and another feeling of fulfillment was just around the corner. *Tomorrow's the day I've been waiting for. Get ready to learn how to be humble, Wayne.*

At the corner, Bob interrupted the quiet. "Pop the clutch, Mom, and peel some rubber."

With a squeal of rubber and a quick applause, they sped toward the Waltons' house, the radio playing more rock 'n' roll music.

Matt felt a satisfied warmth. The feeling was strong. What was it? He gazed out the window and searched within himself for the answer. It's not about Bonnie. It's not about Wayne. And then it came to him. *It's the music—It's the music! Rock 'n' roll is music with a different beat and lyrics for teenagers and their idols to sing.*

Three straight hours of listening and dancing to the music had made a great night for him. It was the beat—It was the story being told. He lived for that music. He loved watching the teenagers on American Bandstand. ... A voice brought him out of his daydreaming. "Wake up back there, lover boy," Bob said. "We're here."

Chapter 80

FINAL PLANS

THE OUTSTRETCHED LIMB of the large oak tree almost touched the window in Bob's bedroom and prevented early morning sunrays from entering the room, but when the sun rose above the limb, its rays came through the windowpane and created a prism that separated the white light into a rainbow of colors on the wall.

Matt stared at the everchanging pattern. He glanced at his watch. Oh my gosh, it's already eight o'clock. He kicked the sheets away from his body. *Brrr—it's cold in here!*

The air conditioner hummed in the other window, and in the bunk bed on the other side of the room, Bob and Billy had pulled the covers over their heads. No wonder he was freezing.

He carefully extended his legs until his feet touched the mattress above him. When he felt John's body sagging down right above him, he put both feet softly in contact and bent his legs for the necessary leverage. With one quick push, he sent John a foot in the air. "Time to get up, John."

"Yeah, John, wake up," Bob said. "We're tired of hearing you talk in your sleep."

"I don't talk in my sleep."

Bob made a smooching sound. "Yes, you do. You were kissing Shirley."

"I was not."

"It was either her or the fat lady behind your curtain."

John grabbed his pillow and leapt off the upper bunk, landing on both feet with a thud. He swung the pillow like a baseball bat and nailed Bob in the back while he still lay face down in the bed.

The bedroom door flew open and Mrs. Walton stood in the doorway. "No pillow fights! Hear me, John?" She reached over and grabbed him by the neck.

"Stop! Yes ma'am ... I quit," John said, laughing.

She released her grip, grabbed Bob by his feet still wrapped in his blanket and pulled him onto the floor.

Matt did a swan dive off his lower bunk and landed on top of the group. On the floor were now three boys and a mom, all laughing.

On top of the other bunk, Billy stared down at them.

It ended as quickly as it began. "Okay boys, let me up."

At the door she turned around. "You boys need to get dressed, make the beds and head downstairs for breakfast. Bob, your brothers and sisters and their friends are already down there. Susie is making her famous pancakes."

The door closed.

"Hey, Bob," Billy said. "Your mom breaks me up. This is the most fun I've ever had at a sleepover. I didn't know any other kids were here. We must have been the last ones home. I didn't see or hear anyone else last night."

"Wait 'til breakfast," Bob said. "You'll see them all. Mom let everyone have a friend stay over last night."

At the bottom of the stairs, Susie cupped her hands around her mouth and shouted up to the second landing. "Hot pancakes on the table. You boys quit your talking and get yourselves down here now!"

"Yes, ma'am. Coming," Bob said.

The breakfast went on for thirty minutes. Susie came out, added orange juice to the pitchers and placed more fried eggs on the center platter. She refilled the fruit bowl, and on her next return from the kitchen, she dropped slices of toast on another plate near the butter and jelly. "Are you children getting full?"

Matt pushed his chair away from the table and stood up and patted his stomach. "I am, Susie. Thank you for a great breakfast, and please excuse me, everyone."

He picked up his plate to return it to the kitchen sink, and Susie stopped him. "Leave your plate there, young Matt. I'll clean up the table today. And that goes for everyone. No kitchen chores today. Scoot!"

"Are you sure?" Billy said.

"It's just the Walton nature," Bob said.

"No, it's just Susie," Danny said. "If it were someone else in the kitchen today, believe me, someone from this table would be washing and the others drying."

Matt stood up. "Hey, guys, I'm going upstairs. Let's meet in thirty minutes in the living room so we can plan the day."

John stood up and downed the rest of his juice like a cowboy in the movies at the bar finishing a drink. Smacking the glass on the table, he said, "Whis-key for my friend."

"He isn't here today, John," Bob said with a jovial laugh. He slithered an egg across his plate, sliding it onto the fork like it was a spoon. Supporting the egg with a finger from his other hand, he shoved it into his mouth. "We're coming, Matt," he mumbled.

By nine a.m., the house was quiet. Matt stood in front of the fireplace in the living room and slowly paced back and forth. He looked intense, and he studied some notes he held in his hand.

John sank deep into an overstuffed chair that was close to the fireplace. Billy took off his shoes and stretched out on the couch that faced the fireplace. Bob plopped down on the floor, laying his head on a pillow that had been on the couch.

"A bag of popcorn would be nice," Bob said.

"I still have a pancake sitting just below my Adam's apple, waiting its turn to enter my stomach," John said, "and you're already talking about popcorn."

"Will we be enjoying popcorn tonight at the movies, Matt?" Billy said.

Matt rubbed his hands together and a smile spread across his face.

"Tonight we will be enjoying popcorn and much, much more. Today is the day, and there can be no mess-ups. Timing will be critical. The movie at the Carib starts at eight o'clock. The doors open at seven forty-five. Billy, you already know what you have to do."

"Right, Matt. I'll meet you at seven."

"Bob, we've finished the phone calls. The final thing you need to do is get in the ticket line at the Carib theater at seven fifteen. You'll be the county fair midway emcee."

"I'll be ready. Master of Ceremonies is one of my favorite roles."

"John, your assignment is the scariest. You need to be at the Atlantic Coastline Railroad Station at seven o'clock. You might take a punch. That okay?"

John nodded. "Sure. Anything for Billy."

Billy patted John on the shoulder. "Thanks, John."

"Okay, John ... If Wayne has taken the bait I put out for him in the phone calls with Bob this week, he'll be at the train station at seven fifteen to steal a note from you that he thinks is meant for someone else. When he reads the note, he'll get in his car and leave. Call me from the pay phone outside the station so I'll know he's got it, and your job will be over. After that, hightail it to the Carib the back way, and stay out of sight."

Matt smiled and rubbed his hands together. "I say, let's get ready! Any questions?"

"Wow," John said. "You look like the wicked witch ready to stir up a potion."

"Almost," Matt said. "The potion will be in the envelope I'm going to give you. Wayne will think you're waiting for someone to pick up that envelope and will waste no time taking it. You need to put up a struggle, but remember, we *want* him to take the envelope."

Matt slowly looked around the table. "That's all for now. Just know, when something happens, everyone will see it happen."

John smiled. "I'm ready. Don't worry about me." He grabbed the glass of orange juice he'd brought from breakfast and lifted it high. "Here's to Billy and here's to the plan and here's to Matt, our buddy who never gave up."

John cupped his ear. "Listen to what's playing on the upstairs radio ... 'Whole Lotta Shakin Going On' ... Sing it, Jerry Lee Lewis."

"There'll be a lot of shaking going on tonight," Matt said.

"That's what I mean. And we know who'll be doing the shaking."

"John, you are a real John Wayne," Billy said.

"Yeah, you should leave the train station on a horse," Bob said.

"How about in a surplus army Jeep?" John said, grasping a make-believe steering wheel. "John Wayne, the GI, not the cowboy."

"You can leave the station any way you want. Just be careful," Bob said. "Sincerely."

"That's right, Bob," Matt said. "You ready to see Wayne's tail between his legs tonight?"

"Yes! I've been waiting to see Wayne get his butt kicked. Hope I get to kick him at least one time."

Billy removed a pencil from a spiral notebook he'd brought downstairs.

"What's the pencil and paper for?" John asked. "Are we going to be tested on this?" He looked up at Matt. "This must be why he gets all A's."

"No. This is my journal. Writing in it has made me feel safe since this started. And more importantly for me, I'll always be able to go back and recount how this all happened."

"So, I guess that means you're ready to hear what I have to say," Matt said.

"I am ready to hear what you have to say," repeated Billy, and he held the pencil in his hand, ready to write.

"Okay," Matt said, "so listen up. Let's start just like in the war movies, and I am John Wayne." He took off his wristwatch and lifted it up, like an auctioneer showing an item to the audience before the bidding begins. "Remember, before a plan was carried out, they would first synchronize their watches. Right? This is just like we did in Doolittle's Raid, but it's ten times as important because we're all going to be in different places."

They all nodded.

"Take off your watches, and let's check our times. My watch says five minutes after nine o'clock. John?"

"Three 'til nine."

"Bob?"

"Nine o'clock."

"Billy?"

"I don't have a watch on."

Matt shook his head. "That's all right. You have one, right?"

"Yes, at home."

"Good. My mom's going to take you home, so we can complete this part then. Now, Bob and John, on my signal, let's set our watches to my time."

They pulled out the stems of their watches.

"Ready?" Matt said. "When I say 'mark,' set them to seven minutes after nine." Matt looked at them both. All he needed was a helmet. It was just like they were on the battlefield. "Ready? Mark," he said, and they pushed in the stems of their watches. "Now, we have our watches in sync."

In the adjoining dining room, Susie had begun vacuuming, and outside, someone started up a lawnmower, but no one reacted to the sounds. Everyone was alert and listening to Matt.

"We're going to catch Wayne with his pants down," Matt said. "If we do this right, he won't expect a thing. The most glorious, exciting and fulfilling thing he thinks *he'll* ever do—will become *our* greatest fulfillment. He will have been sucked in and spit out by a group of 'seventh grade twerps.' The beauty of our story is that most of the people he thinks are involved don't exist. We are making up a story and placing Wayne in it."

Billy raised his hand like he was in class.

"What, Billy?" Matt said.

"Are we characters in the story?"

"No. We all have a part in making the story happen, but in the end, we are just onlookers. Thank you for trusting me."

The three looked at Matt with blank faces.

He picked up the metal poker and gave it a swift sweep like it was a sword. "The day Wayne hung Billy on the post—in my mind—I became a matador. I would find a way to beat the bull—fool Wayne with a cape, and in the end, he would meet the sword. The bull meets his sword of death. Wayne will meet our sword of humility. Are you all ready to help me with this?"

Billy wiped his eyes with his forearm and looked over at John and Bob. "Yes, ready."

John gave Matt a "thumbs-up" sign. "Yes, Matt. Today, you're the man!"

Bob clapped his hands softly. "Ready, Matt. We're with you."

The room became eerily quiet.

John picked up his baseball mitt, took out the ball and started throwing the ball into the mitt.

"Let's finish up here," Matt said. "We're all getting uptight. John, your assignment is the scariest, but I know you can handle it. You okay?"

John nodded.

"Okay, it all starts with you."

Billy raised his hand again. "What does Wayne think is happening?"

"Wayne thinks the second half of the map has been found after twenty years. He thinks he is stealing the envelope that will direct him to a rendezvous where he will get some gold coins and the second half of the map that was just discovered, so he can find an incredible buried treasure of gold, gems, silver ingots and jewelry fit for a queen."

Billy checked his notes. "And Lucille and I will meet you tonight behind the Carib at seven o'clock, right?"

"Right," Matt said. He pulled a folded piece of paper and an envelope out of his bag. "John, there's a pay phone at the train station. Call me at the pay phone outside the Carib. Here's the number on this piece of paper. And here's the envelope with the note for Wayne to take away from you. It's sealed with just one strip of Scotch tape so it will open easily."

He handed John the envelope. "Guard this well, but let him have it after a believable struggle. 'Lay on, Macduff, and damned be him that first cries, 'Hold! Enough!'"

John slipped the paper in his pocket and grinned. "Damn, Matt. There you go again. I don't know who said that, but it sure wasn't Yogi Berra." He looked carefully at the sealed envelope. "And don't worry, I'll take good care of this and Wayne will get it, if he shows up. There will be no slip-ups."

Chapter 81

THE TRAIN STATION

JOHN WALKED INTO THE HOUSE and found his brother Bill slouched on the living room couch with an Ace bandage wrapped around his shoulder and holding an ice bag in place. The medicinal smell of the salve used on pulled muscles and small bruises filled the room. "Heard you beat Plant High … at a price, I see."

"Always a cost," Bill said. "They have an all-western conference linebacker who looked into my eyes—helmet to helmet—all night, and finally messed up my shoulder. Dr. Hagan says it's just a bad bruise. I'm going to school in a little while and get in the whirlpool. Need a ride somewhere?"

"No thanks. I'm going downtown this afternoon, but I'll ride my bike. He wrinkled his nose at the odor in the room. "I might need that smelly stuff next."

"How's that?"

"We're finally paying back the hood that's been after Billy, and I've been chosen to get the plan going."

"Not that Tyson guy that's almost my age."

"Yep. The same. He's a badass."

"You'll get him. What's Matt's job?"

"It's a secret. He's going to surprise us."

"Maybe he'll bring Gargantua, that gorilla from the Barnum and

Bailey circus."

"No, we got something better than that."

"What?"

"It's got scales."

"I don't want to hear any more. Don't make me have to come to the jail like Dad almost had to do last weekend."

John's face turned red and he blew air out his nose as he laughed. "It's going to be good, Bill. Oh God, it's going to be spectacular."

"Stay safe and be careful," Bill said.

"I will. Tell you my story tonight."

John left the empty house and jumped on his bicycle. Wayne Tyson was a tough guy when you were twelve, even if you were John Hollis. He knew what was going to happen soon. He would take all the back streets. He didn't want to see Wayne before he was supposed to meet him, but he knew he had to get out of the house. He needed to keep moving. He had to feel tough himself.

He secured his bike to a post in the alleyway behind his mom's store, using a combination lock. The combination numbers gave him another scare. He reached in his pocket and felt the paper. He pulled it out. Written on the paper was the phone booth number. He hadn't lost it. Good God, he'd forgotten all about the phone number.

He went into the back of the store and took new inventory out of boxes and separated it by size and style. He chuckled. He'd never let Bob see him doing this or he'd be on the other side of the jokes, but he liked doing it, it helped his mom and it was helping him pass the time. He looked at his watch for the hundredth time: six o'clock. Time to get going. His mom was with her last customer. He walked by her so she could see his face and mouthed the words, "Goodbye. See you tonight."

Before she could respond, he was out the door. He left his bike locked up and walked up the street and around the corner. The station was only a ten-minute walk and he'd decided the best place to wait would be at Harn's Feed Store, a large, red-frame building which sat along the railroad tracks behind Brown Brothers, half a block from the Atlantic Coastline train station. It stayed open late on Saturdays to accommodate its customers, and it was always busy.

He'd be able to look down the train tracks from the platform outside the loft of the store and see the station, but not be seen from the street—and use the outside stairs to get down to the tracks when it was time to leave.

To break up the time, he walked up and down the aisles of Woolworth's, sat on a stool at the closed lunch counter for a second and got nervous and walked back out on the street. None of the stores along the rest of the way were open.

The sidewalks that were filled with shoppers an hour before were almost empty, and he had difficulty staying out of full view of cars driving past him. John walked around the block and through the Harn's customer parking lot into the busy store and climbed the stairs to the loft.

He walked past the bags of grass seed that lined the walkway to the open wooden door, stepped onto the platform suspended above the loading dock and looked around.

The second rail line, where train cars were left beside the store to be unloaded, was empty except for one tank car way down where the spur came off the main rail. Behind it was an empty brown boxcar which, if necessary, would be another place to hide.

He looked at his watch: six thirty-five ... twenty-five minutes to go.

He chewed on his fingernails as he waited. He was nervous about getting the envelope to Wayne. He'd rather be throwing punches. Suddenly, a train horn sounded. The hairs on his arm stood straight up. *A train now? Matt didn't say anything about a train. Oh God ... it's a passenger train.*

He walked to the wobbly wood railing, aware that a wrong step might send him to the ground. He leaned forward and saw the bright beam of the engine's headlight moving back and forth. He looked at his watch: six forty-five.

A second blast pierced the air as the train came toward him, slowly crossing the last intersection before reaching the station.

He ran down the outside stairs and crossed the tracks as the engine, a dining car, four passenger cars, a baggage car and one last passenger car inched closer to the station, the train's steel wheels grinding against the steel tracks. He could hear his heart beating. For the first time, he admitted to himself that he was scared. He was not afraid of being roughed up by Wayne. He could handle that. His fear was about getting everything right so the plan would be carried out.

Why did you give me this job, Matt? Why not Bob? That dirty bird … he probably said, 'John is the best one for the job.' I'll get him for this. I'll get Matt too. Oh Lord, just let me do this right … Please.

He stopped running and began walking at a slow pace. Don't be noticed. When he reached Cleveland Street, the train engine was only fifty feet from him. He stopped and looked at his watch. Six fifty. He was ten minutes early. Matt said to stay hidden until seven and the pickup wasn't until seven fifteen.

A porter pulled a baggage wagon from the station and parked it perpendicularly to the train, right between the engine and the first car. Stacked high with suitcases, trunks and other bags that had *US Mail* printed on them, the wagon looked like good cover.

Standing out in the open, he felt very noticeable and he wasn't ready for Wayne to see him yet. He stopped beside the wagon. Thank you, porter. It was a perfect hiding place. He peeked around the wheel of the wagon and watched the first passengers as they got off the train, stepping on a stool on the ground in front of the door. He looked at his watch: seven o'clock.

The open area between the train station and the passenger cars filled with passengers getting off and passengers getting ready to get on, and porters helping them all, progressing at about the same speed as a school fire drill. *This is insane. Come on, seven fifteen!*

He bent down and looked through the large wooden spokes of the wheel. He scanned the crowd.

He did not see Wayne—*good!* His hiding spot started to move—*bad!*

The porter moved the wagon, still piled high, to the open baggage car, and he moved with it—staying between the wagon and the train— trying to look like a kid playing hide and seek.

Five minutes later, the porters had emptied the wagon and he leaned against the station wall, close to the pay phone. He looked at his watch: seven ten. Wayne had to be somewhere close.

Midway between the engine and the last car, the conductor stood holding a large pocket watch on a chain attached to his pants. "All aboard!" he yelled. After some last-minute kissing and saying goodbye, the people in the area quickly changed from a lot standing near the train, to only a few.

The engineer gave two short horn blasts, and the train started to move. John looked at his watch: seven thirteen.

He walked out in the open area and looked around, but didn't see Wayne. Probably on the other side of the train. He wiped a wet drop of sweat running down his nose.

Out of the corner of his eye, he caught a glimpse of two guys in leather jackets, jeans and black boots approaching him, and they were coming fast. The hoods had arrived. It was Wayne and Bruce. Seven fifteen—right on time.

Wayne ate the carrot ... He took the bait ... It's going to happen.

His heart raced. He braced himself. Instinctively, he wanted to run, but he didn't. The train picked up speed and he knew he was too close to the tracks.

"Give me that envelope," Wayne yelled over the sound of the train.

He waved the envelope in front of their faces. "This is for somebody else, not you."

Wayne and Bruce ran toward him.

He lowered his head and hit them both hard. All three went down. They hit the ground and rolled close to the moving train with their legs tangled.

John stared at the steel wheels rolling by, almost touching their heads. One wrong move and all three of them would be pulled under the train.

"Nobody move," Wayne yelled, "or we're dead."

Wayne grabbed for the envelope in John's outstretched hand, but his hand hit the ground inches from the rail, and a wood splinter from a cross-tie jabbed his hand. The loosely sealed envelope blew into his face and stuck there for an instant, but the wind from the train pulled it under the train and onto the tracks.

Two cars left. It was almost over. The three boys froze.

John's heart stopped. With his squinting left eye mashed in the rocks beside the rail, he could see the last car. Something long and black hung down from it—a pipe was coming right toward Wayne's head. Something terrible was about to happen. *Poor Wayne.*

He closed his eyes, clenched his teeth and prayed. *We wanted to get him, but not like this.*

A loud bang and then a scream, "Owwwwwwww." Wayne shot off him and spun across the wood ties. Bruce yelled and rolled toward the station. Wayne lay motionless beside the tracks. His head was wet, but not bloody.

John lifted his head and got a good look. A rubber hose—not a pipe—hung from the car at the back of the train. The note lay ten feet down the tracks, fluttering between the rails.

Bruce stood up and brushed himself off. "You okay, Wayne?"

Wayne sat up, shook his head slowly and looked around. His cheek was red and swollen. "I think so. What hit me?"

"I don't know," Bruce said.

"Just a wet noodle," John said. "You were lucky."

Wayne looked at the disappearing train. "Shut up, prick! Bruce, get the note. It's on the tracks."

Bruce picked up the note and brought it back to Wayne.

Wayne stood up. "Don't you tell anyone I got this note, big man, until after eight o'clock. If you do, I won't even tell you what I'm going to do to you next, but you will pay."

John stayed on the ground and watched as Wayne read the note in the fading light, shoved it back in the envelope and sprinted down the tracks, Bruce beside him.

His hands were shaking like a hot wire was shocking him. He wiped train soot from his blurred eyes with a fast sweep of his forearm and looked down at his watch: seven twenty. Right on schedule!

He reached in his pocket and pulled out the folded paper. Time to make the phone call to Matt.

Chapter 82

HE'S GOT IT!

THE SUN WAS SETTING and the scary moment on the train tracks a few minutes earlier was now a hazy memory. The train horn blew in the distance.

Wayne could see Bruce's car parked in the lot a block north of the station. He looked over his shoulder and saw John still sitting beside the tracks. He pulled the note out of the envelope and read it again. He had the information he needed. He didn't have much time to get to the Carib and intercept the package meant for someone else. "Let's go, Bruce. We gotta get the fuck outta here." He took a deep breath and started to run. "Let's go," he yelled. "I'm driving."

He would find the buried treasure. His name was Tyson. It would have belonged to his dad, so he had every right to find it ... and keep it!

That little scumbag Matt was trying to cheat him out of it, and he wasn't going to let him do it. He felt an exhilaration he'd never known before, and he almost tripped because he wasn't watching where his feet were landing.

His lungs burned. He needed more air. He stopped and put his hands on his knees. He wished he were an athlete. The car was still fifty feet away. He coughed and choked. He wished he didn't smoke.

Bruce stopped beside him, panting. "What did the note say?"

Wayne caught his breath. "Tell you in the car. Hurry!"

"Don't forget—the driver's door is jammed shut," Bruce said. "I have to get in first on the passenger side and slide over."

"No," Wayne said. "I said I'm driving. We don't have much time."

★

John looked over at the phone booth beside the train station just as a man dressed in a suit and tie stepped into the booth and closed the door.

"Damn!" He walked over to the booth and the man turned his back to him. John tapped on the glass door, but the man ignored him. He started to pull the door open. "Please, mister ..."

The man continued to talk ...

John knocked on the door again and tried to pull it open. The man hung up the phone and turned around. "What's wrong, son?"

John squeezed by him through the hinged panel doors. "Sorry, mister."

"The bathroom is inside the station."

"I know, sir. Gotta make a very important phone call."

His hand shook as he put the dime into the slot and dialed the number.

Click—on the first ring. "Does he have it?"

"He's got it."

"Get on down here." Click!

John let his legs collapse and he sunk to the floor, feeling a settled relief. He sat on the floor and thought about what he'd done. *It's over! I did it! No screw-ups! Take over, Matt and Billy!*

"Yes!" he shouted. He sat on the floor of the telephone booth for a few moments relishing his accomplishments and then sighed. *Get going, John old boy ... Got to watch what Matt has planned ... Don't miss it!*

★

Wayne sprinted for the car. This was his operation and he was in charge. With Bruce a yard behind him, he jumped through the driver's window into the driver's seat like a stock car driver, flopped his feet over the steering wheel, scraping the dashboard, and ended with one foot on the gas pedal, the other pushed down on the brake and his hands tightly grasping the wheel.

Bruce jumped in the passenger seat and held the car keys dangling from the ignition switch. Sweat beads rolled down his red face. His eyes narrowed to slits. "Listen to me. We're not going anywhere 'til you give me some answers. Before I let you start up my car, you talk to me."

"What's going on?" Cracker Jack said from the back seat. "Jimmy and I've been sitting here patiently waiting and here come you two dudes, runnin' like the cops are after you."

Jimmy leaned up so his head was between Wayne and Bruce. "What happened? Did you get what you wanted?"

Wayne banged the wheel with both hands and glared at Bruce. "Get your hands off the keys, you bastard."

Bruce watched as the evil look in Wayne's eyes changed to a look of frustration. He took his hand off the keys. "Okay, start driving, but tell me where we're going."

Wayne turned the key with one hand and turned on the headlights with the other. The starter growled and the engine came to life. A soft yellow light shone on the pavement. He stepped on the small silver-colored knob on the floorboard with his left foot, clicked it and the bright lights came on. They had no effect yet, but he wanted them on. "All I can tell you is we're wasting time. We need to get moving."

"Moving where?"

"The Carib theater, dammit!"

He turned to the boys in the back seat and waved the note at them so they could see it. "I grabbed this note from John Hollis at the train station, and it says a secret drop-off is going to be made in front of the Carib in ten minutes. We're going to a drop-off to find something—and the something is a treasure."

He looked back toward the station. "Hollis is gone!" His face began to get red again. "If he gets there before we do, they'll know I got the note instead of the man who was supposed to pick it up, and they won't put it out. Get it?"

"Got it," Bruce said. "Let's go!"

With the clutch pushed in, Wayne jammed the accelerator down and gunned the engine. The engine roared, the mufflers popped and the sound of the glass packs echoed off the downtown building walls. He threw the gear into reverse and backed out.

Chapter 83

THE CARIB THEATER

"LOOK BILLY, the line at the box office has to be over a hundred feet long," Bob said. "I think half the seventh grade class is here."

"Well, Matt told us to get the word out and it looks like we were extremely successful," Billy said with a grin. "I even see teachers. There's Mr. North and his family, and our biology teacher, Mr. Cantor. The sidewalk's packed."

"Do you see John?"

"Not yet."

Billy checked his watch. If all was going according to Matt's plan, Wayne had the note, and John should be joining them in line. He peered out into the twilight, waiting for John to walk out of the shadows. "I'm not worried yet, but I hope he shows up soon with a big smile and both thumbs up."

"Where's Matt?" Bob said. "He didn't tell us where he was going to be. He seemed more excited about surprising us than getting Wayne."

"That's because whatever happens to Wayne … happens," Billy said. "He'll get his satisfaction when he sees us. He told me that Wayne will receive the ultimate lesson and we're going to love it."

★

Wayne pulled out onto Cleveland Street. "What time is it now?"

"By my watch, almost seven twenty-five," Jimmy said.

"Good. We have five minutes before the drop-off and we are two minutes away. I hope your watch is right."

"It's right. It's a Timex. I just got it as a present for starting junior high."

Wayne shifted into second at fifteen mph. The car crept along. His voice changed. "Okay, here's the story. My dad found part of a treasure map a long, long time ago with a friend, and they searched but never found the missing half of the map." Wayne looked around the car and smiled with a look of satisfaction. "The other half of the map has been found, and they don't want me to know."

His face changed. The smile disappeared. "But I found out. First, we get the treasure and then I'll deal with them. That's for another day. They tried to keep the secret from me. But careless tongues talked, and I was told all about it by a confidant who knew it was wrong."

Wayne's hands held the steering wheel tightly. His knuckles turned white. His biceps flexed. "They were going to take it from me. But now I know. I know it all. Them sons of bitches. I'm getting what's mine."

He made a fist and banged the wheel in a fit of anger. "We're on our way to intercept the drop-off and get the newly found missing part of the map so I can claim my half of the hidden treasure. Those little butt-twerps found out and were stealing it from me and keeping my half. But I learned their scheme. When I have it, they won't get a penny."

Wayne talked fast. He licked his dry lips and tried to moisten them. "The treasure is pure gold coins and jewels, and there is some gold in this drop-off just to show what's in the mother lode ... more than we could spread out on our beds. First off, I will buy a big diamond ring, put it on my ring finger, form a tight fist and stick it right in front of their noses. I'll fix those weasels."

"Gold coins and a treasure map? Why didn't you say so?" Bruce said. "My dad was involved in that treasure hunt too, cousin. It was a family thing and I've heard that story thousands of times. You going to share it with all of us?"

"Damn right."

"Well, let's go get it!"

In the back seat, Cracker Jack moved his arms back and forth like

465

an orchestra conductor and began singing "Money, Honey."

"How much money in the treasure?" Jimmy asked.

"No money. The treasure is gold coins and jewels and stuff like that, not cash. You'll see soon. The note says there are gold coins with this drop-off. It was in a bag along with the lost half of the map."

"Why did you turn here?" Bruce said, watching Wayne's every move carefully now.

"The note said it would be on the same side as the Carib, just a short distance down on the sidewalk to the west. We were on the wrong side. Plus, I want to go right beside the lines of kids waiting to go in the movies." He pulled a comb out of his back Levi's pocket and ran the comb down the sides, redefining his D.A. "Got to look cool for the twerps."

"Okay, we're on it," Wayne yelled as they approached the theater, his excitement starting to interfere with his voice. "And we're on time. We'll drive by slowly and then we look for something sitting on the sidewalk."

*

"I don't see them, but I hear Bruce's car," Bob said, standing on the edge of the curb, looking east.

"How do you know?" Billy asked.

"I'd know Bruce's car if I was surrounded by a dozen guinea hens with cotton in both my ears."

"The sound, huh?"

"It's distinctive," Bob said. He pointed up the street at the light. "I'm right, as always. It's them. Here they come."

Bob looked around. "Where's John?"

"He'll be here. He's just being careful so Wayne doesn't see him. I bet Matt's last words to him were 'Take no chances.'"

*

Wayne pushed the dimmer switch with his left foot. The headlights dimmed. He pushed again. The bright beam cast a light way up in front and spread outward like an expanding triangle. "Definitely bright. It's getting dark, but we'll see it with that light."

Jimmy looked at his watch. "Slow down. The package will be just past the Carib, right? Don't get there too early."

"Yeah," Bruce said. "Not too early. Not before they put it out. What are we looking for?"

"Something up on the sidewalk, near the curb," Wayne said. "No more questions. When we get past the movie line, start looking. I'm feeling so good. Look at the line up there. Be sure and shoot our favorite twerps a bird, Jimmy. If you see Matt or Bob, yell out and tell them their ass is grass."

Wayne slowed the car and shifted back into first gear. The car was creeping. "Roll down the windows."

"They're already down," Cracker Jack said.

"I've never seen this many kids at the Carib," Jimmy said.

Wayne pushed in the clutch, then pushed down the accelerator and steered the car close to the curb. The engine screamed and the mufflers sounded like a gun battle under the theater canopy. "Bang! Bang! Bang!"

The sound ricocheted off the sidewalk. Startled adults ducked, but most of the kids knew the sound. They put their hands over their ears and laughed.

Wayne took his foot off the gas. The engine quieted. The glass pack rumble settled back to a hum, and the car slowed almost to a stop. Bruce sat in the front passenger seat with his arm resting on the open window frame, his biceps flexed inside his clean white T-shirt sleeves, rolled up and revealing a pack of Winston cigarettes.

Jimmy sat by the rear window near the theater, his right hand outside the window, elbow resting on the frame, hand pointed upward with his fingers formed into a perfect "bird" that he kept still like a stone Greek statue. He gazed out into the crowd, with a smile that he hoped would be seen as a cool smirk. He spotted Billy and thought he mouthed, "Not for long." He pointed his bird right at Billy and heard Bob say to Billy, "Jimmy's shit-eating grin," and Billy answer, "That's what I'm talking about."

Jimmy stuck his other hand out the window and birded them with both hands. "Eat this," he said.

"Serve your shit to the driver," Bob yelled.

Cracker Jack pushed into the window beside Jimmy and stuck his head out. "I see you, Walton. You're pretty big when you're around the girls."

"Call me when you're *ever* big," Bob yelled back.

Cracker Jack pushed on the door to get out of the car, but Jimmy restrained him.

The car crawled by the line of teenagers and traffic backed up behind it.

Wayne stuck his arm out and motioned the cars around. They glared at him as they passed. "Quit your bitching. The road has two lanes."

"Do you see the twerps?" Wayne said, slowing down even more. "Look hard. I know they're there."

"Just Bob and Billy," Jimmy said. "No Matt or John ... too many people in the crowd to find them, but I'm sure they're here."

"I know they're here," Wayne said. "Shoot 'em another bird." He stuck his arm up above the roof and shot a bird himself. "The little turds ... I'm going to get them again. They're so much fun to get ... the little assholes." Wayne pulled his arm back into the car. "Still see the little two?"

"I see them," Jimmy said.

"What are they doing?"

"They're smiling at us."

Wayne pressed on the dimmer switch again. It went to low beam. He pushed the switch back to high beam. "Okay, here we go. We're right on time. Soon we'll be rich. Wave goodbye to the twerps."

★

"John's here," Billy said to Bob. "He ducked down behind that 'old man' car parked right across from us."

"The Buick Roadmaster?"

"Yeah, right under the streetlight. See him? He's crouched down. Has his hand on the taillight. Looks like he's ready to run over here."

"I see him."

John jaywalked across the street, close behind Bruce's car, bent over like a soldier not wanting to be seen.

"God, what happened to you?" Bob said.

"I'm fine. He took the carrot. This is going down … By the way, I heard a lot of cussing going on while I was waiting on the other side of the street, and I think the voice I heard sounded a great deal like yours."

"I was into it, John. I was having so much fun I couldn't help myself."

"Well, this hypocrisy—*Ah say, this hypocrisy*—has gone too fa'. *Ya hear? Ah say, Ya hear me, Bob?*"

"How did it go at the train station?" Bob asked.

"Good … kind of."

"Bad?"

"Almost."

"Well, everything seems okay now, but you look a little roughed up."

"Yep."

Bob stepped out a little farther into the street. "Well, tell us all about it later. Let's enjoy the show. All I need is some popcorn."

Billy pointed down the street. "Bob, John … look! I see someone down there … It's Matt … He has something. Oh my gosh, it's a brief-case … a huge briefcase. It's Matt! See him?"

Matt set the briefcase down and disappeared into the darkness. Inside a circle of light from the streetlight above, the briefcase sat alone.

Bob smiled. "It's Matt's stage. The curtain is open, the spotlight is on and we await the final act."

"Wow, Bob, you sound like Tim Johnson when he played the Stage Manager in *Our Town* last year at the high school," John said.

Bob laughed and slapped John on the back. "It feels like that, doesn't it? We have a great view. We are in the front row."

"Oh boy, it's about to happen," Billy said. "The trap is set and ready to be sprung. No jinxes now. You're right, John. It's going down. We're in the Sputnik countdown."

Down the street, Bruce's car closed in on the briefcase. The brake lights flickered.

"They see it. Oh my gosh, they see it for sure," Billy said.

The car passed the briefcase but didn't stop.

"What happened?" Bob said. "Did they not see it?"

"Hold on," Billy said.

"God, did I jinx it?" John said.

The car sped up, waited for an oncoming car, made a squealing U-turn and headed back in their direction.

Billy put his hands together like he was praying. "Whew ... we're okay. They're being cautious. We need to get back on the sidewalk."

"They saw it," John said. "Don't you know there's excitement in that car now. Okay boys ... come on back. Let this car going past us get by them and then they'll turn back around."

"Turn, dammit," Bob said.

John turned and looked at Bob and gave him the "watch your language" look.

"Damn is quite appropriate here and now," Bob said.

"Okay," Billy said, crossing his fingers. "Turn around, car. You know, they must be worried someone else might pick it up. Whip that car around and go get that briefcase."

The car slowed, moved into the center over the yellow line, waiting for the other car to pass, and made another U-turn, this time quietly with no squealing tire rubber sounds.

"Yessss," John said. He put his arm around Billy's shoulders. "There's some handshaking going on in that car right now."

The brake lights went on again and the car angled toward the curb.

"Guys," John said, "*this* time the briefcase goes into the car."

"Show time," Bob yelled to the crowd.

"Where?" someone in line yelled.

"Hey, Bob ... we're ready," Brad yelled.

"John ... Crow and I are here too ... Right behind you," Bum said.

Bob pointed down the street. "Okay everybody, watch that souped-up car that just went by us."

"I see it," Bum said. "And, I recognize that car ... It belongs to Bruce Tanner. What a jerk."

"What you're about to witness was planned," Bob shouted to the crowd. "There's a bully in that car and he is about to get his payback. Don't feel sorry for him. He humiliated our friend at school. He's a bully hood."

"Boo to the bully."

"No tears from us."

"Right … this lesson is deserved," Bob said. "Laugh and enjoy. No one is getting hurt … especially not Lucille."

"Who's Lucille?"

"Where is she?"

"You'll see," Bob said.

The movie line broke apart and people stepped out on the street near the boys. Wolf whistles echoed off the walls of the building.

"Get ready," Bob said. "They are about to be introduced to Lucille."

Dee looked at Bonnie and then at Brad. "I'm confused. I don't know anyone named Lucille."

Brad shrugged his shoulders. "Guess we're going to find out soon enough."

"Who's Lucille?" Rocky said.

"A seven-foot-long, gigantic black snake with an attitude," Bob said. "And … she's not kind toward bullies."

"Does she know him?" Rocky said.

"Oh yes, she does," Billy said. "His picture is pinned on the side of her cage."

The people in the crowd who knew Billy cheered when they heard his voice.

"Bring her on," Rocky said. "I can't wait to see these guys get what's due them. Where's Matt?"

"He's with Lucille," Bob said. "You'll see him after the show."

★

"There's a car right behind me," Wayne said as he slowed down and pulled the car close to the curb."

"Do you think he sees the briefcase too?" Jimmy said. "Maybe that's the real pickup person."

"Who cares," Wayne said, "because we're getting it. We'll make it look like the high school track guys transferring that stick."

"Baton," Cracker Jack said.

"You know what I mean. I don't follow that crap."

"I know what you mean," Jimmy said. He looked over at Cracker Jack and mouthed, "Why did you say that?"

Cracker Jack shrugged his shoulders.

"Jimmy, I'm going to pull near the briefcase. You open the door and when we go by, grab it and pull it into the car," Wayne said. "Did your asshole buddy beside you understand?"

"I understand," Cracker Jack said. "Don't give me any crap. You just drive without running over it. Jimmy and I will grab it and pull it into the car."

The front wheel scraped along the side of the curb.

"Okay. Here we go," Wayne said.

"Can you see it?" Bruce yelled. "The light shines right on it. It's shining down like a rainbow pointing to a pot of gold."

"I see it," Wayne said. "Tell me when I get beside it, Jimmy."

Jimmy leaned his head out the window. "Okay. Go slow ... slower ... stop!"

Jimmy opened the door and grabbed the briefcase. "Got it. It's in the car."

The door slammed and the car pulled away from the curb.

★

"Oh my gosh," Billy said. "They've got it. They've got the briefcase inside the car. Lucille is in that car."

The car barely moved.

"Wayne's going slow," Bob said. "He wants to see his jewels and gold."

John laughed hard. "And he's saying, 'Show me, Jimmy, show me, Jimmy.'"

Bob pulled an old paper program from his back pocket, rolled it and placed it up to his lips. "Ladies and gentlemen, boys and girls, I am your Carib midway announcer. The door was opened, now it's closed. The briefcase is in the car. Soon we expect to hear screams and the car should start to weave. And then ... who knows?"

★

Wayne let off the accelerator and the car coasted. He did not want to go fast yet. He wanted to know what was in the briefcase. "Open it ... Is it gold coins or what?"

Cracker Jack and Jimmy lifted the flap and yanked the top open. They stared into the dark cavern of the old brown leather briefcase.

"What's in it?" Wayne yelled. "Tell me!"

"Can't tell," Cracker Jack said. "It's heavy, but it's too deep to see anything in this light."

He stuck his hand into the top of the open case.

"Do you see it?" Wayne said. "What's the problem?"

"It's dark in the bottom. I'm feeling for it. Coins and a map, right?"

"Right. They're probably on the bottom."

Cracker Jack yanked his hand out of the briefcase. "Shit. There's something alive in here. *Ahhhhhhhhhhhhhhhhhhhhhhhh ...*"

"What is it?" Wayne yelled.

"*Ahhhhhhhhhhhhh,*" Cracker Jack yelled.

Wayne pushed on the gas pedal and the car jerked forward. "What is it ... money or a map?" he yelled over the screaming. He looked into the rearview mirror. Cracker Jack had a terrified look on his face. The briefcase was on his lap.

"Money, my ass," Cracker Jack yelled. "It's a goddam snake, Tyson! At the bottom of this case is a snake—a big snake—coiled and hissing and spitting at me. It's ready to jump out."

"Then close it!" Wayne yelled.

The snake's head peered from the case opening, its tongue shooting out.

Wayne could see it in the mirror. He hit the accelerator and jerked the steering wheel. "Close it, dammit!"

Cracker Jack began screaming again.

"*Ahhhhhhhhhhhhhhhhhhhhhhhhhhhhhhhhhhhhh.*"

The car zigzagged and when the right front wheel hit the curb, it jumped in the air and bounced back, coming to rest on the sidewalk. The front grill rested on a light pole and the back left wheel had stopped in the gutter. "*Ahhhhhhhhh*" ... the screams got louder.

Cracker Jack pushed the briefcase away and kicked it. It hit the sagging fabric covering the ceiling and fell back toward him, landing on the back seat with the large, wriggling snake trying to get out.

The snake slithered out and lay on the seat between Cracker Jack and Jimmy. For a moment it was still—except for its head moving back and forth.

*

The line to the ticket office became a crowd gathered on the sidewalk, watching the car.

Brad bent over and held his stomach as he laughed. "Sounds like someone's being murdered in that car down there."

Bob yelled to the crowd through his makeshift megaphone: "A nine-inch stiletto stuck deep into the stomach—through the belly button with blood shooting out everywhere—the victim coughing up red-black blood that's running down his chin … You think? No! How about a live slithering serpent loose in the car?"

*

Wayne looked in the back seat. Jimmy's red freckled face was white. Cracker Jack looked seasick.

The snake swayed back and forth, hissing, its tongue darting in and out, and then moved up the back seat, its head level with Jimmy's eyes. The huge black snake pulled its head backward, forming an S with its body.

"It's a monster!" Wayne yelled. "It's going to bite you. Grab it, Jack!"

"My ass," Cracker Jack yelled. "I'm outta here."

"Me too," yelled Jimmy.

Jimmy and Cracker Jack pushed their doors open and scrambled out, arms flailing. As they fell out on the ground, they kicked the doors shut and tried to crawl away, but their hands and knees were moving and they were going nowhere.

*

"Look at them come out of that car," Billy shouted. "The snake is going crazy! I bet she left the back seat and headed for the front! She's coming for you, Wayne!"

"Hey Jimmy, Cracker Jack … we see you. Is that a new dance step?" John yelled, bending down and hitting his knees as he laughed.

"Oh yes," Bob said. "Where's Lucille now? Somewhere in the car? What's she doing? She's a seven-foot monster, and she hates bullies."

Laughter spread throughout the crowd.

✶

Inside the car, the snake slid over the front seat toward Bruce, its head close enough to nip his ear.

"God, don't let it bite me," Bruce said. He moved and the snake lunged. With a quiet scream deep in his throat, he dove for the door, pushed the handle down and hit it with the top of his shoulder. The door opened and he fell out, hitting the pavement on his lower back and rear end.

The door sprung back and he pushed it closed with his feet. BANG!

Bruce was out and the snake was not. He jumped up, ran down the sidewalk and crossed the street.

Jimmy and Cracker Jack got to their feet and headed off in the same direction.

✶

Lucille lay coiled on the passenger seat with her head a foot in the air. Her scales glistened in the light shining down through the windshield.

Wayne pushed down the handle and tried to open his door. The door didn't move, but the snake did. He looked at the snake's open mouth, heard its hisses and saw the long black tongue darting in and out. The snake was so close to his face, he could see right where the tip of its tongue split into a fork.

His body trembled. "Help! Please help," he yelled. "I'm trapped. I can't get out of the car." He felt the cold, scaly body wrapping around him. Fear sapped his energy. Silence overcame him. He tried to climb out through the open window of the jammed door with the snake wrapped around his body. He stopped. He was stuck with half his body still inside the car.

★

Hidden in the middle of a hedge of large hibiscus bushes only ten feet from the car, and resting on his knees and the toes of his tennis shoes, Matt watched it all happen.

Up the street, laughter spread through the large crowd, and some of the junior high students moved down the sidewalk toward the car.

"I bet that snake has a hold of him," John said to Bob. He cupped his hands around his mouth and yelled in the direction of the car, "Protect your privates, Wayne! Snakes sometimes eat their babies!"

★

Wayne struggled to move and the snake clung to him. He tried to push himself out the window, but couldn't. He pushed himself back inside the car and leaned toward the passenger door.

The snake still clung to him.

His foot hit the steering wheel and his knee pushed on the horn. The horn blew again—and again. He twisted and struggled. He yelled. He cried. He cussed.

His shirt was pulled up near his neck and the snake wrapped itself tighter around his bare waist. The cold scales touched his skin. His heart pounded. He no longer could scream. He gave one final push against the passenger door. The snake released its hold on him and he fell out the door onto the pavement. His nose hit the ground first, and the snake dropped right on top of him.

★

Smoke hissed from the crunched grill of the car. Under the streetlight, it was as bright as mid-morning. Wayne's face was ashen. His lips were blue.

Matt watched from his hiding place in the hedge. It was a scene he would never forget.

The crowd in front of the Carib laughed and cheered. "That snake is huge," Rocky said. "Ha-ha, I think it chased him out of the car."

"I certainly hope so," JB said. "That guy deserves everything he's getting."

★

Wayne tried to get up, but the snake moved onto his shoulder and wrapped itself completely around him again. A small puddle of blood lay under his nose in a circle on the asphalt. His cheek was pushed up into his eye and his face looked distorted. Lucille held on to him like she had her prey wrapped up, ready to finish him off.

Matt walked over and stood over him.

"Help me! Please help me!" Wayne mumbled.

"Hey, Wayne," he said very clearly so he could be sure Wayne recognized his voice. "A lot of money in the briefcase?"

He looked down at the helpless hood, initially feeling great satisfaction watching him lying there, scared and barely moving. But as fast as the satisfied feeling of joy filled him, it left him, replaced by sadness and even some shame, of what he had planned and what they had done. He knew Wayne deserved this, but the feelings were all still there within him.

★

Billy smiled and winked at John. "I'm going to help Matt get Lucille back in her burlap bag. Stay here. If you see my guest arrive, send him down."

John winked back. "I'll do it."

Bob and Billy stood beside Matt and looked at Wayne stretched out on the sidewalk, face down, wrapped in the snake.

With a satisfied grin on his face, Billy bent down closer to him. "Hello, Wayne. Everybody up at the Carib is watching, you know ... you snake in the grass. Now you know what it feels like to look like an idiot in front of a bunch of people who know you. Just wait until the next time you see them at school."

"Yeah, Wayne," Bob said. "What a movie! Where's your girlfriend? Is she somewhere watching or is she going to hear about it from some of her girlfriends? You're not looking very tough or handsome right now. It might be hard to get this snake off of you before it kisses you. Snakes love snakes, you know."

Wayne struggled to get up on his hands and knees, but fell back on the sidewalk, still face down. "Help me, Matt. Get this goddam snake off me, please."

"Okay, we will," Matt said. "Just lie still for a minute and let her calm down."

Matt walked back to the hedge, picked up the snake stick and burlap bag and handed the stick to Billy. Billy gently prodded her with the stick. She loosened her grip around Wayne and fell to the sidewalk.

Billy pinned her down and gently picked her up. Matt opened the burlap sack and Billy lowered her through the opening, releasing her once her body settled on the bottom of the sack.

Wayne struggled to his feet and with blood dripping into his cupped hand, he walked behind the car and blended into the dark shadows without saying a word.

Under the canopy of the theater, laughter and cheers exploded.

Bob ran back to John and they slapped hands and exchanged congratulatory high-fives. Brad, Robin, JB and Rocky joined in. The girls jumped up and down, clapping their hands.

Bonnie ran down the sidewalk where Matt and Billy stood holding the bag with the snake. She put her arms around Matt's neck and hugged him. "I was so scared for you!"

Matt handed the burlap bag to Billy and planted a little peck on Bonnie's lips, swung her around and set her on the ground. "It's over."

Bonnie stared over his shoulder and her smile faded. "Oh no!" she whispered.

Chapter 84

SHOW ME WHAT YOU'VE GOT!

WAYNE JUMPED OUT from behind Matt, his eyes bloodshot and watery and a tire iron tightly clasped in his right hand. He reached for Bonnie with his free arm, pulled her to him and held her tightly around the neck.

The crowd in front of the theater became silent. John grabbed Bob by the arm. "Come on. He needs help."

Matt spun around. "Let her go, Wayne."

Wayne tightened his grip and pulled Bonnie close to his cheek.

"Now!" Matt said in a calm, quiet voice.

Wayne looked down at Bonnie. "I've got *your* treasure here, asshole."

"Don't regret this, Wayne. Let her go."

"Make me, punk."

Matt pulled John's trick and winked at Wayne. "You're too easy. I'll show you."

Wayne's eyes became slits. He pushed Bonnie aside and lifted the tire iron high into the air. Foamy bubbles stuck to his lips as he mumbled something unintelligible.

"Come and get me, Wayne, ole boy. Show me what you've got," Matt said with a smile on his face.

"You're going to get it now, you fucking twerp."

Wayne charged and swung the heavy tire iron at Matt's head. Matt jerked his head backward.

The tire iron swept by his ear and continued to swing, pulling Wayne's arm around his own waist and distorting his body into a corkscrew. He regained his balance, pulled the tire iron from deep down between his legs and arched it over his head like a crazed lumberjack ready to strike a felled log with an ax. "Short and sweet, dead boy."

Matt ducked his head and used his arm to direct Wayne's second blow toward the pavement.

The iron rod smacked the pavement with such force that the stinging vibration in Wayne's hand loosened his grip, and the weapon bounced down the sidewalk twenty feet.

Matt moved forward. He struck Wayne in his solar plexus and followed with a lightning-bolt jab to the bottom of his chin. Wayne's head lurched back, and he collapsed on the sidewalk like a puppet with its strings severed.

Jimmy stepped out from behind the streetlight. A hissing sound still spurted from under the hood of Bruce's car. He kneeled down beside Wayne. "He doesn't look so good," he said to Matt.

"Get Bruce and your other buddy and drive him home when he comes to."

"Are you sure? I'm scared he's dead."

Matt kicked Wayne's motorcycle boot and watched Wayne's eyelids flutter. "Snakes die at sundown, Jimmy. He made it. He's alive. I know what death looks like. And, Jimmy ... there *is* a right and a wrong. Right now you live on the wrong side. Start listening to your heart."

Matt took Bonnie's hand. "Come on, guys. Let's get out of here and let Wayne's buddies take care of him."

John grabbed Billy and pulled him into his chest, squeezing him hard. "What an amazing ending, snake man. You did a good job!"

Bob rubbed Billy's head and messed up his hair. "We got him, Billy! Way to go!"

"When we saw Billy hanging from that post, I felt so embarrassed for him," Dee said to Bonnie. "And right now I feel so happy for him." She looked around at Matt, John, Bob and Billy. "I don't think you'll have to worry about Wayne Tyson anymore. Thank you, guys, from all of us. What a lesson."

"I knew you had it in you, Matt," John said.

Matt smiled. "I'm just sorry we had to take it this far."

Billy put his arm around Matt's shoulders. "Matt, that boy got what he deserved. Only you would feel sorry for him now. Thank you."

Matt rattled car keys up in the air. "Lawrence Fraley gave me his keys to open his car trunk. I'm putting Lucille there and I'll be right back."

"Wait just a minute, Matt Parker," a voice yelled from the crowd still waiting in line outside the theater.

Matt recognized the voice, but couldn't place it.

"You got here, Justin! You're home!" Billy shouted.

He ran back to Justin and gave him a hug. "I'm so glad you're here. It's over. The snake in the grass is lying back there on the sidewalk and our snake is snuggled in her burlap bag. Matt was amazing, Justin! Sorry you missed it ..."

Chapter 85

A NEW DAY

THE BEDROOM DOOR OPENED and the silhouette of a body stood tall and still in the bright light of the hallway. "Four o'clock and all is well. Dark as pitch and cold as hell ... If you're going fishing with me, young man ... get your butt out of the bed."

Matt pulled the covers up over his head. "Oh, Dad, I feel like I just closed my eyes. Fifteen more minutes?"

"No time. I've already given you that fifteen. Only the bored lie in bed. Take a cold shower. That'll jump-start your engine."

Matt lay under the covers and took a moment to savor his success the night before. He had slain the evil dragon inside Wayne. *Only time will tell if that dragon comes back to life.* A smile of satisfaction spread across his face and goose bumps tickled his skin.

He folded the covers back and touched his face—no scratches, no shiner. The goose bumps were his red badge of courage. He and his team had met the enemy and were victorious—no cowards in his group.

He closed his eyes. He saw Billy standing over Wayne. He saw Bonnie ready to be swept away. He saw Bob and John running down to the streetlight yelling and laughing. He saw the appreciation in Justin's eyes. Mission complete!

He kicked off the covers and jumped out of bed. Five minutes later, he stepped through the swinging doors into the brightly lit kitchen. "I'm ready, Dad. Let's go fishing!"

His dad sat at the kitchen table changing the line on his Ambassadeur casting reel. "Almost finished here. We're going to be fishing in some heavy lilies today—twelve pound test won't cut it."

Matt pulled open the door of the refrigerator. "What are you putting on?"

"Twenty pound."

He grinned at his dad and poured himself a glass of orange juice. "If that fish wraps around the stalk of a lily, you're still not getting him."

"You're not supposed to get them all."

"Well, *we* got 'em all last night."

"You sure did," Mr. Parker said.

"And we'll know how *you* will lose the big one today ..."

Mr. Parker sipped on his coffee and smiled. "Yeah, you're probably right. So, what's your strategy, Ted Williams?"

"I'll stay with the twelve pound test on my spinning reel. I'm starting with a Dalton Topwater and I'll cast to the edges of those lure-eating lilies, and then when you get tired of getting tangled up in the lilies and move to the grass, I'll fight 'em on my own terms."

"The big ones are in the lilies in this hot weather."

"You always know the skinny, Dad, but I got the vibes, and I bet I put more fish in the boat than you do today ... and they won't be mudfish." Matt cringed. "Ugh, mudfish."

"Hey, your mom's tea has steeped. How about taking her a cup? I'll be finished here in a minute. I'll meet you outside."

"She awake?"

"She's waiting."

Matt poured a cup of tea and walked into his parents' bedroom singing "Lawdy, Miss Clawdy," one of his mom's favorite Elvis songs. "G'day, Mom."

His mom sat in the bed, propped up on pillows, smiling. "G'day, dear. Such a luv you are. Singin' a little Elvis for me?"

Matt laughed. "Boy, everyone's perky this morning. No need to say 'keep your pecker up' today."

His mom's eyes twinkled. "I learned from you boys that's not a

SORRY YOU MISSED IT...

good saying to use here in America."

"You're a riot, Mom."

"Thanks for the tea, Matt. You men have a good day and bring me home some fish."

He leaned down and kissed her on the cheek. "We always do. See you tonight. Love you."

"Love you too. Ta-ta."

Garage door down ... truck engine running ... concrete driveway illuminated by the lights of the boat trailer hitched behind the truck ...

Matt stepped out into the darkness and headed to the truck.

Mr. Parker walked slowly around the boat, kicking the tires and pulling on the strap holding the boat tight to the trailer. His white baseball cap with Washington Masonry printed on it in green glowed in the red lights on the back of the boat trailer. "Doing my pre-flight check. Climb in and hit the brake."

Matt jumped into the truck and touched the brake pedal with his foot. "Brake lights working?"

"Yep. Slide over and let me have the wheel, Captain, so I can drive."

Mr. Parker looked down at his tan workpants and faded, long-sleeve, blue cotton shirt, and then at Matt's outfit. "Shorts? No jacket?"

"I put some jeans in the boat last night. It's September, Dad." He rolled down his window and opened the corner triangular window. "I love my jet fan."

Mr. Parker pointed to the old black thermos bottle on the seat beside him. "There's plenty of coffee if you need a sip to warm you up later, and a sweatshirt under the seat. Bet you're chilled in half an hour."

"Dad, it's seventy-nine degrees."

They pulled out of the driveway and his dad lit up a Pall Mall cigarette.

"Where are we headed?" Matt asked.

"Haines Creek."

"Great. Thanks for letting me get a little extra sleep this morning."

"I understand. Thought you might need it today. And a day on the water might do you some good too."

The truck turned east and soon the road was bordered on both sides by citrus groves barely visible on the moonless morning. Away from the lights of town, stars lit up the sky. In the dark truck with only a dim light coming from the instrument panel and a glistening red ember at the end of a cigarette in the hand resting on the steering wheel, Matt caught a sweet smile visible on his dad's face.

In front of them, the white center lines reflected the headlights and shone brightly. When the occasional oncoming vehicle approached them, with a push of his left foot, Mr. Parker hit the dimmer switch on the floor, switching the lights from bright to dim. At the limits of the headlights, the road was black and an occasional animal darted across in front of them. Behind the truck, beyond the glow of the boat trailer's red taillights, darkness ate up the road quickly.

Hardwood forests replaced the citrus groves, and an even darker landscape spread out around them. The white lines of the highway snapped by as the truck made its way between walls of trees.

Matt closed the triangular window vent and pulled out the sweatshirt tucked under the seat and pulled it over his head. "You were right," he said with a grin.

His dad smiled and handed his coffee cup to Matt. "Pour me a little more, please."

Matt unscrewed the lid of the thermos and released the catch of the small cork cap plunger. It popped out, and Matt held it between his legs while he filled the cup with the black, oily coffee. He put the cup into his dad's outstretched right hand and put the thermos back together. The aroma of coffee filled the cab of the truck.

Mr. Parker took a sip of his coffee. "You know, Matt, I'm very proud of you. These last two weeks you've become a man. I think you can put Wayne Tyson behind you and get on with your studies and the fun of junior high. You handled him well and you handled yourself well."

"Thanks, Dad. I'm so glad I finally realized what my hang-up was. I had no trouble with holding back last night. And you know what? I've decided I'm still going to look for that stolen treasure so Mom can go back to Australia and visit all her family, and if I find it, I might even share some of it with Wayne and Bruce and Jimmy. What would you think of that idea?"

"I'd say that's a great idea ... but guess what?

"What?"

"You and your mom are going to Australia next summer whether or not you find the treasure."

"What? You're kidding me, Dad."

"No, I'm serious. I got a call yesterday from the deacons at the Presbyterian Church off Indian Rocks Road, and they want me to build their new church. I'm going to be really busy with that job, and I think this will be a perfect summer for you and your mom to make the trip."

"So do I, Dad. Thanks. And just for the record ... I'm still going to keep looking for that treasure. It's still out there somewhere, right?"

"Well, let's just say it's never been found. But like I told you, Bill and I made that map as a joke. Don't think you can use it to help you find it. You'll have to do some research and see what you come up with."

Silence settled into the truck cab as the tires of the truck followed a straight highway—no approaching headlights, not a curve in sight. An hour later, the black sky in the east began to turn gray.

Slowly, new colors appeared. Pink spread through the gray like dye being poured into water. Yellow started to hug the road in the distance and a red hue grew out of the yellow. Like the butterfly in its womb, a metamorphosis was in action.

"Oh wow! I see magic—on the horizon ... See it, Dad?"

"We're seeing the birth of a new day," his dad said. "Always magnificent, never the same."

"We're watching it from the beginning, Dad."

Matt leaned forward in his seat and began tapping his fingers on the metal dashboard like it was a snare drum—*Ta ... Ta-Ta-Ta ... Ta ... Ta-Ta-Ta ... Ta ... Ta ... Ta.* "This is one of my favorite songs you play on the record player. What's the name of it, Dad? At first, it's only a flute and a snare drum, then a clarinet and an oboe join in, and then the rest of the woodwinds and then the strings and then the brass until the whole orchestra is playing ..."

"Ravel's 'Bolero.' Don't stop. It's perfect. It fits the moment."

Matt kept tapping and began to softly hum the melody. His dad started to hum in a soft baritone voice.

The light grew brighter and Matt began conducting their two-man orchestra like he'd seen Mr. Frederickson do in class, hands close to his chest, waving only a finger on each, back and forth for a quiet three-quarter time.

They gradually began to hum louder and louder as if the rest of the instruments were being added, and Matt's moving hands and fingers became moving arms, hands and fingers.

The bottom edge of the ball of fire rose above the horizon, and the sun separated itself from the earth. Its beams struck the windshield, creating rainbow mosaics that reflected off the metal dash and splashed across their faces.

They looked at each other and grinned as they opened their mouths, and their humming became a roaring *La ... La-La-La ... La ... La-La-La ... La ...*

"There's our 'Bolero' crescendo, Dad. It's the sun's message to me. A new day is here."

Matt squinted his water-filled eyes as he looked at the new glowing sun. "That beautiful sky reminds me of a song from *Oklahoma!*"

His dad looked over at him, nodded his head and together they belted out Curly's song, "Oh, What a Beautiful Mornin,'" as beams of light doused the inside of the cab.

"A new day. It's perfect, Dad. I'm rolling up my sleeves. ... Next?"

EPILOGUE

THE RED TWELVE blinked on the bedside radio.

He drifted in and out of a semi-comatose sleep. He felt alone. In the dark room, he reached across the bed and searched for a warm body. Empty. He sat up and rubbed his eyes. He felt full of energy, and that was good because the day was going to be busy and full of emotion. The evening before, when he got home from making rounds at the hospital, he felt tired and aware that he was sixty-five.

He got out of bed and headed toward the strong aroma of coffee coming from the kitchen.

"I guess the power went off," he said to his wife.

"Sometime during the night. Thank goodness we don't wake up to an alarm clock. You've got plenty of time."

"Oh, to be a kid again," he said with a little giggle, "and sleep until you're stirred by a shake."

"Are you okay, Matt Parker?" his wife of forty-three years asked, her back to him, while facing the coffee maker. She poured him a cup.

"I'm okay."

"I'll ride over to the airport with you, if you want."

"Thanks, but I think I'll try it alone. It'll be a good time for reflection. Besides, it'll give Billy and me time to talk—you know—catch up."

"How long has it been?"

He rubbed his eyes. "A long time … we were in our twenties. The last memory I have is popping him on the arm while we were standing at the 'Pier Pavilion' on the beach. John was with me and he popped him too. Billy was still working on his PhD at Indiana University, and he'd come home to visit his mom and dad."

He thought about that day and smiled. "Yep, we sure gave Billy a hard time. The last time I saw Billy, I was taking protein pills and vitamins. Now I take beta-blockers and gout medicine."

Bonnie laughed. "You're still funny. You have a lot of memories. Try to remember them all."

"Let me shower, dress and get out of here. The next time you see me, I'll be pulling along an old fart."

He cranked up his Toyota Tundra, hit the pedal and listened to the sound. Sweet. The upgraded exhaust system sounded like a truck out of the fifties. He turned on the radio, already set to the oldies station, and backed out the driveway. His destination: Tampa International Airport.

When he reached Courtney Campbell Causeway, he opened all the windows. The smells of Tampa Bay took him back to another time. He knew they would. Sadness overtook him. Then out of nowhere, he began to laugh.

Oh, how he was blessed. He watched a pelican glide beside him along the bridge, following the wind currents beside the railings. An osprey sat high on a bridge light. Fishing boats anchored up ... a guy throwing his cast net ... each picture took him to another memory, another adventure.

He turned off his engine. He was deep in the parking garage. He pulled a card from a holder beside the elevator. Wright Brothers was written on it and he was glad. He didn't want to have Billy with him and not remember where he parked the car. "They remember every-thing for you these days," he thought.

He reached the terminal, took the elevator down to Level Three and walked to the waiting area for deplaning passengers.

Would he recognize him? Maybe he should have made a sign like in the TV commercial. Dr. MacDonald. No, he knew he'd recognize him.

He sat and waited. He was early. The flight from Los Angeles blinked on the arriving information sign. It was late ... almost an hour.

As the tram doors opened, travelers poured out. He liked to watch people and he really studied them. He watched each person and played in his mind what they must have looked like when they were young. Old people had young lives.

The time finally came. He watched the first tram open its doors. Only a smattering of people stepped off. The first was a young mom carrying an infant. Two young children ran to her and embraced her legs, squeezing them tightly ... the beginning of a new generation's story.

Matt could see through the windows of the next tram. It was packed with people. Out they came. Businessmen headed for the escalator, bypassing the waiting greeters. They pulled their cases. They were in a hurry. Get to the rental car agencies, be first and get to that meeting or whatever.

No one knew Matt. He was only a statue. He wanted to yell, "Slow down," but he knew they wouldn't notice. They all had cell phones to their ears.

"Get off that tram, Billy. Let's slow down the earth. Stop the spinning, at least today."

And then, he stepped off the tram. He was the same ... still had short hair—all white ... still small—no belly ... casually dressed—no tie ... looked lost. Matt wiped away a tear. Some things never changed.

"Billy, over here," Matt said. John would have yelled, "Hey Boney Maroney, you need to be fed some liver," but there was only *his* voice.

Billy turned, and his smile was big. He got close, dropped his suitcase, stepped around it and grabbed Matt. They hugged a long time and finally stepped back and studied each other.

Matt smiled. "You look the same, except for the white hair, professor. John would've called you Dr. Einstein."

"It's been too long," he said to Matt, and tears rolled down his cheeks. Before Matt could pick up his suitcase, Billy stopped him with a frog to his upper arm and then grinned. "We're even for the moment."

Matt tossed Billy's suitcase into the bed of the truck and climbed in behind the wheel.

Billy fastened his seat belt. "I'm ready to smell the salt air," he said.

FRED HOSLEY

"I'm not crying for John today, I'm loving John today. I'm wanting to remember all those good times with him."

Billy was silent for a moment.

"We lived in another time, Matt."

"I know."

"And now John is gone. Hear him laughing?"

"Today and every day."

Matt opened the windows to let the salt air enter as they passed under the traffic light on Rocky Point and began their drive across the causeway.

"I've been thinking about Bob," Billy said. "He was so young when we lost him ... right before our senior year. That was a difficult time for his family and all of us who were friends with him."

"I know," Matt said. "I love to imagine what he might have been if he hadn't fallen asleep at the wheel coming home from Tallahassee early that morning. A movie director? A dad with lots of kids? He'd have probably found a crazy woman like his mom—what a pair. I loved them both. You know, I still can't go up US 19 without thinking about him."

"He was such a great guy ... Oh, to be kids again ..."

"Want to pull off and put your feet in the water?"

"I'll wait for Clearwater Beach."

"Okay."

"Matt, let's talk about all of us back when we started seventh grade. I'm serious. That's when I first met John and Bob and the others. You guys got me through one of the roughest times in my life."

"Where should we start?" Matt said. "That morning in front of Mr. Weller's house the weekend before we started classes at Clearwater Junior High School? I'm getting goose bumps."

"Me too."

"Let's drive around and talk for a while and then go and pay our respects to John's family."

"Good. I'm respecting John right now, thinking about us guys starting that first year of junior high and how you all did what you did."

491

"What a way to start junior high. Those were our first major 'growing pains,'" Matt said.

"To put it lightly."

"We can circle the old school property and then drive down Cleveland Street and across the causeway over to the beach. They've built a new bridge, you know."

"School's gone?"

"Yep, they bulldozed the building after it burned. I'll drive by really slowly. We might hear voices. Maybe see ghosts of the past."

"They never rebuilt?"

"Nope."

"I'm sure they're there."

Matt parked his truck on the side street that had separated the main school buildings and the Phys Ed building and turned off the engine. "Want to walk around?"

Billy smiled and rubbed the skin on his arms. "I'm good to just sit here a while and talk. This is the street where the post was, isn't it? Where Wayne's threat became my reality."

"Yes. That's the oak tree that grew beside the girls' volleyball court."

"I remember when Coach Shank helped you and John and Bob get me off that hook on the post. I was ready to cry. You put your hand on my shoulder, and for the first time, I felt safe. I was surrounded by friends. My life changed after that."

A big smile spread across Billy's face. "In the end, we taught Wayne a real lesson, didn't we? Remember the look on his face as he lay on the ground with Lucille wrapped around his body?"

Matt leaned his head back. "How could I ever forget it?"

ACKNOWLEDGMENTS

I WOULD LIKE TO EXPRESS my sincere thanks to everyone who helped me turn these words into a book.

First and foremost, to my wife, Camille, for her ceaseless encouragement during the many days of unimaginable pressure to keep writing. And to Camille and her cousin Mary Harris, my team who spent countless hours on the computer turning the handwritten pages of my sometimes rambling, rough draft into printed pages ready for me to review and revise.

To Bart Lewis, my first critical reader, who saw potential in my story and led me to Joseph Campbell.

To Margaret Langstaff, veteran professional book editor, whose thoughtful and sensitive editing significantly improved my manuscript. She told me that it should be shortened, that the days of *War and Peace* and *Gone with the Wind* are gone because they are too expensive to produce, and people today prefer shorter books and faster reads. I didn't listen, but I learned later that she was right. Thank you, Peggy, for all you did for me.

To *My Word Publishing* founder Polly Letofsky for her help with creating a marketing plan and to her extensive network of talented professionals, including Kirsten Jensen, publishing consultant, who recommended that I divide the manuscript into two books because of its length and who made the self-publishing process painless with her expertise and enthusiasm.

To Bobby Haas, my second professional book editor and an outstanding writing coach, who brought me through the home stretch and showed me how to use an ax to cut … cut … cut and separate this novel from an unwieldy manuscript while preserving the balance for another novel at another time.

To Jennifer Jas of *Words with Jas,* our proof editor, whose knowledge of grammar and attention to detail was amazing. And, to Victoria Wolf of *Wolf Design and Marketing,* cover and interior book designer, who nailed it every time with her recommendations and designs.

And there on the cover is the art of Steve Littlefield, my dear friend and talented artist, who listened to my feelings about my story and its setting and created this beautiful picture.

Special thanks also to Bill Bruce Hines, my Wyoming army buddy, who introduced me many years ago to the novels of Larry McMurtry and to the experience of reading for enjoyment.

To the late Bob Buckner, whose dental office was across the hall from my first office, who encouraged me to continue to write after retirement as he did, and then gave me his tattered copy of the Dean Koontz book *How to Write Best Selling Fiction* after he published his novel, *Dark Moon.*

To Jerry Schwalje and Mike and Ruthi Winter for their positive comments as they read parts of my manuscript during the writing process and for their interest and support through the editing and publishing of this novel.

Also, to Harv and Dave, my dental colleagues who loved to tease me as I pulled out my writing pad to work on this book, year after year, during our annual group scuba diving trips in the Caribbean—accept criticism and grow! I love you guys!

And finally, to Kit Challoner, who tackled an early draft and gave me helpful feedback and encouragement, and Sarah Caudell, who provided me with old photos and historical information about the town that does more than exist in my imagination—it really is out there, although it has now grown into a city.

ABOUT THE AUTHOR

FRED HOSLEY was born in Melbourne, Australia and grew up in Clearwater, Florida.

He began his college studies at the University of Florida in 1963, but his education was interrupted when he was drafted into the army, sent to Ft. Benning, and served his two-year commitment at Valley Forge General Army Hospital in Pennsylvania. He returned to Florida to continue his college studies, and in 1976 graduated from the Emory School of Dentistry in Atlanta, Georgia.

He practiced dentistry in Clearwater for thirty-five years.

Fred told stories about his teenage adventures to his children and later to his patients and then decided it would be fun to write some of them down. He took writing courses, participated in writing workshops and began writing before he retired. "Sorry You Missed It ..." is his first novel.

He is a lifelong saltwater and freshwater fisherman and scuba diver. He currently lives in Florida on the backwaters of the Withlacoochee River with his wife, Camille, and their golden retriever, Sunday.

Made in the USA
Columbia, SC
15 August 2020